**"The name Bertrice Small
is synonymous with passionate historical romance."***

Praise for the novels of Bertrice Small

"Bertrice Small creates cover-to-cover passion, a keen sense of history, and suspense."
—*Publishers Weekly*

"Bertrice Small doesn't just push the limits—she reinvents them."
—**The Literary Times*

"Ms. Small delights and thrills."
—*Rendezvous*

"[Her novels] tell an intriguing story, they are rich in detail, and they are all so very hard to put down."
—The Best Reviews

"Intriguing . . . fascinating."
—*Affaire de Coeur*

"[A] captivating blend of sensuality and rich historical drama."
—Rosemary Rogers

"Brimming with colorful characters and rich in historical detail, Small's boldly sensual love story is certain to please her many devoted readers."
—*Booklist*

BERTRICE SMALL

A DANGEROUS LOVE

 NEW AMERICAN LIBRARY

New American Library
Published by New American Library, a division of
Penguin Group (USA) Inc., 375 Hudson Street,
New York, New York 10014, USA
Penguin Group (Canada), 90 Eglinton Avenue East, Suite 700, Toronto,
Ontario M4P 2Y3, Canada (a division of Pearson Penguin Canada Inc.)
Penguin Books Ltd., 80 Strand, London WC2R 0RL, England
Penguin Ireland, 25 St. Stephen's Green, Dublin 2,
Ireland (a division of Penguin Books Ltd.)
Penguin Group (Australia), 250 Camberwell Road, Camberwell, Victoria 3124,
Australia (a division of Pearson Australia Group Pty. Ltd.)
Penguin Books India Pvt. Ltd., 11 Community Centre, Panchsheel Park,
New Delhi - 110 017, India
Penguin Group (NZ), cnr Airborne and Rosedale Roads, Albany,
Auckland 1310, New Zealand (a division of Pearson New Zealand Ltd.)
Penguin Books (South Africa) (Pty.) Ltd., 24 Sturdee Avenue,
Rosebank, Johannesburg 2196, South Africa

Penguin Books Ltd., Registered Offices:
80 Strand, London WC2R 0RL, England

First published by New American Library,
a division of Penguin Group (USA) Inc.

First Printing, October 2006
1 3 5 7 9 10 8 6 4 2

NEW AMERICAN LIBRARY and logo are trademarks of Penguin Group (USA) Inc.

LIBRARY OF CONGRESS CATALOGING-IN-PUBLICATION DATA:

Small, Bertrice.
A dangerous love / Bertrice Small.
p. cm.
ISBN 0-451-21978-3 (trade pbk.)
1. Great Britain—History—Edward IV, 1461–1483—Fiction. I. Title.
PS3569.M28D36 2006
813'.54—dc22   2006014345

Set in Goudy
Designed by Ginger Legato

Printed in the United States of America

PUBLISHER'S NOTE

This is a work of fiction. Names, characters, places, and incidents either are the product of the author's imagination or are used fictitiously, and any resemblance to actual persons, living or dead, business establishments, events, or locales is entirely coincidental.

The publisher does not have any control over and does not assume any responsibility for author or third-party Web sites or their content.

For Maryl Killmeyer, a friend

Chapter 1

"Adair! Adair! Now, where has that child gotten to this time?" Nursie asked herself aloud. Pray God she hadn't slipped out of the hall, as she so often did. Not now. Not when the Lancastrians were prowling the countryside, causing havoc. Especially when she had been specifically told not to wander about in these dangerous times. Not that Adair Radcliffe ever listened to anyone except herself, Nursie considered. "Adair!" she called again impatiently. "Oh, bless my stars!" the servant cried, jumping back as her charge leaped out from behind a high-backed chair.

"Boo!" Adair Radcliffe said, grinning wickedly at her keeper.

"You bad thing," Nursie cried. "You have given me quite a fright, child, but come. Your mother and father want to see you in the hall. Hurry along now, my precious. You don't want to disobey your parents."

"They've burned the village," the six-year-old girl said. "I was up in the west tower, and I could see it. And the fields as well."

"These are terrible times," Nursie muttered, catching the child's hand and leading her from the corridor into the great hall of Stanton. She saw her master and mistress at the far end of the room. They stood by the large open fireplace in earnest conversation. "Here she is, my lord, my lady," Nursie said as they reached the Earl and Countess of Stanton. She curtsied, and then moved away, but Jane Radcliffe bade her remain.

"What we have to say concerns you as well, Nursie." The Countess of Stanton looked both worried and sad. "Come, and let us all sit down."

1

Adair climbed into her father's lap, waiting to hear what her mother would say.

"You must save the child, Nursie," Jane Radcliffe began. "The Lancastrians are moving toward the hall. My husband and I are known Yorkists. They have burned the village and killed everyone they could lay their hands upon. They showed no mercy to old or young, we have been told by the few who managed to flee to the hall. They will kill everyone here when they come. You must take Adair to he who fathered her. You must take her to King Edward. He recognized her at her birth, and when you tell him what has happened here, the king will take her into his own household. The queen will not be pleased, for she is a cold woman, but when I left her service, she swore she would remember me with kindness. Tell her for the peace of my soul to render that kindness to my child. It is my dying wish."

"My lady!" Nursie cried, paling.

The Earl of Stanton put Adair from his lap. "Go and comfort your mother, my child," he told her. Then he turned his attention to Nursie. "You are not a young woman any longer, Elsbeth," he began, "but Jane and I must entrust you with our most precious possession, our daughter. The Lancastrians have almost finished marauding through the village and fields. It is several hours until sunset, and they will attack the hall before then. They will kill all they find. They must not find Adair."

"But how can we escape them, my lord?" Nursie quavered. It was true she wasn't young, but neither was she old. She wanted to live.

"There is a tunnel beneath the hall. At one end are horses, saddled. Their bags contain food for several days. And water. By tomorrow at this time the Lancastrians will have departed. You will exit the tunnel. Ride south, Elsbeth. For London. Someone will know where to find the king. Take Adair to him. When you have found King Edward, tell any who would stop you that Adair is his daughter, her ladyship the Countess of Stanton, come to seek his protection. Do not allow anyone to prevent you from getting to the king, Elsbeth. Do you understand me?"

Nursie nodded. "I will go and pack what I can take for my little mistress," she said, standing. "With your permission, my lord."

He nodded. "Go."

Nursie left the hall quietly.

"She is loyal, thank God and his blessed Mother," Jane Radcliffe said.

"The last of my grandfather's bastards," he replied. "We were born in the same year. I always remember how shocked my mother was by Elsbeth's birth. Why my mother thought he was no longer interested in things of the flesh as an old man, I do not know. I was five when he died, and I still remember coming upon him in a corridor going at a maidservant with robust vigor. He had the girl up against a wall, and from her cries it was obvious he was giving her pleasure."

"John," the countess murmured softly, "these are not stories for Adair's ears. We have more important things to discuss with our daughter."

"Aye," the Earl of Stanton agreed. "We do." He sat next to his wife on the settle and, taking Adair from her mother's lap, set her before them. "Now, Adair, I would have you listen well to what we have to tell you. King Edward the Fourth got you on your mother. I was unable to give your mother a child, and the king desired her. But your mother is an honorable woman. She refused him. He persisted and came to me. I gave them my permission to lie with each other, provided he created Stanton into an earldom, and that he recognize any daughter born and provide her dower. But I would recognize a daughter too, and give her my name. I did not sire you, Adair, but you are my child nonetheless, and I have always loved you. Now, however, you must use your connection with the king to help you to survive what is to come. And always remember you are a Radcliffe."

"What if I had been a boy, Da?" the little girl asked him.

"The king would not have recognized you. Only I would have," the earl explained. "But there is one other thing. Upon my death you become the Countess of Stanton in your own right, Adair. And I will be dead by the morrow."

"Da!" the little girl cried, stricken. Her violet-colored eyes were large in her pale face. "No!"

"Adair, I cannot flee in the face of this Lancastrian incursion. Stanton has been my family's home for centuries. Once it was only the

Scots we fought. That we English now fight one another pains me, my child. Thrones mean little to simple folk. But I will defend my home until my last breath, and your mother has elected to remain by my side, though I would wish it otherwise," the earl told Adair.

"Mama?" the girl looked at her mother. "Would you leave me?"

"Nay, Adair, not willingly. But I will not leave your father to face the futile wrath of the Lancastrians alone. We will defend Stanton together. Know this, my daughter: I did not love your father when we were first wed. But that is not unusual for people like us. Those of our station do not marry for love. I brought your father land and coin. However, I came to love him, and because I cannot imagine life without him, I will die by his side as I have lived by it. And because you are strong you will survive, and you will remember that I love you," Jane Radcliffe told her only child quietly.

Adair began to weep. "I am only a little girl," she said piteously. "I need you!"

"Cease that caterwauling immediately!" Jane Radcliffe commanded her daughter sternly. "You do not have the luxury of sorrow now, Adair. Not if you expect to survive past this day. I did not bear you to see you needlessly slaughtered by a pack of rabid partisan fools! You must seize the future, my daughter, and live to rebuild Stanton one day. The king, your sire, will see you have a husband, and by agreement with your father that husband will take our name. The Radcliffes will eventually return to Stanton. The Lancastrians can slay us, but if you live, we defeat them for good and all."

Adair swallowed back her sobs. She stood tall and straightened her little shoulders. "I hate the Lancastrians," she said in a grim voice.

"Hate," the Earl of Stanton said, "is a wasted emotion, my child. Do not waste your passions on hate, Adair. Escape Stanton, and live for our family. Come, now, and give me a kiss, my child." John Radcliffe held out his arms to her, and Adair flew into them, struggling to hold back her anguish. He stroked her sable hair gently, and then, after kissing her on both cheeks, he turned Adair to her mother.

Jane Radcliffe struggled with her own grief, but she would not give in to it. Enfolding her only child in her arms, she held her close for a long moment. Then she, too, kissed Adair on both of her cheeks. "Be brave, my child," she said quietly. "John Radcliffe willingly gave you his name, and you are his daughter, though another sired you on me. Always remember that, and bring no shame on the Radcliffes."

Adair stepped back and looked at both her parents. She was only six years old, but suddenly she felt so much older. "I will remember everything," she said, "but especially I will remember that I am a Radcliffe."

"We can ask no more of you than that," the Earl of Stanton told her.

Nursie came back into the hall carrying a small bundle. "We are ready," she said.

"Did my serving woman give you the money pouch, and have you put it on?" Jane Radcliffe wanted to know. "There are two gold coins and a goodly number of silver coins inside it, Elsbeth. And did she give you Adair's garnet velvet skirt? There are five gold coins sewn in the hem of it."

"I have them both, my lady," Nursie replied.

"Go south," the earl said. "Where the sun rises is east. Where it sets is west. North is over the border into Scotland. South is away from it. Do not travel the roads. Keep to the fields, and be very cautious. Trust no one, Elsbeth. Adair must reach her sire safely. It is her only chance of survival. And yours."

"My lord!" The bailiff ran into the hall. "The Lancastrian rabble are approaching the hall. We've barred the doors and shuttered the windows, but there is little else we can do. They will break in soon enough."

"Rally those you can," the earl said quietly, and the bailiff ran out with a nod.

Nursie picked a torch from the wall holder.

"Come," John Radcliffe said. He led his wife, daughter, and Nursie from the hall, stopping to take a small lantern and several candles from a small cabinet as he went down into the cellar of the building. A large wolfhound arose from before the fire where he had been sleeping, and ambled after them, walking by Adair's side.

"Beiste wants to come with me," the little girl said, putting her hand on the animal's head as they hurried along.

" 'Tis not a bad idea," the earl noted. "He's intelligent and obedient, and will defend his mistress. Yes, Beiste will go with you, my child."

Down into the deepest part of the hall they went, and down a narrow, dark corridor. When they reached the end of the passage the earl reached out, feeling about, and then suddenly a small, low door sprang open with a noisy creak. "Here is the mouth of the tunnel," he said. Then he gave Nursie the candles he carried, and lit the lantern from her torch. "The other end of the tunnel is well hidden," he told the older woman. "It opens out a goodly mile from the hall in the wood by Stanton Water. Do not come out until you are certain the Lancastrians have been long gone. Turn to the right when you exit the tunnel, and you will be headed south. Godspeed, Elsbeth, my kin."

Nursie took up the earl's hand and kissed it. "God bless you, my lord," she said. "I will keep the bairn safe. My life on it!"

The earl picked Adair up and kissed her on the lips. "Be brave, daughter, and remember you are a Radcliffe."

"I promise, Da," she answered him as he set her back down again.

"And remember how much your mother loved you, my darling daughter," Jane Radcliffe said softly. There were tears in her violet eyes, but she would not shed them. "And be certain you tell your sire that the Radcliffes stood strong for him." Then she hugged Adair before pushing her into the narrow little tunnel. "Farewell, Adair. God bless and keep you," she called as her husband closed the hidden door and pulled a decrepit cabinet in front of it to conceal it even further.

"Mama?" Adair's voice trembled at the sudden separation and the darkness around her. She jumped, frightened, as a hand touched her sleeve.

" 'Tis me, my precious," Nursie's comforting voice said. "Come along now. We must reach the tunnel's end as soon as we can." Elsbeth—or Nursie, as Adair called her—knew that the sounds of the battle in the house above them would not be entirely drowned out by the depth in which they now stood. She did not want the little girl's last memory of her parents and Stanton Hall to be that of screams and dying. So she hurried the child along the underground passage lit only by the scant light from the flickering lamp. The air was fetid, but chill. As they went she noted the corridor they traveled, while dug from the dirt, was buttressed with stone along the walls, and wooden beams above them. She had lived in this place her entire life, and never known of this tunnel's existence.

The wolfhound went before them, sniffing, alert. When they reached the end of the passage it opened into a small cave with a narrow opening to the outside. There were, to Nursie's relief, three stalls in which the two animals the earl had promised them were now saddled and tethered, placidly munching upon the hay and grain in their feed boxes. Beiste immediately went to each horse and sniffed and nuzzled it. The horses replied in kind.

"Now listen to me, Adair," Nursie said quietly. "You must be very, very quiet. We do not want those wicked Lancastrians to find us here. They would kill us. Do you understand me?" Her mild gray eyes looked into the child's violet ones.

Adair nodded. Her ears seemed to pick up just the faintest sounds of shouting, and she was almost certain that she smelled smoke, but she said nothing.

Nursie went to the horses and took the two blankets from the rear of their saddles. Entering the empty stall, she spread the blankets out. "Come, child. You must sleep now," she told her.

"Will you sleep too?" Adair asked her.

"Not yet, my precious, but later," Nursie promised as Adair lay down. She spread her wool cloak over the little girl. "What fun to sleep in a lovely bed of sweet-smelling hay," she told the child.

"Will the Lancastrians kill my parents?" Adair wanted to know.

"Yes," Nursie answered her.

"Why?" Adair's eyelids were growing heavier, but she needed an answer to her question.

"Because they are loyal to good King Edward, and the Lancastrians are loyal to the mad old king, Henry of Lancaster," Nursie explained as best she might. "Now that King Edward has returned to England he has been welcomed by the commoners, and the mad king sent packing. The Lancastrians are angry. They strike out at Yorkists whenever and wherever they can, my precious. But they will not get you! I have given my word to your father and your mother, my little lady. Nursie will keep you safe. Now you must go to sleep, for we have several hard weeks of traveling ahead of us."

Adair yawned. "Good night, Nursie," she murmured, and was fast asleep, the wolfhound stretched out by her side, his great head next to hers.

Elsbeth sat in the hay, her back to the wood of the stall, listening. A great troupe of horsemen thundered by just a short distance upstream of the cave. The smell of smoke became stronger. Then there was the sound of thunder, and the rain began to pour down outside of the cave, but inside they were dry. The horses stirred restlessly once or twice, and finally, convinced they would be safe for the night, Elsbeth allowed herself the luxury of sleep, curling up on the other side of the child.

She awoke as the faint light of the new day shone beyond the thick brambles hiding the entrance to the cave. Again she heard the sound of horses, but this time they stopped briefly at Stanton Water. Beiste raised his shaggy head up, listening. She tensed nervously. Then she realized the men outside her hidey-hole were only watering their animals and relieving themselves. They were shortly on their way again. The dog laid his head back down. But she waited until the sound of the troupe had faded into silence again. Then Elsbeth leaned over and gently shook Adair.

"I must leave the cave for a short while, my precious," she said. "You will remain until I return. Beiste will stay with you and keep you safe."

"Do not be long," Adair said sleepily, lowering her head back down again. Her eyes closed, and the dog pressed closer to her.

Elsbeth stood up, brushing the hay from her skirts. Then, going to the entrance of the cave, she listened hard before drawing the greenery aside and sidling out. The day was gray. The rain was still falling, but now it was a fine mist. All around her it was silent. There was not a note of birdsong, or animals lowing. Carefully Elsbeth slipped through the woods and quickly crossed the open meadow before Stanton Hall. What had been a gracious home was now a smoking ruin. The air was heavy with the smell of wet, burned wood, for the rains had tempered some of the destruction. Bodies were everywhere, and Elsbeth recognized many of them.

She found the Earl of Stanton where he had died fighting before his home, his sword still in his hand. Lady Jane, his wife, was in another area. She had been stripped naked and obviously violated before her throat had been cut. Her delicate limbs were all skewed crookedly, her fair skin bruised and beaten. Elsbeth could not help but weep at the sight of her gracious mistress so abused. She had to bury them. She could not leave them here for the birds and beasts to ravage. She looked about for something with which she might dig a grave. Finding nothing, she wept harder. What was she to do? And then she knew, although the realization pained her deeply. Turning, she left the scene of destruction and returned across the meadow into the woodland and to the cave where Lady Adair Radcliffe, the Countess of Stanton, was waiting for her Nursie. Adair was her first priority. The dead were dead. Their pain and travails were over now. Adair had to be saved. She had to be taken to the man who sired her so she might grow up and return to Stanton one day with a fine husband who would rebuild it all.

"I was becoming frightened," Adair said as Nursie reentered the cave. "Where were you? You were gone so long." She had awakened and was walking nervously about the little cave.

"I went to the hall," Elsbeth said candidly. "They are all dead, my lady. Now we must leave here. The countryside is like a tomb. Not a creature is stirring."

"I have shaken the blankets and rolled them up," Adair told Nursie. "But I am too little to replace them on the horses."

"I will do that," Elsbeth replied. "Are you hungry?"

"Yes," Adair answered her. "I should like some oat porridge and ham."

"I can give you bread, a sliver of cheese, and an apple," Elsbeth said quietly.

Adair pressed her lips together with disapproval.

"We have no fire, no kettle, no oats, or a larder," Elsbeth continued, "and many like us have not what we have, my lady."

Adair sighed deeply. "Give me what you can then, Nursie," she said.

Elsbeth portioned out the food carefully. Who knew how long it would be before they would run out of the supplies the earl had seen packed for them? Or where they would be able to purchase more? If they were fortunate they might come upon a monastery or convent, and beg a night's shelter and a meal or two. But she suspected they would be traveling rough for most of the way south to London. There might be inns here and there, but such places were to be avoided. They were peopled by thieves and dishonest folk who would consider her and the child she shepherded vulnerable to their chicanery. No, the weeks ahead of them would not be easy. She quickly fed the child.

Then she led a horse from its stall, tightened its cinch, replaced the blanket behind its saddle, and looked to Adair. "Have you relieved yourself, child?" she asked.

Adair nodded solemnly.

Elsbeth picked her up and set her astride the animal. Then she tightened the cinch on the horse she would ride, put the second blanket behind the saddle, and tied on the small bundle she had packed the previous day. Then she clambered up onto the horse, and with the wolfhound by their side they exited the cave. The woman turned her mount to the right as they came forth, remembering the earl's instructions. For several hours they followed Stanton Water, which flowed in a fairly straight line through the trees into the fields. When the stream turned east they left it behind. Around them the countryside was both silent and desolate. The herds of cattle belonging to Stanton were nowhere to be found. They saw no one. The raiders had done a fairly good job of destroying and stealing, although Elsbeth knew there would be some who had hidden away like themselves, and escaped the fury of the Lancastrians.

It was several days before they saw any sign of life, but those few people they saw hurried by them in the fields or woodlands, eyes averted. No words were exchanged at all, only furtive glances to ascertain whether they were dangerous. One man did look enviously at their horses, but Elsbeth's hand went immediately to her belt, where a large knife was visible, and Beiste growled menacingly. The man lowered his eyes again and passed by.

After almost two weeks of travel they had the good fortune to come upon a convent just at sunset. The nuns took them in, and when they had heard the story Elsbeth told them—although she was wise enough to leave out Adair's natural paternity—the sisters invited them to remain for a few days to rest their animals and regain their strength. They bathed Adair, fed her a good hot meal of vegetable potage and buttered bread, then put her in a comfortable bed, and Elsbeth wept as she thanked them for their kindness.

They remained two full days, and then departed. Elsbeth had dug out two silver pennies from her little hoard and left them on the altar of the convent church, as was the custom for visitors. She knew the nuns would be surprised to find them, and she smiled to herself as they rode along again. The farther south they traveled, the more difficult it became to keep from the roads, which it seemed were everywhere. And villages—there were so many of them. Elsbeth had never been more than five miles from Stanton, and as they traveled she realized how different the rest of England was from the wild Northumbrian countryside along the Scottish border. It frightened her, but she would show no fear before her charge. And Adair was fascinated and intrigued by what she saw. Especially the towns. But Elsbeth would not go into them. Seeing them from a distance, she would circle about them until she could head south again.

The autumn was almost upon them. The days were growing shorter, and their hours of travel were fewer. Adair had caught a cold, and Elsbeth was worried it might develop into something worse if they did not reach the king soon. The child had always had good health, but these past weeks of long travel, little food, and sleeping outdoors on the damp ground were beginning to take their toll. They both

needed an end to their journey, and warm shelter. Then one afternoon they were forced to cross a wide, high road, and Elsbeth saw a
sign. Unlike many women of any class, Elsbeth could read. It had
amused her ancient father to teach her in the months before his
death, when he had grown too frail to do anything else. The sign
read LONDON, and pointed toward one of the four roads before her.
Elsbeth considered. Perhaps now that they were so far south it would
be safer and quicker to follow the road, especially considering Adair's
worsening health. She turned their horses in the direction the sign
indicated.

They saw only a few folk as they moved along the road, and as with
those they had seen in the woodlands and fields they traversed, everyone was minding their own business. Elsbeth began to feel that perhaps she had made the correct decision. And then she heard behind
her a troop of horses. Reaching out to grab the reins of Adair's animal,
she struggled to get out of the way, but she was not quick enough.
They were quickly surrounded by mounted men. Elsbeth pulled her
mount and Adair's to a halt, that the others might at least pass them
by. But to her surprise the others came to a halt too.

The gentleman leading the troop—for by his apparel she could see
he was a gentleman—detached himself, and rode over to where Elsbeth and Adair now sat upon their horses. "Woman," the gentleman
demanded, "what are you doing out on the road in these dangerous
times? And with a little maid. Where are you from, and to where are
you journeying with only this great wolfhound for your protection?"

Elsbeth opened her mouth, but she was so frightened she could not
speak for the life of her. What had she done, coming onto the road?
Why had she not obeyed the earl's directive? Would they now be
killed for her foolishness? But the gentleman addressing her was very
handsome, and of slight stature. He was commanding, but did not
seem menacing. She swallowed and tried again to speak, when to her
surprise Adair did.

"I am Lady Adair Radcliffe, the Countess of Stanton, sir. I have
come to seek the protection of the king, as my parents are now dead,
slaughtered in his good cause."

The gentleman reached out and pushed Adair's hood from her head, ignoring the dog's deep growl. He nodded. "You look like your mother," he said. "I remember her."

"And who, sir, are you?" Adair demanded in a slightly imperious tone that caused the gentleman to smile, obviously amused by her bravery.

"I am your uncle Richard, Duke of Gloucester, my lady Countess of Stanton," the gentleman said. "I think it fortunate that I have come upon you instead of someone else. Is your servant without speech, Adair Radcliffe?"

"Nay. I think you have frightened her, my lord. She has been very brave these past weeks, and I owe my life to her," Adair answered him truthfully. "Her name is Elsbeth, but I call her Nursie, and my hound is Beiste."

Richard of Gloucester nodded, turning to the woman. "You need not fear me, Mistress Elsbeth. I am King Edward's brother, and I will take you to a place of safety. You cannot reach London today, and he is not there now. Tomorrow I will send you on with two of my own men to guide you and protect you. You must go to the queen's household, and she still is in sanctuary at Westminster with her children."

"Thank you, my lord." Elsbeth had managed to find her voice again.

"The child looks ill," the duke said to Elsbeth.

"I fear the conditions in which we have been forced to travel have caused it, my lord," Elsbeth said wearily. "We have had little to eat, and have sheltered mostly out-of-doors. It has not been easy for my little mistress. Only the dog's warmth has kept her from worse harm."

He nodded. "No, it would not have been easy," he agreed. Then, reaching out from his saddle, he lifted the startled child from hers, setting her before him. "You will ride with me, Adair Radcliffe," he said, and drew his fur-lined cloak around her little body. Then he looked to the great dog, who was now baring his teeth. "Come, Beiste!" he commanded the animal, and, recognizing the voice of authority, Beiste obeyed.

Instinctively Adair snuggled against the duke's chest. Her eyes grew heavy as they moved off, the even gait of the horse rocking her into slumber as they rode. Richard of Gloucester looked down on the child for a long moment. Yes, he did indeed remember Jane Radcliffe. She had been a great beauty, although she was genuinely unconscious of that beauty. Her ebony hair, her violet eyes, and her serene face had attracted his brother. And Edward had never been able to resist a beautiful woman. Richard had been only a boy then, but he remembered.

Fascinated, he had watched as his elder sibling pursued the lovely Jane Radcliffe. But she, a lady-in-waiting to the king's wife, and a married woman herself, had carefully avoided Edward as much as she could, for she was an honorable woman. But Edward could not be deterred. He had gone to her husband, gotten his permission to futter Jane, and Baron Stanton had become the Earl of Stanton. And when Jane had conceived a child she had left court, never to return. He had learned later from Edward that the child had been a girl, and that Edward had acknowledged her birth, setting aside a dower for her.

Richard of Gloucester, now a young man, looked down at Jane Radcliffe's daughter. She was her mother in miniature. There was nothing of her sire about her, thank God, but he thought that her assured manner was much like his own mother, Cicely Neville. His sister-in-law, the queen, would not be pleased by this addition to her family, but he knew his brother, the king, would keep the child safe. *I will take her myself*, the duke thought, *if need be*. He was interested to learn Adair's story. Why and how had her parents met their untimely end at the hands of Lancastrians?

They reached the monastery where he intended sheltering that night. The gates of St. Wulfstan's swung open for them, for they had been expected. The prior was a distant cousin, and his hospitality would be generous. A young monk hurried to take the duke's horse, not just a little surprised to see a woman, a child, and a great wolfhound among the party. Elsbeth was quickly off her horse. She reached out to the duke, and he handed Adair down into her arms before dismounting himself. Beiste was immediately by their side, and followed along.

"Come with me, mistress," he said to her, and she followed him into the building, carrying the little girl. The duke appeared to know exactly where he was going and, reaching a large carved double oak door, opened it, ushering Elsbeth inside.

"Dickon!" A portly man with a youthful face arose from a chair by the fire. "And what, or who, cousin, is this that you bring with you?" He peered at Elsbeth, and then at Adair, who had just been set down upon the floor, stepping back as the wolfhound came immediately to the little girl's side.

"Peter, I have brought Lady Adair Radcliffe, the Countess of Stanton, and her servant. I found them wandering out on the road. Edward sired the child several years ago. Now she is seeking the king's protection."

"Are you certain the child is who she says she is?" Prior Peter Neville asked the duke. "What proof can be offered that this is not a fraud? The queen will not be pleased, Dickon. You know how jealous she is of even her own children. If it were not for Lady Margaret I do not know how they would fare."

"The child looks exactly like her mother, and I remember Jane Radcliffe well, Peter," the duke said. "Look at her. She is delicate and has fine features." He held out his hand to Adair. "Come, little one, and make your curtsy to Prior Peter."

Adair stepped forward and curtsied to the cleric, but she was silent.

"How far have you come, my child?" the prior asked her.

"From Stanton Hall," Adair answered him. "It is burned now."

"And where is Stanton Hall?" the prior pressed further.

"In Northumbria, on the border with Scotland. You can see the Cheviots from my bedchamber window, sir," Adair replied.

"Her accent is northern," the prior admitted.

"Peter, the child, her dog, and her nurse have been on the road for several weeks now. They are tired, half-starved, and frozen to the bone. They need dry beds and hot food. You have an abundance of both at St. Wulfstan's," the duke said. "I ask you to shelter them tonight. Tomorrow I will send them to Westminster to the queen."

"The dog too? She will not be pleased," Prior Peter repeated.

"But she will take Adair and her party in, for it will please my brother, and Elizabeth Woodville is always prepared to please Edward," Richard of Gloucester murmured softly.

"And what if she refuses?" the prior asked.

"Then I will take my niece into my household," was the reply. "She is my blood kin, after all. I will be marrying shortly, and my bride loves children even as do I."

"I do not need the queen," Adair suddenly spoke up. "If my sire, the king, will give me a rich husband I can rebuild Stanton. I would trouble no one but for that."

Prior Peter looked astounded by the child's blunt speech, but the duke laughed.

"One day, Adair, you will be given a husband," he said, "but now is not the time. You are too valuable a prize, poppet, to be given quickly or squandered rashly."

"I? Valuable? I am poor, my lord, I assure you. All I have Nursie carries. That, two horses, and a wolfhound."

"You are the Countess of Stanton, poppet," the duke told her. "You will bring your husband a title and an estate. That makes you valuable, my lady Adair. And the king is your sire, which but adds to your value. And you have a fine dower, for my brother promised it at your birth. He will not have forgotten that."

"Indeed, my child, you can be considered a wealthy female," the prior declared. Adair's boldness in speaking up for herself had surprised him, but then he had decided he liked her. Reaching for a small bell on the table next to him, he rang it loudly, and immediately a young monk answered his call. "Take my lady the Countess of Stanton, her dog, and her servant to the women's guesthouse. See that they are all well fed and made comfortable."

"Yes, Reverend Father," the monk replied.

Richard of Gloucester knelt down and took Adair's small hand in his. "I will come and see you before you go to sleep. I would like to learn why you have come to seek your sire's protection. Go with your Nursie now, my poppet."

"Are you really my uncle?" Adair asked him softly.

"I am indeed," the duke replied with a smile. This little girl had already caught at his heartstrings.

Adair threw her arms about his neck and hugged him. "I am so glad!" she said. Then, releasing him, she took Elsbeth's hand and followed the young monk from the room, the wolfhound following in their wake.

"Tell me how Edward managed to sire that fairy child," Prior Peter said. "Pour us some wine, Dickon, and come sit with me."

The duke did as his cousin suggested. Then he told Prior Peter the story of King Edward's seduction of Jane Radcliffe. "She pleased him but briefly, for she was an honorable woman, and not content to be my brother's leman."

"I am surprised, but not shocked, by her husband's behavior, though while the lady had honor, her husband, it would seem, did not," the prior said.

"He was childless and had, I am told, come to the conclusion that after three wives his lack of an heir lay with himself, and not his wives. He was forty. Jane was sixteen, and my older brother's reputation preceded him. John Radcliffe wanted an heir. Edward tells me he asked for the earldom in exchange for his wife's virtue. A lad resulting from such a liaison would be recognized only by the earl as his son and heir. But the king would recognize a daughter, though Radcliffe would give her his name, and make her his heiress if no other children came. Which, of course, they did not."

Prior Peter shook his head. "Cousin Edward's behavior has always amazed me. He is like a stag, forever in rut. How the queen bears it I do not know."

"Elizabeth Woodville stomachs it because she is queen, and as long as she keeps producing children for him and makes no complaint, she will remain queen. The woman's ambition for herself and her family is horrific. Of them all only her oldest brother, Lord Rivers, can be called a gentleman."

"You have never liked her, Dickon, have you?" the prior remarked.

"No," the duke admitted. "I have not. Warwick had negotiated a good marriage for Edward with the French princess, Bona of Savoy,

King Louis's sister-in-law. We needed that alliance, and it would have brought honor to the house of York. But Edward let Elizabeth Woodville lead him about by his cock, and into a secret alliance. My brother had also managed to promise marriage to Lady Eleanor Butler before he seduced Elizabeth and married her. What was different about Elizabeth Woodville I will never understand. And then we lost Warwick's friendship over it. Another disaster because of that damned woman."

"I hear that Henry of Lancaster and his son, Prince Edward, are both dead now," the prior remarked.

"And Warwick too, the bastard," the duke said. "I was to marry his daughter, Anne, but after the breach with my brother Warwick gave her to Prince Edward of Lancaster. She's widowed now, and we will marry when her mourning is over for her father and her husband. We have loved each other since we were children."

"I am told your brother, George, who is wed to Warwick's elder daughter, Isabel, opposes your match with the Lady Anne," the prior murmured.

"Do not take sides, Peter," the duke warned his Neville cousin. "Though George is reunited with Edward and has begged his pardon for his treason, I have ever been loyal to Edward, as all know. I will have my way in this. George is greedy. He wants all of Warwick's inheritance, not just half. He doesn't care whom I wed. He just doesn't want me to get any of Warwick's lands or wealth. And believe me, he will betray Edward again should the opportunity arise and he thinks it of benefit to himself. It is his nature."

The cleric drank down his wine and rose to his feet. "It is the dinner hour, Dickon, and I am hungry. Aren't you?"

Richard of Gloucester stood up with a small smile. "Aye, I am hungry," he agreed. "And you always set a fine table, Cousin Peter, despite your vow of poverty."

Prior Peter chuckled as he led his guest into the refectory of the monastery. They took their places at the high board, and after having blessed the food to come, the cleric motioned his guest and his monks to sit down. Immediately the silver goblets at their places were filled with fragrant wine. The duke doubted the monks shared in the exclusive bounty accorded the prior's high board, where he sat with his cousin and half a dozen of his right-hand monks.

The servers began to offer the dishes to the high board first. There was broiled salmon, mussels with a sauce of Dijon mustard, and creamed cod to begin with, followed by duck, ham, and beef. The high board was offered artichokes steamed in white wine. The bread was still warm from the ovens of the bake house. There were several cheeses, and finally apples baked with cinnamon and honey. Richard of Gloucester noted that the tables below the high board were served creamed cod, a rabbit stew, bread, cheese, and fresh apples. The wooden goblets were filled with beer.

When the meal had concluded the duke arose, thanked his cousin, and departed for the women's guesthouse, a small building near the monastery gate. There he found Elsbeth bathing Adair in a small oak tub by an open hearth. "Have you eaten?" he asked her. "Was there enough?"

"Yes, my lord. They brought us good hot rabbit stew, bread and cheese, and wine," she answered him. "I never tasted anything so good."

"You probably have"—the duke chuckled—"but after several weeks on the road I know that hot food does taste especially good. I have been on campaign enough to understand that." He took a drying cloth from the rack before the fire and, wrapping it about Adair, lifted her from the tub. "And you, my poppet, has your hunger been assuaged now?" He dried her little body gently, and took the chemise that Elsbeth handed him to slip over Adair's childish form.

"Let me do her hair, my lord," Elsbeth said. She was amazed and touched by the kindness the duke was showing to her mistress. She brushed Adair's long black hair until it shone with reddish lights. Then she braided it into a single plait. When she had finished she said to Adair, "Now, my precious, tell the duke what had driven us south to seek the king's protection."

Richard of Gloucester picked Adair up, and, sitting in the single chair by the fire while Elsbeth went about the business of tidying up, he cradled the child in his lap. "Are you warm enough now, Adair?" he asked her.

"Aye, my lord," she whispered. She felt so safe, and she had not felt safe since the night her father and mother had pushed her into the escape tunnel at Stanton Hall.

"Aye, Uncle Dickon," he corrected her gently. "All my nieces call me Uncle Dickon, and while you may not be a princess, Adair, you are my niece too. Now, tell me what happened at Stanton that you were forced to flee."

"The Lancastrians came," Adair began. "In the morning just before sunrise they came, and they burned the village. Then they burned the fields and the barns. They drove off or slaughtered the livestock. Many of our folk were killed. Others fled. My da and mama put me in a tunnel with Elsbeth and Beiste. The horses were already waiting for us. They told us to flee."

"Who told you that the king sired you?" he asked her, curious.

"Mama, but Da said I was still a Radcliffe, and should be proud," Adair answered him. "They said the king would protect me. And Mama said that the queen had told her when Mama left her service that Mama would always have her friendship. I was to ask the queen that that friendship be offered to me, for it was my mama's dying wish."

The duke nodded, then turned to Elsbeth. "You are certain both the earl and his wife are deceased?"

"Aye, my lord," the serving woman replied. "I went up to the hall myself the day after, before we departed for London. I saw both of their murdered bodies lying slaughtered in the courtyard of the hall. I had to leave them there, and it has troubled my conscience ever since, my lord. But I had no means of burying them, and no one to aid me in such an endeavor. The earl had ordered me to get my little lady to safety, and that was my first obligation." Elsbeth wiped the tears that had begun to flow from her eyes.

"You did your duty well," the duke praised her. "You have naught to regret, mistress. Why, though, I wonder, was Stanton attacked?"

"When word came of King Edward's victories and the final defeat of the Lancastrians, one of the Percys decided to attack the few York-ists in the region in an effort to avenge King Henry. And, I expect, to steal their lands. The Radcliffes were more prominent than most, and the earl, while never involving himself in the politics of it all, had also never hidden the fact that he stood with King Edward."

"Why was Stanton not better defended?" Duke Richard wanted to know.

"Stanton Hall is not a castle, my lord," Elsbeth explained. "It was a large stone house alone out on the moor. It had suffered destruction in the past, but was always rebuilt. I once heard my father bemoan the fact that the Radcliffes could not get permission to fortify our home or build a castle. The house was built upon a hillock. And a moat had been dug around the bottom of the hillock. The Scots who came call-ing over the border were usually just looking to steal our cattle, our sheep, or a pretty girl."

"You are not near Berwick then?" the duke asked.

"Lord, no!" Elsbeth exclaimed. "We are closer to Cumbria, on the border with Scotland. The region is very desolate, my lord. Those who attacked us were not near neighbors. But if the Radcliffes were killed then the land was for the taking."

He nodded and then, looking down at Adair, smiled softly. The child had fallen asleep in his lap. "Poor little mite," he said, stroking her dark hair. Then he looked to Elsbeth. "Listen well to what I tell you, mistress. My brother will accept his responsibilities with regard to this daughter of his. And the queen will not move against the child for the promise she made to Jane Radcliffe. But do not trust the queen. She is a cold and venal woman whose clever wiles managed to ensnare my lustful brother into wedlock. Even her own children fear her. Her first husband was a Lancastrian knight. Her grown sons from that union are dissolute and greedy, as are most of her relations, save her eldest brother. Did your master give you any coin for the child?"

Elsbeth nodded. "I wear a pouch beneath my skirts, my lord," she told him. "And there are gold coins sewn into the hem of one of my little lady's gowns."

"Keep a few for your mistress, but tomorrow you will give me the bulk of your funds. I will place them with Avram the Jew in Gold-smith's Lane," the duke said.

"A Jew? In England? I thought there were none," Elsbeth said, surprised.

"There are exceptions to every rule, mistress. London is a city of great mercantile importance, and the Jews are the world's bankers. Therefore Avram does business in Goldsmith's Lane even while England's laws prohibit Jews from taking up residence here. I will put Adair's little fortune to him, and the receipt will be with my own household treasurer. You are free to draw upon the monies for the child's care when you need it, but it cannot be stolen from her by any in the queen's household. And should you ever need the aid of Richard, Duke of Gloucester, mistress, you have but to ask.

"I was yet a boy when King Edward took Adair's mother for his leman. Once when my brother George was bullying me she stepped in to protect me from a beating. As you can see," he said, "I am not like either of my older brothers, who are sturdy of frame. I am slender and slight." He smiled. "George was practically a man, but delicate Jane Radcliffe stepped between us and said in her gentle voice, 'It does not behoove your reputation, my lord of Clarence, to abuse your younger sibling, who has really done you no offense.' I remember the look on George's face. It was pure outrage that this beautiful young woman had reprimanded him.

"My brother George is overweening proud, as you will eventually see. But she was Edward's current mistress, and greatly in his favor. Certainly more so than George. He turned on his heel without a word and left us. Then Lady Jane took a silk handkerchief from her sleeve and wiped the blood from my cheek where George's ring had cut it when he struck me. 'You must get that attended to, my lord,' she told me. And then she left me. And another time, when George took all the candied violets from the dish so there were none left for me, Lady Jane gave me some from her own plate. She was always doing kind things like that, mistress. I think I fell in love with her for a short time, and was even jealous of the king. And then she was gone from the court."

Elsbeth's eyes were filled with tears. "She was a very good woman, and a good wife to my lord earl, God assoil both their poor souls." And Elsbeth crossed herself, as did Richard of Gloucester. "But you are a good man too, my lord. It is not my place to thank you for your kindness to my little lady, but I do." Elsbeth caught up the duke's hand and kissed it.

"Thank you," he said. "I recognize Adair as my blood kin, and I will always be there for her as I am for my brother Edward's children. The princesses Elizabeth and Mary will be her playmates. Little Cicely is not even three yet, and little Prince Edward will be a year next month."

"The queen's nursery is a busy one then. But Adair will be no trouble, for I will look after her," Elsbeth said.

"The queen has little to do with her children," the duke responded. "The royal nursery is the province of Lady Margaret Beaufort, whose son, Henry Tudor, is considered the new heir to Lancaster. She is a strong-minded woman, and ambitious for her son. But she is also fair and devout. Adair will be safe under her guidance, and you safe in her service." He stood up, Adair still sleeping in his arms. "Show me the child's cot, and I will put her there. I will come to see her before you depart on the morrow. Midmorning will be soon enough for you to reach Westminster the same day. I shall have two of my men escort you." He followed Elsbeth into another room, Beiste by his side, and, laying Adair down where Elsbeth indicated, drew the coverlet over her as he placed a kiss on her brow. "Sleep well, my lady Countess of Stanton," he said. And then with a brief nod of his head to Elsbeth he left them.

When he had gone Elsbeth sat down upon the pallet cot next to Adair's. Reaching out, she patted the wolfhound's head while reveling in the warmth coming from the wood brazier. God was obviously watching over them, if today was any indication. To have been rescued from their long and miserable travels by the king's brother was more than simple good fortune. And to have that great lord remember Jane Radcliffe with kindness, and to publicly accept Adair as his own kin, was a miracle. Her little lady was warm and dry and well fed for the first time since they had fled from Stanton. Elsbeth whispered a prayer of thanks to God and his blessed Mother. She offered her prayers for the souls of the earl and his wife. Then she lay down to sleep, certain that they were finally safe. As long as Adair was safe nothing else mattered.

Chapter 2

It was the bells sounding for prime that awakened both Elsbeth and Adair. The older woman arose slowly, calling to the child as she did so. "Time to arise, my precious. Today we go to Westminster to meet the queen. You must look your best." She walked to the door of the little guesthouse and, opening it, let the dog out. Then, undoing the bundle she had packed for Adair, she drew out a gown of soft jersey, crimson in color. She spread the garment out on her cot, smoothing the wrinkles from it. Then she poured a little water into a brass basin and directed her charge to get up and make her ablutions.

When Adair had washed her face and hands and scrubbed her teeth with the cloth, Elsbeth slipped the gown over the child's sleeved camise in which she had slept. The garment was cut with fullness from the neckline, and without any waist emphasis. The neck opening was square, and the sleeves tight from shoulder to wrist. The gown had a small train and the hem was trimmed with a darker red silk ribbon. Elsbeth sat her little mistress back upon the cot and brushed her long, dark hair until it was shining. She fit a pair of dark leather shoes upon the child's feet, and set a narrow jeweled band above her forehead. Around her neck she hung a thin gold chain with a small crucifix.

"There!" she said, standing back and viewing the girl. "You are ready to meet the queen and make your case for protection, my precious. Now sit down while I hurry and dress. The duke has promised to come to see you before we go." She hurriedly washed herself in the basin and drew on a dark blue gown similar in design to Adair's. Braiding her nut brown hair, she pinned up the plait and tucked it beneath

25

a soft white cap with a stiff turned-back brim. Then she slid her feet into a pair of worn but still serviceable round-toed leather shoes. Hearing Beiste whining at the door, Elsbeth hurried to let him inside again. He nuzzled her hand with a wet nose as he reentered the guesthouse.

Shortly afterward a young monk came bearing a tray with two small bread trenchers filled with hot oat cereal, and a goblet of cider. "The duke says he will be with you shortly, my lady," the monk addressed Adair. He drew a large bone from his robes. It was yet thick with scraps of meat. "For the animal," he said, and offered the bone to Beiste, who took it from the young man's hand, even allowing the monk to pat him. Then the monk hurried off without another word.

"Do not get your gown stained with food," Elsbeth warned as they began to eat.

They devoured all the hot cereal and ate every bit of the stale bread trenchers, sharing the cider between them.

"Who knows when we will eat again this day?" Elsbeth said. When they had finished she quickly packed up the few things she had unpacked the previous evening.

Richard of Gloucester arrived, and was pleased to see them ready to depart. "How pretty you look, poppet," he complimented Adair. "Crimson is a color that suits you, as it did your mother." He knelt so they might speak face-to-face. "Now, you will remember to make your parents proud, my lady Countess of Stanton. You will behave with grace and dignity no matter the situation. Some at the court are high-flown with reason. Others have little reason. Your mother always spoke gently no matter, and you will make me proud if you do as well." The duke slipped a little gold ring with a tiny green stone from his smallest finger. He placed it upon Adair's middle finger. It just fit. "My gift to you, my lady Countess of Stanton. I will see you again soon." He stood up and spoke now with Elsbeth. "The queen and her household will remain at Westminster for a few more weeks until all is finally settled. It is safer. Make certain Adair reminds the queen publicly of her promise to Jane Radcliffe. Elizabeth Woodville is most careful of what she considers her good name and good word. And my brother, the king, will not deny Adair. He is an honorable man. You may not see him for several weeks, for we are yet mopping up pockets of Lancastrian resistance. I have assigned two of my own soldiers to escort you to Westminster. You should reach there by late afternoon today."

"Thank you, my lord," Elsbeth said. "I do not know how we would have managed without your kind intervention." She curtsied to him. Then she handed him her money pouch. "This is my mistress's fortune, my lord. You wished to put it with the Jew in Goldsmith's Lane," Elsbeth reminded him.

"You managed quite well yourself, mistress," he complimented her. "I am amazed you got this far without incident. You are a brave woman." He took the pouch from her. "You have counted it?" She nodded in the affirmative. "I will place it with the banker," he told her. Then, turning away from her, he picked the little girl up. "I must go, Adair. Be a good little maid, and I will see you soon. Will you give your uncle Dickon a kiss, poppet?"

Adair wrapped her arms about his neck and kissed him twice on both of his ruddy cheeks. "I will give you two kisses," she told him. "One for now, and one for later to remember me by."

Richard of Gloucester chuckled. "I can see you are a minx," he told her as he set her down. "You must not be so free with your kisses with anyone else but me, my lady Countess of Stanton."

"Will you come to see me?" Adair asked him, her young voice anxious.

"I will visit with you each time I am at court," he promised her. "Now go and bid Prior Peter farewell, and thank him for his hospitality," the duke said. He set Adair's cape about her shoulders, pulling the hood over her dark head.

Adair curtsied to him, then took Elsbeth's hand, and they hurried off to find the cleric before terce began. Beiste walked by Adair's side, carrying the large bone in his jaws. The prior was just breaking his fast, but he received his two guests. Adair thanked him nicely for their shelter and the food he had given them.

"And Beiste thanks you too for his fine bone," Adair said sweetly.

Prior Peter looked at the great dog. He was a fine animal, if perhaps a bit scrawny. "The dog wants fattening up," the prior remarked.

"He has had to hunt for his food as we journeyed," Adair explained.

"Indeed," Peter Neville said. "Come now, child, and kneel. I will give you my blessing." He looked to Elsbeth. "You, too, woman! You'll both need my prayers." And when they knelt before him he prayed over them and blessed them.

"Thank you, my lord prior," Adair said, rising, and she kissed the cleric's outstretched hand. "I hope you will remember my parents, and the good folk of Stanton so grievously slain, in your prayers. They were good people."

"I will pray for them, child," Prior Peter promised.

Outside of the prior's dwelling they found their horses and two men at arms awaiting them. They helped Adair and Elsbeth to mount their animals, and then with Beiste alongside them the little party departed the monastery and turned in the direction of Westminster.

They rode for the next four hours, and then stopped to rest the horses. The prior's cook had packed a basket of delicate foods for the two women. The soldiers carried oatcakes and strips of dried meat for their own fare. After an hour they were on the road again, and by three the towers of Westminster came into sight. The duke's men knew exactly where they were going, and brought Adair and her companion to the queen's dwelling within Westminster's vast compound as the darkness fell.

The queen's majordomo was called forth. He looked haughtily upon the duke's men, for he knew his mistress liked her husband's brother no better than the duke liked Elizabeth Woodville. "What is it you want?" he demanded.

"Our master, the Duke of Gloucester, asked that we deliver my lady the Countess of Stanton into the queen's care. He found her yesterday with her servant on the high road seeking the king, who is her natural father. Her family has been slain by Lancastrians, and she is alone in the world."

The majordomo raised a skeptical eyebrow, but the duke's man did not budge. "Who is her mother?" he demanded to know. "I have been with the queen since before the days of her marriage to King Edward."

"My mother was Jane Radcliffe," Adair spoke up quietly.

Suddenly the majordomo softened his attitude. "Lady Jane Radcliffe?" he said. "Yes, I remember her well. Unlike some, she treated my mistress with the greatest respect." He stared at Adair. "You are your mother's image, my lady. Come in! Come in!" He waved a dismissing hand at the duke's men. "You may go. You have done your duty, and I will see that my lady the Countess of Stanton is presented to the queen." He looked at Beiste. "Take the dog to the kennels as you leave."

"Nay, Beiste remains with me," Adair said in a commanding tone. "He is mannerly, sir."

The majordomo shrugged. "Very well," he replied. "Come along now, my lady."

Turning a moment, Adair thanked the duke's men for their service. Then she, Elsbeth, and Beiste followed after the queen's majordomo as he led them into the house, up the stairs, and into the queen's hall, where Elizabeth Woodville was seated with her women and two eldest daughters listening as a minstrel sang. A fire burned in a large stone hearth. The high board was set with plates of cold meats, bread, and cheeses. There was a bowl of both apples and pears.

Elizabeth Woodville looked up as her majordomo came into the chamber. Seeing the woman, the child, and the wolfhound accompanying him, she cocked her head to one side. "What is this, Roger?" she asked him as he came before her.

"Your Highness, may I present to you Lady Adair Radcliffe, the Countess of Stanton. It is not my place to tell you her tale." He stepped back.

Adair came forward and curtsied prettily. "Your Highness, I beg that you give to me the friendship that you once promised to my late mother, Jane Radcliffe, who served you loyally. My parents have been slain by renegade Lancastrians, and I was forced to flee for my life with my servant and my dog. Before they sent me to safety my parents told me the truth of my birth."

"Did they?" Elizabeth Woodville said softly. Had the child looked anything like her sire the queen knew she would have hated her on sight. But Adair Radcliffe looked exactly like her mother. *Perhaps*, the queen thought, *I should still hate her*. But she couldn't. Jane Radcliffe had done everything she could to keep from the king's bed. In the end it was her husband who had sold her for an earldom. Not that it had actually cost Edward a ha'penny, for his leman's husband had land aplenty. "I remember your mother well, Adair Radcliffe. The king must decide what is to be done with you, but until that time you are welcome in my household. Your servant and dog as well," Elizabeth Woodville said with a smile. "How old are you?"

"Six, Your Highness, this August past," Adair answered.

"Elizabeth, Mary, come here to me," the queen called to her two eldest daughters. "Come and meet her ladyship the Countess of Stanton, who will now be in the nursery with you." As the two little girls came forward the queen introduced them. "This is the Princess Elizabeth, who will be seven in February. And Princess Mary, who was five on the sixth of August."

"Oh!" Adair said excitedly, "we share the same birthday, my lady."

Mary of York looked haughtily at Adair. "I do not share my birthday with anyone," she said in a hard little voice. "I am a king's daughter."

"So am I!" Adair snapped back, and then she clapped her hand over her mouth.

Elizabeth Woodville laughed softly. "You do not look like your sire," she remarked, "but you have his pride, I see. Well, the cat's escaped the bag, and there is no help for it. Adair was sired by your own father, my daughters, which is why she will have our aid and comfort, for she is your blood kin. Where is Mags?"

"I am here, Your Highness." Lady Margaret Beaufort came forward. She was a tall woman in her late twenties with chestnut-colored hair that showed from beneath her headdress, and fine dark blue eyes. Although her son was the heir to the house of Lancaster, she was nonetheless a trusted member of the queen's household, and the royal governess. Her intellect and serene manner were much admired.

"This is Adair Radcliffe, the Countess of Stanton, Mags. She's one of Edward's bastards. Her family has been killed, and she has been sent to us. She is a bit younger than Bessie. I'm putting her in the nursery with the girls. You will have charge over her," the queen said. "She has her own servant."

"Very good, Your Highness," Lady Margaret Beaufort said. She looked at Adair. "The dog is yours?"

"Yes, my lady." Adair's little hand rested on Beiste's head.

"He goes into the kennel. I will not have a dog in my nursery," Lady Margaret said in a no-nonsense tone.

"Then I shall go into the kennel with him," Adair said stubbornly. "I will not be separated from Beiste. He is my best friend, and all I have left of Stanton."

"You will not like the kennel," Lady Margaret remarked dryly.

"Probably I will not," Adair admitted, "but I will not send Beiste away. It would be cruel. And I am all he has left of Stanton."

Margaret Beaufort looked down at the little girl standing so politely but defiantly before her. There was something about this child that reached out and touched her heart. "There are cats in the nursery," she pointed out.

"Beiste loves cats," Adair quickly assured her. "There was one who slept with him in my father's hall. And he does not shit indoors but goes out. Even in the rain. And he is a wonderful watchdog as well."

The queen laughed. "I think, Mags, that my lady the Countess of Stanton has made a good case for her wolfhound, don't you?"

Margaret Beaufort allowed a small smile to turn up the corners of her mouth. "I suppose a good watchdog would be a fine addition to the nursery," she agreed. "Very well, child. The dog may come with us. Bessie, Mary, it's time to return to our quarters." She looked at Elsbeth. "You have a name?"

"Yes, my lady. Elsbeth, although my lady calls me Nursie."

"You will continue to have charge over your mistress, but now and again I may ask service of you. Do you understand?"

"Yes, my lady," Elsbeth said. *No nonsense with this one*, she considered. She was yet young, but she was tough.

Adair took her leave of the queen, thanking her for her gracious welcome and curtsying politely. Then she and Elsbeth followed Lady Margaret back to the children's quarters of the house, Beiste trotting along beside them. The nursery was made up of several chambers. The infant prince, Edward, had several of his own rooms for himself and his attendants. Adair was assigned a sturdy pallet cot in a bedchamber with the three princesses, who slept in a large curtained oak bedstead. Cicely, the littlest princess, was between two and three years of age. She was not considered old enough to visit her mother in the hall. The queen came now and again to coo over Cicely and her baby brother. The children's personal servants slept in a small adjoining room.

Elsbeth immediately commandeered a serving man to find her a small trunk for the Countess of Stanton, who had fled her burning home with what she could carry in a cloth wrap. "Damned Lancastrians!" Elsbeth muttered to the man. With a sympathetic nod he found what she needed, and she thanked him with a tear in her eye.

Lady Margaret Beaufort watched Elsbeth's dramatics, amused. The woman would prove useful to them all in time. She was clever and loyal, although her reference to the Lancastrians would have to be softened eventually. But then, it was unlikely that Elsbeth knew that Lady Margaret's only child was the heir to Lancaster. She would learn that fact in time, and guard her tongue once she did. But for now, unawares, Elsbeth unwrapped the shawl in which Adair's possessions were contained, and laid them carefully in the trunk.

In the days that followed Adair's life became quiet and orderly again. Each morning the little girls were wakened just before prime. They quickly washed and dressed and went to the first Mass of the day. A breakfast of hot oats, bread, and cheese followed. Sometimes on feast days there was meat. Lessons followed the meal. Lady Margaret Beaufort had a deep passion for learning. Her charges learned to read, to write, and to do sums. A lady must know sums so she could be certain that her servants were not stealing from her, Lady Margaret said. Adair had never heard any language but English spoken in her short life. Now she learned to speak her mother tongue without a northern accent. And she learned French as well, for highborn ladies must speak French, Lady Margaret said.

There were other lessons as well. Lessons in housewifery. A lady must know how to do many things if she was to direct her servants properly. Adair was taught remedies for dosing and caring for the sick. She learned how to make soap and candles. She was taught how to salt meat and fish; how to make butter, cheese, jams, preserves, and comfits. She candied violets and rose petals. These were mostly tasks to be done by her servants, Lady Margaret said, but if she did not know how to do them herself, she would not know if her servants were doing them properly. Adair and Elizabeth of York found these tasks fascinating, but the princess called Mary did not.

The girls were taught to sew and to weave. They learned how to fashion tapestries. It took Adair three years, but she designed and made a tapestry of Stanton Hall from her memory of it. Lady Margaret complimented her greatly when she had finished it, and Adair was pleased, for a genuine compliment from Lady Margaret was rare.

And finally the day came some weeks after her arrival at Westminster when she met the king who had sired her on her mother's body. Edward of York was tall, with deep blue eyes and golden hair. He was charming, and had the ability to remember the name of every man or woman he had ever met. It gave the illusion to those who came in contact with him that he really cared, that he was warm and kind. He looked down at Adair and remembered the beautiful and reluctant Jane Radcliffe. He remembered how he had overcome her natural modesty and made her shriek with a passion that later embarrassed her.

"My child," the king said, and he picked Adair up in his arms and held her there while he spoke with her. "You know who I am, Adair Radcliffe? I am your father."

"Nay," Adair said boldly. "You are he who sired me, but my father was John Radcliffe, the Earl of Stanton."

The king looked surprised, and then he laughed. "Why, I believe you are right, Adair Radcliffe," Edward said. "Still, I have an obligation to you, my lady Countess of Stanton, and I will not shirk my duty toward you."

"I am grateful for your kindness, and that of the queen," Adair told the king.

"You have been with us but a month and already have the tongue of a courtier," the king noted with a grin. "I can see you will one day be of great use to me, Adair Radcliffe. Is there anything I might give you now for your pleasure?"

"If Your Highness would be so generous," Adair said sweetly, "Nursie and I could use some cloth for new gowns. We are not really fit for the company of your court in our country garments, and we escaped Stanton with little. And perhaps some new shoes. Ours are quite worn, I fear. I do not wish to appear greedy, my lord, but Lady Margaret will attest that our need is an honest one."

"Indeed, my liege, Adair is truthful as always," Margaret Beaufort confirmed.

"You may have whatever you think is necessary for the care and well-being of this natural daughter of mine," the king told the royal governess. "You need not ask again. For as long as Adair Radcliffe is in our custody she shall be provided for, even as are the children of my queen."

Margaret Beaufort curtsied politely. "Thank you, my liege," she said, and afterward she took Adair herself to the room where bolts of material were stored. Together they chose enough cloth for three gowns. The older woman was pleased to see Adair had an innate sense of what would be suitable for a girl of her station. It was a rare talent, and especially in one so young. The colors she chose were a violet, a dark green, and a deep red-orange.

"Nursie must have something too," Adair told her companion. "She has but one gown, and it is difficult to keep it clean for daily wearing."

Lady Margaret cut cloth from a dark gray-blue bolt, and another from a warm brown bolt. "I think these will suit," she said. "And we will need some soft cotton for camises, and lawn and crepe for veils."

"What of our footwear?" Adair wanted to know, loath to let Lady Margaret forget that the king had promised them new shoes.

"You and Elsbeth will visit the royal cobbler," was her answer.

The new shoes were forthcoming once the cobbler had taken measurements of their feet; and Elsbeth sewed diligently for several weeks to come on the new gowns. Adair, however, did her part, hemming each garment as Elsbeth cut it, and sewing each together. She had been careful in her choosing, picking material that was relatively plain, for Adair knew it would not do to outshine her royal half sisters.

England had finally settled down to peace. With King Edward's successful return after his brief forced absence, all pockets of resistance were cleared up. Henry VI had been returned to the Tower of London, and died shortly thereafter under murky circumstances. His queen, Margaret of Anjou, had been captured and brought to the Tower on the same day her husband had perished. It was rumored that she was forced to view his body as it was carried from his apartments. Their son had died at the battle of Tewkesbury. Warwick the Kingmaker, whose allegiance to York had been withdrawn when Edward married Elizabeth Woodville, had died at the battle of Barnet, which preceded Tewkesbury. The king's middle brother, George of Clarence, had begged his forgiveness, and it had been granted. But Clarence was unable to contain his ambitions, and was a constant source of trouble. Finally, in 1478 King Edward clapped him in the Tower, where it was said he drowned in a vat of malmsey wine.

On the frequently troubled borders of Scotland, Richard of Gloucester kept order. Adair looked forward to his visits to court. While he made a great deal of fuss over his brother's growing family, it was Adair who received much of his free time. The queen's children were a little wary of their father's brother, for Elizabeth Woodville no longer bothered to hide her distain for Richard. Adair, however, felt no loyalty to the queen, and she adored Richard, or Uncle Dickon, as the children all called him.

The duke had married his childhood love, Anne Neville, the widow of Henry VI's son, Edward, prince of Wales. A son, named Edward, was born to them at their home, Middleham Castle, Yorkshire, in December of 1473. He was a frail child, as was his mother, and the duke worried over both of them.

Adair rarely saw the king, for with stability and peace he was free to indulge himself with his many mistresses, of whom a goldsmith's wife, Jane Shore, was his particular favorite. And yet he loved his queen. Their family grew in size to ten children, most of whom were daughters, although three were sons, two of whom survived infancy. Adair had been in the royal household four years when the king took an army ten thousand strong into France, where he was to be met by his brother-in-law, Charles the Bold, Duke of Burgundy, and another ally, the Duke of Brittany. Edward meant to conquer France.

But neither Charles nor the Duke of Brittany appeared as they had promised to back up the ten thousand English. Fortunately King Louis XI was a shrewd man, and had no desire to squander his resources in a war. And Edward, without his allies, could do little more than cause damage to the French countryside. So when Louis offered to buy him off, Edward accepted, and returned home again to his life of feasting and women. Three years later, when war between England and Scotland threatened, the king mounted a large army, but was unable to lead it, as he seemed to lose his strength. The authority was given to Richard of Gloucester, who kept the Scots at bay.

And afterward, when he visited court for the first time in several years, he was amazed to find that Adair was now verging on womanhood. Richard was a pious man who, like his mother, had a deep devotion to the church. Unlike his elder brother George, he was utterly loyal to the king. His own motto was "Loyalty binds me." He adored his wife and son. He deplored drunkenness and overindulgence, and if he kept a mistress it was not known who or where she was. Now he looked at the little girl he had rescued some ten years ago and found himself reminded of how much time had passed since that dreary day he had come upon Adair Radcliffe and Elsbeth and the great wolfhound, Beiste, wandering on the high road.

"How old are you?" he demanded to know as he detached her from around his neck. "My God, you are practically a woman, my lady Countess of Stanton."

"I'll be sixteen just after Lammas," Adair told him. "Do I really look grown-up, Uncle Dickon? Am I pretty? No one ever says it, if I am. Lady Margaret says a woman should not be prideful if God has made her beautiful."

"You are beautiful," he told her. "Why, you were all arms and legs the last time I saw you, Adair. Now, however, they must be considering which match would suit you. You will bring your husband an earldom, so you are to be considered a prize."

"I don't want to marry yet," Adair said. "Bessie and I have decided we will marry in the same year. And Lady Margaret seems content with that too. The queen doesn't care, and neither does the king. They live their own lives, and we live ours. Now tell me, how is the Lady Anne? And little Neddie?"

"Both well at the moment, praise God and his blessed Mother," the duke told her.

"Good! Now come and greet your other nieces and nephews, Uncle Dickon. They are quite jealous when you come, for it is obvious that I am your favorite," Adair said a trifle smugly.

The duke laughed aloud. "That is something I have always loved about you," he told her. "You say what you are thinking, poppet."

"Not always," Adair said. "Only to you, for I know you understand me."

The duke chuckled. "Aye, I believe I do understand you, my lady Countess of Stanton. And you are still a proper minx."

Adair slipped her arm into his. "Come along now," she said. "The others are waiting for you."

"Where is the queen?" he asked her.

Adair laughed. "Not waiting for you," she told him. "She likes you no better than you like her, my dear lord."

"Are you as blunt with the others as you are with me?" he wanted to know.

"Certainly not!" Adair told him. "I am a paragon of exemplary breeding and good manners, according to Lady Margaret. It would distress her greatly to learn that all her hard work had gone for naught. No, Uncle, I am a perfect little courtier."

"One day you may have to fly your true colors, Adair," he warned her.

"And I will," she promised him as they entered the section of the castle where the royal children lived.

Elizabeth, the eldest and now fully sixteen, came forward to greet the duke. Next to Adair she was his favorite. The others were lined up in order of their births. Next came Mary, almost fifteen now, but appearing frailer than the duke had ever seen her. Cicely, named after the king's mother, was thirteen. Edward, the first of the princes, nine. Richard, his brother, six. Anne, named after the duke's wife, was four; Catherine, in her nurse's arms, not quite a year; and the queen was enceinte with another child. Two children, George and Margaret, had died in their infancy.

The duke greeted each child by name, and drew forth from the pockets of his robe sweetmeats and small toys, which he distributed among his smaller nieces and nephews. To Mary he gave a rosary of small amber beads with a delicate silver crucifix. She smiled, pleased with the gift. And for Elizabeth and Adair he had pretty gold chains.

They all thanked him prettily, and he smiled. "I am a man of the world, and I know that ladies appreciate fine jewelry," he told the girls. Then, looking to young Edward, he said, "I've brought you and your brother border ponies. They are very well trained, and my own son loves his. I hope they will please you. They await you in the courtyard."

"Oh, go along," Lady Margaret said. Then she turned to the duke. "You spoil them, my lord. But then, no one else does. It is not easy to be a king's son."

"I would not know," the duke said, "for I was not a king's son, but I know how lonely it is for a growing boy when he rarely sees his sire. The beasts I brought are gentle, Mags. The lads will be safe on them."

She had flushed at his use of the sobriquet the queen had given her. "You are good to the children, my lord, and they love you for it. How is your son?"

"Frail, and Anne is not strong enough to bear another child, I fear," the duke said.

"Come and have wine and biscuits," the royal governess invited the duke.

The children had disappeared but for Elizabeth and Adair. A subtle nod from Lady Margaret told them that they were invited to join the duke for refreshments. The quartet sat talking for some time. Then Adair, curious as always, spoke up.

"In your travels along the border, Uncle, have you been in the vicinity of Stanton?"

"I have. Your parents have been buried, with stones to mark their graves on the hillside. Those not slain in the raid have rebuilt the village and cleared the hall of debris. When I saw what they were doing I sent a small purse and a few of my own people to help them. You told me it rained shortly after the hall was fired. Those rains saved your home, Adair. That and the fact that the house was stone. The roof was gone, but I have had it replaced with slate. It will not burn again. A good deal has been pillaged from among the furnishings, but your home is still there. I told the Stanton folk that you had escaped with Elsbeth and were in the king's care. They are glad to know it."

"I want to go back to Stanton so very much," Adair said earnestly.

"You will go back when you have a husband," Lady Margaret said. "You would be wed by now but that Elizabeth desires your company until she is married."

"Why can I not go back now?" Adair asked. "The king could appoint a bailiff for me from among his own trusted servants. Stanton should have its mistress overseeing it again, and I am old enough now to go. And have you not taught me everything a good chatelaine needs to know to manage her own estates, dear Lady Margaret?"

"You are a maid of good birth and gentle breeding," Lady Margaret said. "It would not do for you to be alone at Stanton, Adair. The king would never permit it."

"I want to go home!" Adair cried. Suddenly, knowing that Stanton still stood had awakened in her a deep desire for Northumbria, her own home, her own lands. She turned to Elizabeth of York. "Bessie, you do not really need me here with you. Tell your father that you would let me go."

"Are you really so unhappy here with us?" Elizabeth of York wanted to know.

Adair thought, and then she answered her half sister, "Aye and nay, if that makes any sense to you, Bessie. I love you all, and I am grateful for all you have done for me these ten years past. But now that I know Stanton awaits me I feel the need to return."

Elizabeth of York sighed. "I love you too," she said. "If it means that much to you, dearest Adair, then I will tell our father that you wish to go."

"I will speak with my brother," the duke said, "and you, my sweet Bessie, will agree with me that it is time for Adair to return north."

"I do not think this is wise," Lady Margaret said. "When it is known that a young girl, the Countess of Stanton herself, is back in the hall, who knows what may happen? We both know, my lord duke, the danger of ambitious men. I fear for Adair alone at Stanton."

"But I will not be alone," Adair said. "I will have my Stanton folk with me, and if danger threatens I will slip out through the tunnel I used as a child, and ride for Uncle Dickon at Middlesham."

"The decision must be the king's," Lady Margaret said, "however, I must let it be known that I do not approve at all. It is a rash and foolish plan you have devised, Adair."

"The king will listen to Uncle Dickon," Adair said, her violet eyes dancing with happiness. "And Beiste is growing old, and should go home before his end."

"The dog still lives?" The duke was surprised.

Lady Margaret nodded. "Do you recall how scrawny he was when they arrived? Well, now he is a mountain of a dog, but I will admit the children all adore him, and he them. I never thought to have a dog in my nursery, but he has been more help than difficulty to me these years past. But Adair is right. He is growing old, and moves slower now than in times past."

"He needs to be before the fire in his own hall," Adair said firmly.

Her companions laughed at her reasoning.

"I think I must speak with my brother soon," the duke remarked.

"Today!" Adair told him firmly.

"Very well, you stubborn minx. Today," the duke said.

Adair grinned archly at him. "Thank you, Uncle Dickon," she said.

The duke stood up. "I will go and seek out Edward now," he told them with a bow. And then he departed. He knew where his brother would be—with Jane Shore. And sure enough, he found them in the king's apartments playing chess.

"Richard!" The king arose to embrace his brother. Then he turned to his mistress. "Run along now, Jane. I will see you later."

Jane Shore arose obediently, and with a curtsy hurried away.

"Thank you," the duke said.

"I know you dislike my profligate ways, as our mother calls them." The king chuckled. He was fat now with his indulgences. "Will you have some wine?" He gestured to his page, who had been standing by, and waved his own large goblet at the boy, who hurried to fill it while handing the duke a goblet of his own. "Sit down, sit down," the king invited his brother. "Anne and Neddie are well? The north is still quiet?"

"The Scots keep to their side of the border," the duke said. "I've come to talk to you about Adair Radcliffe. She wants to go home to Stanton."

"Isn't it a ruin?" the king asked.

"No. The walls were stone. The roof burned, but I have had it repaired so the house would not deteriorate. Enough villagers survived and have rebuilt Stanton village. But they need their mistress. The girl will be sixteen shortly. Lady Margaret has taught her everything she needs to know about being a chatelaine. It is time."

"She'll need a husband," the king said.

"She doesn't want one," the duke told him. "At least, not yet. She wants time to renew her acquaintance with Stanton without a husband overseeing her every move. She wants a bailiff from among your servants to help her." The duke quaffed half of his cup, then looked directly at his brother. "It's a reasonable request."

"Jasper Tudor has a bastard he particularly favors, and has been hinting to me through Mags that a marriage between the lad and one of my daughters, not Elizabeth, would suit him. I'm not of a mind to give him one of the queen's girls, but I could give him Adair. Any disappointment Tudor felt would be mitigated by the fact that his son would gain an earldom by the marriage."

"Adair will not have it," the duke said quietly.

"I am her sire, and she will do what I tell her," the king replied stubbornly. "If she would go home to Stanton then she must take Jasper Tudor's son for her husband. It is the solution to both of our problems, Richard." He chuckled. "Mags lobbies again for a marriage between her son, the Lancaster heir, and my Bessie. But I think to match my oldest daughter with the young Dauphin Charles, Louis's son. She will be queen of France, Richard, and that is far better than Countess of Richmond, you will agree."

"I do," the duke said. "But why give Adair, then, to the Tudors?"

"Because Jasper has asked for one of the king's daughters, while Mags lobbies for her son, Henry Tudor of Lancaster, to wed my Bessie," the king repeated. "While I will refuse Mags, I will honor Jasper, and thus keep the Tudors in check. Eventually I may give one of my other girls, Cicely perhaps, to Henry. But my Bessie will be a queen."

"I think Adair will not cooperate with you, Edward," the duke warned his brother.

"It is true I do not know her well, Richard, but on the occasions I have seen her she seemed placid and sweet enough. She will do as she is told, brother."

The duke laughed loudly. "You do not know her then, Edward. Adair may look like her mother, Jane Radcliffe, but she is your daughter in that she is stubborn and will have her own way in spite of it all. When you attempt to force her to the altar you will learn that to your sorrow."

"If she is that difficult then it is time she had a husband to keep her in check. That company of women she keeps with Mags and my daughters is not good for Adair. She has obviously begun to think above her station," the king decided. "She will marry Llywelyn Fitz-Tudor as soon as I can arrange it." Edward drank down the content of his goblet. "And if Jasper's by-blow quickly puts a son in her belly, so much the better."

Richard of Gloucester shook his head. Adair wasn't going to like this at all. The duke considered his options, and decided it would be better if his favorite niece were made aware of the fate awaiting her. Perhaps she could convince the king of his folly in attempting to match her without her consent. Concluding his visit with his brother, the duke left the king and sought out Adair once more. Taking her aside he said, "I have news for you of a nature you may not like, poppet."

"The king will not let me go home," Adair replied, shaking her head wearily.

"Oh, he will let you go home, poppet, but the price for your return is that you must take a husband of his choosing. And he has chosen Jasper Tudor's favorite bastard for the honor," the duke said.

"I won't marry him," Adair said quietly.

"If the king says you will marry, you will marry, poppet. You must gain his ear and reason with him. No one else can," the duke advised her.

"I know the Tudors seek to align themselves with the king's family," Adair said slowly, "but I am hardly that link. I have no importance."

"But you are my wily brother's natural daughter, poppet, and you are recognized as such. So the Tudors get one of the king's daughters as well as an earldom in a union with you. And Bessie is kept for bigger things," the duke pointed out.

"The Dauphin Charles," Adair said. "I know that those negotiations are ongoing, Uncle, but why force me to the altar with a Tudor?"

"Mags also seeks a match for her son, Henry Tudor," the duke replied. "You, of course, would not suit, given the circumstances of your birth, but one of Edward's younger daughters would. Mags is satisfied. And her brother-in-law, Jasper, is satisfied, for while you are the king's brat, his son also comes from the other side of the blanket. And you bring the lad a title."

"I remember you once told me of the value I had by just that alone," Adair said slowly. "But, Uncle, I am not of a mind to marry a Tudor. Especially one I don't know. Where is this fellow that he has been kept from court? What is his name?"

"He is Llywelyn FitzTudor," the duke said. "I know nothing more of him other than that, poppet. Speak to the king. It is your only chance, Adair. Remember that you owe him for all these years he has sheltered and cared for you. You must do your duty."

Adair sought out the king. In the ten years she had lived in the royal nurseries she had spoken with him but briefly on perhaps half a dozen occasions. But as he was still alone she dared to ask for an audience. She was ushered into the king's privy chamber.

"Come in, come in," the king said. "Let me look at you, child. You have grown into quite a pretty young woman, I see. Your mother was your age when I knew her."

Adair curtsied low to the king. He did not ask her to sit down. "My liege, my uncle, the duke, says you would match me shortly so that I might return to Stanton. I do not wish to wed yet, if it would please you."

The king looked at Adair with blue eyes that suddenly turned hard. "It does not please me, mistress. The decision on your marriage, my lady Countess of Stanton, will not rest with you. Jasper Tudor wishes one of my daughters for one of his sons."

"One of his bastards," Adair said sharply.

"Then it is fitting that one of my bastards marries one of Jasper Tudor's," the king replied cruelly, giving her a cold look. "Remember that I am your father as well as your king, my lady Countess of Stanton."

"You may have sired me on my mother, my liege, but you have never been my father. John Radcliffe, God assoil his good soul, was my father. I bear his name. He recognized me as his own. You will not call me misbegotten because of your unbridled lust." She stared back at the king angrily, refusing to lower her eyes before him.

"By the rood, you are my blood nonetheless!" Edward of York said angrily. "I have sheltered you these ten years past. You have never been mistreated in my house. I am your lawful guardian, and you owe me your duty, Adair Radcliffe. You will marry whoever I say you will marry. And I have chosen Llywelyn FitzTudor for your husband. There will be no further discussion of the matter. Do you understand me, my lady Countess of Stanton? It is time you had a husband to teach you your place. You will wed Llywelyn FitzTudor, and the sooner the better, I am thinking!"

"Nay, I will not!" Adair shouted at the king. And then she ran from the chamber.

Edward watched her go, a small smile touching his lips. *Now, if her mother had had the spirit and fire of this royal brat*, he thought, *I should have never let her go.* He shouted for his page. "Fetch the Earl of Pembroke to me, my lad," he said to the boy.

The page hurried off, returning almost an hour later with Jasper Tudor in tow.

"Give him some wine," the king ordered the page; then, turning to the Earl of Pembroke, he said without any preamble, "I will give you my natural daughter Adair Radcliffe, the Countess of Stanton, for your natural son Llywelyn."

The Earl of Pembroke's face showed no reaction at all. "I had hoped for one of the queen's girls," he said quietly.

"Adair's dower is goodly," the king replied. "And your son will become Earl of Stanton by his marriage to her, for she is countess in her own right. I want someone in the north I can trust. Someone who will keep an eye on the Nevilles and the Percys for me. I do not give Adair lightly, my lord."

"Tell me her worth, my liege," Pembroke said matter-of-factly.

"A large stone house in good repair. Much grazing land. A village that has been rebuilt over the last ten years, with its own church, mill, and blacksmith's foundry. She will have one hundred pieces of gold from me, as I promised the Radcliffes when she was born. She has jewelry, garments, linens, other items too numerous to mention, and a servant," the king said. "She is an heiress, and a virgin of good repute."

"Livestock?" Pembroke asked sharply.

"Driven off by the Scots and the Radcliffes' neighbors," the king admitted. "But your lad should bring something to the marriage besides his carcass, my lord."

Jasper Tudor laughed, but it was a cold sound. Then he nodded. "I'll pay for a new herd of cattle," he said.

"Including a young bull," the king bargained.

"My lord!" the Earl of Pembroke protested. " 'Twill cost me dearly."

"I'm giving you a king's daughter for your bastard," Edward of York reminded the earl. "No matter how she was conceived she is my blood, and raised with my legitimate progeny as if she were a princess. What good is a herd of cows without a bull? And the herd must be at least one hundred beasts. Young. Heifers. And I will check."

"Would you beggar me then, my liege?" Pembroke protested. "Fifty is the best I can do, for healthy heifers are difficult to come by in these times."

"Seventy, or I shall seek elsewhere for a son-in-law," the king responded implacably. "It's a good match, Jasper, and you know it." Edward of York held out his hand to the Earl of Pembroke.

Jasper Tudor did not hesitate. He thrust his own hand forward and shook the king's. "Done!" he said with a small smile. "It is a good match. When shall we have the wedding, my liege?"

"As soon as can be arranged," the king said, returning the smile.

Chapter 3

Adair ran through the castle seeking Elsbeth. She found her by the fire in the children's hall, Beiste at her feet. "We are leaving here as soon as possible," she told her nursemaid. "And no one is to know. Not even Uncle Dickon."

"What has happened, my precious?" Elsbeth asked her young mistress. "Sit down with me, child. You are as white as a sheet."

"They want me to marry," Adair said. She remained standing.

"Of course you will marry one day," Elsbeth replied mildly.

"Nay! They want me to marry now! To one of Jasper Tudor's by-blows. The king has other plans for my half sisters. Bessie will be queen of France one day. They will give Cicely to Mags's son, Henry Tudor, for Mary is not strong enough for marriage. And I am to be handed over to Jasper Tudor's son. I won't do it, Elsbeth! We are going home to Stanton. Uncle Dickon says the hall is livable. His people put on a new roof, and the villagers who escaped the Lancastrians have rebuilt the village. If I am gone then the king will have to make other plans for this Llywelyn FitzTudor. He won't bother to send after me up into Northumbria. I am not that important. Get up, Nursie! I would go now before they can stop me." Adair tugged at Elsbeth's arm. "Hurry!"

Elsbeth stood up. "If you would go then you will," she said quietly. "But no one will expect such behavior from my lady Countess of Stanton. Remember, though, that the way is long, and you surely do not want to leave behind your possessions, my precious. I will need time to pack for us."

"Nay. Leave everything. I do not want it!" Adair cried.

"We will need coin to ease our way," Elsbeth advised.

"I have enough coin to get us north. The bulk of my small fortune is with the Jew in Goldsmith's Lane. I can draw on it from anywhere," Adair replied.

"Half the day is gone," Elsbeth said. "Let us go on the morrow."

"It is just past the noon hour," Adair responded. "It is June. The day is long. I would go now, Nursie. Now!"

"Very well," Elsbeth answered her. "Tell me what to do."

"Go to the stables and have our horses saddled. I will go to my chamber and collect our cloaks and the coins from where I've hidden them," Adair told the woman. Then, turning, she hurried out of the hall.

Elsbeth sighed. This was, she decided, a very foolish move on Adair's part. But she owed her loyalty to Stanton, and Adair was the Radcliffe of Stanton. Then she thought to herself that they would be caught by the king's men on the morrow for certain. "Come along, Beiste," she called to the dog by the fire. "We're going home."

In the small chamber that she shared with Elizabeth, Adair went to the hearth and, reaching into it, pulled a little block of stone out of the back of the cold fireplace, setting it on the floor. Reaching into the dark cavity she drew out a pouch of coins. Lifting her skirts she tied the pouch strings to the drawstring on her camise. Then, replacing the stone, she took their cloaks and ran from the room.

Elsbeth and Beiste were waiting with their horses in the stable yard. "Do we need a groom to go with us, my lady?" Elsbeth asked innocently.

"Nay, we are just riding down into the town," Adair told the stableman as he boosted her into the saddle.

"There be a fair in Windsor today, my lady. Beware of the Gypsies," the stableman advised.

"Oh, thank you, we will," Adair responded.

The two women rode out from Windsor Castle, the great wolfhound loping along by their side. Out of sight of the guards they turned onto the road north, and put their horses into a canter. Adair never looked back, and for the first time in ten years she realized that she was truly happy. Happy and free of the king's house. Free of the barely concealed scorn of certain courtiers. It wasn't that anyone had been unkind to her. They hadn't. She rarely saw the king. The queen was happy to bear children for the king, but hardly interested in them afterward.

Adair's world had consisted of Lady Margaret Beaufort, Elsbeth and her half siblings. They had lived an orderly and quiet life. The boys were prepared to rule, and the girls were prepared to marry. But it had come too soon to suit Adair. Why should she be married before Elizabeth, who was but six months her senior? And to someone she didn't even know, had never heard about until today? No! She would not marry Llywelyn FitzTudor. And when they discovered she was gone that would be an end to it.

But Lady Margaret Beaufort had been laid low with a wretched summer flu. And the Princesses Elizabeth, Mary, and Cicely were off visiting their paternal grandmother, Cicely Neville, who was known as Proud Cis. And because Elsbeth took care of Adair, there was no one to take note of the fact that the Countess of Stanton was among the missing. It was several days before anyone realized it and brought it to Lady Margaret's attention.

Lady Margaret arose from her sickbed and sought out the queen. "Your Highness, Adair Radcliffe has gone missing," she said.

Elizabeth Woodville looked annoyed at this news. "Missing?" she said. "What do you mean by missing?"

"She has not been seen for several days; nor has her servant, Elsbeth. They are nowhere to be found in the castle, Your Highness," Lady Margaret answered.

The queen looked even more annoyed. It had been a lovely summer so far. Her three oldest daughters had gone to their grandmother's, thus saving her the usual burden of entertaining the king's mother, who made no secret of her dislike for Elizabeth Woodville. She didn't want to be bothered by this problem, and it was certain to be a large problem if Adair Radcliffe had run off with some squire, which was undoubtedly the case. "I will call for the king," the queen announced.

"He must be made aware of this dilemma, and it is he who must decide what is to be done." She signaled to her personal page. "Go and fetch your master, my lad. Tell him it is urgent."

The page ran off, and the two women sat waiting in silence. It was close to an hour before the king arrived in the company of his brother, Richard. The queen glowered. She did not like Richard of Gloucester, nor he her.

"What is so urgent that you take me from my council, madam?" Edward demanded of his wife. "I ended a meeting that needed to be continued."

"Adair Radcliffe has gone missing. Her servant also," the queen said. "Mags can tell you more, for I know nothing of it." Her blue eyes already indicated her boredom.

The king looked to Lady Margaret Beaufort. "Madam?" he said questioningly.

"I have been ill, my liege, and was not made aware until today that both Adair and her servant, Elsbeth, are nowhere to be found," Lady Margaret said. "Her usual companions are off with your mother, and only this morning did a little maid note that her bed hadn't been slept in for several nights. We have scoured the castle, but she is nowhere to be found, yet all her belongings are in her chamber."

"What about that great dog of hers?" the duke wanted to know.

Lady Margaret thought a long moment, and then said excitedly, "You are right, my lord! The dog is gone too."

"Adair has run away," Richard of Gloucester pronounced.

"What the hell do you mean, she has run away?" the king demanded.

"Did you tell her that she was to wed Jasper Tudor's bastard, Edward?" the duke asked his elder brother.

"Aye, I did," the king said. "And the sooner the better."

"And what was her reaction to such news?" the duke pressed his sibling.

"She said she didn't want to marry yet. That she wanted to go home to Stanton Hall and reacquaint herself with her lands and her people," the king said.

"A reasonable request," the duke murmured, "but knowing you, Edward, you persisted in impressing your will upon Adair. Unfortunately, Adair is much like you in temperament." He chuckled. "You would have your way, but so would she."

"Adair is my brat, and should be grateful that we took her in when her family was slaughtered," the king snapped. "She is almost sixteen, and ripe for bedding. It is time she was married, Richard. And it is time she begin repaying her debt to me by taking a husband of my choosing, helping me to unite once and for all York and Lancaster."

"I will not disagree with you, Edward, but a touch more diplomacy would have served you better here than your iron determination to be obeyed. You know little about Adair other than that you fathered her on Jane Radcliffe in a bout of lust. The girl is intelligent, and she is devoted to the house of York. The only thing she knows about the house of Lancaster is that some of its adherents murdered her mother and foster father. That she was driven from her home at a tender age. Yet you chose for her husband the bastard of one of the most important men of Lancaster. While I understand your reasoning, Adair did not.

"You did nothing, Edward, to prepare her for this event. To explain to her the small part she would play in helping to unite the two warring houses. She is very fond of Lady Margaret. Admires her. If you had spoken with Mags and told her of your plan, she could have aided you in readying Adair for this marriage. You did not treat your daughter with the respect that she is due, and now she has run away. The fact that she took none of her possessions but for the dog who was hers to begin with tells me she has washed her hands of you, would not be beholden to you again in any manner," the duke concluded. "Would you like me to go after her for you?"

"Nay!" the king snapped. His younger brother's words had stung him deeply. Adair had no right to attempt to dictate to her king what she would or she would not do. "She will marry the FitzTudor lad, and I do not need her presence to manage that union," the king said. "I am Adair's legal guardian. I have agreed to the match, and the marriage will be celebrated by proxy. One of my daughters can stand in for the bride."

Richard of Gloucester shook his head. "Edward, do not do this," he advised his older brother. "You can accomplish what you want if you will just wait a short while and let me speak with Adair. Why must you rush this union?"

"Because I would have Jasper Tudor satisfied that Lancaster and York can live peaceably, Richard," the king said. "A union with our houses will accomplish that. I have made my decision!" Then he turned and stormed from the queen's privy chamber.

"Am I wrong?" the Duke of Gloucester addressed Lady Margaret Beaufort.

"Nay, you are not. But neither is the king," she answered him. "My brother-in-law is an impatient man, my lord. He wants a wedding, and he wants it now. He will not be pleased to learn it is to be a proxy wedding. I will tell him that her ladyship the Countess of Stanton has gone north to prepare her long-deserted hall properly for the arrival of her bridegroom," Lady Margaret, said her dark blue eyes twinkling.

The Duke of Gloucester laughed in spite of himself. "Now, you, madam, show great promise as a diplomat," he told her. "As for me, I had best ride north myself so that my niece is made aware of her fate before it arrives on her doorstep. How old is the bridegroom?"

"Fourteen," Lady Margaret said softly.

"Christ's bones," the duke swore softly. "She will eat him alive, Mags. No lad, even Jasper Tudor's son, will be able to control Adair. She needs a man grown." He sighed. "I think I shall not tell her that he is a mere stripling. Let her discover it herself."

"I would agree with your decision, my lord," Lady Margaret Beaufort said.

"Could you not convince your brother-in-law to wait for this union?" the duke wondered.

"He is every bit as stubborn as the king," she replied. "He wants what he wants."

"You are both giving me a headache," the queen announced. "My lord husband has made his decision. You will both help him to see it is carried out." She waved them impatiently from her privy chamber.

Together the Duke of Gloucester and his female companion walked from the queen's apartment and into one of the castle's small gardens, speaking together in low and confidential tones.

"I shall do what I can to delay my brother-in-law," Lady Margaret said. "There should be a negotiation of Adair's dower portion to be agreed upon. And, of course, her possessions must be taken north to Stanton, and she should have a small trousseau."

"And while the marriage may take place sooner than later," the duke noted sagely, "the winter could come before young FitzTudor can go north. He might not be able to reach Stanton until the spring, when the snows have gone."

"A distinct possibility," Lady Margaret agreed with a brief smile.

"We are in accord then, madam? We will both do what we can to ease my lady the Countess of Stanton into this marriage that her sire wishes of her," the duke said.

"Indeed, my lord, we are in agreement," Lady Margaret replied.

And in the weeks that followed, despite the king's desire for a swift marriage, summer fled into autumn. Finally the marriage contract was drawn up. The king would give his natural daughter Adair Radcliffe in marriage to Llywelyn FitzTudor, son of Jasper Tudor. FitzTudor would have to assume the surname of Radcliffe, as the king had long ago promised John Radcliffe. It was a sticking point that delayed the union, with both Jasper Tudor and his son arguing against it, but in the end they agreed.

The bride would have a dower of one hundred gold pieces, full weight, not clipped; a dozen silver spoons; two chased silver cups; a trunk of linens for both table and bed; three new gowns; three bolts of cloth; new leather shoes; a gold chain; and two gold rings, one with a pearl, and the other with a ruby. There would also be a pair of silver candlesticks, a wedding gift from the queen; and two horses, a palfrey for the bride, a stallion for the groom, from the king.

And while her fate was being decided without her, Adair had reached Stanton in just under a fortnight. The trip home had taken much less time, given that they might travel the roads, and those roads were safe again. Still, it was a miracle that two women alone but for a large dog had managed to reach Stanton without incident. They rode into her village, and, recognizing Elsbeth, the villagers flocked from their cottages. One look at the girl riding with her and the villagers fell to their knees, some of them sobbing.

"What is it, Mama?" a little boy asked his parent. "Why do you greet?"

" 'Tis the young mistress come home to us, laddie," his mother told him as she wiped her eyes with the back of her hand. "Once again there is a Radcliffe on the land. Praise be to our sweet Lord Jesu and his blessed Mother!"

An older man arose and bowed to Adair. "Welcome home, my lady. I am Albert. My da was your father's majordomo. I am pleased to say the hall is most habitable. Good Duke Richard came several years ago and told us of your miraculous escape. His men restored the building's roof, and we have kept the hall clean."

"Thank you, Albert," Adair said, looking at him from her saddle. "Thank you all for your welcome. Tell me, does your da still live, and is he able to return to his duties?"

"Alas, my lady, my da died fighting at the earl's side," Albert replied.

"God assoil both their good souls," Adair said quietly. "Will you then take your father's place in my hall?"

"I am honored that you would ask me, my lady, and right gladly I will serve you," Albert answered, and he smiled broadly. Then he grew more sober. "We lost many furnishings in the fire, I fear, my lady. With your permission I will order the craftsmen to begin making new for you. And I will gather together a staff for the hall. While many were slain that terrible day, many survived. And with the winter coming there will be more hands to help before it is time to prepare for the spring."

"Walk with me up to the hall," Adair said, moving her horse forward. "Have we any cattle, or was it all lost that day?"

"What wasn't lost was eventually stolen by our neighbors, both Scots and English," Albert said.

Adair nodded. "We will replace them come the spring. No sense in buying them now and having to feed them through the winter," she reasoned.

"My lady, if I may be so bold," Albert said. "How did you and Elsbeth escape the carnage? I should not have known you but that you resemble your dear mother so greatly. And is that poor weary creature one of your father's dogs?"

"There is an escape tunnel from the hall. My parents put Elsbeth and me into it along with Beiste that day. They had horses waiting for us at the other end. We remained until the raiders had gone. I was sent to King Edward, as he owed my father a debt. I have been raised in his household these ten years past. It was Duke Richard who found us on the road as we neared Westminster, where the queen lay in sanctuary," Adair explained, making her story as simple as possible. There was no need for any other here except for Elsbeth to know the truth of who really sired her. She would not shame John Radcliffe, who had always been so good to the child she once was.

"When the good duke came and told us that you lived we counted it a miracle. He promised us that you would return one day, my lady," Albert said. "And you have."

"First I will settle in," Adair told him. "You must tell me who survived, what is left, and then we will decide how to proceed."

They reached the hall and entered the courtyard, which was, Adair noted, well swept, but otherwise barren. The roses and other plantings her mother had so lovingly tended were obviously long gone. Probably destroyed in the fire, Adair considered sadly. In the spring they would replant, for it was too late now, and the frost was already in the soil this far north. Albert took a key from the pocket in his breeches and fit it in the door of the stone building. The key turned easily, and he flung the door open.

They stepped inside. It was cold and dank within. The only light came from the weak midmorning sunlight coming through the few unshuttered windows that were unbroken. Adair walked forward, remembering the corridor leading to the great hall as her favorite place to play and hide from Nursie. It was the same, and yet it wasn't. The house was so very, very quiet. There was no life to it at all, but neither was it filled with any haunts of those killed here on that awful day so long ago.

"Can the villagers spare any wood, Albert? We must get some warmth back into the house before nightfall," Adair said. She looked about her as they entered the great hall. It was virtually empty but for two high-backed wood chairs behind a ramshackle table that sat where the high board had once been, and a low-backed wooden settle by the large hearth. The hearth had no firedogs. The tapestries were gone from the walls.

"The roof and the interior burned," Albert explained. "The walls stood, which is why we were able to save the hall, my lady."

"Were the contents of all the rooms damaged or pillaged?" she asked him.

"All but the kitchens below the great hall, my lady. The upper stories and the hall were fired individually, and the contents carried off, but the kitchens were not thought important. The women who survived to return packed everything away in the cupboards for the family's return one day. We knew you would come home to us."

Elsbeth had been silent, but now she seemed to recover from her shock of seeing what had once been a gracious home destroyed. "Fetch the wood," she told Albert. "And see if any would be kind enough to loan us pallets, and not ones filled with fleas, if you please. Her ladyship will sleep in the hall temporarily until we can get some furnishings made. And we'll need a staff. And everything that's broken must be repaired as soon as possible, for the winter will not be kind to any of us."

"Indeed, Mistress Elsbeth, it won't," Albert said. " 'Tis good to see you home again too. You'll have some grand stories to tell, I'm sure."

"I'm not one for telling tales," Elsbeth responded.

"Oh, Nursie"—Adair fell back for a moment on her old form of address for Elsbeth—"I'm sure Albert and the other Stanton folk would love hearing your stories of the king and the court. There is no harm in it."

"If it's all right with your ladyship, well, then, perhaps I can recall

56

a few moments that might entertain," Elsbeth said slowly. "But I'm no gossip!"

Albert grinned at Elsbeth. He was a stocky man of medium height with mild blue eyes and a fringe of brownish hair beneath a bald pink pate. "I'll look forward to it," he told her with a mischievous wink.

"Now, you mind your manners," Elsbeth scolded. Then her tone softened. "How is your mother? I remember her so well."

"She escaped the carnage. They weren't interested in an old woman," she said. "She will be happy to see you, Elsbeth."

"And your wife? You have certainly taken a wife, Albert?"

"Nay. There was no time," he answered her. "At first there were only a few old men and women and some younglings left after the raid. I had been injured and left for dead. Over the next few months some of the younger women returned, many with big bellies. And finally about a dozen of the other men, young and of middle years. I was, it seemed, in charge. We have managed to rebuild the village, keep the hall safe, and plant enough to just get by." He turned to Adair. "I have had to act as sheriff and magistrate, my lady. We were forgotten here in Stanton until the duke came. If I have overstepped my authority, my lady, I hope you will forgive me," Albert finished.

"Nay," Adair told him. "You have done nobly, Albert, and you have my undying gratitude and thanks for your loyalty to Stanton. But for the duke it is likely we will continue to be forgotten. Now, you had best arrange for that wood and our pallets. I am going to walk about my home now and reacquaint myself with it." With a nod she left the hall.

"She looks like her ma," Albert said.

Elsbeth nodded. "Aye, she does. But she's stubborn. She's run away from the king's house, and best you know it now. She thinks they'll not come after her, but I disagree. She has value to the king."

"Run away? Why?" he asked.

Elsbeth motioned Albert to a chair. "Sit a moment, and I will tell you."

"Let me get the wood first and begin a fire to warm the hall," he said to her. "Then we can speak, and I will listen to what you have to tell me."

She nodded to him. "Go on then." And she sat down as he went out. It seemed that he was gone a very little time, but when he returned it was with several men and women bearing all kinds of items. Enough wood for several days was stacked by the large hearth. The wobbly table was removed, and in its place a great high board was set.

"Now, where did that come from?" Elsbeth wanted to know.

"It's the original," Albert told her. "It was badly scorched by the fire when the roof over the hall fell in, but then the rains came. We were able to save and restore it. It's been in a shed in the courtyard. I'd forgotten about it until old Wat reminded me."

Elsbeth nodded. She walked over to the great table and slowly ran her hand over it with a small smile. Then she turned to the villagers. "I know she'll thank you all for this. To be able to sit at the same high board her mama and da sat at will be a comfort."

The women gathered about smiled and nodded. And then they began placing food upon the table. One drew a silver goblet studded with oval green stones from her skirts. She placed it carefully on the high board where Adair would soon sit.

"We saved several items that weren't stolen," Albert said quietly.

Having done their duty for now, the villagers departed the great hall. Elsbeth noted there were now two thick pallets in the bed spaces by the fire, each set upon a sheepskin, and with a small coverlet. She nodded, pleased. It wasn't grand, but they would be warm, dry, and comfortable for the first time since they had left Windsor.

"Come on, lass, and tell me what I should know," Albert said, motioning Elsbeth back to the settle by the fire.

Elsbeth sat down with a sigh. "The king wants her to marry. She didn't want to wed yet. Nor did she approve of his choice of a husband for her—the by-blow of an important Lancastrian. The king is attempting to make a more permanent peace between the two factions. He's plenty of daughters of his own, but the eldest will probably be queen of France, the next eldest is too frail for marriage, and the third girl is to go to the Lancastrian heir, Henry Tudor. The others are too young yet by far. To show his good faith toward the Tudors the king decided to marry Adair off first. She is his ward, a noblewoman in her own right. Marriage to her will give her bridegroom the earldom, and the king promised her a generous dower portion. But my lady did not wish to be wed to a Lancastrian. They killed her parents, and orphaned her. Nor did she wish to marry yet. She is younger in age than Princess Elizabeth. She wanted to come home, Albert. And she did. She thinks the king will forget about her and find another lass to wed the Tudor's by-blow. But he won't.

"The king is a stubborn man, and he rules with a smile, and an iron fist in a silken glove. Servants know more than their masters, as you well understand, Albert. My lady has spent these last ten years well sheltered in the royal nurseries with the king's children. They know little of what goes on in the outside world. King Edward is a charming man, and well loved by his people. But he is also a man who will be obeyed. If he says our lady is to wed, then wed she will be. I am frankly surprised no one came after us in our flight these twelve days past."

"I am surprised you got there and back in safety without an armed escort," Albert remarked with a shake of his head.

"Going south was hard," Elsbeth admitted. "It took us over a month, but I followed the earl's orders and kept from the high road. The countryside was so upset that everyone went quickly about their business. The dog, of course, was in his prime then, and no one sought to tangle with him. Returning, however, was a far different matter. We rode hard, and at times my lady took the dog up and laid him across her saddle, for he could not keep up. She loves that creature fiercely, but he's old, and I think he may not live too long now that we are home," Elsbeth said.

"How could my lady even be certain that Stanton still existed?" Albert said. "Many families who once had homes and land along the border are long gone."

"The Duke of Gloucester told her. It was he who found us as we sought to reach London. My lady calls him Uncle Dickon, as all the king's children do. She adores him, and he has always treated her with favor—more even than he shows the others. He is a man who loves children," Elsbeth said.

"Aye, I could see that on the occasions he came to Stanton," Albert agreed. "He always brought sugared treats for the bairns."

"There is absolutely nothing left above stairs," Adair said as she reentered the hall. "Not a stick of furniture, or a carpet, or hangings."

Albert quickly stood up. "The burning roof fell in and destroyed all," he explained. "The floors, being stone, protected the chambers below. We saved what little was not looted and hid it away. The Scots were raiding then. Most of the cattle went over the Cheviots with them." He bowed to Adair. "With your ladyship's permission I'll be going now. There's food for the night on the high board. And I have posted men at the door of the hall. They will protect you from any harm. On the morrow we'll be bringing from hiding what we rescued, and then you will be able to determine what you are going to need for the hall."

"Bedsteads, for one thing," Adair said wryly.

Albert chuckled as he left them. "Good night, my lady. Elsbeth."

"Come and eat, my precious," Elsbeth said, drawing Adair to the high board. "The women from the village have brought food, and it is still hot." She beckoned to Adair, and seated her in one of the two high-backed chairs at the board. Then she served her a rabbit stew, ladling it into a bread trencher. She poured some cider from an earthenware pitcher into the silver cup.

"Sit down," Adair said, gesturing Elsbeth to the seat beside her.

"It isn't meet that I sit at the high board," Elsbeth replied.

"It's only the two of us," Adair answered.

"Nonetheless, we will observe the proprieties, my lady. You are the Countess of Stanton, and this is your seat. I'll eat later."

"This was my mother's cup," Adair noted as she looked at the silver vessel before her on the table. "Where on earth did it come from?"

"Our people rescued what wasn't looted, burned, or stolen. They hid them away until the day a Radcliffe returned to Stanton," Elsbeth explained.

Adair felt the tears welling up in her eyes. "It is good to be home," she said.

Within a short time Stanton Hall began to come to life again. The furnishings from the upper floors had been all destroyed in the fire, but the local craftsmen began fashioning new beds, tables, chests, and chairs to replace them. Elsbeth discovered that the chamber deep in the cellars of the hall where Jane Radcliffe had kept fabric in cedar chests still held its contents. Curtains and hangings for the bedchambers were now sewn from the fabric. The cloth had not mildewed because it had been protected by the cedar.

Much of the contents of the kitchens were still intact. New furniture was built for the hall. The wooden shutters for all the windows were replaced. Jane Radcliffe had not liked rushes on the floor of her hall. She had brought with her as part of her dower portion two carpets that had been woven in Arabia. The carpets, however, were gone, as were the tapestries from the walls. Adair set Albert to finding her mother's loom if it still existed, and when it could not be found a new loom was built for her. She found the proper wools and threads to weave new tapestries in a cedar trunk in the same room that had held the materials.

Each day a few items belonging to Stanton Hall found their way back to the hall. Adair had offered positions in her service to any in the village who would serve her. Albert chose those young men who could be trained as men at arms, and put them in the custody of his cousin, who was known as Dark Walter. It was rumored that Dark Walter had Moorish blood in him, but how that had come about no one knew for certain, not even Dark Walter. Elsbeth would run the household with Albert. Together they chose a cook and others for the kitchens, and several little maidservants to help keep the hall clean. As the feast of Christ's Mass drew near and the hall was decorated with green branches and holly, Stanton appeared almost back to normal.

Adair organized two hunts, and together with the villagers they managed to slay three roe deer and a young boar. The meat was butchered and hung in the cold pantry. Adair gave one of the deer to the village. She permitted one day a month for the hunting of rabbit and game birds, as well as fishing twice a month. The grain that had been harvested in late summer and autumn was stored in a single granary at the castle. Each family was given two measures a month, which the miller ground into flour for bread. Apples and pears had been harvested and stored, with carrots and onions. Elsbeth had coaxed Jane Radcliffe's herb garden, which grew in the shelter of a kitchen wall, back into existence with judicious pruning and generous helpings of manure. It would produce until a hard frost sent it into a winter's rest. A smaller garden of kitchen herbs still flourished by the kitchen door: rosemary, parsley, sage, thyme, shallots, and leeks.

Adair spent the late autumn making candles for the house, and soap. She sent to a cooper in another village to come and make her a bathtub of hard oak. The cooper returned to his own village to tell others that the young Countess of Stanton had returned to her hall, and that Stanton had come to life again. The cooper's master, old Lord Humphrey Lynbridge, was interested to learn this fact. He had had his eyes on Stanton lands, and had hoped to eventually gain them for his family.

"Has she a husband?" Lord Humphrey asked the cooper.

"Don't know, my lord, but the only man with any authority that I could see was her majordomo, Alfred. And I didn't hear the maidservants gossiping about any master." The cooper shuffled his feet nervously.

"Go on about your business," his master said, waving him away.

"What are you thinking, Grandfather?" Robert Lynbridge asked. He was his grandfather's heir, as his father was dead.

"If the girl is unwed we could make a match with your brother. If you were not married I might make the match for you, and the Radcliffe lands would be ours. But if your brother gets them 'tis almost as good."

"How old can the girl be, grandfather? Fifteen, sixteen, seventeen? I do not see her guardians, whoever they might have been, allowing her to come back to Stanton alone. There has to be a husband," Robert Lynbridge said. "Besides, Andrew feels no need to wed. Why should he?"

"Because I say so," the old man snapped. "I want the Radcliffe lands. Do you want them falling into the hands of strangers, Rob?"

He glared at his eldest grandson, his blue eyes sharp and clearly filled with annoyance.

"If you would have it then you would have it," Robert Lynbridge said mildly. He knew better than to argue with his grandfather. The white-haired old man was a fierce fighter. "But I think first we should determine if the girl is wed or pledged."

"It matters not," the old lord said. "If she is wed, the husband can meet with an accident. If she is not, there is nothing wrong with a little bride stealing, laddie."

Robert Lynbridge laughed aloud. His pretty wife, Allis, sitting by his side, just shook her head wearily. "Let us begin at the beginning, my lord," Rob suggested. The only advantage he had—any of them had—over Humphrey Lynbridge was that the old man was virtually crippled in his final years. It was difficult for him to get about. Not impossible, just very hard. "I will ride over to Stanton Hall before the winter sets in, and take Andrew with me. We'll get a good look at the girl and learn what we need to know about her and about her situation."

"Good! Good!" his grandfather said. "Praise God you are a sensible man, Rob, and not stubborn like your brother."

"He's just like you," Robert Lynbridge said with a laugh. "Exactly like you, if the truth be told, my lord."

"*Merde!*" the old man protested. "He is nothing like me."

"Who is nothing like you?" Andrew Lynbridge had come into the hall. Unlike his older brother, who was of medium height with light blue eyes and brown-blond hair, Andrew was tall with coal black hair, and gray eyes with tiny flecks of gold in them. He looked more like his Scots mother, while Rob resembled their father's family.

"You!" his grandfather snapped.

"We look nothing alike," Andrew agreed.

"In temperament," Rob explained, "you and Grandsire are much alike."

Andrew Lynbridge grinned wickedly. Like his elder sibling he knew when to back away from an argument with his grandfather.

"Grandsire is planning to marry you off," Rob said mischievously.

"Bloody hell he is! I'll pick my own wife when I wed," Andrew said.

"The Radcliffe wench is back from wherever she was sheltered after the hall was attacked. Damn fool John Radcliffe, flying York's banner in the face of all."

"Yet York rules England," Andrew murmured softly.

"I heard that, my lad. Aye, they rule, and we have peace at last. But that's not the point. I've always wanted the Radcliffe lands. Their cattle meadows are the finest about, but of course they have no cattle now. Scots got them all," the old man said.

"I seem to recall a few strayed in our direction," Andrew baited his grandfather.

The old man cackled. "Perhaps they did. Perhaps they did," he admitted. "Well, the Radcliffe girl is back. She'll need a husband. Rob has a wife, and I have to say Allis has done well by him. Twin lads, and her belly is full again. We might wait to see if she dies in this next childbirth, but I think not. Allis has always been a strong, healthy lass."

"Grandsire!" Robert Lynbridge looked outraged.

"Thank you very much, my lord," Allis Lynbridge said dryly from her place by the fire, where she had been both sewing and listening.

Lord Humphrey ignored them both, continuing on with his train of thought. "So it's up to you, Andrew, to woo and win the Radcliffe lass. Then her lands will be ours."

"If I were of a mind to wed, and if I wed this girl, the lands would be mine," Andrew Lynbridge said quietly. "But I am not of a mind to wed some horse-faced heiress right now, Grandsire. And I repeat, when I marry, I will chose my own bride."

"Bosh, lad! All cats look alike in the dark," Lord Humphrey said. "Besides, who says she is ugly? Have you seen her? Her mother was a beauty. Besides, it's past time you took a wife. You're nearer to thirty than you are to twenty," his grandfather said.

"Nay, I have not seen the girl, and I am twenty-eight," was Andrew's answer.

"Then what is to prevent you and your brother from riding over to

Stanton Hall tomorrow and paying our respects to the girl? 'Tis but a half day's ride. Soon the snows will come, and there will be no opportunity for you until spring. Once word gets out that this wench is home again all the Nevilles and the Percys will come calling in an attempt to win her and grab her lands. Why should they have all the wealth hereabouts?" the old man grumbled irritably. "Lancaster's toadies, most of them."

Andrew Lynbridge laughed. "Very well, old man, if it will make you happy we shall ride to Stanton Hall and see the girl."

The following morning Robert and Andrew Lynbridge rode from their home and directed their horses in the direction of Stanton. It was the last day of November, and they had attended early Mass celebrating Andrew's name day. The air was crisp, but there was no wind. A weak sun shone down on the barren hillsides.

"I suppose you think I should marry too," Andrew said to his older sibling.

"There will always be bed and board for you at Hillview Court, little brother," Robert said. "But don't you want your own home, and a forever woman? You have never been a man to be beholden to any, even your family. I thought when you returned from fighting in the service of the Duke of Gloucester that you would settle down, but you have not. The Radcliffe girl might be the answer for you. Our families would be near one another, and you would have your own lands. I would hope you will marry eventually. Sooner or later some angry father will come to Hillview demanding you wed with his big-bellied daughter and accept your responsibilities."

Andrew Lynbridge chuckled. "I've kept my activities to the other side of the border, brother," he said. "And none know my surname."

"I have heard it said you are called Amorous Andrew," Robert replied with a grin. Then he grew serious. "Don't get caught and forced to the altar by some farmer's lass. At least since you must wed, marry to your advantage, and our family's."

"Not for love?" Andrew teased Robert.

"Love may come, as it has with Allis and me. Her parents are noble, and while she was the youngest of fourteen she came with a good dower portion: a herd of twenty-four healthy heifers, and a young bull. But I will say I liked her from the start, and she showed her respect for me immediately. She is a dutiful wife," Robert said.

"She is a sweet woman, but too dull for my taste," Andrew remarked.

"Sweet and dull is a comfort to a man when he has more important matters to attend to on a daily basis," Robert replied. "Grandsire sits in the hall and barks orders, but the responsibility of Hillview is mine, and has been for close to ten years."

"Nonetheless, I would need a woman with more spice to her than your good Allis," his brother remarked. "I want a woman who sets me afire with just a look."

"You're thinking with your cock and not your head," Robert said, grinning.

Andrew laughed again. "Aye, perhaps I am. Is that Stanton Hall?" He pointed.

"Aye," Robert answered. "It doesn't look as if it was touched by disaster at all."

The two brothers rode down the hillside into the sheltered valley where Stanton Hall stood. The fallow fields were well cared-for, Robert noted as they came. The village was neat, the cottage roofs well thatched, the cottages themselves freshly whitewashed. There was a small church at one end of the village and a mill at the other, but it did look deserted. The two brothers followed the road to the hall, and guided their horses into the courtyard of the great stone house. Stableboys ran out to take their horses. The door to the house opened to reveal a stocky man who stood blocking their entry.

"Welcome to Stanton, sirs," he said. "I am Albert, my lady's majordomo. Do you have business with her?" He was polite, but he did not move.

"I am Robert Lynbridge, heir to Lord Humphrey, and this is my brother, Andrew. We have come to pay our respects and those of our grandfather to the lady of the hall."

A smile now creased Albert's face, and he stepped aside to usher them into the house. "My lady is in the great hall," he said. "If you will but wait here, good sirs, I will tell her you are here." He hurried off.

"House seems to have survived the raid nicely," Andrew noted.

"Duke Richard came and made repairs," Robert informed him.

"What is his interest in her, I wonder?" Andrew said.

"Good sirs, if you will come this way." Albert had returned. "My lady is ready to greet you." Turning, he led them into the great hall of Stanton, where Adair stood waiting to receive her visitors.

Both men were surprised by the girl's beauty. They bowed, and Robert kissed her hand gallantly. "My lady, I am Robert Lynbridge of Hillview. I bring you greetings from my grandfather, Lord Humphrey. He knew both your parents."

"I remember your grandfather, sir. He once called at Stanton when I was a child."

"May I present my younger brother, Andrew Lynbridge," Robert said.

Boldly Andrew Lynbridge locked his gaze on Adair, and to his surprise she did not look away. He kissed her hand, his eyes never leaving hers. "My lady," was all he said as he bowed to her.

Adair took back her hand. "Come and be seated by the fire, sirs. Albert, wine for our guests." She turned to Robert. "How is your grandfather?"

"Crusty as ever," Robert replied with a small smile. "He will be delighted you recalled him."

"I remember you too," Adair surprised him. "But you were far too grown-up to be bothered paying attention to a little girl of five," she said. "It was at the midsummer fair the year before the troubles came upon us. But I do not recall your brother."

"I left Hillview to join Duke Richard's forces when I was sixteen," Andrew said.

"Ahh!" Adair's face lit up. "You fought with Uncle Dickon?"

"And went to France with him as well," was his reply. "Why do you call the duke Uncle Dickon, if I may be so bold, my lady?"

"After my parents were murdered I was raised in the king's nursery," Adair explained. "The Duke of Gloucester is very beloved of all the children there. When my nurse and I had almost reached London it was he who found us and saw we were taken to the queen in Westminster. He asked that I call him uncle."

"Ah," Robert said. "So that is where you have been all these years. In the king's house. We had wondered where you had fled for safety."

"Yes," Adair said. "I was with the royal family."

Albert came now, offering wine and biscuits to the guests.

"Why have you come home to Stanton now?" Robert inquired.

"I thought it was time," Adair said. "Ten years is a long while to be away, and Uncle Dickon said the house was habitable. My Stanton folk have worked very hard to help me refurbish it. We discovered chests of fabric that had not been found and looted. It has allowed us to make curtains and bed draperies. And they built a loom for me. I have begun a tapestry, the first of several I will do to replace the ones stolen."

"And when will your husband be joining you?" Robert asked pleasantly. "He will undoubtedly be pleased to see the excellent progress you have made in restoring your home. We shall look forward to seeing you both in the spring at Hillview. I know that would please our grandfather greatly."

Adair flushed, and then, drawing a breath, said, "I have no husband, sir."

"I should not have thought that the king would allow a maiden of your tender years to return to her home alone," Andrew Lynbridge said softly, watching Adair closely as he spoke. The talk of a husband had turned his serene hostess edgy.

"I am sixteen, sir, and quite capable of running my own house. Albert watches over all, and I have appointed Dark Walter as captain of my men at arms. England is at peace, and the Scots are not raiding currently. But if they did we should be able to protect Stanton now. In my father's time it was thought we were too isolated to be bothered with, but I am wary of all. I have known since midmorning that you were coming to visit. I have watchers in the hills," Adair told him.

"A wise precaution," Robert agreed, nodding. "And most clever."

"You must remain the night," Adair said. "With winter upon us it is already almost sunset. There is no moon to guide you home." She turned to Albert, who had been hovering in the background. "Tell Cook we have guests."

"Yes, m'lady," he said, and hurried off.

"I thank you for your hospitality," Robert responded.

"And in the years I have been away," Adair said to him, "have you both taken wives and sired children? I'm sure that would please your grandfather."

"I have a wife," Robert told her. "She has given me twin lads, and will birth another child in late winter. And aye, Grandsire is pleased."

"And you, sir?" Adair asked Andrew. "Have you a wife?"

"Nay," he told her. "I haven't found a woman who pleases me enough. Yet."

"Albert says we have guests." Elsbeth now bustled into the hall.

"Robert and Andrew Lynbridge, old Lord Humphrey's grandsons from Hillview," Adair told her. "Sirs, this is my nurse and dear companion, Elsbeth. It was Elsbeth who took me to the king."

Both men nodded, murmuring almost simultaneously, "Mistress Elsbeth."

"I have asked them to remain, as the night is upon us," Adair said. "Will you see that a guest chamber is prepared for them?"

"Bed spaces in the hall will be more comfortable, and warmer," Elsbeth said, eyeing both young men suspiciously. "Does Brenna still lie with your grandfather?"

"More to keep the old man warm now," Andrew Lynbridge said with a grin. "You know Brenna, Mistress Elsbeth?"

"We are kin," Elsbeth replied tartly, "although I rarely admit to it, for Brenna is no better than she ought to be, and never was."

Andrew Lynbridge laughed loudly. "She's a wicked piece, and always was," he agreed, "but she has a kind heart and is good to the old man. She cares for him like her own babe, and best of all, she makes him laugh. He is much infirm now, but she rarely leaves his side. She'll always have a place at Hillview."

"Agreed!" Robert echoed his younger brother.

Having satisfied herself, and none too subtly, that the two men were who they said they were, Elsbeth left the hall to get the bedding and make up the two bed spaces that the Lynbridge brothers would sleep in tonight. Robert appeared a sensible man, and settled, but the younger sibling, Andrew, was, Elsbeth suspected, a proper hell raiser. It was plain to see no woman had yet tamed him.

Neither of them, especially that Andrew, was going to get above the hall tonight, Elsbeth decided. Adair had her reputation to protect. She was young, innocent, and beautiful. But there was no other woman of rank in the house who could attest that her virtue was intact come the morning. The word of a servant was rarely accepted as legitimate. No. Their visitors would remain in the hall tonight. And she would alert Dark Walter to station some men at arms discreetly in the upstairs hall.

In the hall Adair entertained her guests with tales of the royal court, totally unaware that Andrew Lynbridge was studying her with a very practiced eye. The lass was indeed a beauty, he thought to himself. All cats might look alike in the dark, he recalled his grandsire saying, but this little kitten was a feast for the eyes in the light. Maybe it was time to consider settling down, he considered.

And as Andrew watched Adair, Robert watched his sibling, and a small, knowing smile touched his lips. The girl was just the sort his brother should wed. She was beautiful, and she had spirit. No milksop of a girl would satisfy Andrew. His grandsire was going to be well pleased with the success of this visit, Robert thought.

And then Albert was announcing that the meal was ready to be eaten. He surreptitiously nodded to Andrew to escort Adair to the high board, watching as he seated her and she turned a smiling face up to him. *Good. Good,* he thought to himself. Then he settled down to eat the very excellent supper that was served them. If Andrew could woo and win the lovely Adair Radcliffe he would be a most fortunate man. After the meal they settled before the fire, and Adair played her lute for them. Then they told of the region which she had left so precipitously as a little girl.

"What are you doing about the cattle?" Robert asked her. "I saw none grazing as we rode your lands, lady."

"There are none," Adair said. "The Scots pillaged them, but I will restock come the spring. I did not think it prudent to do so now. There would not have been enough to feed cattle over the winter months.

My parents left me a small inheritance, and I know they would want me to bring Stanton back to its small glory." She arose. "Now I will bid you good night, sirs. My day begins early. Elsbeth has made up your bed spaces on either side of the hearth. You will be quite warm." She curtsied to them and left the hall, followed slowly by an aged wolfhound.

"She is not horse-faced," Robert said softly to his brother.

"Nay, she certainly is not," Andrew Lynbridge answered.

"You will come courting in the spring?"

"I will come courting this winter," Andrew said. "None shall have her but me."

"Grandsire will be pleased," Robert noted.

Andrew laughed. "Aye, he will, the old devil. But Stanton lands will be mine, Rob. I will not share them with Grandsire. You and I understand each other, but the old man can be greedy."

Robert Lynbridge nodded. "Agreed. But first you have to get the lass to accept you, little brother."

"Make no mistake, Rob, I mean to have her. If she cries nay I will convince her otherwise, even if it means forcing her to the altar. Women will generally come around if you handle them properly and love them well," Andrew said.

"You're ruthless, like Grandsire," Robert remarked.

"Perhaps I am," Andrew Lynbridge agreed slowly, "but God's foot, she is lovely! I can't let anyone else have her. And Grandsire is correct in one thing: Why should the Nevilles and the Percys have all the land hereabouts?"

"She has spirit," Robert replied. "Treat her gently and you may win her over. But should you woo her too roughly she will fight you."

"I enjoy a good challenge," his sibling said with a wicked grin.

"I suspect you have found one," Robert responded, grinning back at Andrew.

Chapter 4

The following morning dawned clear again, but there was a hint of snow in the wind that blew from the northwest. As the good chatelaine she had been taught to be, Adair was up long before her guests. She saw the servants brought them water in which to bathe, and there was breakfast at the high board almost immediately. Adair joined the Lynbridge brothers as a trencher of bread filled with hot oat stirabout was placed before each of them. Newly baked bread was set upon a cutting board along with half a wheel of hard yellow cheese. Cups were filled with sweet cider.

"You keep a fine table, Mistress Adair," Robert Lynbridge complimented his hostess. "When the spring comes I hope to visit you again, and mayhap I will bring my wife, should she be recovered from her childbed."

"I will certainly welcome you both," Adair replied graciously.

"I will come before the spring," Andrew Lynbridge said.

"Why?" Adair surprised him by asking.

"I would ask your permission to court you," Andrew answered her.

"I do not choose to be courted," Adair told him frankly. "I have just returned home after ten years away. Do you not think I know my own value? Every man who says he will court me wants my lands, sir. But I am not ready yet to give up my newfound freedoms for the marriage bed and childbirth."

"Nonetheless, I will come courting," Andrew said, "whether you will or no, Adair Radcliffe, and I shall not be the only man on your doorstep suing for your hand. But I will be the only man worthy of you."

"Indeed, sir, and you have a fine opinion of yourself, I can see," Adair responded tartly. "I can but wonder what others say of you, but I shall ask, you may be certain."

"Our families have been neighbors for many years," Robert Lynbridge said quietly. "It would please both my grandsire and me should you accept my brother's suit."

Adair smiled at the older of the Lynbridge brothers. "I am flattered, sir, by the attention that your family would lavish upon me," she said, "but I need some time to myself before I consider any marriage I would make. And I would want Uncle Dickon's advice and blessing on any union I might consider contracting," Adair told them.

Robert nodded. "I understand, and you are, of course, correct. I know my brother would certainly accept the duke's decision in the matter." He stood up. "The weather is unusually fair this day, and I think that Andrew and I should take the opportunity to journey home before the day is much further advanced." He nodded to his younger, brother, who also arose.

Adair now stood. "Elsbeth, fetch a jar of the plum preserves I did in September." She turned to the two men. "For your grandsire, sirs. As I remember he had a sweet tooth for my mother's plum preserves, and I have used her recipe."

Andrew chuckled. "He still has that sweet tooth, sweetheart, and I shall tell him you sent the preserves to him with a kiss."

Adair burst out laughing. "How is it that two brothers can be so different?" she asked him. "You are quite wicked, sir."

"But you like it," he teased her, and chuckled again when she blushed.

"Here is the jar," Elsbeth said, coming up to them and shoving it into Andrew's hand. "Try not to break it, my fine laddie, before the old man has a taste."

Adair escorted her guests into the courtyard, where their horses were even now awaiting them. It was at that moment they heard the blare of horns and the thunder of hoofbeats, but before they had a chance to consider it a large party of horsemen swept into the courtyard, led by Duke Richard.

Adair's face lit up when she saw him, and she ran to his horse as he dismounted, kissing the beringed hand he held out to her. "Uncle Dickon! Welcome to Stanton!"

The Duke of Gloucester kissed his niece on both cheeks, and then, setting her back from him, said, "You have been a very naughty girl, poppet. The king was most disturbed when you departed court so precipitously. It was most rash of you."

"You know why I left," Adair said softly.

The duke nodded, and then his eyes swept over the two young men. "Andrew Lynbridge," he said. "And this must be your elder brother."

"My lord duke," Andrew said, bowing low. "It is good to see you again. And, aye, this is my brother, Robert, our grandsire's heir."

"Your brother was one of my finest captains, sir," the duke addressed Robert. "What brings you both to Stanton Hall?"

"We are neighbors, and our grandsire asked that we pay our respects to Mistress Adair," Robert answered the duke.

"Good neighbors are a blessing," the duke said.

"You were here the night?" A richly dressed young man by the duke's side spoke.

"Aye, sir, we were," Robert Lynbridge replied.

The young man turned to the duke. "This is untenable, my lord! That my wife should have been alone in her house with two men, and no chaperone. Is she unchaste, then, that she was sent from court? My father did not believe for one minute that tale that Lady Margaret told of the bride going north to prepare her estate for my arrival."

"Wife?" Andrew Lynbridge said softly. His glance flicked to Adair, who looked astounded by the peacockish young man's statement.

"Aye, my wife, Lady Adair Radcliffe," came the reply. "I am Llywelyn, born FitzTudor, now Radcliffe, the Earl of Stanton."

"I have no husband!" Adair cried furiously. Her heart was beating with her outrage at the young man. "How dare you speak such an untruth!"

"Perhaps, poppet, we should all adjourn to the great hall, and I will tell you what you need to know," the duke said quietly. "I am sure Lord Humphrey will be interested to learn of your marriage."

"I am not married!" Adair shouted.

"I am afraid you are, poppet," the duke told her ruefully. Dismounting, he took her arm and led her back into the hall, the others following behind them.

"I am not married!" she protested angrily, pulling away from him, her dark green skirts swirling about her legs. She glared at the young man with the duke. He was practically a child, she realized, certainly younger than she was.

"You are a wedded wife, poppet," the duke told her firmly. "You knew the king wished you wed to the Earl of Pembroke's son."

"The Earl of Pembroke's bastard!" Adair snapped.

"A fitting match for a king's brat," the young man sneered. He was at least an inch shorter than Adair, and wore a richly decorated short-skirted doublet of plum velvet and cloth of silver. His woolen hose were natural in color, and his short black boots had turned-back cuffs. On his head was a hat covered in beaver fur that trailed several silk streamers of plum and silver. About his neck was a heavy gold chain with a pendant.

The Lynbridge brothers looked at each other, surprised, for they understood the meaning behind the young man's words.

"I did not consent to any marriage, Uncle Dickon, and I was certainly not present at any wedding ceremony," Adair said firmly. Her heart was beating wildly, and she suddenly felt like a rat in a trap.

"Your consent was not necessary. It was the king's decision," the duke reminded her. "The ceremony was a proxy one, with Princess Mary standing in for you," he explained. "Llywelyn FitzTudor has taken your family's name for his own, as John Radcliffe had demanded of the king many years back. My brother is not a man to go back on his word, Adair. I told you a long time ago, poppet, that your value would be in your title and your lands. The Earl of Pembroke is pleased with this union, and so is the king."

"And now, madam, you will welcome me properly to Stanton," Llywelyn FitzTudor said. "I will forgive you your surprise and your ignorance, for you are only a weak woman." He held out his hand to her, waiting for her to kiss it.

Adair stared at him as if he were mad. She slapped the hand away. Then, turning, she ran from the hall. They would not see her cry. And she needed time to figure out how she was going to escape from this nightmare that had been visited upon her.

But Elsbeth remained in the shadows, for she needed to know more. She listened as the Lynbridge brothers took their leave of the duke and his party.

As they departed the hall, Andrew Lynbridge murmured softly to Elsbeth, "Call if she needs us, mistress. This laddie cannot last." Then he was gone.

Elsbeth nodded slightly, her eyes making brief contact with his. Then she turned and listened as the duke attempted to soothe the boy's anger at Adair's behavior.

"I was told she would welcome me," Llywelyn FitzTudor complained to the duke as Elsbeth gave the boy a goblet of wine. "My father thought it odd the bride had a proxy, but the king assured him all was well. And how, after days on the road, am I greeted? With shouts, anger, and bad manners! My father will not be pleased when I write him. This bride is a termagant! I can see I shall have to beat her into obedience."

"I think, perhaps, my lord, you would do better to win her over with gentle manners and a subtle wooing," the duke advised. "Adair was told she was to be married, but she did not believe it would happen so swiftly. She is surprised, of course, by your arrival, for no word was sent ahead, or the knowledge that the deed is done. She wanted to come home after ten years and reacquaint herself with Stanton and her lands. She barely escaped with her life that night when her parents were slain. She is a good maid, and if you will be patient she will come around. I shall stay the night so you two may begin to experience some familiarity with each other beneath the eye of a friend."

Llywelyn FitzTudor held out his goblet to be refilled. "I hope you are correct, my lord," he said sulkily. But his mood did not improve when Adair refused to return to the hall that night. He was shown to an apartment at the far end of the corridor, where the bedchambers were located, by the house's majordomo, who introduced himself as

Albert, and politely addressed him as "my lord earl," which allayed Llywelyn FitzTudor's bruised ego. But instead of the wedding night he had anticipated, he slept in a cold bed alone.

The duke attempted to reason with Adair the following morning when he came down to the hall to find her going about her daily duties. He suddenly realized how lovely she was, and how much she had grown up in the few months she had been away from the court. She wore a simple loose housedress of violet wool that matched her eyes, and her long black hair was braided into a single plait. They sat by the fire together on a gray morning, and the duke gently scolded her.

"If you had stayed we might have avoided this," he told her. "We could have reasoned with the king. Postponed the wedding until you had had the opportunity to grow used to the idea."

"How old is he?" Adair demanded to know.

"Fourteen," the duke responded honestly.

"He is two years younger than I am. He has a face pockmarked with blemishes. He had a fine idea of his own importance, Uncle Dickon, and I suspect he knows nothing about running an estate such as mine. Yet he is not wise enough to allow me to do it, and will ruin Stanton if permitted."

The duke sighed. "You are probably right," he agreed, "and so you will have to find a way around him so that Stanton remains prosperous."

Now it was Adair who sighed. "I know," she said. "The snows will soon come, and I must weather the winter with this pompous boy, but come spring I mean to send him back to his father and seek an annulment, Uncle Dickon."

"Adair, you refuse to understand. The king wants this marriage. Giving you to the Earl of Pembroke's favorite by-blow gives the boy a title of his own. It binds the Tudors to the house of York," the duke explained.

"The Tudors will never be truly loyal to the house of York," Adair said. "How could the king have been so unkind as to give me to the very people who killed my parents, Uncle Dickon? If I do not slay the little wretch myself it will be a miracle."

The duke could not help but laugh. "Poppet, do not do anything rash," he pleaded with her. "Perhaps you will come to like young Fitz-Tudor."

Adair looked at him with a jaundiced eye. "More than likely not," she said. "Why is it that no one understands? I wanted time to myself again."

"Noble folk do not have such luxury, poppet," the duke told her. "We have responsibilities to our lands, our people, and our rulers. My brother sired you and acknowledged his paternity of you. When your parents were slain he took up the responsibility for you and your well-being. He did not shun you, Adair, but rather saw you raised as his legitimate children were raised. He has never showed any partiality toward any of his offspring, trueborn or otherwise. But he is also your king, and you owe him your loyalty as such. You also owe him your devotion and obedience, poppet, for his devotion and kindness to you over the years."

"If you were king you would not have forced me into such a marriage, Uncle Dickon," Adair said.

"No, I should not have, but then, I know you better. If I were king and I had wanted this marriage, I would have taken time to see you and young FitzTudor got to know each other. I would have convinced you of the advantages of such a union to our house, the house of York," the duke said, reaching out to caress her cheek with a finger. "But I am not your king. I am the king's brother, and my first loyalty has always been to Edward and his wishes. I have never betrayed him, nor will I ever betray him. The king wants this marriage, Adair, and therefore you must accept his wishes even if you do not want to accept them. Loyalty must be your first consideration in all things, as it is mine, poppet." The duke leaned forward and kissed her cheek. "When you are a king's brat, Adair, there are few choices, I fear."

A tear rolled down her cheek. "I want to do as you say, Uncle Dickon, but I cannot be wed to this boy. He is overproud, and ignorant to boot, I fear. Did you see how he attempted to lord it over everyone last night? And telling me he would forgive me? It is untenable! I cannot be like you. I would send him packing tomorrow if I could." She impatiently brushed the tear from her pale skin.

"There is nothing I can say to dissuade you then?" Duke Richard said.

"I think it best you go home to Middleham today," Adair told him. "The weather is certain to turn after such a lovely and unexpected day as we had yesterday. We are due for snow, I fear. I will deal with this boy in my own fashion, and I think it better you not be here, Uncle."

"You cannot kill him," the duke told her quietly.

"I won't," Adair said. "But neither will I be his wife, or let him lord it over me and my estates. I will house him and feed him, but no more. Who was his mother, and how was he raised, Uncle?"

"His mother was a girl said to be descended from the house of the great Llywelyn himself. She was a poor orphaned cousin in service to one of Jasper's wives. She caught his eye, as so many have, and died giving birth to his son. But the Tudor is a decent man, and the boy was raised in his father's house, treated well and with respect. For some reason that I cannot see, the lad became a favorite of Jasper Tudor's," the duke said.

"He is not worthy of me, Uncle. I was sired on a baron's daughter by a king. He who called himself my father was an earl. My lineage is better than this boy's," Adair said proudly. "I shall tell him so without hesitation." She arose from where they were seated. "Give my dearest love to the Lady Anne and little Neddie. If you are home in the spring, and when the snows have gone, I will come and visit you, Uncle," Adair said, in effect dismissing the Duke of Gloucester.

He stood with an amused smile. "Come and bid me farewell in the courtyard, poppet," he said, and together they walked from the great hall of the house. Outside the duke called for his men, and they were shortly all mounted. "*Adieu*, poppet," Richard of Gloucester said, giving her a quick kiss upon her cheek and then mounting his steed.

"*Adieu*, dearest Uncle Dickon," Adair replied, curtsying prettily to him. Then she watched as the duke and his men departed the courtyard and galloped off down the road leading south to Middleham Castle, the duke's favorite home. Turning back to the house, Adair took up her daily duties. She was not surprised when Albert came to her as she was totaling up the estate's accounts.

He stood, respectfully awaiting a sign that he might speak, and then she looked up and nodded to him. "My lady," he began slowly, carefully. "What are we to do about the young earl?"

"Who?" For a moment Adair looked puzzled.

"Your husband, my lady?" Albert said.

"Oh, him? You are to do nothing. Treat him respectfully, and the servants may follow his simple commands for things like food and drink. But anything else he requires or demands must be brought to me first. You are to carry out no orders that he may give you; nor are any of the other servants. Do not argue with him. Just say, 'Very good, my lord,' and then come to me. I mean to return him to the king come spring."

"My lady, forgive me, but much was heard in the hall last night, and the servants are asking questions I am unable to answer." Albert looked very uncomfortable, and he was shuffling his feet nervously, something he had never done before.

Adair flushed, but then, drawing a deep breath, she said, "My paternity is not something I ever wished to discuss, Albert, but the duke, and this boy who calls himself my husband, have spoken too freely before all. Here is the truth of it: John Radcliffe did not sire me on my mother's body. King Edward did. He desired my mother, and offered him I called Father the earldom in exchange for my mother's virtue. I was born from the king's seed and my mother's loins."

"My lady!" Poor Albert was now quite red in the face.

"The king acknowledged me as his own child, his blood, and agreed to dower me one day. He declared that if no son was born to my parents that I should become Countess of Stanton in my own right on John Radcliffe's death. He who wed one day with me would take the Radcliffe name for his own, and should become Earl of Stanton. That is the whole truth of it, Albert," Adair told her majordomo. "Tell the others so they will stop guessing and speculating on it all. But first tell them what I previously told you about the boy FitzTudor. He is an arrogant lad, but if he is made comfortable I believe I can control him easily."

"Yes, my lady," Albert said. He turned to go, almost bumping into

Elsbeth as he did. "Your pardon," he said to her, and hurried from the chamber.

"The servants were gossiping. I told Albert the truth, and to tell them," Adair said.

Elsbeth nodded. " 'Tis better now that the cat's been loosed from the bag," she agreed. "What else? I know you well, lassie. There is more."

Adair laughed. "You know me much too well," she said. Then she went on to tell Elsbeth of her plans for Llywelyn FitzTudor.

"Do you think it wise to treat the lad so?" Elsbeth asked slowly. "He will expect his husbandly rights sooner than later."

"Well, he shall not get them from me," Adair said firmly. "I will not have that boy attempting to bed me, Nursie. He is pockmarked, and despite his fine clothes he smelled," she remarked. "Nay. In the spring he goes back to his father. Did he have any servants with him when he arrived yesterday? I could see only the duke's men."

"There is one. A little dark Welshman who calls himself Anfri. He attempted to chat the servants up last night in an effort to learn about us," Elsbeth said.

"Warn Albert to speak to the others. The man is to be tolerated, but told nothing that might be of value to him," Adair said. "If he is a good servant he seeks to gain information that would allow his master an advantage over us. It shall not happen."

"He was just coming down into the kitchens when I came up," Elsbeth said.

"Is the boy up and in the hall yet?" Adair wanted to know.

"Nay, I have not seen him," Elsbeth said.

"He has the habits of a sluggard then," Adair noted. "Well, so much the better. He will be out of our way."

Llywelyn FitzTudor came to the hall in early afternoon. He found Adair at her loom weaving on her tapestry. The piece was half-done, and showed a good rendition of Stanton Hall on its hill, the gray stone house against a blue sky, the ground beneath it green. Adair was working on some cattle in the meadow below the house.

"I am pleased to find you in suitable womanly pursuits," FitzTudor said. He was wearing a beautiful short-skirted doublet of pea green and gold brocade with long hanging sleeves. His trunk hose were pea green, and the sollerets upon his feet were heel-less. The same heavy gold chain she had seen yesterday was upon his chest. His mousy brown hair was cut to a medium bob. He was not unattractive, but neither was he attractive.

"Sit down, my lord," Adair said, ignoring his remark about womanly pursuits. "Have you eaten yet this day?" She didn't bother to look at him, concentrating instead on her stitches in the tapestry.

"Yes, my servant Anfri brought me food, madam. We must discuss our marriage now," FitzTudor said.

"There is nothing to discuss, my lord," Adair replied. "The king and your father made this match without my permission. Had I been there I should not have agreed to it, and holy Mother Church would not have forced me to the altar. I will return you home come spring. For the king's sake I will keep you safe for the winter, for you would not have the time to return south before the snows, which began in late morning while you slumbered in your bed."

"Whether you will or no, madam," FitzTudor said, "you are now my wife, and I shall claim all my rights of you. It is the king's will, and that of my father. Our marriage is meant to unite our families, Lancaster and York."

"Arrogant boy!" Adair snapped. "Do you really believe the union of two bastard-born such as we are can accomplish such a high purpose? Nonsense! Perhaps a marriage between Henry of Lancaster and one of my half sisters will create a cohesive union between York and Lancaster, but you and I will not. We are merely the first payment in a possible arrangement of such magnitude. We are not important, either of us. By the time I return you home, the proper matches will have been made. Your father will seek a comfortable heiress for you, and I will wed where I please one day."

"I doubt my father will find another countess in her own right to pair me with," FitzTudor said sarcastically. "What made you so desirable to my father, madam, other than your paternity, was the earldom you would bring your husband."

She was surprised. He was not as stupid as she had assumed he was. "You are two years my junior," she said. "You are shorter than I am. I do not like you," Adair told him, finally looking up from her tapestry work. "What do you know of managing one's estates, my lord?"

"Nothing," he said candidly. "It is not for me to manage an estate. That is what one has servants for, madam."

"Servants, even the best of them, will steal when not properly overseen. It is a great temptation for them, my lord. Do you know how to purchase cattle?" she asked.

"Why would I?" he returned.

"All the cattle from these lands were stolen when my parents were killed. In the spring I will have to replace them."

"You have been home several months," he responded. "Why have you not already done so, madam?"

"Because the Stanton folk are few, and not able to grow enough grain to feed a large herd through the winter. And why should we feed them when someone else will? The spring is the best time."

"Oh," he answered. "My father is sending us a herd of heifers, and a young bull," FitzTudor said. "I did not ask when they would come."

"Your father's people will understand, and not send them until spring. By that time you will be back with the Earl of Pembroke, and he will not have to send them. I would not take his cattle under false pretenses," Adair answered.

"You are my wife!" the boy said angrily.

"Temporarily, and in name only," Adair replied calmly. She almost expected him to stamp his foot at her.

Llywelyn FitzTudor jumped up from the settle before the fire where they had been sitting. He yanked Adair up. Putting his arms about her he tried to kiss her, mashing his mouth against hers desperately. "You belong to me now!" he raged at her.

Not only was he shorter than she, he was slight of body. Adair, almost gagging on his bad breath, broke his hold on her and shoved him away. "Do not ever dare to accost me in such a manner," she snarled at him. "You disgust me, my lord!"

FitzTudor struggled to his feet and lunged at her again, but suddenly he found himself facing a large and snarling wolfhound who bared yellowed but still sharp fangs at the boy, who screamed in fright as he was backed away by the dog.

Adair waited until her would-be husband had been pushed into the settle, where he fell, half sobbing. "Enough, Beiste. As you can see, my lord, I have protection against such assault as you have just committed. Touch me again and I shall order the dog to tear out your throat. Do we understand each other?"

"Bitch!" FitzTudor cursed at her.

Adair laughed at him. "Boy," she taunted him.

Outside the windows of the great hall the snows began to come down in earnest, the cold outside matched only by the cold inside. By Christ's Mass the countryside was hidden beneath a deep coverlet of white. Adair passed out gifts to her servants and her villagers. She did not include FitzTudor in her largesse; nor did he present her with anything. Twelfth Night came and went. They barely spoke. In fact, they barely even met except now and again in the great hall, when FitzTudor would come to the high board and join her for a meal.

January ended, and February was ushered in with a great blizzard and snows that reached the eaves of some of the cottages on the outskirts of the village. The Stanton folk were kept busy keeping open the road through the village and up to the house. The servants kept to the hall. To Adair's surprise and delight, Beiste had sired a litter of pups, who were born early in the month. He would sit almost grinning by his mate's side, guarding her while she nursed their offspring. But he also continued to watch over Adair, the hair on his back bristling whenever FitzTudor came into the great hall.

Llywelyn FitzTudor was not happy with the situation, and he complained to his manservant, Anfri. "I am master here by right, and yet I am not."

"Your every wish is obeyed, my lord," Anfri said, "is it not?"

"Aye, but I can tell it is not because I am the earl, but because she told them to obey me. These Stanton folk do not see me as their lord. They behave as if I were a guest who has overstayed his welcome," FitzTudor grumbled. "And she is worst of all. She is my wife under

God's law and the king's law, but she practically ignores me. And I cannot get near her because of that damned dog. Miserable old cur. Beiste. He is well named. I hate the damned creature!"

"If you could get near your wife what would you do?" Anfri murmured boldly.

"I would place her on her back and fuck her until I put a babe in her belly," FitzTudor said. "Then she could not send me away. But as long as she maintains her virgin status she has grounds for annulment. I will be made a laughingstock in my father's house. She is a beauty, isn't she, Anfri? My cock hardens just thinking about her. At least in my father's house I had women on which to ease my lust, but not here. It has been pent up for several months now."

"Then surely your seed is at its strongest now, my lord," Anfri said. "You should look to catch the lady when the dog is guarding his mate. She is most vulnerable then. I believe part of this dilemma is that she has a virgin's fears. If you could soothe those terrors she would surely be more amenable to you, my lord." His black eyes glittered as he spoke to his master.

"And just how do you suggest I do that?" FitzTudor demanded.

"By putting your manly cock within her love sheath, my lord. Nothing cures a maiden's alarm of the unknown like a strong familiarity with her fears," Anfri replied.

"You give me food for thought," FitzTudor said thoughtfully, and after that he began to watch Adair more closely. And by doing so he saw one day after the main meal had been served and eaten that his wife went to her chamber alone. Looking about, he saw that the old dog was snoring with his mate and their puppies by the fire. Fortified with several goblets of rich, dark wine, Llywelyn FitzTudor followed Adair upstairs, watching as she entered her chamber. He listened carefully, but did not hear the key turn in the lock as he did each night. Slowly he crept down the dimly lit corridor. He put his hand on the door's latch and felt it give way. The door opened. Surprised, he stood for a moment in the open door, and then he quickly stepped through into the bedchamber, shutting the door behind him and quietly turning the key in the lock.

Adair heard the door open and, assuming it was Elsbeth, asked, "What is it, Nursie? Can it not wait until I have cured this wretched headache?"

"I think I have waited long enough, madam, to exercise my rights over you," Llywelyn FitzTudor said. His young voice almost squeaked in his excitement, and he could almost taste his victory over her as he walked across the room.

Adair was up and off her bed in a trice. "How dare you enter my bedchamber without my permission, boy!" She wore no shoes. "What do you want?"

"It is past time, madam, that you became my wife in every way," FitzTudor answered her. He began to loosen his trunk hose and doublet.

"Get out!" Adair said in a cold, hard voice.

"No! I shall have your virginity of you, madam, and none shall say I was not man enough to do the deed," he told her stubbornly. He tossed his upper garment aside.

"You shall have nothing of me," Adair said angrily. "Not my lands, nor the title, nor my virtue, my lord! When the snows go, you go! Now get out of my chamber or I shall begin to scream for help."

"The door is locked, and it is my right to have you," FitzTudor declared. He moved around the bed in an attempt to corner her.

"Get back!" Adair warned him. "Get back, take your clothing, and go. If you do not I will do what I must to defend myself."

He laughed aloud. "You are a mere girl," he sneered. "A weakling of a female."

Adair said nothing more. Reaching out, she grabbed the earthenware pitcher from the table by the bed and smashed it over his head as hard as she could. His legs gave way and he began to fall. Adair walked around FitzTudor and, going to the door, opened it and shouted, "Beiste! To me! To me!" The dog came up the stairs of the house with a roar that emanated from deep within his furred chest. "Take him away," Adair ordered the dog.

Beiste went over to where FitzTudor lay in a crumpled heap. He sniffed at the boy just as FitzTudor opened his eyes and, seeing the creature, made a strangled whimpering sound in his throat. Beiste snarled. Then, opening his mouth, the dog clamped his teeth gently about the boy's still-shod foot. FitzTudor fainted, his eyes rolling back in his head as Beiste pulled him from Adair's bedchamber out into the hallway.

"Good dog!" Adair praised her animal. "Go back to Anice and the pups now." She shut her chamber door and relocked it. Spring, she decided, could not come soon enough for her. What in the name of all heaven had possessed FitzTudor to attempt to assault her? She intended on moving him to a bed space in the great hall and posting a man at arms at her door each night. Elsbeth would sleep on the trundle in her room until Adair had sent the boy back to his family.

She would plead with Uncle Dickon to convince the king to arrange for an annulment, and if the Earl of Pembroke objected to it she would threaten to tell everyone in the kingdom that his by-blow was incapable of mounting a woman and doing his duty by a wife. It would be her word against the boy's. And she would wager that Jasper Tudor would not wish to have his family embarrassed publicly by a cry of impotence against his son. Adair smiled, pleased with herself and her plan.

February faded away and March quickly followed. FitzTudor complained about having to sleep in the great hall, and berated Anfri for his bad advice. April came, and with it Andrew Lynbridge, who rode up to Stanton Hall early one morning. Finding Adair in the great hall, he greeted her.

"There is an early cattle fair to be held today at Brockton. Would you like to come? The beasts will be a bit scrawny, but the farmers who have housed them over the winter won't want to feed them any longer, as they are low on feed," he told her.

"Albert, do we have feed? And how many can we take?" Adair asked her majordomo. "And how long until the meadows can be grazed?"

"Another few weeks for the meadows, my lady, but we have feed enough. Stanton folk will be happy to see cattle back again. We can easily care for two dozen."

Adair nodded. "Aye, I should like to go with you then, Andrew Lynbridge."

"Go where?" FitzTudor demanded as he crawled from his bed space.

"To Brockton," Adair said impatiently.

"I cannot allow my wife to travel in the company of another gentleman without me," FitzTudor said.

"I am not your wife," Adair said wearily. "Why must you persist in this fantasy? The snows are gone. I shall send you and your wretched servant south this week."

"You will not leave Stanton Hall without me by your side," Fitz-Tudor insisted.

"Come along then, my lord," Andrew Lynbridge said jovially. "We will need all the hands we can get driving the cattle back from Brockton."

"Very well, if you insist on coming, then come," Adair echoed, "but in the name of heaven, FitzTudor, do not wear one of your fancy garments. No one will be impressed by them, and the traders will try to charge me more than I need to pay for the cattle." She turned to Andrew Lynbridge. "Cider, sir? A bit of bread and cheese before we go?"

They traveled to Brockton in the company of Dark Walter and a dozen of his men. They would be needed to get the cattle back to Stanton Hall. FitzTudor had actually taken her counsel, and wore a leather jacket instead of a velvet or silk brocade half doublet. Andrew Lynbridge murmuring advice in her ear, Adair purchased thirty head of thin but sound beasts that would be the nucleus of Stanton's new herd. It was early afternoon when they began to drive the animals back the seven miles to the hall. The animals were docile and moved along well, but when they were almost in sight of Stanton a party of horsemen appeared at the crest of the hills.

"Jesu!" Andrew Lynbridge swore softly. "Scots."

"What do they want?" FitzTudor asked.

"The cattle, you fool!" Adair said. "They want the cattle."

"We're evenly matched, my lady," Dark Walter said.

"Aye, they may decide 'tis not worth the fight," she agreed. "The cattle are scrawny, after all." But Adair had a sinking feeling as the Scots moved slowly down the hill toward them. "Keep going, lads."

"Protect your lady first," Andrew Lynbridge said to Dark Walter. "The cattle can be replaced, but she must not be harmed."

"I am capable of protecting my own wife," FitzTudor said irritably.

Adair looked at him, astounded, and laughed. "You, boy? I do not think so, but not to fear. Dark Walter will see we are both safe."

The two groups advanced toward each other, finally stopping, each party blocking the road ahead. The cattle milled about, lowing.

" 'Tis a fine group of beasties ye hae," the leader of the Scots said casually.

"These poor starving cows?" Andrew Lynbridge replied easily.

"Thin they are, aye," the Scot agreed, "but yet they would make a tasty supper for our folk over the next few weeks, and they would fatten themselves up on our good Scots grass." He smiled at them, showing several broken teeth.

"You would do better to wait until they have fattened up on good Stanton grass," Adair remarked. "You've had my cattle before, I am told, sir."

The Scot laughed. "I have, my lady, but 'twas some years back. Now, to show your good faith I would have you turn a few of these creatures over to us today. We'll come for the rest in a few weeks' time, I promise you."

"Nay, good sir, I cannot," Adair replied. "I must rebuild my herds, starting with these cows. If you will but give me a year or two I promise you the wait will be well worth it." She grinned at him wickedly.

"Yer a braw lassie," the Scot said. "I think you might be worth it. Perhaps I shall take you and leave the cows." He returned her grin.

"How dare you, you low Scots varlet! How dare you speak to my wife in such a manner," FitzTudor demanded as he pushed his mount forward to face the Scot.

"Jesu!" Dark Walter muttered low.

"I am the Earl of Stanton," FitzTudor continued, "and if you do not immediately give way I shall send the duke's men after you and have you arrested for your presumption." He glared at the Scot and his men.

They burst out laughing. "This bantam cock is your husband, lady?"

"No, he is not. The king sent him, but I will not have him," Adair explained.

"The king sent him? Now why would the king be bothered with a little border lass such as yourself?" the Scot wanted to know.

Before Adair might say a word FitzTudor was speaking again. "Why? Because the Countess of Stanton is his natural daughter, that is why! Now, move aside and allow us to pass with our cattle."

"Perhaps you are worth more than your cattle, my lady," the Scot slowly mused.

"Nay, sir, I am not. And I am not in the king's favor at all, I fear. And I will be even less so when I send this pompous boy back to him and demand an annulment," Adair said lightly. "He is quite useless."

The Scots burst out laughing again, and then their leader said, "For a man to be useless with you is a tragedy, lady. Very well, we will take six head of cattle now, and return for the rest at summer's end." He nodded to his men to begin cutting the animals out of the herd.

Dark Walter looked to Andrew Lynbridge, who nodded in silent agreement. At a signal from Adair's captain the Stanton men drew their weapons, and a brief battle was on between the English and the Scots as the cattle scattered into the nearby meadow and began to graze. Swords clanged against one another. Horses whinnied in fright, their hooves kicking up dust from the narrow road as the short skirmish raged. Realizing he was outnumbered, the Scots' leader had thought better of it, and now reached out to grab at Adair's reins. She slashed at him with her dagger while struggling to maintain her seat.

Then, to her surprise Llywelyn FitzTudor came to her aid, his sword drawn, but he was no soldier. The Scot parried his opponent's flailing blade. FitzTudor managed to briefly get beneath the man's guard and bloodied his arm. The Scot swore angrily and then swiftly thrust his sword directly into the boy's chest, drawing it slowly out as FitzTudor, a look of complete surprise upon his young face, fell forward onto his horse's neck. With a shout to his remaining men the Scot galloped off, followed by those who were still a-horse. No other Stanton men had been killed, although several of the Scots had.

Llywelyn FitzTudor fell slowly from his horse. Adair was immediately on the ground by his side, cradling his head in her lap. "Now, boy, that was very foolish of you. Gallant, but foolish," she scolded him gently. She could feel tears pricking at the back of her eyelids at the futility of it all, for she could see the wound was a mortal one.

"I could . . . have . . . loved you," Llywelyn FitzTudor whispered with his dying breath, and then his weak blue eyes glassed over. He was gone.

Adair stared down in shock. She had not liked this husband the king had forced upon her. She had fully intended to send him back to his family. She had not been kind to him at all; nor had he been kind to her. He had even tried to rape her. Yet he had come to her defense when he thought her in danger. "He has died bravely," she said softly. "I will tell his father that he died bravely in my defense, but if he had not insisted upon coming this day he would still be alive. How odd a moment's decision can lead to death, yet if he had remained at Stanton Hall he would have lived."

"Aye, he did a noble thing," Dark Walter said. "I would not have expected it of him, my lady, if you will pardon my saying so." The captain slid from his horse and bent down. "Let me take him, my lady."

Adair looked up, her face tearstained now. "Aye." She nodded. "We'll give him a fine funeral, and bury him on the hillside with my parents."

Dark Walter lifted FitzTudor's body up and carefully slung it across the back of the boy's horse. Andrew Lynbridge had dismounted, and now helped Adair to rise from the ground where she had been seated. She staggered against him for a moment, and his arm tightened about her, steadying her as he helped her to her mount.

"Can you ride alone?" he asked her low. " 'Tis no shame if you can't."

"If I give way now," she told him, "I will not be able to do what must be done. For all I did not want him; for all the marriage was no real marriage in any way; he was my lawful husband. We did not treat each other well in life, but I will give him the honor he deserves as the Earl of Stanton in death. I will ride alone, Andrew."

He helped her to mount, his heart contracting, for she had called him by his given name for the first time. Hearing it on her lips had set his pulse racing and his blood pounding in his ears. Once she was firmly in her saddle he mounted his own horse. The Stanton men at arms were busily gathering up the cattle from the field to which the animals had fled in a panic when the battle had begun. And then they were on their way again.

When they reached the hall the servants came out and, seeing the body across the horse's back, looked in surprise to Adair.

"We were accosted by Scots on our return home," she said. "The young earl was slain, I fear. Take his body and lay it out in the great hall. Where is his man, Anfri?"

The dark little Welshman slid out from among the other servants. "Have you killed him then?" he whined. "I shall tell my master, the Earl of Pembroke, of your unkindness to his beloved son. I shall tell him!"

"Watch your mouth," Dark Walter said grimly as he slid from his horse. "My lady has not the heart for murder. The young earl was killed defending his wife when we were attacked by Scots borderers who sought to take the cattle we purchased today." He turned and carefully took the body from its mount. "Come along with me, little man. You will help the women prepare the boy's body, which will lie in the hall."

With a black look at Adair, Anfri scuttled after Dark Walter.

"You had best send to Duke Richard to help you in this matter," Andrew Lynbridge said to Adair. "I can see the Welshman is determined to make trouble for you. You have to protect yourself from his slanders. Write a message, and I'll take it to Middleham myself. You can write, can't you?"

"Of course I can write," Adair said irritably. "And read, among other accomplishments. It's late. Don't go until morning, please."

"I'll stay," he agreed.

"Thank you," she said softly; then she turned and went into the hall.

He turned and handed the reins of his horse to a stable lad, and followed her into the hall.

"Now there is a fine figure of a man," Elsbeth said to Albert, who stood by her side. "He would make us a suitable earl, don't you think?"

"Aye," Albert agreed.

"She'll keep a proper period of mourning," Elsbeth said.

"Let's hope the king don't send another bridegroom to her," Albert remarked.

"I think the duke will help her avoid that trap," Elsbeth said. "Besides, she is now of little importance to the king. He has other matters to consider that will take precedence over a bastard daughter's well-being. My lady served the royal purpose. She was wise to come home when she did. King Edward has the Tudors to contend with, I'm thinking. They will not be easily satisfied. Peace, I learned at court, is all very well and good. But with folk of high degree it is power that is more important."

Chapter 5

Middleham Castle had been constructed in north Yorkshire in the year 1170. It was one of the largest keeps in England. It had been built upon the southern hills. Its great gray stone towers and walls stood tall above the little village of Wensleydale, and near the town of Leyburn. The curtain walls, gatehouse, and moat had not been added until a century later. As he rode toward it, Andrew Lynbridge could see the white boar pendant of the Duke of Gloucester flying high in a brisk spring wind. As the day was coming to an end he hurried his horse toward the refuge of the castle. He was tired, and he was hungry. He would find generous hospitality within Middleham's walls, as well as old friends. Crossing the moat bridge he was recognized and waved through by the smiling man at arms. In the courtyard his horse was taken away, and he entered the castle going to the great hall, where he knew the duke was likely to be at this hour of the day.

Andrew stopped a serving man. "Would you tell your master that Andrew Lynbridge is here with a message from the Countess of Stanton?" he said.

The servant nodded and hurried off. Andrew watched him, and so saw him stop by the duke's chair and murmur in his ear. Richard of Gloucester looked up and around. Andrew stepped from the shadows, and, seeing him, the duke beckoned him forward. Andrew Lynbridge obeyed the command and came to kneel politely by the duke's side. Having kissed the hand extended to him he arose and drew the folded parchment from where it had rested between his skin and his shirt.

"Do you know what is in this?" the duke asked as he took the message.

"I do, my lord," Andrew replied.

Richard broke the seal on the parchment, and, opening it out, swiftly read the contents. When he had finished he folded the communication back up, laid it aside, and asked, "Was it an accident? Or did she kill him?" The startled look on Andrew Lynbridge's handsome face gave him the answer before the man even spoke.

"We were returning from a cattle fair near Stanton," Andrew said. "A party of Scots borderers attacked, attempting to steal the animals. FitzTudor went to the aid of his wife when their leader made to carry her off. Frankly I wouldn't have thought he had the balls, my lord, but he did. Alas, he was no soldier. Did his father never have him taught better? The Scot skewered him easily."

"There was no saving him?" the duke asked.

"My lord, the wound was mortal. The Scot slew his heart. The lady jumped from her horse and comforted her husband, but he died in her arms," Andrew Lyndbridge said.

"Then my niece had become reconciled to the marriage?" the duke queried.

"Nay, my lord. She despised him, and he, I think, thought little better of her. But he had great pride in being the Earl of Stanton, and he tried hard to be possessive of her, and master of Stanton, but she would not allow it," was the reply.

"Do you think there might be a child?" the duke said.

"You would have to ask her women that question, but I would wager he never got into her bed, my lord," Andrew Lynbridge replied.

The Duke of Gloucester nodded. Then he sighed. "I do not fear telling my brother this news, but the Earl of Pembroke is another matter. Jasper Tudor doted upon the lad, though frankly I never understood why. The boy was ignorant and prideful. He had little to recommend him that I could see. I tried to talk the king out of making the match, but my brother would not listen."

"Perhaps the Earl of Pembroke had a particular fondness for the boy's mother," Andrew suggested.

The duke nodded. "That could very well be it," he agreed. "She died when her son was born, and dead mistresses, I am told, always hold a warmer place in one's memory than discarded mistresses. Well, the boy is dead, and there is an end to it. Perhaps I will wait a bit before informing the king of these unfortunate events."

"I should not, my lord," Andrew said. "The young earl's body servant, a Welshman called Anfri, believes that the countess caused her husband's death. He said so, and the morning after the lad was slain he was gone from the hall. I suspect he has fled south to tell Jasper Tudor his version of what has happened. As he was not there he has nothing but his suspicions and dislike of the countess to speak on to the Earl of Pembroke. That could cause great difficulty for the countess."

"And you would not like that," the duke said slyly.

Andrew Lynbridge grinned. "I will admit that before I learned that she was the Countess of Stanton, and not simply the lady of the hall, I considered courting her. And before the king sent her a husband. My grandsire was extremely annoyed to learn that. He has always coveted the Stanton grazing meadows."

"And would the lady consider your suit if you approached her?" the duke pressed.

"I have no idea, my lord," Andrew replied candidly. "Once I learned she was wed I did not even consider it."

"You're a baron's son," the duke said. "Your blood is every bit as good as Radcliffe blood. John Radcliffe was a baron, and gained a greater title only by letting my brother futter his pretty wife. Jane served the queen, and though Edward pursued her she would have nothing to do with him. So my brother made an arrangement with Radcliffe, and Radcliffe told his wife to please Edward. They are no great family."

"But the lady is the king's blood," Andrew Lynbridge said.

"If you care for her, court her before my brother decides to barter her off again to some minion in order to obtain something he wants," the duke advised. "I would not be unhappy to see a loyal ally at Stanton Hall. Adair is strong for a woman, but I do not see her holding her home against the Scots. They have been restless and raiding of late. Now that it is known she is back, a young, pretty widow alone and ripe for the picking, she is in danger. My wife's relatives, the Nevilles, will be interested, as will all the Percys. I am Adair's uncle, and I would approve a match between you," Richard of Gloucester said with a small smile. "I can certainly assure my brother of your utmost loyalty."

"She will want to mourn FitzTudor, if for no other reason than good etiquette," Andrew Lynbridge said. "She is proud of her name, my lord. And any who weds her must take that name, for the king promised John Radcliffe."

"You could be the Earl of Stanton," the duke tempted him. "Six months mourning a boy you didn't know, and who was with you less time, is enough. We have a border to protect, and having one of my former captains at Stanton would please me."

"I'm not even certain she likes me," Andrew said slowly.

"She didn't like FitzTudor, but had he been a man he would have gotten between her legs, and it is possible her attitude would have changed. I have known Adair since she was a little girl. She needs a man she can respect first. Gain her respect, and you could gain her heart," Richard of Gloucester said quietly.

"Perhaps," Andrew Lynbridge said, "when I return to Stanton Hall with your message of condolence, you might tell the lady that you would wish me to stay on to oversee the defense of her home, as the Scots are being troublesome of late. She does have a good captain of her men at arms, Dark Walter, but he is not as experienced as he could be. I know she loves you, my lord, and if you wrote her that it would please you, then she would acquiesce, I am quite certain," he concluded.

The duke chuckled. "A worthy and clever plan, Andrew. Go now, and pay your respects to my wife. We will speak again before you depart back for Stanton tomorrow."

Andrew Lynbridge bowed politely and left the duke. He found the Lady Anne with her women in the solar.

The Duchess of Gloucester looked up with a sweet smile as he entered. "Andrew, how good to see you. What brings you to Middleham?" She was a pretty young woman with pale blue eyes and long golden hair, the braids of which were looped up about her small head. She was not strong in body, but Richard of Gloucester adored her.

He kissed the delicate little blue-veined hand she offered him, and then at her invitation sat down to tell her his tale.

She listened with great interest to what he had to say, and when he had concluded his narrative she said, "Poor little Adair. I know she did not want a husband now, but still, to lose him in such a manner. Of course Jasper Tudor will not be pleased at all by this turn of events."

"The boy was brave," Andrew Lynbridge said.

"Did she love him at all?" the duchess wondered.

"I do not believe she did, my lady," he replied.

"She will be alone now," the duchess remarked. "Should she be alone, I wonder? We must invite her to Middleham to visit. Little Neddie adores her."

"The duke has asked me to return to Stanton and take charge of its defenses," Andrew told the duchess.

"Aye, that is wise," Lady Anne agreed. "I have a cousin, Rowena Neville, married to Baron Greyfaire. Their keep, much like Adair's, is on the border. Of late my cousin writes that the Scots have been raiding more frequently. A young girl alone would be considered fair game to any of the border lords."

"I will do my best to keep Stanton Hall safe," he promised her gallantly, and the Duchess of Gloucester smiled at him.

"He misses you," she told Andrew Lynbridge.

"I miss my good lord's company too, my lady, but I am, it seems, good only for warfare," Andrew replied. "Praise God and his blessed Mother Mary, England is a peaceful land. Yet it is difficult for a soldier in peacetime, my lady. My brother is our grandfather's heir, and he has sons already. I am grateful for my lord's desire to see the defenses at Stanton Hall strengthened, and for his faith in me to do it. I hope the lady will be as grateful to her uncle for his concern."

The duchess chuckled. "Adair is a bit prickly at times," she said. "But you have charm, Andrew, and I am certain that you will win her cooperation easily."

* * *

Andrew Lynbridge was reminded of Anne Neville's words several days later, when he returned to Stanton Hall to tell Adair what the Duke of Gloucester had requested of him. He had stopped first at Hillview Court on his return to tell his brother and grandfather what the duke desired of him.

His grandfather had nodded. "Then you'll be back in Gloucester's service again," he said. "He's given you coin for your trouble, I hope, eh? Give it here, lad. We're always short of coin in this family."

"He's given me his blessing if I can convince the lady to marry me," Andrew replied. "I think that's more than enough, Grandsire."

"He should have given you coin," the old man grumbled.

"I can't stay," Andrew said. "I want to reach Stanton by nightfall. Farewell, Grandsire."

"He gave you coin," Robert said as he walked with his brother back to the courtyard where his horse was waiting.

"He did," Andrew admitted, "but I may need it myself."

"Aye, you may," his brother said. "The old man doesn't need it. He's just a greedy bugger." Robert chuckled. "Do you think the girl will marry you if you ask her?"

"My first order of business," Andrew answered, "is to see to the proper defense of Stanton. I barely know the girl, nor she me. Good marriages, I have seen, come about when friends marry friends, as you and Allis did."

"You'll be an earl if you can wed her," his brother remarked.

"And I'll be a Radcliffe, for it was her father's request of the king, and he agreed. Any man who marries Adair Radcliffe must take her surname. Grandsire will hardly take kindly to that." Andrew chuckled. He mounted his horse. "Farewell, Robert."

"Farewell, my lord," Rob gently mocked him.

And now in the same day he found himself standing before Adair Radcliffe as she read the Duke of Gloucester's missive. He watched as her brow darkened in annoyance. Then she looked up at him. "You know what is written in this letter?"

"I do, my lady," Andrew said politely.

"I do not like it," Adair said, looking him straight in the eye.

"Nay, I imagine that you do not," he agreed pleasantly. "Nonetheless, it is the duke's wish that Stanton Hall be better fortified, as the Scots are becoming more active again along the borders. Had the hall been better fortified in your parents' time it might not have been taken then. The duke feels it is important that all the great homes in this area be protected better. He desires your safety above all, my lady."

"How is he?" Adair's tone had softened.

"Well, and the Lady Anne too. He is content being his brother's voice here in the north. He keeps his own court at Middleham."

"Have you eaten?" Adair asked him, and when he answered in the negative she ordered food be brought and led him to the high board to sit down, pouring liquid into his goblet. "My uncle Dickon does not like the queen or her family. He thinks them upstarts, and the queen has proven most greedy, as have her relations. He loves the king, but he has never been one for the court his brother keeps. And since their brother George was slain four years back, he has stayed away almost entirely. He blames the queen for that death. They say the Duke of Clarence drowned in a vat of malmsey, but he was imprisoned in the Tower at the time for the latest of his rebellions against the king. I would not have thought they had so large a supply of malmsey in the Tower," Adair mused. "But Uncle Dickon loved his brother for all his imperfections. He was always attempting to teach him the same loyalty that he practices. But George would not learn, and his spirit was so restless. Three such different brothers. The king a man who indulges his lusts, loves luxury and having his own way in everything to the point that he wed an unsuitable wife. Yet he has proven a good king, and the people love him unquestioningly. Then George of Clarence, jealous of Edward's every accomplishment and possession except perhaps the queen. And always in the midst of some plot or scheme to bring down the king so he might have his crown. And finally Uncle Dickon, totally devoted to his eldest brother. A man of discipline, strong faith, ethics, and deep loyalties. He would never betray the king, or any he loved.

"Did you know that when Lady Anne was widowed of her first husband, Prince Edward of Lancaster, George, who was wed to her older sister, Isabel, attempted to prevent Uncle Dickon from wedding Lady Anne? And why? Because he didn't want to share the Warwick inheritance, which had been divided between the two sisters. But Uncle Dickon and Lady Anne had been in love with each other since a shared childhood. Only that her father insisted, and made her wed Henry VI's son, were they separated.

"I was not sorry to see George dead. Few were except Uncle Dickon. He always believed that he could help his brother to change his ways, but of course he could not. Uncle Dickon believed the queen and her minions were responsible for Clarence's death. After that he came rarely to court, preferring to remain here in the north. The queen would bring him down if she could, but she can't. Everything he does is for the benefit of King Edward. He is no rebel like Clarence."

"Aye, and there is a matter upon which we will always agree," Andrew Lynbridge said quietly. "The duke is an honorable man."

"How long were you in his service?" Adair asked.

"Many years, and now it seems I am again," he answered her.

"Dark Walter has trained his men at arms well," Adair said. "We can defend ourselves against the Scots. Did you not tell the duke that?"

"Call Dark Walter and Albert to you, my lady," Andrew said. "Let me explain to you exactly what it is the duke wants. Then see what they have to say."

"That is fair enough," she agreed, and sent for the two men.

Andrew Lynbridge plunged a spoon into the trencher of rabbit stew that had been placed before him. Used to eating on the run, he had it finished by the time Dark Walter and Albert had arrived. He sat back and listened as Adair began to explain.

"The duke thinks we need to strengthen our defenses against the Scots—" she said.

"Aye!" Dark Walter interrupted her. "We do. And I hope he has sent the wherewithal to do it, my lady."

"He has," Andrew spoke up. "He wants walls built. The hall is not a castle, but six-foot walls about the house could help to deter an assault."

"Aye, they surely could," Dark Walter agreed, and Albert nodded.

"I thought this was to be my decision," Adair said pointedly.

"The duke assumed you would see the wisdom of his plan once I explained it to you," Andrew Lynbridge said smoothly. "He does not want to see you dead in your courtyard like your poor mother, my lady. He seeks only your safety."

"Where is the stone to come from?" she demanded.

"The wagons should begin arriving in a day or two," Andrew answered her.

"He wants his man to remain to oversee our security," Adair told Albert and Dark Walter. "Could you not do it, Dark Walter? Is it necessary for Andrew Lynbridge to stay?" she demanded of them.

Dark Walter nodded. "It is, my lady. I have not the experience in defense that he does. I was naught but a common soldier. Captain Lynbridge is a skilled man, and in the good duke's confidence. 'Tis an honor, Captain," he said, bowing politely from the waist. "I know you spent many years with the duke. He will have the authority that I know you want someone in his position to have, my lady. Hesitation in a siege is no benefit to those under attack. I am glad for his aid, and bid him welcome."

"Thank you," Andrew Lynbridge said quietly. "But 'tis you who are the captain of arms here. And so you shall remain. I did not come at my lord's request to replace you, Dark Walter. I came only to help, to direct, to teach you and your men."

The older man bowed, and the two men's eyes met in perfect understanding.

"If Dark Walter remains my captain," Adair said irritably, "then what are we to call you, sir?" They were making decisions without her, and she was the lady of Stanton.

"Andrew?" he suggested, and there was a twinkle in his eye. "It is my name."

Albert and Dark Walter chuckled, and Adair was forced to laugh.

"Very well," she agreed, "then Andrew it will be."

Elsbeth decreed that Andrew Lynbridge would sleep in the hall. "It is not meet he go above the stairs," she said tartly. "You are a girl alone, and must be wary to mind your reputation if you are to wed the proper man one day," she reminded Adair.

"I know you will make me comfortable, Mistress Elsbeth," Andrew replied, "and I agree that the lady's good name must not be besmirched."

"Well, then, you have more common sense than most men," Elsbeth said sharply.

"I think you will find that I do," he agreed soberly, and Elsbeth looked at him, not certain that he was not mocking her, but his handsome face remained impassive.

Several days later the carts carrying the stones that would become a wall began arriving at Stanton, along with a stonemason who quickly trained several of the local men so they might help him with the construction. Every few days, as the carts emptied, others carrying more stone would arrive. Adair was never certain how the workers knew when they had enough, but then one day there were no carts. And several days later the wall that stood six and a half feet in height was completed. The old moat had been redug, and a channel from nearby Stanton Water was opened so that the moat would always be filled. The blacksmith made a portcullis for the main entry between the walls, and heavy oak double doors, reinforced with iron bands, were hung. A wooden bridge was built over the moat.

"Why not stone?" Adair wanted to know.

"It takes too much effort to destroy a stone bridge," Andrew told her. "If the walls are breached we can burn the bridge and hold off the invader longer, because they cannot easily reach us without the bridge. And the moat prevents the hostile from laying siege ladders against the house."

"It's more a castle now," she remarked.

"Not really," he explained to her. "You have no battlements. And you would have needed royal permission to raise a castle. But you did not need royal permission to reinforce the defenses of your house."

It had taken all spring and half of the summer to complete the new defenses. Adair now saw to the raising of new barns within the stone enclosure. She would house her cattle safely from the winter snows. They had seen small parties of riders now and again, but their apparent readiness to defend what was Stanton's seemed to deter any attacks. The cattle Adair had purchased early in the spring had grown fat upon the lush Stanton meadow grass. Several of the young heifers were showing signs that they were with calf. Adair was very pleased. She would not buy more cattle until next year. The Stanton folk had worked hard through the summer months to grow enough grain to feed the new herd. They harvested and threshed the grain, and stored it within the walls in a new stone granary, along with two fat tomcats to patrol its perimeter and keep the mice population to a minimum. The two felines were very fierce.

As August came to an end Adair received an invitation from the duchess Anne to come for a visit at Middleham Castle. She was loath to go, as she felt there was too much to do before the winter, but Elsbeth and Albert insisted.

"It's been a hard year for you, my chick," Elsbeth said. "First you faced the difficulty of dealing with a husband you did not want; then he died, and now you have spent these last months overseeing everything here at Stanton. You have forgotten you are a lady. A visit with the duchess will remind you of your station. And you know the duke will be happy to see you, and you him."

"And I will escort you," Andrew Lynbridge said. "The duke will want a report on what we have done here at Stanton."

"Perhaps you will not have to come back," Adair said carelessly. Having been raised in a household made up mostly of women, and under the tutelage of Lady Margaret Beaufort, she resented Andrew Lynbridge's interference in her life. She had been taught to be a capable manager of a large estate. But there was an air of authority about Andrew. Her servants deferred to him, even Albert. And Dark Walter adored him with a slavish devotion that grated upon Adair's nerves.

"Perhaps," he agreed pleasantly. He had been attempting for months to get close to the lady of Stanton, to win her favor, her friendship. But the truth was that he had been so busy with the walls and all that went with them, there had been little time for pleasantries. And Adair had been just as busy overseeing the planting, the haying, her kitchen garden, making candles and soap, salting meat and fish, and preparing other foodstuffs that would be stored away for the winter. By day's end they were both so tired there was little time left for banter, although sometimes they did play chess.

They traveled the few days south into Yorkshire, reaching Middleham on an early September day. The weather had been pleasant, as it usually was at this time of year.

The duchess welcomed Adair warmly. "I have been wanting to see you for some weeks now," she said, linking her arm through Adair's as they walked into the hall. "How pretty you look. Orange tawny suits you. Did I see you were riding astride?"

"It's more comfortable for me," Adair admitted. "A bit hoydenish, Lady Margaret would have said, I fear." She smiled. "You are looking well, your grace."

"I have had a good year," the duchess admitted. "The air here in the north is good for me, except in the winter when I remain indoors. Still, the quiet life suits me better than any other, Adair. How do you enjoy it? You have been back well over a year now."

The two women sat down on a broad settle by one of the great hall's hearths.

"I have never been busier in my life," Adair admitted. "The fate of Stanton and its people rests upon my shoulders now. I never realized how heavy a burden it would be, and yet I am happier than I have ever been in my life."

"It is unfortunate, then, that your husband was killed," the duchess said.

"FitzTudor? He was no husband to me but in name," Adair replied. "And his pride was such that he was more trouble to me than help. I have never known so ignorant a boy. He could but scrawl his name, and could not read. He truly believed that he had been brought into this world to be served. He had no useful skills and knew nothing of managing an estate of any size. I was planning to return him to the king when he was slain. I am shocked he was not better educated or trained. He got himself killed."

"Yet it was a gallant gesture," the duchess said softly.

"Gallant? Aye. But foolish. He had no skill with a sword, poor lad," Adair replied. "Still, in death he received what he could not get in life. I buried him next to my parents, and the stone marking his grave states he was Earl of Stanton."

"Still," the duchess said, "you must have a husband, Adair. How old are you now? Seventeen, if I recall correctly, and still a virgin."

"But just last month," Adair defended herself, blushing.

"I was fourteen when I married Prince Edward," the duchess remarked. "And sixteen when I wed my Dickon. Our Neddie was born when I was seventeen. Like me you have lost a first husband tragically. You must remarry."

"Why?" Adair said pettishly. This was not a subject with which she was comfortable. Could she not be allowed time for herself?

"Why, for Stanton, my dear," the duchess said. "Stanton must have an heir."

"But who would marry me?" Adair wanted to know. "I am far from court, and I will not wed a man I do not know, or like, or, most important, respect. The king sent me poor FitzTudor, and I despised him on sight. Only good fortune saved me from a lifetime of misery. I cannot go through that again, my lady Anne."

"You know Andrew Lynbridge," the duchess said. "He is most eligible. I do not know if you like him, but certainly you respect him."

"Andrew? Is that why Uncle Dickon sent him to Stanton? So I would consider him worthy to be my husband?" She laughed. "How clever of him."

"Yes, it was," the duchess admitted. "Andrew Lynbridge is old Sir Humphrey's grandson, as you know. The family has held its lands as long as the Radcliffes. Your blood is slightly better by virtue of your paternity, but in all other ways the Lynbridges are equal to the Radcliffes. As Andrew was in my husband's service I have known him for many years. He is a good man, Adair. He would not mistreat you, and he would make you a good husband," the duchess concluded.

"He seems to know and understand the land," Adair replied. "And the Stanton folk do like him. So much so I am almost jealous," she admitted.

"Your people want a master, Adair. Aye, you are the countess, the acknowledged daughter of Earl John, but they need a man to guide them, I fear. It is their way. Country folk are simple and uncomplicated in their outlook."

Adair sighed. "I suppose you are correct," she replied. "I just don't like turning over my responsibilities to someone else. Lady Margaret always taught me that a woman is perfectly capable of managing her own affairs."

"Lady Margaret is a strong woman, as all her husbands and her son would attest, but her place in our world is greater than yours, Adair."

"I am the Countess of Stanton in my own right," Adair said proudly.

"But Lady Margaret descends from King Edward the Third. She is mother to Lancaster's heir. She stands high in favor at court. She may think and say things other women might not, and few will think badly of her. She is a most unique woman of eminent common sense."

"I have always admired her," Adair admitted.

"But you cannot be just like her," the duchess responded. "You are indeed the Countess of Stanton in your own right. But the countess must have a husband now, Adair. Dickon has kept my Neville relations and the Percys from your doorstep all summer by virtue of the fact that you are supposed to have been mourning young FitzTudor. They cannot be kept at bay much longer. Stanton lands are very good lands. You cannot protect them alone. And your neighbors have sons and other male relations they need to match favorably. Is there someone upon whom you dote and would wed? If he is suitable I am certain Dickon would permit it. When your unfortunate husband died my husband asked the king for your wardship. Edward was more than glad to grant it. The Earl of Pembroke was very saddened by his son's death, but grateful for your respect of the boy."

"He sent me no message of condolence," Adair said. "Perhaps Fitz-Tudor's servant, Anfri, poured his poison into Jasper Tudor's ear."

"If Anfri went south he never saw the earl," the duchess said. "I know, for Dickon inquired about it."

"How odd," Adair responded. "He was gone from Stanton the day after FitzTudor's death. No one has seen him since."

"You have not answered me," the duchess told Adair. "Is there someone you would wed?"

Adair shook her head. "Nay," she admitted.

"Then will you accept the duke's wish that you marry Andrew Lynbridge?"

"I suppose better the devil you know than one you don't," Adair replied pithily. "But he must take the Radcliffe name, your grace. That was Earl John's wish, and the king agreed it would be so. If Andrew would be the Earl of Stanton he will be a Radcliffe earl. I wonder if his family will like that. His grandsire has always wanted my lands for his estates, but the Radcliffe name must remain. And I must have a little time in which to grow used to this decision of Uncle Dickon's. Has anyone bothered to speak to Andrew about it? He may not agree."

"He will agree," the duchess said. "He has never failed the duke in anything."

Adair laughed softly. "You make it sound like some military campaign that Uncle Dickon would plan, and Andrew execute."

Lady Anne laughed too, her soft blue eyes twinkling. "It is, in a manner of speaking," she agreed. "I know that Dickon will be very pleased with your agreement and sensible manner. Most of us do not get to marry for love."

"You did," Adair said.

"Aye, but not until the second time. You will remember that my father was not a man to be disobeyed or thwarted when he made up his mind, Adair. When he fell out with King Edward and turned on him to support poor old Henry the Sixth and his son he was determined that I be queen of England. God forbid! I barely knew Edward

Lancaster, but I was married to him nonetheless. And because my father trusted no one we were put to bed, and the prince forced to con-
summate the match so there might be no annulment later on the
grounds of nonconsummation. That unfortunate prince did not want
me for his wife, and he had a mistress he loved at the time. Still, we
were wedded and bedded for the sake of political expediency. It was
not a happy time. But you have the advantage at least of knowing Andrew Lynbridge. He is pleasant-looking, and seems kind."

Adair considered the duchess's words. "Aye, I suppose he is
pleasant-looking, and I have never seen him unkind. And he was the
duke's captain. When we marry he will be the Earl of Stanton. Will he
still be kind then?"

"It is a chance all women take when they wed," the duchess answered. "The ram sheep may turn out to be a wolf garbed in fleece. But
women, once they have gotten the lay of the land, usually manage to
cope, Adair."

"And if they are clever, rule the roost," the younger girl said mischievously.

The duchess smiled. "Shall I tell my husband then that you are
agreeable to a marriage with Andrew Lynbridge?"

"If Andrew will agree then so will I," Adair said. "For Stanton, and
its future."

And while the duchess had spoken with Adair, her husband had
been speaking with Andrew Lynbridge on the very same matter.

"Marry the lady?" he said, surprised by the duke's overture.

"She is now my ward," Richard of Gloucester replied. "She needs a
husband to hold Stanton for the king. I prefer a man whose loyalties I
can count upon, and not another FitzTudor. I do not trust the Lancaster faction, despite the deaths of Henry the Sixth and his son.
There is still a Lancaster heir, and Margaret Beaufort is ambitious for
her son."

"It would please my father," Andrew said slowly.

"There is, however, one small drawback to marriage with Adair,"
the duke said. "Before Jane Radcliffe bore her child it was agreed that
if that child was a female, and the earl fathered no legitimate sons,

Adair would be the Countess of Stanton in her own right. That you already know. But you may not know that the king decided that her husband would have to bear the surname of Radcliffe, and forgo his own family's name before he might become the earl. I know Lord Humphrey will not be pleased to learn that, and certainly you are not. But can you accept this condition?"

"I would be Earl of Stanton if I did, wouldn't I?" he asked.

"Aye," the duke replied.

"And I would have all the rights a husband has over his wife's property?"

Richard of Gloucester nodded. "You would."

Andrew Lynbridge chortled. "When my grandsire began casting covetous eyes on Stanton, I told him that if I could wed Adair the land would be mine and not his. And will it not be clearly more so if my surname is Radcliffe, my lord?"

The duke saw the humor in the situation, and laughed himself. "Indeed it would, Andrew," he ageed.

"Then I shall do it," Andrew said.

"You must be kind to Adair, and respectful of her," the duke warned the younger man. "I have had a great fondness for her since we first met. She was such a brave little girl in the face of such terrible tragedy. She has grown into a lovely, if headstrong, young woman. She's like a fine but yet wild young mare. You will tame her if you treat her with gentleness. And you will not be sorry for it. Adair understands loyalty."

"This matter should be settled before the winter sets in," Andrew said.

"It should," the duke replied. "I will have the marriage contract drawn up, and if my niece is willing we will celebrate your union before you return to Stanton. Go now, and find her. Make your peace with her."

Andrew left the duke's privy chamber and went to the great hall. There he found Adair sitting by a fire as if she had been waiting for him. There was no one else about. "May I sit by you?" he asked her. "I have spoken with the duke. He would have a marriage between us. Will you have it?"

She motioned him to sit by her side. "I have spoken with the duchess. I will consent to a marriage between us. I did not wish to wed a year ago because I wanted time to become familiar with my home again. I did not choose to marry a stranger, especially the son of a Lancastrian. I can never forgive them for murdering my parents. I am sorry the king did not consider that when he made the match for me with Pembroke's son, and then celebrated a proxy marriage without me. All was done for his benefit, not mine. I will assent to a match between us because I know, though I am capable of much, I am not able to defend Stanton and hold it for the king by myself. I need a husband to do that. I know you, Andrew Lynbridge, and you would seem a good man."

"I am a good man," he told her seriously. "I will care for you, and I will defend Stanton," Andrew said, reaching out and taking Adair's hand in his. Raising it to his lips, he kissed the delicate little hand. "I will not fail the duke, or Stanton, or you, Adair. You have my word on it."

"And you will accept the Radcliffe name in place of Lynbridge?" Adair said.

"I will," he responded. "You understand, however, that this marriage shall be a real and complete marriage, and not in name only. You are a grown girl, and I am a man. I want a bedmate as well as a helpmate. And we will need heirs."

Adair felt her cheeks grow warm. Bedding Andrew had been the farthest thing from her mind. She was doing this for Stanton. But as Duchess Anne had gently pointed out, Stanton did need heirs, and one did not get heirs by just wishing for them. "I understand," she agreed, nodding.

"You are a virgin?" he asked, looking into her face for the truth. It didn't actually matter to him, but he did want to know.

Adair's fair skin blotched scarlet. "Of course I am a virgin!" her voice squeaked angrily. "Do you believe I am some wanton creature?"

"You did have a husband," he reminded her. She was untouched! He thought it would not matter, but it did.

"Do you really believe I let that pimply boy put his hands on me?" she demanded of him. "I should have gone into a cloister first, sir!"

"Andrew," he said quietly. "My name is Andrew, Adair, and I expect you to address me by my name when we are together."

"So there is no mistake between us, Andrew, I am a virgin," Adair said. Did he think she was unable to control her emotions, like the man who sired her?

He tipped her face up with a half-closed hand, and kissed her gently. "Good," he said. Her mouth was sweet beneath his. It softened with her little gasp of surprise, but she did not draw away from him. His kiss deepened as his arms slipped about her to draw her closer to him. He felt the softness of her breasts pressing against his chest as he suddenly realized how very much he had wanted to kiss her these past months.

Adair's heart raced with excitement as he kissed her. She had never been kissed but for that one time FitzTudor had mashed his wet mouth against her mouth. This was completely different. It was thrilling and tender all at once. She kissed Andrew back, and felt the nipples of her breasts tightening even as a delicious shiver raced down her spine and her belly heaved with tiny eruptions of excitement.

Finally he stopped kissing her, but he kept his arms around her, and his warm gray eyes smiled into her violet ones. "If you keep kissing me like that I shall want more than I should have at this time, Adair."

"I think I want more too," she admitted boldly.

"Then shall we tell the duke we are of one mind, and will wed as soon as it may be arranged?" he asked her.

"Aye, I think it best," Adair agreed. "We need to return to Stanton before the wicked weather sets in, Andrew."

"Would you prefer to wed at Stanton?" he asked her thoughtfully.

A smile lit Adair's lovely features. "Oh, yes! Do you think it would be permitted, Andrew? Do you think Uncle Dickon would allow it?"

"If the betrothal papers are all signed by both parties, by the duke and his priest, and witnessed by the duchess and another, I do not see why not," Andrew told her.

"It would so please the Stanton folk," Adair said. "They have been so loyal to me, and I know that they will be loyal to you, Andrew."

"Then I shall speak with the duke, sweetheart," he said, and he did.

The duke agreed it would be an excellent idea for Adair to be married at Stanton, in her own hall surrounded by her own people. It would bind them all closer. He had the papers drawn up. Both Andrew and Adair read the agreement that would unite them as husband and wife. The priest read the contract and approved it. Then, in the duchess's private chapel at Middleham Castle early on a late October morning, the papers were signed by the couple and the duke, who was Adair's guardian. The sun was not even up, but its colorful advance was evident in the clear blue sky. The priest then blessed Adair and Andrew, and while a marriage ceremony at Stanton would be held, they were now for all intents and purposes man and wife.

The Mass was then held, and afterward they ate a meal of poached eggs in a cream sauce, thin slices of country ham, oat stirabout in bread trenchers, and fresh-baked bread still hot from the ovens. There was ground pepper in the cream sauce, and a silver crock of sweet butter, and several dishes of summer preserves on the table. The goblets were filled with fresh sweet cider or October ale, depending on the diner's preference. And after they had eaten, Adair and Andrew were escorted to the courtyard by the duke and his wife to begin their journey home to Stanton. They would be escorted by a large troop of the duke's men. Richard of Gloucester would take no chances on his favorite niece being harmed.

Adair knelt before him for his blessing, which he gladly gave her, raising her up to kiss her on both of her cheeks and her forehead. "I believe that this husband will make you happy," he said with a small smile.

"Thank you for seeing what I could not, Uncle Dickon. Look after yourself, I pray you, for you worry far too much."

The duke nodded in acknowledgment, and passed her to his wife.

The two women embraced.

"Tell Neddie I am sorry he had to stay in bed today, and give him a kiss for me," Adair told Anne.

"I will," the duchess said. "It is his lungs, and he will persist in riding, though the weather has grown cold. You will find a mother has but so much control over her sons, I fear, my dear Adair. Be as happy with your Andrew as I am with my Dickon." The duchess kissed Adair as her husband had. "God bless you both," she told them.

Adair and Andrew mounted their horses and, surrounded by the duke's men at arms, rode out from Middleham Castle, heading north and west toward Stanton. Their journey took them several days. It was arranged that they would overnight at several convents and monasteries along the way. The duke had sent ahead to make the arrangements. Finally Stanton came into view and, unable to help herself, Adair surprised Andrew and the men escorting her by putting her horse into a gallop and riding fast for home. Once over their astonishment, Andrew and the duke's men followed her.

The Stanton folk gleaning in the fields saw her coming, and waved to her. Adair waved back, beckoning them with an arm to follow her to the hall, which they did. And there in the courtyard she spoke to them from her mount, Andrew by her side.

"My good people, I have returned to you from our good duke with a new earl," she said. "Andrew, born Lynbridge, has taken the name Radcliffe as both my father, Earl John, and King Edward wished. Tomorrow in the great hall we will wed, and you are all invited. Welcome Andrew Radcliffe, Earl of Stanton, home!"

And the Stanton folk cheered mightily, pleased and contented by this turn of events. They knew Andrew. They both respected and liked him. And it was past time that the lady had a husband, and that Stanton had a real earl again.

Chapter 6

"My baby is getting married," Elsbeth said excitedly. " 'Tis past time. Why, when she was your age your mother already had you. He's a lovely man. Not the comeliest I've ever seen, mind you, but nice enough looking. You're a fortunate lass."

"I'm marrying for Stanton, Nursie," Adair said. "If I don't, who knows if the king might send me another like poor FitzTudor, or worse?"

"I know you're marrying for Stanton," Elsbeth replied. "You have to if we are to have heirs for the estate. But if you must take a husband to your bed—and you must—it does not hurt to have an attractive man by your side, my lass. I've heard it said he's a good bedmate," she concluded with a knowing wink.

"Heard it said by whom?" Adair demanded to know. "I'll put up with no mistresses from a husband of mine!"

"Word gets about the countryside," Elsbeth said knowingly. "But your man is a will-o'-the-wisp where women are concerned. He has no favorites I've heard named on either side of the border. But the lasses smile and nod when they hear his name spoken."

"Either side of the border?" Adair raised a dark eyebrow.

"There is no line drawn in the hills," Elsbeth said. "A man goes where he will. If he sees a pretty girl and wants her, it makes no difference if it be this side of the border or the other. All the men hereabouts are like that. The new earl is no different."

"I see I must speak with Andrew," Adair replied darkly. "I will have no nonsense with other women, or bastards scattered about the countryside."

"Now, now, my dearie," Elsbeth cautioned, "I do not believe the earl would either hurt or shame you. Do not embarrass him by making demands you should not."

"I do not want a husband who is always in someone else's bed," Adair said stiffly.

"Then make certain he is content in his own bed," Elsbeth replied pithily.

Adair flushed. "You well know that I have never been with a man," she said.

"Well, tonight you will be, and knowing you're a maid he'll show you the way," Elsbeth replied. "Passion can be a grand thing with the right man, my lass."

"What if he isn't the right man?" Adair wanted to know.

"Plain lust is pleasurable, no matter what the church may say." Elsbeth chuckled. "Now come along, m'lady," the tiring woman said, helping her mistress from her bed. "Your bath will be ready and awaiting you in the day room. Nothing stirs a man's desires like a sweet-smelling woman. I've put some of that nice scent in the water that Lady Margaret gave you on Twelfth Night two years past."

They went into the little room off the bedchamber where an oaken bathtub was kept set up. Adair's mother had wanted a separate bathing space, and her doting husband had been happy to comply with her wish. Cauldrons of hot water were hauled up from the kitchens by means of a wooden platform within a stone shaft that opened next to the tub. Two sturdy serving women would draw the platform up and tilt the large kettles into the tub. Then they would lower the platform back down to the kitchens for another cauldron of water. It was a far more efficient means of filling the tub than employing a line of serving men with buckets.

The servants were gone now as Adair entered her bathing chamber and climbed into her tub. She washed her dark hair. The water was nicely hot, and the fragrance of the gillyflowers was sweet. She soaped and rinsed herself, taking her time. The sky outside was still dark. To all intents she was already wed. The priest would bless them after the first Mass of the day. And Adair had declared a holiday for the Stanton folk. They would be invited into the hall for a feast. She had no idea what day of the week it was. The month was November, and before Martinmas, she knew, but the rest really didn't matter. She had a husband, and her life was going to settle into a pattern revolving around the estate. And there would be children. It was a startling thought, but that was why you took a husband, wasn't it? To have heirs. And she wanted heirs for Stanton.

She stepped from her tub, and Elsbeth swathed her in a large drying cloth. Then, sitting by the fire, Adair rubbed the water from her black hair with a smaller cloth and a brush. Slowly her long hair dried until it was silken and soft. "I will wear it loose," she said. "There was no real marriage with FitzTudor, and I am yet a maid."

"I've brought the violet damask gown you chose last night," Elsbeth said, gesturing to the garment now laid upon the bed.

It had a draped neckline, and was cut with fullness from the neckline to its ribbon-trimmed hem. It had long tightly fitted sleeves. The gown was all of one piece, although the Duchess Anne had told Adair that at court a new fashion was just coming into being where skirts, bodices, and sleeves were all separate, allowing a wearer to interchange the pieces. It made it appear as if a lady had more costumes than usual. Here in the country, however, Adair had no time for such fashion. Her wedding dress was the best dress she owned, and she had worn it now for two years. The fabric had been a Twelfth Night gift from the king. He always gave his daughters a bolt of fabric as a gift, and she and Bessie had always shared their fabrics with Cicely so they might have larger wardrobes.

Adair ran her hand over the silk damask. "It was the nicest cloth he ever gave me," she said softly as she drew a clean camise on, and then her gown over it.

"Do you miss the court?" Elsbeth wondered aloud.

"Nay, not at all. I prefer Stanton, and my own company," Adair said. "I wonder if my sisters think of me. I must write Bessie today. Perhaps I can get a message south before the snows. I'll send it to Middleham. Uncle Dickon will send it with his own Christmas correspondence." She straightened the gown's neckline. "Give me a jeweled headband, Nursie. The one with the pearls and little purple gemstones." She held out her hand, and when Elsbeth had placed the required item in it, Adair fit it upon her head.

"You look beautiful, m'lady," Elsbeth told her mistress. "Your parents would be very proud that you are being married here, and I know they would approve of Lord Andrew. He'll be a good earl to us."

Would he? Adair wondered. She barely knew the man who was now her husband by virtue of the contracts that they had both signed at Middleham several days back. The man to whom she would pledge her troth today before the local priest who lived in Stanton village. Adair barely knew him either. He had not been at Stanton in her childhood. Father Gilbert, he was called, and she could not tell if he was an English borderer or a Scot by his accent. Still, she was grateful to have a priest, even if he was a bit old, and slightly deaf. Her people were comforted by his presence.

"Time to go down," Elsbeth said, interrupting her mistress's train of thought.

"Can you tell me nothing of tonight, Nursie?" Adair asked her servant.

"It isn't for me to educate you, my lady. Your husband will do that. It would be different if your mother, God assoil her good soul, were alive, but she isn't, and it isn't my place. I've said what I could, and I'll say no more."

"And when the babies come, Nursie," Adair asked dryly, "can you help then?"

"Then I can help," Elsbeth replied with a small smile. "Now, the bridegroom awaits you, m'lady. You don't want him to think you're reluctant. You did agree to this marriage before God, Duke Richard, and his good duchess."

"I did," Adair agreed. "Let us go down." Then she looked startled as a knock sounded upon her bedchamber door.

Elsbeth hurried to answer it, and the open door revealed the new earl.

"May I come in a moment?" he inquired of her politely. "Elsbeth may remain."

Adair beckoned him forward. "Are you so anxious then, my lord, or do you fear I shall cry off?" she asked him.

"You can't cry off," he told her. "Legally we are already wed, but I am not fearful you will run away from me as you did the court, Adair. Before we left Middleham I sent word to my grandsire and brother of the match the duke had made between us. They have both just arrived at the hall. I want you to know that I did not invite them. I wanted to have some time for us to live together as man and wife before I inflicted my grandsire upon you," he said ruefully. "He is a hard old man, and he will, I have not a doubt, have something to say about my taking the Radcliffe name. How he managed to ride over I do not know, as he is quite crippled with his age. Will you be patient with him?"

"Will you?" Adair asked him.

"Probably not," Andrew admitted. "You've met my older brother, Rob."

"If they are here then they are here, and there is naught we can do but welcome them as kin," Adair told him. "Tell me what your sister-in-law is like."

"Allis is patient and wise. She tolerates my grandsire," Andrew said.

"I cannot promise to be patient, and I do not know if I am wise or not, but I will tolerate your grandsire while he is in our house because he is your blood, Andrew. I have come to respect you while you have been at Stanton."

Andrew took her two hands up, and kissed them. "Thank you," he said softly.

Adair colored prettily. Then she said, drawing her hands from his, "If Lord Humphrey and your brother are here we had best go down to greet them together, my lord."

He nodded, and with Elsbeth following they descended to the great hall below. There they found Lord Humphrey Lynbridge sprawled in a large chair by the fire, a goblet of ale in his fist. It was obvious that the early morning ride had exhausted him quite thoroughly. Robert Lynbridge stood by his side. His mild blue eyes lit up as Andrew and Adair entered the hall, and he smiled warmly.

Seeing the state her guest was in, Adair went immediately to his side. "My lord, what on earth possessed you to make such a journey? I was given to understand that you were no longer able to ride."

"The day they can't get me a-horse is the day they'll put me in my coffin," Lord Humphrey growled. "Well, come closer, girl, and let me look at you. Aye, you still look like your mother, and she was passing fair. I see nothing of the Radcliffes in you. What is this foolishness about my grandson taking the Radcliffe name?"

"It was my father's wish when he became Earl of Stanton. The king agreed. It is not an unheard-of thing, my lord," Adair said quietly.

"He's a Lynbridge," the old man snapped.

"He is the Earl of Stanton, my lord, and Stanton earls are Radcliffes whether it be by choice or by birth," Adair retorted.

"Why the hell would King Edward agree to such a thing like that?" Lord Lynbridge demanded of her.

"He agreed because he is my natural father, my lord," Adair said. "The man I called my father did not sire me. Edward of York did. Not that he was any father to me. John Radcliffe, who loved me as if I were his own flesh, was the father I knew."

"You're the king's brat?" The old man's bright blue eyes snapped at her. "Well, damn me for a fool! I always wondered what great service John Radcliffe did for the king that he would have an earldom created for him. But it wasn't John at all. It was your sweet mother, Jane, who did the king a service." And Humphrey Lynbridge slapped his knee and laughed heartily. "How long did you know of your paternity, girl?"

"You will speak to me with more courtesy than you have exhibited so far, my lord," Adair said coldly. "I am not 'girl' or 'lass.' I am her ladyship the Countess of Stanton. You may address me as such, or because I am wed to your grandson you may call me by my given name, Adair. In future, however, you will not address me as if you were speaking to some servant wench."

The old man's mouth fell open with surprise, while beside him Robert Lynbridge swallowed back the laughter that threatened to overcome him. He fixed his gaze upon his younger brother, who was struggling to manage himself as well. "Well, bless my soul," Lord Lyn-bridge managed to say, but then he quickly recovered himself. "You have a fine opinion of yourself, my lady," he told Adair.

"Indeed, my lord, I do," she agreed pleasantly.

"So my Andrew's to be a Radcliffe, and no more a Lynbridge," he said.

"Aye, he is. But with the name comes an earldom, my lord, and that is surely worth the name, is it not?" She looked directly down into the old man's face.

"Perhaps," Lord Lynbridge said slowly. "Our families have inter-married for centuries. Did you know that? John Radcliffe's grand-mother was a Lynbridge. Andrew will sire no fewer sons on you, my lady, for changing his name. At least FitzTudor, for that was your first husband's name, didn't give you a child."

"FitzTudor was not allowed the privilege of my bed," Adair told him quietly.

"But my grandson will be," was the reply she received.

"Aye," Adair agreed. "He will. Andrew and I have come to know each other. I did not know FitzTudor, and besides, he was a fool. Your grandson is not."

"He died conveniently," the old man said slyly.

"He died tragically and foolishly," Adair retorted. "I did not have him murdered. But I did intend on returning him to his father, and de-manding an annulment from the church. The king had no right to send me a husband when I had already said nay."

"The king needs the borders held close," Lord Lynbridge replied.

"FitzTudor could not have done it for him, and we have peace," Adair answered.

"There is never real peace in the borders," was the dour answer.

"His lordship, the Earl of Stanton, will hold this land," Adair said.

"Aye, my lady, he will," Lord Lynbridge agreed. "If there is one thing my grandson Andrew knows how to do well, it is fight. There is no better man in a battle than Andrew Lynbridge."

"Andrew Radcliffe," she gently corrected him, and he nodded.

"Aye, Andrew Radcliffe." Then he looked at her and said, "Robert tells me you keep a good table, my lady. I am famished. Am I to sit here starving?"

"You will have your meal after the Mass, my lord. While we have been speaking, Father Gilbert and two lads have been setting up the altar on the high board. While the marriage contract was signed at Middleham, the blessing of our union will be this morning in the presence of my Stanton folk. It is a fortunate coincidence that you have come now. I am glad Andrew's family will be here to witness our marriage." She signaled to Albert and said softly, "Have two sturdy men take the old man in the chair and set it before the altar so he may be part of the ceremony."

"At once, my lady," Albert said, and went off to do her bidding.

"It is good to see you again, my lady," Robert Lynbridge said, and he bowed.

"Please, Rob, you will call me by name. You are now my brother, and I have always wanted an older brother." She gave him her hand, and he kissed it.

"You handled the old man well," Andrew murmured low. And he slipped a proprietary arm about her waist. "He's a bully if allowed."

"I have never allowed any man to bully me, even the king," Adair said sweetly.

Rob laughed. "Can it be you have met your match, little brother?" he teased.

"Perhaps Adair has met hers," Andrew answered with a chuckle.

"We shall see, my lord," Adair replied.

The altar was now set up upon the high board. Old Lord Lynbridge was carried before it so he might see all. The great hall was filled with the Stanton folk. The Mass began. The candles flickered while the voice of the priest spoke and sang the ancient service. And when he had concluded the Mass, Adair and Andrew came and knelt before him. Father Gilbert blessed the union that had been formally contracted almost two weeks back. Then he raised the couple up and turned them to face the Stanton folk, who cheered heartily, bringing smiles to the faces of both the bride and the groom.

The candles on the altar were snuffed, and the servants hurried to clear the high board while the Stanton folk brought the trestles and benches from the sides of the hall, where they had been pushed and stacked so the Mass might be said. The house servants began hurrying forth with the food. Bread trenchers of hot oat stirabout were put on all the tables. The oats were sweetened with honey, and bits of apples and pears. Platters of ham and hard-cooked eggs along with freshly baked loaves were brought, with tubs of butter and dishes of honey. Wooden cups were filled with October ale. At the high board the eggs were poached in cream and marsala wine. There were baked apples with honey and cream as well.

Lord Lynbridge had been carried to the high board and seated to the left of the bride. He said little, but the murmurs from him and the smacking of his lips indicated his approval of the meal set before him. Albert himself saw that the old man's goblet was never empty, Adair noted, well pleased. After the meal Lord Lynbridge declared that he and Rob would return home that same day, but Adair prevailed upon him to sit by the fire for a brief while. There Humphrey Lynbridge fell asleep.

"It was too much for him," Adair said. "You and your grandfather must spend the night, Rob. Unless you have pressing business that requires you to leave sooner, I think it better you go in the morning. How long a ride is it to the court?"

"It is several hours' riding," Robert Lynbridge answered.

"Dear heaven, what time did you leave this morning?" she exclaimed, for they had been at her door before sunrise. "At least there was a border moon to ride by, but it had to be cold and damp. How old is your grandsire?"

"Seventy-three years, he says," Robert answered her. "And we departed the court just after two of the morning."

"Why was he so determined to come today?" Adair asked frankly.

"I believe he thought you would be back by now. He was distressed that Andrew would take your name and cast off ours," was the candid reply.

"It is better I did," the new earl said. "This way Grandsire can have no illusions that Radcliffe lands are Lynbridge lands. And you know that he has always coveted the grazing meadows belonging to Stanton. Now he must put those thoughts from his head."

Adair arose from her own place. "I must go and tell Cook that our guests will be remaining until the morrow," she said. Then she hurried off.

"She is lovely," Robert Lynbridge remarked. "And strong-willed. Did you see how she stood up to Grandsire? And he was not in the least taken aback by her."

"I have no idea what it is to be married, Rob," Andrew said suddenly.

"No man does at first," Robert replied with a grin, "and even after several years have passed it is still confusing, little brother. Marriage is a game, but it is your wife who will make the rules for the game. Those rules will always be changing, but you will not necessarily be told of those changes, yet you will be expected to know all about them." Robert Lynbridge chuckled. "Just remember that the house and the servants are hers. And the children when they come. The rest is yours to manage."

"I expect that Adair will want the rest as well," Andrew said. "She loves Stanton and is devoted to both the lands and the people."

"Then share it with her until she is ready to let you have it," Rob counseled wisely. "She will eventually. Jesu, Andrew! You're an earl. Richard has married you to an heiress who came with a title for her husband. My brother, the Earl of Stanton." He laughed. "It falls easily from my tongue. Have you bedded her yet? Is she as—"

Andrew cut him off. "Until last night we were on the road from Middleham. And I did not wish to press the issue until the church had blessed the union."

"So then tonight will be your wedding night," Robert said.

"Adair is yet innocent. I will wait until you and Grandsire are gone, Rob," Andrew told his brother.

"You must like the little wench," Robert observed. "I have never known you to be so tender with a female's feelings."

"I have to live with her, Rob, and I should prefer a peaceful house. I have known enough war in my life," Andrew said.

But to his surprise, that evening Adair excused herself from the high board after the meal, and murmured in his ear, "If I am asleep when you come up, waken me, my lord. We have a final duty to do for Stanton this day."

Hiding his astonishment, he nodded. She wanted him in her bed tonight? Well, that boded well, didn't it? He refrained from smiling at her. "You are sure?" he asked.

"My lord," was all she said before turning to his grandsire. "Elsbeth herself has made up the most comfortable bed space in the hall next to a hearth for you, my lord. There will be a servant in attendance the night through should you need anything." She curtsied to him. "I will bid you good night now." Then, turning, Adair departed the hall.

Lord Lynbridge watched her go. "She may look like her mam, but she has her sire's grit and backbone," he noted. "Her mam was a gentle and obedient lass. Had she not been, John Radcliffe could have not easily sent his wife into King Edward's bed. I can see, Andrew, that your wife is someone who understands the meaning of duty. I don't expect she will be easy to live with, but she'll be a good wife to you, and a good mother to the children you breed upon her. Go to her now, grandson. I am proud of you. Your service to the duke has paid you a handsome dividend." He drained the last of the wine from his goblet and then banged the vessel on the oaken board, demanding more. "Your wife keeps a good table, and has a good cellar." Then he sipped from a newly filled cup.

"You'll be warmer by the fire, my lord," Albert murmured in the old man's ear, and before he might say yea or nay the chair was lifted up from its place and carried again to the great hearth with its blazing logs. Lord Lynbridge held his goblet tightly.

"Her servants are well trained," Robert noted. "You have come into a well-ordered household, brother. Do you think Adair really is a virgin? Young FitzTudor seemed a determined sort."

"He was no match for her," Andrew said with a smile. "She says she is untouched, and I must accept her word unless it is proven false. I will treat her like a virgin tonight, and if she is indeed one it will please me mightily. But if she is not then I must be concerned that she lied, and consider what else she has lied about."

"I do not see Adair as devious," Robert remarked. "She is actually quite straightforward in her manner. Have you cause for suspicion, brother?"

Andrew shook his head in the negative. "Nay." He stood up. "Good night, Rob. I will see you on the morrow before you and Grandsire depart." The earl strode from the hall and climbed the staircase up to the second floor of the house, where his bride would be awaiting him. When he reached the bedchamber door, however, he found Elsbeth waiting. "Is Adair ready to receive me?" he asked.

"When did you last bathe?" Elsbeth demanded of him.

"Bathe?" He looked surprised by her words. "Why?"

"My mistress has a delicate nose, my lord. She bathes regularly. She says you must be bathed before you enter her bed. The master's chamber and the mistress's chamber share a little room my lady's mother had built. It is for bathing. Come along, and I will help you. You have no manservant of your own, but Albert will find a lad to suit you. Tonight, however, I will do what needs to be done," Elsbeth said.

"I am capable of washing myself," Andrew protested.

"My lady says I am to do it," Elsbeth retorted in a tone that did not bode well, he thought, should he continue to argue with her. "Come along, my lord."

She led him to the little room where the great oak tub was set up. Andrew was so fascinated by the accommodations that had been made to deliver the water that he did not notice at first that Elsbeth had begun to pull his clothes from his lean frame. He sat to allow her to yank his boots from his feet, blushing as she tched over their condition. "You'll be needing new boots, my lord," she said. "I'll tell Albert, and we'll get the cobbler to come and measure these big feet of yours."

"How do you empty the tub?" he asked her as he climbed into it, gasping at the hot water. "Jesu, woman! Would you scale the skin off of me?"

"There's a plug of cork at the bottom, on the side of the tub," Elsbeth said. "We have a small hose that fits into a stone drain by the window." She climbed up the two steps next to the tub and, taking a small pitcher up, dumped its contents over his head. He sputtered with surprise, but Elsbeth paid him no mind. Scooping a handful of soft soap from a dish on the tub ledge, she began to wash his dark hair. Her fingers dug strongly into his scalp, and he yelped briefly as she scrubbed at his head. Another pitcher of water was poured over his hair, then another bout of suds, followed by more water, and Elsbeth began to pick through his hair. "No nits," she said, satisfied, and handed him a small rough cloth. "You do the bits you should, and I'll take care of the rest," she told him with a grin.

"Did you bathe FitzTudor too?" he asked her.

"That bairn had his own man he brought with him from the south. I wanted naught to do with them. He was more perfumed than washed. They kept much to themselves once they saw the lay of the land," Elsbeth said with a chuckle.

"And how did they determine the lay of the land?" Andrew asked as she scrubbed his neck and shoulders.

"FitzTudor snuck up to her chamber one evening and tried to force himself upon her. She hit him over the head with an earthenware pitcher. He fell to the floor dazed, and then she called to Beiste, who dragged the boy from her chamber by his velvet-shod foot." Elsbeth cackled as she remembered the incident. "After that he gave her a wide berth, he did. She's a virgin, which is what you've been getting at with all your questions, my lord. You treat her gently."

"Have you explained to her what is involved in a man and woman's coupling?" he asked the older woman.

"Not my place, my lord," Elsbeth said. "She has no mother, and so it is you as her husband who must guide her along love's path. Have you done the bits I cannot mention? If you have then you're done, my lord. I'll leave you to dry yourself. That door"—she pointed to a small portal—"leads into my mistress's bedchamber." She curtsied to him. "Good night, my lord."

He remained in the tub, enjoying the heat from the water, until he realized it was beginning to cool. So young FitzTudor had attempted to have her and been soundly rebuffed. Well, he couldn't blame the lad. Adair was a toothsome morsel. She said she was a virgin. Her servant said she was a virgin. He sighed. *A virgin.* How in hell did one approach a virgin? And especially one as matter-of-fact as his new wife. He had not expected to bed her for at least several days, during which he had planned to woo her with kisses and caresses that would grow bolder with time until she was curious enough, and ready enough, to be breached. But when she had left the hall after whispering to him they had a duty to perform, he had been astonished. Aye, making a new heir for Stanton was important, but he wanted a bed partner who would enjoy being with him.

Andrew suddenly realized he was growing cold, and so he arose and stepped from the tub. Reaching out, he drew the drying cloth from its rack and toweled his body and hair free of water. He looked about and could see no garment to wear. Shaking his head, he reached for the door handle and opened the door into his wife's bedchamber. He stepped into the room, pulling the door shut behind him. There was a fire in the hearth, and draperies drawn over the windows. He drew the curtains back that enclosed the large oaken bedstead and saw her sitting straight up, pillows behind her, awaiting him. Her eyes widened at the sight of his naked body, but she said nothing. He could see she was without clothing as well, for her shoulders and arms were bare as she clutched the coverlet against her breasts.

"We don't have to do this tonight," he said quietly. She was afraid. He could see it in her dark violet eyes. He did not want her afraid.

"Aye, we do," she whispered. "Your grandsire will demand to see the bloody sheet on the morrow. If we do not have one to display he will assume I was not a virgin. And if you tell him you did not breach me, he will call you coward before everyone in the hall. I will not let him shame us before our Stanton folk, Andrew. It would erode our authority. Get into bed, my lord, before you catch the ague." She threw back the coverlet.

He climbed in next to her, drawing the coverlet back over them. "Give me your hand," he said to her, and she slipped a hand into his. "I am sorry to say you are correct, Adair. There is a bit of the bully in my grandsire. Your strength tonight won his grudging respect. And your understanding of our situation is well thought out. If my grandsire had not come this day we might have had the time we needed to really become acquainted. But we do not. However, let me suggest something to you. Let us cuddle together until you feel brave enough for us to couple. We have until the dawn to do what must be done. We need not do it immediately, Adair." He slid down beneath the coverlet, drawing her with him. His strong arms wrapped about her. "There. Isn't that better, wife?" His lips brushed her forehead, and the scent of gillyflowers arose from her dark hair. "I never expected to wed," he told her. "I had nothing to offer a wife." The feel of her young, supple body against his was intoxicating. Andrew struggled to maintain a semblance of self-control. He could not allow his lustful body to overcome his common sense. This girl was the wife to whom he would be married for all his days.

"From what I have just now observed, my lord, you have more than enough to offer a wife," Adair said with a naughty giggle. She had looked well at him as he had come to her bed. He was the first naked adult man she had ever seen. She did not need a great deal of experience to know he was well made, and he was.

Andrew chuckled. "I couldn't tell how hard you were looking in the dim light."

"The light was bright enough for me to observe your attributes, my lord," she told him. "I have naught to compare them with, but I suspect they are considered more than satisfactory by the ladies you have honored. I believe I am safe in saying that I am the only virgin in this bed tonight." Her cheeks felt hot with her bold words.

"Aye, you are the only virgin here," he agreed. "I lost my virginity when I was fourteen, and I have since known several women. But I am not careless with my affections. Are you always so candid in your speech, Adair? I have never known a woman to be so open with her thoughts."

"Lady Margaret always advised me to be more careful in my discourse. She said those who did not know me might think me bold—or worse, wanton. But I have always said what I am thinking. I was never any good at the games they play at court," Adair noted. "I am too honest, I suppose." His body was firm, and there was a comfort being enclosed in his arms. She felt safe for the first time since she had been a child. And his skin was smooth and smelled good. She wondered what Elsbeth had put in his bathwater. She would have to remember to ask her.

"Why did you stay so long then at court?" he asked her, unthinking.

"My lord, I was only six when Lancastrians slaughtered my family. I had no one else to go to but the king. My sire has great charm, as you must surely have heard. Most who enter into his presence are enchanted by him. His manners are flawless, and his memory for faces and names is incredible. He can make strangers feel welcome and mere acquaintances as if they are close friends. And he comprehends his duty as king of this realm.

"But I could not really like him or the queen. Both are totally self-involved. The king indulges himself shamelessly with women and rich living. The queen's only interests lie in advancing the members of her family. They bred their children like a litter of puppies, and afterward ignore them, believing their duty done. Were it not for Lady Margaret Beaufort we children would have been lost. It was she who provided us with a structured life. She who taught us our manners, our faith, and our morals. She saw that we were educated as befitting our station as the king's children. And never once did she mistreat me or differentiate between me and my half siblings. She is a good woman, Andrew."

"Yet you ran away from court," he said. "Why?"

"I have always felt my duty was to the king, but my second duty was to Stanton. I did not want to be treated like a possession to be disposed of by the king. And that is how he treated me. I tried to reason with him, but he would not listen. The Lancasters wanted a king's daughter for one of their own, and I am the king's daughter. But as I am bastard-born and not considered important, I was the one chosen for FitzTudor, who had also been born on the wrong side of the blanket, but dearly loved by his father. And because I brought my husband a title, the Earl of Pembroke could not be insulted or dissatisfied. It was cleverly thought out but for one thing: No one thought to consider how I would feel, being saddled with a husband I did not want."

"Yet this is how marriages among our class are arranged, Adair. Wealth and the advantages to both parties are the deciding factors in arranging matches among our kind. The duke arranged our union, and you agreed. Why?"

"Because I know I must have a husband, for even I am not foolish enough to believe I could hold Stanton alone against the Scots," Adair told him frankly. "And as your grandsire pointed out, our families have intermarried before, and we are neighbors. *And* I know you, Andrew, and you know me. You were willing to have me, weren't you? And not just because Uncle Dickon asked you."

He smiled to himself in the dim light. "You know I planned to come courting you, Adair," he said softly, and he kissed her brow. "I did not know when I first met you that you were the Countess of Stanton, and that your husband would be the earl. But you were the fairest lass I had ever seen, and I wanted you. I still do. But had this not been so I would have done the duke's bidding, for I owe him my loyalty, having served him before. You should understand that I am a man who does what must be done."

She was silent now.

The fire crackled in the hearth, and there was the faint sound of wind beyond the closed draperies. He shifted their bodies so that she now lay on her back. Raising himself up on an elbow he slowly drew the coverlet back, revealing her nakedness. She had perfectly round little breasts, each topped with a cherry of a nipple. Looking down on them he felt a distinct tightening in his groin. Andrew swallowed softly and let his eyes meander down her body. Her waist was narrow and her torso long. Her hips and thighs were shapely. Her Venus mons was plump, pink, and smooth, for a lady of the court, he knew, would have been taught to pluck the hairs from it, as was fashionable. She had dainty feet. Each foot was slender with a high arch. Her body was every bit as fair as her face, and Andrew found he was having difficulty looking away.

"Am I pleasing to you?" her voice inquired softly.

"Aye, most pleasing," he told her.

"I have heard it said that men like to touch women's breasts," Adair said. "Would it please you to touch mine?"

"Aye." He nodded, reaching out and cupping the rounded flesh in his hand. It nestled in his palm like a small dove. He fondled it, and heard her indrawn breath. The ball of his thumb rubbed at the nipple, and he watched as Adair's eyes grew wide. "My touch should give you pleasure," he said, and, lowering his dark head, he kissed the nipple.

"*Oh yes!*" Adair replied breathlessly as his mouth closed over that nipple and began to gently suckle on it. "*Yes!*"

Raising his head as he released the nipple, he said softly, "I need very much to kiss you, Adair." And his mouth closed swiftly over hers. The lips beneath his were sweet, and they softened beneath his as she attempted to follow his lead. He coaxed her to caress his tongue with hers, which she did shyly, shivering at first contact. And when he had decided that she had had enough, he drew her into his arms again, holding her close.

"Why do you not just mount me, and have done with it?" Adair asked him.

"Did you not enjoy the kissing?" he responded.

"Aye, but you have not answered my question," she said.

"Animals mount one another when they breed. There is no emotion to it. Their need to fuck is pure instinct," he began. "But we are not animals, Adair. I want to enjoy possessing you, and I want you to gain pleasure from it too. Therefore we prepare each other with kisses and caresses."

"Oh," she responded. "I may touch you then?"

"Aye," he said. "I should like it if you did." He rolled onto his back.

Adair now raised herself up. Her small hand reached out to touch his chest. "You are smooth," she noted. "I have seen men in the fields with furred torsos. I like this better." Her hand brushed over his skin. "And you have nipples, but mine are nicer, I think, and I will suckle our children with them." The little hand moved boldly to his belly. "You are very flat here." The hand reached farther to touch his muscled thigh. "What is this?" she asked him, running a finger over a slightly raised scar.

"An old battle wound. I received it in my first engagement," he replied.

"You are very furry here," she said, fingers ruffling through the black curls surrounding his manhood. "Why do you not pluck?"

Andrew gritted his teeth. "Men do not," he answered her slowly. *Jesu!* Did she know nothing about a man's body? He struggled to control himself, but he could not, and when her slender finger closed around him he groaned.

She released him quickly. "Am I hurting you? I did not mean to hurt you. 'Tis the manroot, is it not? It seemed of a moderate size before, but now it seems to be growing much bigger."

"Hold it in your hand," he ground out harshly.

Adair wrapped her fingers against the column of lengthening and burgeoning flesh. It was warm in her grasp, and she thought she could detect a faint throbbing.

"You are not hurting me, lovey. You are giving me pleasure," he told her.

"I have heard it said that the manroot is inserted into the woman's body," Adair said. "How is it done? Will you do it soon?"

"Lie upon your back again," he responded, and when she had complied he ran his hand down her torso, her belly, and placed it for a brief moment over her mons. He could sense the heat emanating from the plump flesh. Adair was too innocent to realize that she was being aroused, and readied for the pleasures they would soon share. He ran a finger down the shadowed slit, pushing gently past her nether lips. Then he smiled, feeling that she was already moistening.

"Wh-what are you doing?" her young voice quavered.

"Giving you the answers you seek," he said, his finger finding that little nub of flesh known as the seed of desire. He rubbed it, and she gasped with surprise as a sudden longing for something she had never before experienced shot through her. The finger kept chafing and fretting her until she was whimpering with her need. But a need for what? She didn't know, and she didn't understand. But she wanted it. Her flesh tingled, and suddenly it felt as if it were bursting, and relief poured over her as she sighed.

Andrew laughed low. "Did you like that?" he asked her.

"Aye," she finally managed to gasp. "But you still haven't answered my question, my lord husband."

In reply he moved the finger past the seed of desire and began to slowly push it into her female sheath. "Here," he murmured against her fragrant dark hair. "The manroot goes in here, Adair." He moved the finger back and forth sensuously, pleased to find her maiden's shield intact. His bride was indeed a virgin.

"You are too big to go there," she replied weakly, her head beginning to spin.

Andrew kissed her lips. "No, I am not too big to fit you, lovey, as you will soon see. Now open yourself to me." He did not wait, but rather gently, yet firmly, pushed her thighs apart as he slid between them. His manhood was as hard as iron, and his heart was beating swiftly and loudly in his ears as he began to press forward.

Adair had not thought to be afraid, but she was. Eyes wide, she watched as he slowly began to insert the thick peg of flesh into her body. How could anything like this give pleasure? she wondered. Her body was being invaded and pried open to satisfy his lust. He moved farther into her, and to her surprise Adair felt her body seemingly opening to accommodate him. Then she gasped and cried out in pain as the tip of his manroot began to press against something within her. "Please stop!" she pleaded with him. "Oh, please stop! It hurts! *It hurts!*

He drew back, to her relief, but then his manhood plunged forward, and Adair screamed as he seemed to fill her. "The pain will ease! The pain will ease," he assured her. "It was your maidenhead, lovey. I am sorry. There is only pain the first time. I swear it." Then he began to move on her again.

Adair sobbed as he did. But the burning was subsiding as quickly as the pain had burst forth to engulf her. Her husband was groaning as he labored over her body. And then he cried out, and she felt the manhood quiver as his juices flooded her. When he collapsed atop her, Adair instinctively put her arms about him in a gesture of comfort. He lay atop her for several minutes, and then Andrew rolled off of her, breathing heavily.

"Why didn't you tell me of the pain?" she asked him.

"You would have been more frightened than you were," he replied.

"I was not afraid!" Adair denied.

"Aye, you were," he said. "But the deed needed to be done, and now my grandsire will leave Stanton content with us both."

"There was no pleasure," she said. "You promised me pleasure."

"You will have it the next time," he assured her. "You were fearful, and your deflowering was painful, for you were a true virgin. It would have been unusual for you to gain pleasure from our first coupling, Adair."

"When will we do it again?" she wanted to know.

He chuckled. "So you are brave enough to try again, are you?" He looked down at her and brushed a strand of her black hair from her face.

"Aye, I am," she said.

"Not tonight," he told her. "You will be sore, but Elsbeth will know how to care for you on the morrow. And when you tell me you are ready we will couple again, Adair. And next time I will strive to see that you have much pleasure. Now go to sleep, lovey. We'll have to face the old man soon enough."

"I think I will be happy with you, my lord," Adair told him, and he kissed her lips softly.

"Aye, I believe we can be happy with each other," he agreed. And then he closed his eyes.

When the morning came Elsbeth awoke them. Andrew went to his own bedchamber next door, and found a man of middle years awaiting him.

"Good morning, my lord. I am Chilton, and it will be my duty to serve you."

"I must get dressed," Andrew said. "My grandsire and my brother will want to leave this morning, and they cannot go until the lady and I have bid them farewell."

"I have water ready, my lord," Chilton replied. He was of medium height, with brown eyes and a bald pate.

The young earl already sensed that Albert had chosen well.

Next door, Adair's needs had been attended to by the faithful Elsbeth, and then the two women had stripped the bedsheet from the bed. Adair was shocked by the large stain, but Elsbeth smiled proudly.

"Well," she said, "that should certainly satisfy the old dragon! His grandson did a fine job, and your innocence is there for all to see."

"I do not think I can walk," Adair complained. "I am too sore."

"Nonsense!" Elsbeth said.

A discreet knock sounded upon the door connecting the two bedchambers, and Chilton's head popped through. "If her ladyship is ready, his lordship is prepared to go down to the hall."

"She's ready," Elsbeth said, and she gathered up the sheet, handing it to Adair. "You have to carry it," she said. "And take it right to the old lord for his inspection."

Adair and Andrew met in the corridor outside the bedchambers, and together they descended. Entering the hall, Adair walked straight to Humphrey Lynbridge, who was standing at the large hearth. She flung the sheet open before him, her look a defiant one.

"There, my lord! You should be well satisfied," she said.

The old man looked at the large brownish bloodstain on the sheet. Then he turned to his younger grandson. "You have a mighty cock like me," he said. "The stain on Allis and Robert's sheet was but half this size. She screamed?"

"Aye," the earl said tersely.

"Good! Now she'll not forget who's master in this house," Lord Lynbridge remarked. He turned back to Adair. "You move gingerly, my lady Countess of Stanton," he mocked her. "I am happy to see my grandson did his duty, and you yours. God bless you both!"

Adair was utterly speechless at his words. Finally she signaled to Albert to bring the morning meal. And when it had been consumed she and Andrew saw their guests off. And at last alone, the newlyweds began their life together. Andrew went off to the cattle barns, and Adair called for her writing box. She had much to write her half sister, Bessie. She wondered if she should tell her all, for one day Bessie would have to face a bridegroom. It was unlikely the queen would explain what was necessary. But then Adair considered that Lady Margaret would never allow her charge to go to the marriage bed unprepared. Finding her writing box, she sat down to write her half sister the news of her marriage, and of how she believed that she had at last found happiness.

Chapter 7

Their life settled into a comfortable pattern that revolved about Stanton and its needs. The winter was a quiet time for the estate. Christ's Mass came, followed by Twelfth Night. The snows had finally made travel impossible, which also meant that borderers on both sides of the border ceased their raiding. The cattle grew fat in their barns as the granaries slowly emptied, until the time came for them to go back out into their pastures with the return of spring.

Andrew was amazed by Adair's abilities to manage Stanton. But to his surprise she was more than willing to share her responsibilities, and taught him all she knew. He realized that she trusted him implicitly, and that she did pleased him. When he mentioned it to her, Adair had demurred and told him that the estate was a man's domain. The house, the servants, and the children were her province.

"I have done what I have done because I had to," she said. "I am happy to pass these obligations on to you, my lord. It is obvious to me that you have come to love Stanton, and will care for it."

They heard nothing from the king. He had sent his daughter no gift to commemorate her marriage. Part of Adair was angered by his dismissal. Another part was relieved. The duke had sent to inquire after them before the snows. He had sent them a footed silver-and-gilt salt dish for their high board. And he had sent Adair a delicate gold chain from which hung a small ruby heart. To Adair he had written, *My dear child, your uncle is so very pleased with you. May Jesu and his blessed Mother Mary keep you safe always. Uncle Dickon.* Adair wept when she read the small parchment missive.

"He has always been so caring." She sniffled against Andrew's shoulder.

"He is the most honorable man I have ever known," Andrew said.

And as the winter slowly passed, the intimacy they shared began to grow deeper. Andrew was a gentle and considerate lover to his young wife. Adair became bolder in her lovemaking. The servants noticed that they sought their bed early each evening. They would nod and smile at each other, and Elsbeth predicted an heir to Stanton before many months had passed. Yet Adair showed no signs of conceiving, and it disturbed her, for she felt her chief duty as the lady of Stanton was to produce the next earl. And she believed it was her fault.

She did not love her husband. She liked him. And she respected him. And after that first difficult night, she had learned to enjoy the lustful moments that they shared. Enjoy? Nay. She relished the moments she lay in his arms. She adored feeling him deep within her, knowing that her body made him weak with his need. But she felt no deep desire for him, as Anne Neville felt for her duke. You could see it when they were together. The air fairly crackled with the passion those two felt for each other. Adair sighed. Admittedly such love between a husband and wife was a rare thing. She wondered if he loved her. He had not said it, but she longed to know if he did.

They had been united in marriage for several reasons, but none of them had to do with love. Adair supposed she was fortunate in that she liked her husband, and enjoyed his hunger for her body, and could reciprocate that lust. At least he was not the pimpled FitzTudor. Even now, especially now that she understood the closeness of intimacy, she shuddered with the thought that he might have possessed her body. She doubted he would have treated her virginity with the care that Andrew had.

"You are restless tonight," he said, breaking her train of thought. They lay abed.

"It is the wild wind screeching about the chimneys, and the rain beating so insistently against the shutters. Spring is coming," Adair answered him.

"It must be," he agreed. "I feel my lust rising like the sap in a tree."

She giggled. "You want to fuck," she said.

"Aye, I want to fuck," he admitted. His hand slipped beneath her nightgown and moved slowly up her legs. When they parted for him, his fingers stroked the softness of her inner thigh before moving to her mons.

"Your touch is always so gentle," she told him.

"I want to be tender with you, Adair," he said.

"Why?" she demanded to know.

"Because I care for you," he answered. His hands moved from her lower extremities up her torso.

"Wait," she said, and, sitting up, she pulled her nightgown off. Then, taking his face between her hands, she drew him to her breasts. "Isn't this what you want?" she asked him low.

"Among other things, lovey," he told her, licking a nipple and laying her back down. "I want everything you have to give me, Adair. All of you!"

"Why?" she persisted.

"I think I may be coming to love you," he answered her. "Would such a thing be displeasing to you, Adair?" He looked down into her face.

She felt her cheeks grow warm with his surprising admission. "Nay," she said. "It would not displease me, Andrew," she whispered. "I would like it if I had your heart."

"Do I have yours?" he wanted to know.

"Aye, you do," she replied, and realized as she said it that it was true. In a quiet way she had finally come to love him, if loving meant being happy and content in his arms, for she had been from the first night. What more was there to love? She had been a little fool, Adair thought, and then his lips met hers in a sweet kiss.

"I love you," he murmured against her mouth, and she echoed his words back to him even as he pushed himself into her body.

"Oh Andrew!" She sighed. She loved the feel of his hard length filling her.

"Oh, lovey," he groaned into her hair.

They loved each other! Surely a child would come of it. But none did. Still, he did not berate her for it. And then in the spring a messenger arrived from the court with a letter for Adair from her half sister, Elizabeth. The king had caught a chill and died suddenly on the ninth day of April. Her half brother, Edward, would be the new king, and the Duke of Gloucester was named his protector at the king's deathbed, much to the fury of the queen. The priests had heard it, and declared it so.

Mama is furious, Elizabeth wrote.

> *You know how she and Uncle Dickon have always rubbed each other. She is rallying the Woodvilles as well as the rest of her supporters, and they have sent for our brother, who has been in the care of my uncle, Earl Rivers, and they have secured the treasury as well. I do not know how this will all end, but Mama is preparing to take our younger brother, Dickie, my sisters, and me into sanctuary at Westminster. Pray for us. The negotiations for my betrothal to the dauphin have ceased. Mama and Lady Margaret return to the possibility of a marriage between me and her son, Henry of Lancaster. I think I should rather have an English husband, Adair, and remain in England. I will, of course, marry where I am told to marry. Uncle Dickon came in early December to see Papa. He told us that he made a good match for you, and that you are content. I am glad for it. Write me when you can, dear one. I remain your most devoted and loving sister, Bess.*

Adair showed the letter to Andrew. "We must send to Middleham to see if we can be of any help to Uncle Dickon," she said. "How typical of the queen to want her own way. She and her odious family would rule through my little brother."

"I'll go to Middleham myself," Andrew said. "But the duke will already know that his brother is dead, and will have already ridden south to protect his interests, as well as those of the young king."

"Follow him," Adair said. "He will need all his good captains. I can manage here at Stanton." Her lovely face was anxious. "The queen would cause a civil war if it meant getting her own way in this matter."

The Earl of Stanton nodded to his wife. "Aye, you're correct. I'll go because I know you can keep Stanton safe in my absence, lovey, but I will miss you."

Andrew Radcliffe departed his home the following morning. He rode with but six retainers at his side. Reaching Middleham, he learned the duke had indeed gone south with all possible haste when he had learned of his brother's unexpected death. The earl rode after him, as his wife had requested. Catching up with the Duke of Glouces-ter, he was welcomed. The news was not good.

The duke had received word from the late king's lord chamberlain of what the queen had managed to do so far. Prince Edward had been proclaimed King Edward V but two days after his father's passing. Preparations were already in progress for the boy's coronation, which was now scheduled for May. The queen had sent to her brother, Lord Rivers, to bring young Edward to her with all haste.

"Aye, the young princess wrote the same thing to Adair," Andrew told the duke.

Richard of Gloucester smiled. "Bess is a wise child. She understands the danger her mother puts England in, and would do her part in an attempt to thwart the bitch. My niece knows her duty, and will always do it. Do you not find it interesting that in this time of crisis a mes-senger was sent with obvious great haste to Stanton? Forgive me, An-drew, but neither you nor Adair is truly important in the scheme of things."

The Earl of Stanton laughed. "Nay, my lord, we are not. And I be-lieve I speak for my wife as well when I tell you that we are quite happy not to be important. But my loyalty is with you in this matter, and Adair agrees that with your other friends I should be by your side until the matter is settled."

"Friends," the duke mused. "If truth be known, Andrew, I have few men like you whom I can count upon as friends. I have not my brother's way with the people; nor would I now seek to be like him. And you know that I did not approve of his licentious behavior, but I did love him. He knew it, else he would not have made me protector of his heir. And our first task will be to secure young Edward before his mother can cause any more harm with her machinations. We must ride hard to reach Lord Rivers before he reaches the queen."

There had been other news in Lord Hastings's missive. Not only had the treasury been secured, but so had the Tower of London. The city had been prepared for possible assault, and the queen's brother, Sir Edward Woodville, had gone to sea with a fleet to protect the coastline from any possible attack. There was no doubt that the queen was making a grab for power, and attempting to exclude her brother-in-law from her plans.

The duke wisely swore a public oath of fealty to his nephew in the presence of half a dozen priests and his troop of three hundred men. He sent a messenger with a letter to the queen reassuring her that all would be well. Then, joined by his ally, the Duke of Buckingham, they intercepted Lord Rivers and his party as they rode toward London. The earl was arrested and his men disbanded. The queen's plot had been foiled, and the resistance crumbled. Sir Edward Woodville sailed into exile, and his brother, Anthony, Lord Rivers, was imprisoned.

The duke's party arrived in London the first week in May. The royal council, the Parliament, and the people of London acknowledged and confirmed his place as protector of the young king. The queen remained in sanctuary with her other children, not yet ready to give up. A month later a conspiracy was uncovered that sought to replace the Duke of Gloucester as his nephew's guardian. Additional troops had arrived from York at Richard's request to help him secure the situation. The queen's coconspirators were arrested, among them, to Richard's sorrow, Lord Hastings, who had first come to his aid. He, Lord Rivers, and several others were, of necessity—and as a warning—put to death.

Young Edward had begged his mother to send his brother to him, and she was forced to comply. Both boys were lodged in the royal apartments in the Tower. Richard had them secretly removed and sent to Middleham to be with their cousin. The powerful were now realizing the dangers of a child king with an ambitious mother. They sought for a way to put young Edward aside, and they easily found it with the aid of the church.

The late king, it appeared, had signed a marriage contract with Lady Eleanor Butler. The contract had not been rendered void, and the lady was still alive when Edward IV had eloped and married Elizabeth Woodville. Therefore the king's marriage had not been a true or legal one under canon law. His children were deemed illegitimate. His sons were therefore not eligible to inherit.

At the end of June Parliament met and petitioned the Duke of Gloucester to take the throne. From her sanctuary Elizabeth Woodville screeched with outrage, but she had lost her grab for power. At Baynard's Castle, where he was housed, the duke accepted the petition brought to him. He considered it carefully, for he knew that if he accepted Parliament's request to rule, many slanders would be spoken of him. But who else was there? The heir to Lancaster? Never! On July 6 the duke was crowned Richard III at a ceremony attended by virtually all the peerage, including Lady Margaret Beaufort.

Andrew had watched the royal procession standing to one side in the front of the church. He wanted to be able to tell Adair everything. The new king had graciously dismissed him from his service once again. When Richard had been declared England's legitimate ruler, the Earl of Stanton took horse and rode north for his home. Arriving, he found his fields green and thriving. His cattle were fat, and the haying was already in progress. The warm greeting he received from his wife convinced him that he had been missed. They kissed each other heartily before the eyes of their delighted servants.

The earl's horse was taken off to the stables, and Adair led her husband into the hall, giving orders as she came for food and wine to be brought for him. He sat at the high board and devoured a trencher of rabbit stew, fresh bread, and a goblet of ale while she waited patiently for his news. When he had finally finished Andrew sat back and sighed with pleasure.

"I haven't eaten so well since I left Stanton in April, lovey," he told her. "I suppose you'll want to know everything that has happened."

"Don't tease me," Adair pleaded.

His eyes grew warm. "But teasing you is so much fun," he said.

"There will be none of *that*, my lord, until I have heard everything," she threatened him mischievously. And the tip of her tongue played a moment with her upper lip as their eyes met.

"Jesu, you're a wicked wench," he said low, feeling the tightening in his groin.

"Speak, my lord!" she commanded him. "And speak loudly, for everyone would hear your adventures. Gather around, Stanton folk, and hear what your earl has to tell you," she called to the servants and others in the hall.

"Richard, formerly Duke of Gloucester, has been crowned your king, the third of that name," the earl began, and there was a collective gasp of astonishment from those assembled listening. Andrew then went on to explain exactly how this had come about. Those gathered were slightly confused by what they were hearing, especially the canon law that would bastardize the former king's children and disinherit them.

"Why wasn't this previous contract brought up when King Edward first wed his queen, and before she spawned all her bairns?" Albert asked candidly.

The earl shrugged. "I am not privy to the reasoning of the church," he replied. "I believe it was decided among the powerful lords that having a boy king could lead to many difficulties, given his mother and her family. They wanted an excuse to set the lad aside and offer the crown to the duke. They found it."

"Where are little Edward and Dickie?" Adair asked.

"King Richard had them sent to Middleham, although this is not widely known. He felt they would be safer away from the seat of his influence. The queen managed to suborn several important men. They were caught and arrested. It was at that point the boys were removed from the Tower. Parliament and the powerful families need the king to be entirely secure. No one wants a civil war, but Elizabeth Woodville and her cohorts cannot see that there will be one if she continues to persist in her efforts to hold on to the reins of power through her sons. They think that by having her bottled up in sanctuary they can contain her. But I will wager she continues to plot and scheme."

"He's a strong and honorable man who will brook no nonsense," Albert remarked. "That will be good for us all. Say on, my lord."

The Earl of Stanton continued his recitation of his adventures. He told them about the coronation, and how just about every noble family of note in England had been in attendance. Even Lady Margaret Beaufort, mother of Henry of Lancaster, had been there. "I stayed no longer than to see the crown placed upon his head, and our good duke anointed and declared the rightful king of England," Andrew said. "Then my men and I took horse to return to Stanton. So now, all of you, hail King Richard the Third," he concluded. Three loud huzzahs erupted from those in the hall. There was no doubt that Stanton would stand for the new king.

Adair's violet eyes were shining. "Uncle Dickon will make a fine king," she said.

"He still has much to overcome, I fear," Andrew answered her. "Elizabeth Woodville hates the king with every fiber of her being. She will continue to cause trouble, and will not rest until one of them is dead. And he is too much of a gentleman to see the bitch killed."

"I would poison her," Adair said. "But tell me, was the new queen there in London? And what about little Neddie?"

"She was there, and crowned with him," the earl told his wife. "The little prince, however, remains at Middleham. You know how fragile his health has been since his birth, poor child."

Adair's eyes filled with tears. "I wonder if he will live to manhood," she said. "And poor Lady Anne has never conceived again. Uncle Dickon may have to one day declare Henry of Lancaster or one of my half brothers his heir, for he will have no other choice, though Buckingham thinks his claim is equal or greater."

"Enough, lovey, of things that do not really concern us," the earl said. "I would take my wife to bed after so long an absence from her."

"You need a bath, my lord," Adair told him. "I know you have not had one since you left Stanton, for you are rank. Let me bathe you, and then we will go to bed."

"Only if you will bathe me with your own little hands," he told her, his eyes twinkling lustfully. "Elsbeth is too rough with me."

Adair giggled. "It is my duty to care for you in all ways, my lord." She arose from the high board where they were still seated. "Let me order that the water be heated before we leave the hall." With a seductive smile and a curtsy she hurried off.

He sat watching the gentle swing of her hips beneath her gown as she went, thinking to himself that he was a fortunate man indeed to have been given such a wife. And he would have had her even without the title she brought him. He tilted his goblet in the direction of the standing server, and it was filled again with ale. He sipped it slowly, awaiting her return, but instead it was Elsbeth who came and murmured in his ear.

"My mistress awaits you in the bathing room, my lord," she said.

Without a word Andrew got up from the high board and, leaving the hall, climbed the stairs to the corridor above. Opening the door to the bathing room, he was greeted by a cloud of scented steam. The fire in the little hearth leaped with the draft from his entrance. He quickly shut the portal. "Adair?" he called to her.

"I am here," she answered him.

He peered through the steam. "Where, lovey?"

"Here." She giggled. "In the tub. If you do not get your clothing off soon, my lord, the water will cool. I can hardly bathe you with my own little hands if I am not here in the tub with you. Did you not think of that?"

It was all the encouragement he needed. He tore his clothing off, his boots, flinging them carelessly aside. Then, walking to the tall oak tub, he climbed the steps and climbed into it, coming face-to-face with his wife as he did so.

"There," she purred at him. "Isn't this nice, my lord?" And taking up a sea sponge filled with soap, she began to wash him. When her hands moved to his genitals she smiled a wicked little smile, for his love rod was already hard with his lust for her. "Just a moment more, my lord. Your hair will need attending to before you may enter my bed." She quickly scrubbed his dark locks, and he grumbled that she was even worse than Elsbeth. Laughing, Adair rinsed his hair with the two pitchers of clean water on the shelf of the tub's wide rim. Then, while he was attempting to get the water from his eyes, she climbed from the tub. "Come along, my lord; do not dally," she said.

Able to see once again, he looked about for her. "Where have you gotten to now, lovey?" he wanted to know.

"I am here waiting to dry you," she murmured seductively.

He exited their tub, and his lust for her was most visible. "Not yet," he growled, and, grabbing her, he backed her against the tall wooden tub. "First, wife, you will take the edge off of my lust. Put your arms about my neck." And as she did so his two big hands cupped her buttocks and raised her up.

Adair squealed with surprise, but she instinctively opened her legs to wrap them about his torso as he thrust eagerly into her body. He was so hard, and she gasped with pleasure as he pumped into her with a fierce, quick rhythm. "Oh, God, Andrew!" Her own passions rose to flood her entire being. "Don't stop. If you stop I will kill you!"

He laughed low. "This is but the beginning, Adair. I have missed you more than I was even willing to admit to myself." His loins banged again and again against her. "I mean to do this with you most of the night long." His lips found hers in a burning kiss.

She almost devoured his mouth. Their tongues fought a pitched battle until her head was spinning and Adair felt entirely out of control of her own body. She moaned deep in her throat, every sense heightened as their wet bodies rubbed and pressed against each other. And then there was no holding her desires in any kind of check. She threw back her head and screamed as a mutual satisfaction overwhelmed them both. Together they collapsed onto the stone floor of the bathing chamber, their combined breaths coming in sharp, quick pants that slowly, slowly grew quieter.

He found his voice first. "I am sated for a few minutes," he said with humor.

Adair laughed weakly. "May I dry you now, my lord?" she inquired of him mischievously. "That is, if I can make my legs stand up."

He struggled to his feet first, and then drew her up beside him. "Attend me, wife," he told her, holding her up.

For a moment she clung to him, but then as the strength seeped back into her body Adair took up a small wet cloth and bathed his manhood, then dried it. Next she lifted a large cloth from its rack before the small hearth and dried him carefully. When she had finished she said, "Go and get into bed, Andrew. I don't want you catching the ague. I will join you when I have attended to myself." She gave him a quick kiss upon his lips and a gentle shove toward the door to her bedchamber. And when she had washed her own sex, she dried herself before hurrying to join him.

He lay upon their bed, his manhood gracefully limp upon his muscled thigh. When he held out his arms Adair ran to join him. There were no words spoken between them for some time. None were really necessary. They lay together, leisurely exploring each other's body, to their mutual pleasure. His absence had changed something between them, Adair realized. Their marriage, begun a few months ago for practical reasons, had blossomed into love. Perhaps, she thought, it was not the wild passion shared between the new king and his queen, but a different, special love between Andrew and her.

She ran a finger down his chest and, leaning over him, kissed him. "I believe I can say with all honesty that I missed you too, husband."

"Did I say I missed you?" he teased. "A moment of weakness, lovey."

"Villain!" She yanked at his mop of dark hair.

"Vixen!" He pulled her back into his arms, kissing her soundly. And with each moment their desire for each other rose once more. Andrew buried his face in her scented hair. "God help me, Adair, I have never wanted any woman the way I want you!" He put her beneath him, and his mouth began to both taste and explore her sweet flesh. His lips closed over each of her nipples in turn, licking, suckling, and then he was nipping with his teeth at the tender buds. Then his kisses moved over her torso with a gentle lust.

Adair's fingers kneaded his shoulders and back. His lovemaking was setting her afire with longing. When finally he slipped his manhood into her well-prepared lover's sheath she sighed deeply, her eyes closing as she allowed herself to be surrounded with the pure sensation of his now-frenzied passion. She soared and flew as the hunger between them grew until it exploded in a fiery burst that left them both gasping for air. And true to his word, Andrew made love to Adair several times that night until, sated herself, she cautioned him that they would need to sleep if they were to perform their duties on the morrow. Then she slept, content with the life she now had, confident in the days that stretched ahead. There would be a child eventually. How could a child not come from the love that now bloomed between them?

In the autumn there came word from Adair's half sister, Elizabeth, still in sanctuary, that there had been some small risings against King Richard in Dorset, Devon, and Kent. *But naught has come of it, and Mama is quite disappointed,* Bess wrote. *She schemes without ceasing, and a match has almost been settled now between me and Lady Margaret's son, Henry of Lancaster, although what good it will do I cannot say, for if I leave Westminster, Uncle Dickon will surely seize me, and in his custody I will not be allowed to wed the heir to Lancaster.*

"Poor Bess," Adair said as she put aside the letter. "Of course she won't be allowed to wed Henry Tudor, if Uncle Dickon has anything to say about it. The heiress to York marrying the heir to Lancaster? It would constitute a threat to Uncle Dickon's authority. Of course, the Woodville woman would like that."

"But the king has only one heir," Andrew noted, "and if truth be told, little Neddie is very frail, as is the queen."

Adair sighed. "I know. If they should die—God forbid it—then Uncle Dickon must wed again for his—and England's—sake. He loves the queen so deeply that I do not know if he could do it."

A small epidemic broke out in Stanton village. Several children and at least three adults ran high fevers, and their cheeks grew quite swollen for a time, but there were no deaths. Adair had never seen such an illness before, but Andrew assured her it would be all right. "I had the swelling sickness when I was a child," he said, "and as you can see I am quite healthy today."

But Elsbeth grew pale when she learned what the earl had said to his wife. She took Adair aside, saying, "It is said that men who have had the swelling sickness at any time in their lives are unable to sire children afterward. I believe this may be why you are not conceiving a child, my lady." Her eyes filled with tears.

"Do not say it!" Adair cried, and then she began to weep. "We must have a child for Stanton. The difficulty is with me, Nursie. I did not love Andrew when we wed, but I love him now. Children are created from love."

Elsbeth took the young woman in her arms and comforted her as best she could. She did not say that Adair's maternal grandmother had produced eleven children, and her mother's two sisters an equal number of offspring. Jane Radcliffe would have had a houseful of bairns had her husband been able to give them to her. And considering the amount of time Adair and Andrew spent in their bed, Adair should already be great with child. But she was not. And in the months to follow her belly remained flat.

In late April came the terrible news that King Richard's little son, Prince Edward, had died. A hue and cry arose over the king's two nephews, who had not been seen in many months now. Few knew the boys were at Middleham. Gossip said the king had murdered them the previous summer, but Adair knew the deeply religious and moral Richard adored all his brother's children. The messenger who brought Stanton the latest news also brought Adair another letter from her half sister, Elizabeth.

I am betrothed, Elizabeth wrote.

The negotiations between Mama and Mags were concluded in late autumn. On Christmas Day my Henry went in procession to the cathedral in Rennes and proclaimed before both God and man that he would have me as his wife. Many do not believe our marriage will take place, but I know it will. Marrying me strengthens the Tudor claim to England's throne. Word has only just come that our cousin, Neddie, died at Middleham. Queen Anne is prostrate with her grief, and the whole court is in mourning. There is a rumor that the king will appoint his sister Elizabeth's son, John de la Pole, the Earl of Lincoln, as his successor, now that Neddie is gone. The queen is too frail to bear another child. My brothers are overlooked, I fear.

A new growing season had come to Stanton, and life burgeoned everywhere except in Adair's womb. She began to wonder if what Elsbeth had told her was truth. Had Andrew's seed been rendered lifeless by a childhood illness? Everyone in the village had recovered nicely, but Adair noticed that the wife of one man who had been quite ill, and who produced a child regularly each year, was not now with child. Nor did she bloom with life in the months that followed.

England remained at peace that summer. Adair relied on Elizabeth for all the news, and her half sister did not disappoint her. Mostly her letters were filled with the minutiae of her daily life, but now and again she would write of some event, news of which might or might not reach Northumbria. In late summer Elizabeth wrote angrily:

> My Henry has been sheltering in Brittany. The king arranged with the duke to turn the Tudor over to him this summer. It is said he means to charge him with treason! Fortunately my Henry was warned in time, and escaped into France, where King Charles VIII has graciously offered him shelter.

Adair laughed when she read this to Andrew. "Of course the French will give Henry Tudor shelter," she said. "They do whatever they can to irritate England."

November came and they had been wed two years. Neither she nor Andrew could address the subject of their childlessness. The winter came and went, and in early April, when the roads from the south were once again open, Adair received the first letter she had had in several months from Elizabeth.

> The queen is dead, Bess wrote.

> She died at Westminster Palace on the sixteenth of March. The king is devastated and heartbroken. In less than a year's time he has lost both his wife and his only child. The queen never really recovered from Neddie's death. She was always delicate, but she seemed to fade away before our eyes with each day that passed. God assoil her good

soul. And now someone is spreading a filthy rumor that the king would wed me himself. He is so horrified that he came to see Mama to swear to her that it was not so. The two of them have made a peace of sorts. But the horrible result of this disgusting rumor is that our uncle will not see any of my sisters or me again lest the gossip ignite once more. Proud Cis, our grandmother, is furious that such a thing should be said of her favorite son.

Adair shook her head. Why would people say such a dreadful thing of the king?

On the fifteenth day of August, as the harvest was being brought in, another letter, a brief one, arrived from Bess.

My Henry has landed at Milford Haven. The Lancastrians are rallying to him, and I do not know what will happen next. Pray for England.

"Is the letter dated?" Andrew asked his wife.

"Aye, the tenth," Adair answered. And then she said, "You must go to him."

"I know," the earl answered her. "I will take thirty men with me and leave you twenty, lovey." He stood up from his chair by the hearth where they were sitting. "I have to go and find Dark Walter. I'll want to leave before the sunrise on the morrow."

Adair nodded, but she was suddenly afraid for the first time in a long while. She pushed the feeling back. Stanton was to be in her hands once more, and she had to be prepared for the worst. What if the Scots came raiding? Their section of the border had been relatively quiet of late, but she knew that once news of a civil war filtered through into Scotland, their borderers would take the opportunity to come raiding. They knew that with the throne in difficulty the local English authorities would be at sixes and sevens. And many of the small castles and halls would be lightly defended.

"*Damn!*" she swore under her breath. They finally had Stanton prosperous, and now the Lancastrians were causing trouble again. She silently wished them all to hell and gone. But had Bess not written they would have never known the king needed their help. Adair hoped that this time her uncle would banish the bloody traitors for good and all.

Andrew came to bed late, but Adair was waiting for him. He wanted nothing more than to sleep. "I'll get precious little sleep in the next few weeks," he told her. "We will make us a fine son when I get back, lovey." Then he kissed her, rolled over, and was soon snoring.

Adair lay awake for some time, finally falling asleep in the hour before dawn. But when he departed their bed she was instantly awake. They dressed together and descended into the hall, where the men were already at the trestles eating porridge from their trenchers. Andrew ate quickly, and then, with a shuffling of benches and a stamping of boots, everyone went out into the courtyard, where the horses were saddled and waiting. He bent down from his mount and pulled her up to him, kissing her hungrily.

"Be good, lovey, and keep Stanton safe for my return," he told her. Then Andrew lowered Adair back to the ground. Raising his gloved hand, he signaled his troop of men forward. Dark Walter was by his side as they rode off.

Adair watched as the cloud of dust stirred up by the animals thickened and then thinned with their passage until the Earl of Stanton and his party could no longer be seen. Turning, she walked slowly back into the house. How long would he be gone? She already missed him. But she had a duty to do, and she would do it. She had never in all her life failed Stanton or its people. She would not fail them now.

Two weeks went by, and then one afternoon a young boy on an obviously exhausted horse arrived at Stanton Hall asking to see the lady. Adair received him in the hall, and immediately recognized him as a page in the service first of the Duke of Gloucester, and later the king. Seeing her, he knelt.

"Lady, I beg shelter and sanctuary of you," he said.

"I know you," Adair answered him. "But I do not remember your name."

"I am Anthony Tolliver," the boy answered.

"You were at Middleham, were you not?" Adair inquired.

"I was. When my master became king he gave me the responsibility of serving his two nephews, Prince Edward and Prince Richard," Anthony Tolliver replied. "I remained at Middleham."

"Then my brothers are alive and safe!" Adair exclaimed.

"No longer, my lady," was the terrible answer, and the lad began to weep. "What could I do, my lady? I was one, and I was afraid."

Adair signaled to Albert. "Bring wine," she said, and led Anthony Tolliver to a chair by the fire. "Sit," she commanded him, and she sat opposite him in her own chair. "Tell me everything. Do not leave out any detail."

The boy took the goblet that Albert handed him, and drank deeply of it. Then, drawing a long breath, he began. "Several days ago one of the king's men returned to the castle to tell us that King Richard and his forces had been defeated at Market Bosworth. The king could have escaped, but he would not go. 'I will not budge a foot; I will die king of England,' is what they say he said. He was finally unhorsed and killed. They took his body, stripped it of its armor, and carried him to Leicester, where they buried him in the Grey Friars Abbey. When the crown fell from his helmet it is said Lord Stanley picked it up and placed it on the head of Henry Tudor, who is now declared king of England."

"Lord Stanley is Lady Margaret Beaufort's husband," Adair told her servants, who were gathered about listening to Anthony Tolliver. "Henry Tudor is his stepson. Go on."

"The battle was but two hours, but many were slain, and those lords who were not were gathered up and executed on the spot," Anthony Tolliver said.

Adair felt a cold chill sweep over her, and she heard the soft gasp of her companions, for they all knew without doubt that the earl was among the dead.

"King Henry immediately ordered the arrest of his chief rival, Clarence's son, the Earl of Warwick. Henry is proceeding to London, where he will be anointed and crowned. After the messenger had delivered his news many of the servants at Middleham fled. But others remained. Several nights ago, as I slept in my masters' chamber, the door opened stealthily. There were two men, and they wore the badges of the Earl of Pembroke. I saw them quite clearly when they turned to depart. The room was dark but for the light from the antechamber. They came purposefully forward, and together they smothered the princes in their bedclothes. Then they removed the boys' bodies from their chamber."

"Why did they not see you, and kill you as well so there were no witnesses?" Adair asked him.

"The princes were afraid to sleep alone, but they were also too proud to admit to it. King Richard knew this, and so it was arranged that I sleep within their room in a far dark corner each night. Few knew, and the light from the antechamber did not penetrate to that corner. But when I was certain these assassins had gone I crept from the princes' quarters, went to the stables, saddled my horse, and fled Middleham through a postern gate. I do not know if these murderers remained at the castle, but I could not take the chance that someone who knew where I slept each night would speak of it.

"I remembered that you lived several days' ride from Middleham, and that you were the king's niece. I thought you would want to know what had happened, and that perhaps you could make a place for me in your household, my lady. I am an orphan, and have nowhere else to go."

Adair nodded. "You may stay," she said. "Albert, take Anthony to the kitchens and see he is well fed. From the look of him he hasn't eaten in several days."

The young boy jumped from his seat, almost spilling the wine remaining in his cup. He caught up her hand with his free one and kissed it fervently. "Thank you, my lady! Thank you!"

Adair smiled briefly, then said to Albert, "Come back when you have settled him."

"Aye, my lady," Albert replied.

She was a widow once again. Uncle Dickon was dead and buried. But most horrifying of all, the Lancastrians had murdered her two young half brothers. And Adair knew why. Both Edward and Richard were a threat to Henry Tudor's ambitions. Their claim to the throne was far stronger than his. His claim could be traced only through his mother, a descendant of John of Gaunt, King Edward III's son. True, Henry's paternal grandmother, Catherine of Valois, had been the widow of King Henry V, but when she had remarried it had been for love, and she had chosen a Welsh knight, Owen Tudor, who had no royal connections at all. The Yorkist claim to England's throne was far stronger, and so the two princes who had been kept in safety at Middleham had to be removed. Adair wondered bitterly if Bess knew. And if she knew, would she still be content to marry Henry Tudor? Then she laughed harshly at herself for being a fool. Of course Bess would marry Henry, and she would do it with a dutiful murmur, for there was no other choice. She would be queen of England.

And then suddenly the sadness and grief Adair had been struggling to contain burst forth, and she began to weep. Andrew was dead. And probably all of the Stanton men with him. She wondered if anyone had bothered to tell Robert Lynbridge and his grandfather. She had not seen either of them in months, but she would send them a message tomorrow out of courtesy. Her shoulders shook with her sorrow. Andrew was dead. Uncle Dickon was dead, and the hated Lancastrians would soon be enthroned. It was not to be borne! She had no husband. She had no child. She was alone. She sobbed harder and harder.

Elsbeth came and, drawing a chair next to Adair's, took her hand and began to stroke it. "There, there, lambkin. We have suffered worse, and prospered in spite of it all. We will overcome this too, my chick."

"He would not make love to me before he left me," Adair sobbed. "He said we would make a fine son when he returned. Now there will be no son for Stanton."

"Nonsense!" Elsbeth said. "When your mourning is over you will seek another husband, and marry again."

"I have not even his body to bury," Adair wept.

"We'll put a marker on the hill with your parents' and young Fitz-Tudor's to commemorate him," Elsbeth suggested. "Many a lord has died in battle and been buried where they fell. There is nothing un-usual about it. It is difficult, surely, for the widow, but there it is, my chick. There is naught to be done about it."

"I cannot start again," Adair whimpered. "I am so tired, Nursie. I can bear no more tragedy in my life."

"Come," Elsbeth said, standing and raising her mistress up. "I will put you to bed, and in the morning everything will look different." She led Adair from the hall.

"Nothing will ever be the same again," Adair said. "*Nothing!* I will waken in the morning and Andrew will still be gone, and I will still have no child to mother for Stanton. I tell you I can bear no more!"

Chapter 8

$\mathcal{S}$tanton was again without a master. None of those who had fought with Andrew at Market Bosworth returned home, and were assumed dead. Adair was not the only one to mourn, but she could not give way to her despair publicly. If they were to survive the winter there were things that still needed tending. The cattle were brought in from the high meadows by the cowherds and their dogs. Repairs were made to any buildings needing them. The grain had been harvested, threshed, and stored in Stanton's stone granaries. Adair gave permission for the Stanton folk to glean what they could from the fields. Her small orchard had yielded a bumper crop of apples. On Martinmas she divided the fruits among her villagers, keeping a few for herself. There would be no visitors at Stanton once the winter set in. No need for hospitality.

Before the bad weather set in Adair rode over to Hillview Court, for she knew that her brother-in-law and his grandfather would have probably not yet heard of the king's demise, or Andrew's. Entering the hall of the house, she was greeted by Robert Lynbridge. Old Lord Humphrey was nowhere to be seen.

Seeing her face, Rob came forward, asking, "What has happened?"

"Where is your grandsire?" Adair replied. "I can speak of this but once."

"On his deathbed, I fear," Robert said.

" 'Tis better then. He need not know. King Richard has been slain, and Henry Tudor reigns over England, Rob. There was a battle at Market Bosworth. Andrew, Dark Walter, and thirty Stanton men are among the dead," Adair told him.

"God's blood!" Rob swore softly. "Aye, 'tis better the old man not know." Then he put his arms about her. "My God, Adair, you are alone again. What will you do?"

"What I have always done, Rob. Survive," she answered him, drawing away from the comfort of his embrace. She would weep if she didn't, and Adair knew that if she began to cry she would not stop for some time. "I have my Stanton folk to care for, and I will."

"Dark Walter and thirty men gone? How will you protect yourselves if the Scots come calling? There have been rumors of several parties of raiders lately."

"Stanton has a reputation of being strong, thanks to Dark Walter, God assoil his good soul," Adair told her brother-in-law. "Hopefully they will leave us in peace, being unaware of our sudden vulnerability. By spring I can have enough men and boys trained to make up for those we lost. What else can I do, Rob? I will not leave my Stanton folk alone or unprotected. We have twenty good men for now."

He nodded understanding, but still looked worried. One large raiding party could wipe out her small defenses. Still, she was right: There was no other honorable choice open to Adair. Stanton was her birthright, and its people were her responsibility. "You'll stay the night," he said. "Allis will want to see you."

"Is the old curmudgeon really dying?" Adair asked him, accepting a goblet of wine from a hovering servant.

"Aye, he is," Rob said.

"Then I think it is best I don't see him. Let him go in peace," she said with a sigh. "He'll know soon enough that my Andrew went before him."

Robert Lynbridge nodded in agreement. "Aye," he said tersely. "Aye."

When Allis Lynbridge came into the hall and as they sat at the high board, Adair told them in detail what she had learned from young Anthony Tolliver. She did not, however, tell them what the young page had told her about the princes' murders. This information was much too dangerous, for Adair did not know if the new king had ordered the deaths of Edward IV's sons. She strongly doubted it, for his own mother was one of his strongest influences, and Lady Margaret Beaufort would have never condoned such behavior. She was not so sure about Jasper Tudor or Lord Stanley. Still, she would take no chances in the matter. She explained young Anthony's arrival by saying he was her Uncle Dickon's personal messenger to her, and had been for the past year. When word of the king's death had come to Middleham he had ridden to tell her, and she had asked him to remain for his own safety, as he had no family.

She left Hillview just as the late-autumn sun came over the horizon, returning with her escort of two to Stanton. The weather grew colder, and several days later there was a light snow that just dusted the ground. Looking out from her bedchamber window Adair saw the moon was almost full, and reflecting itself against the snowlit night landscape brightly. She sighed. It was so beautiful, but it would have been more beautiful if Andrew had been by her side sharing it. How odd. She loved him more now that he was dead than she had when he had been living.

December came and went. There was little celebration at Stanton. Their mourning was deep, and lasted the winter long. She had not heard from her half sister in many months. Not since before the battle that had brought down Richard of Gloucester, and put Henry of Lancaster and Elizabeth of York upon England's throne. But one bright early spring day a party of horsemen arrived at Stanton Hall.

"I have a message for your mistress from my lady Queen Elizabeth," the captain said to Albert, who greeted him.

"My mistress is out in the near meadows counting the calves," Albert said. "I will send for her immediately." And he dispatched a servant to find Adair.

When she came into the hall, the captain jumped from the chair by the fire, where he had been seated enjoying a cup of ale. He bowed to her.

"I am the Countess of Stanton," she told the captain. "You have a message for me from my lady the queen?" She held out her hand.

"The message I bear is a verbal one, madam. I have been ordered to escort you with all due haste to the queen at Windsor," the captain said.

"It will take my servant several days to pack," Adair replied.

"Nay, madam." The captain looked uncomfortable. "We must leave on the morrow, and you can bring no one with you. A woman from the queen's household has traveled with us to serve you."

"Is the queen all right?" Adair asked anxiously.

"Aye, madam, her health is excellent. The queen is with child, or so the rumor goes," the captain said.

"Praise God and his sweet Mother for that blessing!" Adair said. "Albert will see to your men, Captain. I will be ready to depart at sunrise. Will you send the serving woman who traveled with you to me?"

Elsbeth was most put out that she was not able to travel with her mistress. "As much as I dislike those long days on the road, I do not like leaving you alone with strangers," she grumbled. "Why, I should like to know, must you travel without me?"

"I think that the queen wishes to see her ladyship as soon as possible," the serving woman who had been sent to escort Adair said. Her name was Clara, and she was a bit dour. "Her Highness did not share her reasons with me."

"Well, you had best take good care of my mistress," Elsbeth said. "I have had her in my charge since she was born."

Clara was fed and given a bed space for the night.

"I don't like her," Elsbeth grumbled. "I don't understand why Lady Elizabeth didn't want you to travel with your own servant. She knows me."

"Perhaps she remembers how much you disliked traveling when we moved from palace to castle and back again," Adair suggested. "Elizabeth has an eye for detail, and has ever been thoughtful of others."

"Humph," Elsbeth said. "I've packed a trunk for you."

Adair shook her head. "We have to travel quickly, the captain said. I'll be riding, and there will be no place for a trunk. We can pack two saddlebags with what I will need. I'll ride astride, and wear breeches. Give me two clean chemises, and two simple gowns, my ribbon crispine with the ruby red jewel, the black pair of sollerets. I'll wear a warm cape over my breeches, shirt, and jerkin, and my boots."

"It's hardly what my lady the Countess of Stanton should be seen in at Windsor," Elsbeth muttered. "What can you be thinking of, my lady?"

"If Bess wishes to see me now then I shall go with all possible haste," Adair answered her serving woman. "If this were to be a social visit the queen would have sent me a missive and given me time to prepare. This is something else, though I have no idea what it is she wants of me. Still she is queen now, and she is my blood. I will go with all possible haste, Elsbeth. I doubt I am being invited for a long visit. But if I am mistaken then Bess will see me decently clothed."

"I should be with you," Elsbeth muttered.

The trip south was quick. The queen's captain was delighted that Adair could ride astride, for it allowed them to cover more miles each day. The serving woman, Clara, hiked her skirts up and rode astride as well. When they finally reached Windsor she brought Adair to the servants' dormitory, where Adair did not recall ever having been. Asked, Clara provided Adair with a basin of warm water and a rag. Adair took the worst of the dirt from her face, neck, and hands. She longed for a bath.

Opening one of her saddlebags, she drew out a gown of orange-red velvet, and carefully unfolded it. It showed scarcely a wrinkle, for Elsbeth had a special way of packing garments. Carefully Adair shook the velvet out, donned a clean chemise, and slipped the gown over her head. It had long, tight sleeves and a small, square neckline. Its hemline was neatly bound. Elsbeth had thought to pack a small cloth of gold girdle that was embroidered with pearls and clear sparkling stones. Adair affixed the girdle about her hips.

Her hair was dusty, but vigorous brushing brought its shine back. Seeking the ribbon crispine with its centered ruby stone, she drew it over her head and down over her forehead. She wished she had a glass in which to observe her preparations. Pulling out her sollerets, she slipped her feet into them. It was already the noon hour, and Adair hadn't eaten since a breakfast of porridge and stale bread early this morning at the convent in which they had overnighted. She was hungry, but Clara was insistent that they go to the antechamber outside of the royal receiving rooms.

"Are you not to take me to my lady the queen?" Adair asked the woman.

"I was told to bring you where I'm bringing you," Clara said.

And when they had arrived Clara departed, leaving Adair amid a crowd of strangers. Amid the crowd of petitioners Adair knew she would be received when she was wanted, but still she went to the majordomo keeping the door and said to him, "I am the Countess of Stanton. The queen sent for me."

The majordomo nodded an acknowledgment, and Adair stepped away. She found a discreet corner with a bench, and sat down to wait. Around her the crowd waited and gossiped. She didn't recognize anyone from her time at court.

"Well," she heard a nearby voice say, "I have it on the most reliable source that he murdered them himself."

"No! Who told you that?" a second voice asked.

"I cannot say, for I should betray a confidence, my lord, if I did," the first voice replied. "He strangled those two poor innocent little princes with his own hands."

"The monster! Where was it done?"

"In the Tower even before he set the crown upon his own head," voice one said.

"But I had heard he had moved them to Middleham," voice two remarked.

"Did you?" Voice one was doubting. "Not according to my sources, sir."

"Did you hear he attempted to bed his own niece, now our queen, in an effort to save his throne? And I have heard he practiced some rather lustful perversions with his own son, and that is why the child died," voice two remarked.

"Well, we are well rid of Richard the usurper. He was obviously a most evil man, and is surely already roasting in hellfire for his wickedness," the first voice said. "Have you heard the rumor that the young queen is with child?"

Adair sat, shocked by the conversation she had just heard. She had wanted to leap up and deny the filth the two men were spewing forth about Richard of Gloucester to those gathered about them and listening avidly. But instead she bit her tongue and remained silent. She had lived at court long enough to know when to fight a battle and when not to. It didn't matter what these nobodies thought. Adair Radcliffe knew the kind of man her Uncle Dickon had been. He had been honorable, decent, and kind. He was a man of great faith, and while she didn't really know who had sent their minions to Middleham to murder her half brothers, she knew it wasn't Richard of Gloucester, for he was already dead when the princes had been killed.

The day waned, and finally the majordomo announced, "Their majesties will receive no one else today. Come back tomorrow."

The chamber began to empty, but Adair remained where she was. Surely Bess would send someone for her soon. The lights in the antechamber were dimmed, and the majordomo came to say that she could not remain. Adair got up and slowly walked from the room. She had no idea of where she should go. On the occasions she had stayed at Windsor as a part of the royal nursery they had been confined to their own apartments and a small garden unless they were invited to ride. Adair had no idea where she was.

She was tired and she was hungry and she was confused. Why had Bess sent for her only to ignore her?

"My lady?"

She turned to see a serving girl. "Yes?" she replied.

"Are you the Countess of Stanton?" the girl asked. "I thought I remembered you."

"I am she," Adair answered. "Can you help me? I have no idea of where I am, or what arrangements have been made for me for the night. The queen sent to Stanton for me to come."

"Of course, my lady. Come with me, and we will find someone who knows," the girl said. "The queen is most thoughtful of her guests."

But no one knew where Adair belonged. No chamber had been set aside for her.

"I have left my belongings in the servants' dormitory," Adair told the young serving wench. "Take me back here, and then will you be kind enough to go to Lady Margaret Beaufort and ask her where I am to go?"

"Of course, my lady," was her reply. The girl took Adair back to where she had changed, and hurried off. When she returned she could not meet Adair's gaze at first.

"Lady Margaret's woman says you are to remain here for the night, my lady." And the servant girl blushed with her embarrassment.

Shock rippled through Adair. What was wrong? She had been sent for, and not come uninvited. She drew a long, deep breath. Perhaps the queen had not expected her so soon, and now there was no time to prepare a chamber for her half sister. Very well, Adair thought. She would remain here, if that was what Mags wanted. She looked up at the girl, who was clearly distressed. "I have not eaten all day," she said. "Would it be possible for you to find me something to eat?"

"Oh, yes, my lady, I'll get you something," the girl said, clearly relieved to be able to escape this difficult situation. Turning, she ran off.

Adair sat down on a narrow cot. It wasn't like Bess to overlook things. Something was very wrong, but what, she would not know until she was able to see her half sister. The servant returned with a small trencher of vegetable potage for Adair, who thanked her and began to eat where she was sitting. She ate it all, including the bread trencher. "Will you bring me something in the morning?" Adair asked her. "I shall have to return to the antechamber and wait until the queen agrees to see me."

"I'll help you on the morrow," the girl replied, and then she hurried off again.

Adair slipped out of her gown and lay down, pulling her cape over her. She did not sleep well, listening as servants came in and out of the dormitory as their shifts began and ended. Her friend came in and lay down on the cot next to hers. Adair pretended to be asleep, for she knew the girl was puzzled by how the queen was treating her own half sister. So was she. Finally, as the gray light of day was being to peep through the narrow windows of the dormitory, Adair arose and dressed herself again. The girl brought her porridge in a trencher, and again

Adair ate it all, knowing it was unlikely she would see any food until after her audience with the queen.

"I will show you back to the antechamber," the servant said, and led Adair back through the castle.

When they arrived Adair dug into her purse and drew out a ha'penny, which she gave the girl. "You have been more than kind," she said. "I don't even know your name." She pressed the coin into the girl's hand.

"It is Mary, my lady, and you are too generous. I was happy to help you, for I remember you when I first came into service here. You were always kind, and always said thank-you. Few do, if they notice you at all." Then, with a curtsy, Mary scampered off down the corridor.

Adair stepped into the anteroom, which was already beginning to fill up. She went again to the majordomo. "I am the Countess of Stanton. The queen sent for me."

"Yes, my lady, I remember you," he replied. "You must wait. You were not on the list yesterday, and I do not see you today, but I will send a page in to tell the king you are waiting."

"Thank you," Adair responded. She found her bench in the corner and waited again, watching as mainly men were called into the royal presence. Some she recognized by their bearing as noblemen. Others were obviously important men of business. There were one or two other women. Finally, to her great relief, the majordomo called out her name, and rising, Adair crossed the chamber and entered through double doors that had been flung open to allow her admittance. She walked slowly down the aisle toward the throne. Elizabeth was sitting to the king's left, her chair just slightly below her husband's. Adair smiled tremulously, but Elizabeth did not even look at her. *How odd*, Adair thought. Then she saw the king's mother, her old governess, seated next to the queen. How elegant she looked, Adair considered. Reaching the throne she curtsied low, and waited to be told to arise.

"Kneel before me, my lady Countess of Stanton," she heard the king's voice command. "Kneel before me, and beg my pardon for your treason."

She was amazed and even startled by his words, but she fell to her knees before Henry Tudor, saying, "But my liege, I have committed no treason against you. You are my king, and I honor you. I will pledge you my fealty now for Stanton."

"Did your husband, the Earl of Stanton, not come to the usurper Richard's aid with a troop of Stanton men, madam?" the king asked coldly.

"Stanton has always supported England's ruler, my liege, and King Richard ruled at that time," Adair explained. "My husband and his men lost their lives at Bosworth."

"In defense of a usurper, madam," the king replied. "An example must be made of those who would betray their country. And Stanton will pay the price for their defense of the usurper. Because your husband died following Richard of Gloucester I cannot punish him. God will judge him. You alone are left to atone, and so I am stripping you of your lands and title, madam. The title will become extinct. The lands I will give to someone who will be loyal to me, and to England."

"But Stanton was not my husband's," Adair cried out. "Stanton is my birthright as King Edward's natural daughter, my liege. Please, I beg of you, do not take it from me!" Adair turned to the young queen. "Bess, you are my blood! We have been friends since the day I arrived at Westminster. Intercede for me, I beg you!"

Elizabeth of York remained silent. She would not even meet Adair's eyes.

Tears were streaming down Adair's face now. "Lady Margaret, I beg you to help me," she pleaded with her old governess, the king's mother.

But the king's mother remained silent as well, turning her head away from Adair.

"Let this woman be an example to all who would betray their king," Henry Tudor said. "I am England's ruler, and I will remain so until my death. The conflict between Lancaster and York is now over and done with. We will speak no more on it."

"I did not betray you, my liege," Adair said. "Nor did my people. It is unjust to punish us. Has England not suffered enough over the years, caught in this war between Lancaster and York? Aye, you are England's *new* king, but that does not mean that those who followed England's old king are traitors to you. This marriage between my royal half sister and Your Majesty settles the matter between your families, brings peace to England at last."

The king stared coldly at Adair, and she felt her anger beginning to get the better of her. She knew better, and yet she could bear no more. Her husband was dead, and now they would take Stanton from her. She rose to her feet. "Yesterday, my liege, I sat in your antechamber waiting for my half sister to receive me. I listened to the foulest slanders against King Richard, and I remained silent. Why do you allow such vile mouthings to be spoken of your predecessor? Your own wife's beloved uncle. It is not worthy of you, for I know the mother who raised you, my liege. She raised me as well."

"You would defend a murderer of children then, madam?" the king demanded.

"Our uncle loved all children! Bess, how can you believe this of Uncle Dickon? You know he would not hurt any child. He kept my half brothers safe at Middleham. It was only after his death—" Adair cried, stopping at the king's thunderous look.

"You forget yourself, madam, and you forget to whom you speak," Henry Tudor said in measured tones. "You will leave our presence, and never come into it again. You are banished from the court. You will not refer to your connections again on pain of further punishment should we learn of it. You are bastard-born, madam, and this day you have shown your true and traitorous colors despite the many advantages that you were given." The king nodded to two of his men at arms. "Escort this woman from the castle. She may take with her what she brought."

"My liege," Adair spoke again. "If you take Stanton from me what am I to do? Where am I to go?"

"We do not care where you go, madam. As for what you should do, you can whore for your bread, like your mother before you," the king told her brutally.

The two liveried men at arms stepped up to stand on either side of Adair. With an elegant curtsy, for she would not allow them to say she had no manners, Adair turned and left the chamber where the king had been receiving petitioners. "My belongings are in the serving women's dormitory," Adair told them. "My horse is in the stable."

They escorted her to the dormitory, waiting outside while Adair changed from her fine gown back into her riding garments. She didn't care what the king said: She was going home to Stanton. It was all she knew, and while she might no longer be the Countess of Stanton, Stanton was her home. The king would neither know nor care where she had gone. Her lands would be given to someone in Henry Tudor's favor who would probably never lay eyes on them, but would just enjoy the possession of them. Lifting her two saddlebags up, she exited the chamber to rejoin her guard. But they were gone, and instead she found a serving woman.

"You're to come with me, lady," the woman said.

Adair did not argue, but followed the servant through a series of dimly lit corridors until they reached a door that opened into a small room where Lady Margaret Beaufort was waiting. "Mags!" Then Adair curtsied. "Forgive me, madam. It is just that I am relieved to see you."

"Come in, Adair," Lady Margaret said. "I am sorry for your troubles."

"If you would but intercede for me, my lady. I don't care about the title, but it is Stanton that means so much to me. You know I am loyal."

"Sit down," Lady Margaret replied. She handed Adair a small goblet. "Drink. I think you need to calm your nerves." She turned to the serving woman. "Wait outside, and when we are done escort Mistress Radcliffe to the stables, where her horse is awaiting her." When the servant had left the little chamber, the king's mother turned back to Adair. "Now, my dear, tell me what you meant that the princes were alive at Middleham after Bosworth. How can you possibly know this?"

"Uncle Dickon removed my half brothers from the Tower after he was crowned. He felt the atmosphere there was not healthy for growing boys. They were taken to Middleham to be with their cousin. I saw them there myself, although I never spoke with them. A young servant who slept in their chamber came to me late last autumn. He told me that they were brought word of Uncle Dickon's death and King

Henry's ascension, and that same night the two men who had come to Middleham crept into the princes' bedchamber. He was asleep on a pallet in the corner of the room, and they did not know he was there. Some little noise awakened the servant, and he saw the men smother the two boys. He could not help them, and was in fear of his own life. After they had left, carrying the coverlet-swaddled bodies of my little half brothers, he fled the castle and came to Stanton, begging me to protect him."

"Did he see any badges of service on these men when they arrived at Middleham?" Lady Margaret wanted to know.

Adair shook her head. "If he did he did not say, and would probably not have recognized such badges, madam," she lied. Better she keep silent for her own safety.

"Unfortunate," Lady Margaret said slowly, her slender, elegant fingers drumming softly on the arm of her chair. "I never thought that Richard had killed the boys, or even ordered it done. But now we shall never know who did." She arose. "You must be going now, I know. Thank you for speaking with me."

Adair had risen too. "Can you not intercede for me with the king?" she asked softly. "Let me keep Stanton. It can be of no use to the king, and who among his court would want property in the northwest corner of Northumbria, my lady?"

"My son is angry right now," Lady Margaret responded, "and he feels the need to solidify his position by making public examples. Why did you speak to him as you did? I know you know better, for you were among my best pupils. But Henry is not cruel or unreasonable. Go home, Adair, and I will see if eventually he can be reasoned with, but in the meantime I will make certain that Stanton is given to no one else. Your title, however, I cannot regain for you. I am sorry."

"The title means little to me, my lady. I will relinquish it gladly if I can retain Stanton. Will I be given an escort home? I am a woman, and cannot travel alone."

"It is barbaric, I will admit, but I dare not order such an escort in defiance of my son's rule. You must make your way on your own, I fear. God go with you, child."

Adair curtsied. "Thank you, Lady Margaret," she said. "You will tell my sister, Elizabeth, that I will pray she delivers a son. She is with child, I am told."

"She is," was the reply. "And I will pass along to her your good wishes. Do not think harshly of Bess, Adair. She was raised to do her duty. She will always be loyal to my son first. I even believe they are growing truly fond of each other. You are unlikely to hear from her ever again."

Adair nodded. "Tell her I understand," she said. And then with another curtsy she left the little chamber to find the serving woman awaiting her.

"I'll take you to the stables, mistress," she said.

Adair followed the woman through another series of corridors until they finally emerged into the stable yard.

"Have you Mistress Radcliffe's horse ready?" the servant called out, and Adair's horse, saddled and ready, was brought forth. The woman stepped close to Adair and said, "My mistress told me earlier to tell you to tuck your hair beneath your cap, mistress. You can pass for a lad at a distance then. She says to beg shelter from convents, and asked that I give you this bag of coins." The servant pressed a small chamois bag into Adair's hand. Then, turning, she hurried off.

"Thank you," Adair called after her. She tucked the bag into her breeches waist, and, taking her cap off, stuffed her braid beneath it. Then she affixed her saddlebags and, mounting her horse, she made her way out of the stable yard and from the castle. It was midday, and she knew if she rode at a fairly steady gait she could reach the convent in which she had sheltered the night before arriving at Windsor.

The next morning she joined a band of pilgrims heading toward York. It was safer riding in a group than riding alone. She gave the leader of the pilgrims a silver penny for the privilege, knowing she was very fortunate to be able to attach herself to this party. When they reached York Adair found a small convoy of merchants going as far north as Newcastle. She joined them, keeping to herself as much as possible, and leaving the merchants just before they reached the town.

For the next few days she rode across Northumbria toward Stanton.

She rested most nights in religious houses, but two nights she was forced to shelter in barns, and one night she spent out on the moors, her back pressed against a rock wall, clutching the reins of her horse. She but dozed on and off that night, fearful of wild animals and bandits. But finally, to her great relief, she gained her own lands, only to find Stanton Hall had been destroyed. Not a stone was left standing, even its defensive walls, but the village remained, and it was there that she found Albert, Elsbeth, and the house servants.

Elsbeth was outraged to learn that her mistress had been sent home in such a fashion. "You could have been ravaged, or robbed, or killed," she said furiously. "What kind of a king sends a helpless young woman out by herself to travel such a distance?"

"I am not in favor with this king," Adair said dryly. "I am stripped of my title and my lands, although Mags says she will try to get the king to relent on my lands. But what has happened to the hall?"

"The Lancastrians finished what they started back when they slew your parents," Elsbeth said bitterly. "A great party of men arrived shortly after you had gone south. They had orders, they said, to destroy the hall, and they did. Albert got them to give us a bit of time to get out your personal belongings, and we managed to save a bit of the furnishings before they began their destruction. They carted away the stones themselves, so, they said, the hall could not be rebuilt. They looted what we couldn't take. Then they burned it."

"The village, the fields, and the livestock," Albert said, "they left, for they said the king would not harm his good people, only their masters who supported a tyrant. What did they mean by that, my lady?" Albert looked suddenly weary and worn, Adair thought.

"This new king has punished Stanton for supporting King Richard," Adair explained.

"What are we to do, my lady?" Albert asked her fearfully.

"We shall go on as we have," Adair said.

"But there is no hall for you," he said.

"Where is Elsbeth living?" Adair asked. "I shall live in the cottage in which she has been living, but if that place is already housing another family you shall build me a new cottage before the winter months set in on us again. I am plain Mistress Radcliffe now, and shall be content with a cottage."

"You are the lady of Stanton, and do not forget it!" Elsbeth snapped, and Albert nodded in agreement.

"We've all been living with our families here in the village," Albert said. "Now that you're back, my lady, we'll begin building you your own house."

"I will be content with a cottage," Adair told him. "We don't want to attract the attention of those who came to destroy Stanton Hall again, do we?"

"And you'll shelter with my sister and me," Elsbeth said. "She's a widow now, and her daughters are married. There is plenty of room, my lady."

"Then it is settled," Adair told them cheerfully. "Now I am going to walk my lands for a bit. Stable my poor horse." She walked away from them, speaking with her people as she went. But finally she was away from the village and out in her meadows. While it was good to be home again, Adair considered what she had to do to help her Stanton folk survive this latest blow. The hall was gone, but at least the king's men had left everything else intact. And she had shelter. She sat down upon a low stone wall to rest a moment. A cold nose suddenly pressed into her hand.

"Beiste!" She reached out to stroke the ancient wolfhound. "Poor baby. You've lost your nice warm hearth, haven't you? But we'll have another by the time the frost sets in. Oh, Beiste, I am so sad. Andrew is gone. Our home is gone. I am so tired of having to start all over again, only to have it snatched away from me." Adair began to cry softly, and the dog laid his great head onto her lap, looking up at her with his dark and very sympathetic eyes. Adair's fingers scratched Beiste's ears, and she brushed away her tears, which were dropping onto his fur. "I have to be brave for them, you know," Adair continued. "They wouldn't know what to do without me. But even I'm not certain what to do now. What if the king won't return Stanton to me? Well, I suppose if no one else comes to claim the land I can remain on it. Someone has to look after the Stanton folk."

"Urrrrrr," the dog said, as if in agreement with his mistress.

Adair gave a watery chuckle. "You always know the right thing to say," she told the dog. Then she stood up. "We had best get back. We're staying with Elsbeth's sister, Margery. She always scared me as a child, being so sharp-spoken," Adair said.

"Did you and the dog settle it then?" Elsbeth asked as Adair entered the cottage.

"How did you know I speak with the dog?" Adair demanded to know.

Elsbeth chuckled. "Ever since you were a wee girlie, you've gone and talked things out with Beiste whenever you are feeling sad or confused. Did you think I didn't notice?"

Adair had to laugh. "You see everything, don't you, Nursie?"

"I do," Elsbeth agreed. "Now, what have you decided?"

Adair took the chair by the fireplace. "We go on as always," she said. "I don't know what else to do. We can't cease our way of life because of the king. Nay. It's almost midsummer. The fields are green, and the cattle are in the high meadows. We will do what we always do at this time of year—we'll make soap and conserves. Were you able to save my apothecary? I should inventory what is there, and begin to gather what is necessary to make new salves, ointments, and medicines."

"You're a sensible young woman, my lady," Elsbeth's sister, Margery, said sharply. She had just come into the cottage, and had stood listening. "The Stanton folk need to feel that naught has changed for them. We're simple folk, after all. It don't matter to us if you're a countess or not. You're our lady. Now, are you hungry? I've got a nice rabbit stew on the boil."

Adair found that to her surprise she enjoyed the simpler life of her villagers. The summer moved on, and the new cottage was slowly being raised up. It was a bit larger, she could see, than the other homes, but she said nothing, for Adair realized that as the Stanton folks' lady she was considered different from them. Still, until she knew that the land was hers again and no one could take away her new home, she could not rest easily. But no word came from Lady Margaret.

The grain ripened in the fields, and was cut and threshed. There had been a bit more rain this summer than in the past, and so the granaries were not as full as Adair would have liked them. Still, she knew from experience that she could get them all through the winter. The day of her birth came and went. She was twenty-one years of age now. Robert Lynbridge rode over from Hillview to tell her that word had come that the queen had given birth to a fair son who was baptized Arthur. Although Adair had written to him about the change in her fortunes, he was still distressed to see the spot where the hall had once stood. And he was unhappy to find her living in a cottage.

"Come back with me to Hillview," he pleaded with her. "Allis would be happy for your company. You have been gently raised, Adair. You should not be living like a common cottager. With Grandsire dead now, there is no one to provoke you."

"I thank you for the offer, Rob," she replied. "But I am most comfortable. My own new home is almost finished, and as you can see it is twice the size of everyone else's cottage. These are my people. I am their lady, whether I be the Countess of Stanton or nay. My place is here."

"The Scots will have discovered by now that you are vulnerable," he responded.

"What is the worst they can do, Rob? Steal some cattle? Let them. I will not leave Stanton ever again," Adair said stubbornly.

"Promise me you will reconsider," he said to her. "And send to me if at any time you feel threatened. I will come with my men, and we will protect you."

After he had gone Elsbeth said, "You could go to Hillview for the winter months, my lady, and no one would think the worse of you for it."

"I'm not leaving Stanton," Adair said quietly. "It was the hall that attracted the Scots. They are hardly interested in a little village."

But Adair had misjudged her neighbors, and one morning in late September a large party of Scots borderers swept down from the hills into Stanton village. The village was filled mostly with women and the elderly. Most of the men were either harvesting apples in the orchards or tending the cattle. The villagers were herded into the square, and the Scots sorted them out efficiently and quickly. The elderly and infirm were told to return to their cottages. They were instructed to take the small children with them.

Adair finally stepped forward. "Who is in charge here?" she demanded to know.

"And who wants to know that, my pretty?" a tall borderer asked, leering at her.

"The lady of Stanton, that's who, you border cur!" Elsbeth snapped.

"Why, you're a hot-tempered piece of goods." The tall borderer chuckled. "You'd keep a man busy and warm on a cold winter's night." He chucked Elsbeth beneath her chin, then, howling, drew back his bloodied hand, for she had stabbed him with her knife. "Bitch!" he roared. "You'll pay for that!"

"Jock!" An older man of medium height with white hair and a commanding presence came forward. "Do not damage the captives. I'll have no rape."

"Are you in charge here, sir?" Adair asked the man.

"I am," the borderer replied. "I am William Douglas. And who be you?"

"I am Adair Radcliffe, the lady of Stanton," Adair responded. "I assume you have come for my cattle, sir. Please take them and leave us in peace."

"Your cattle, your grain, now that you have so nicely threshed and stored it, and captives, lady," William Douglas answered pleasantly. "While the cattle have more value, of course, there is a good market for slaves at the Michaelmas fair in the borders. I will, of course, be happy to accept a ransom for you, if you will direct me to where I may apply for one, lady. Where is your husband?"

"Dead," Adair said. "But recently."

"And your bairns?"

"We were not wed long enough," she replied.

"Your parents?"

"On the hillside, sir," Adair answered.

"And your relations?"

"Alas, I have none living, sir," she told him.

"Have you gold hidden away that can buy your freedom?" he inquired politely.

"If I had gold hidden away, sir, and I do not, what would my guarantee be that you would take it, and leave us all be?" she asked him.

"I am a man of my word, lady," he told her with the utmost seriousness, "but if you have no gold then I have no choice but to take you with me and sell you at the Michaelmas fair. I am a poor borderer, and must make my living where and when I can."

"Sir, I beg you, leave us be," Adair said softly.

William Douglas smiled gently at her. His face, in contrast with his white hair, was a youngish one. Tipping her chin up, he met her gaze. "Madam," he said, "I regret I must refuse someone as fair as you are, but I must." His blue eyes were as cold as ice. Turning away from her, he said to Jock, "Are we ready to go?"

"Aye, milord, we are," Jock replied. "I'll signal for the carts to be brought. It's a good haul of strong women and younglings. You'll make a pretty profit on this lot."

Hearing the tall borderer, Adair thought to herself, *Why am I standing here letting this happen to us?* She bolted from the group and dashed up the village street. *"Run!"* she shouted to her Stanton folk. *"Run!"* Behind her she heard the others scattering, the Scots swearing, and then a great deal of shrieking. Where were the men? she wondered. Why hadn't they come to her aid? She heard the sound of hoofbeats behind her as she reached Margery's cottage. She screamed as she was scooped up and deposited across William Douglas's saddle.

Then, to her dismay, Beiste came forth from the cottage with a fierce roar. He leaped for the horse's throat, but he was old and missed the mark. Still, his devotion to Adair bade him act to save her. But as he jumped again at the horse, William Douglas severed Beiste's head from his shoulders with a single clean stroke. Adair caught but a glimpse of her dog, dead in the street, as William Douglas rode back with her to where the three wagons were now being filled with sobbing women and older children of both sexes. Unceremoniously he dumped her into a wagon, and suddenly, to the Stanton folks' amazement, Adair began to cry. Astonished, they could but gape as she sobbed, not understanding this sudden outpouring of great grief on her part.

They could not have comprehended that Adair wept not because all of their lives were about to be turned upside down. She wept for everything that had happened to her in the last fifteen years. For her mother and father murdered so cruelly, and a childhood cut too short. For Richard of Gloucester, her beloved Uncle Dickon, who had loved her. For Andrew, the husband she had accepted and come to love. Aye, even for poor FitzTudor, whose young life had been cut short by these damned Scots. And for Beiste, her beloved wolfhound, who had died not gently on a warm hearth, as he had deserved to do, but in a gallant attempt to save her.

The carts began to rumble away from Stanton. Ahead of them was a great cloud of dust being kicked up by Adair's herds, which were being driven off. The herds were followed by several carts carrying Stanton's grain, stolen from her granaries. The raid had been well thought out and well planned. As they passed by the orchard a great cry went up from the women. The Stanton men had been slain, and lay among the trees where they had fallen.

Elsbeth stuffed her hand in her mouth to keep from shrieking when she saw Albert's body lying by a basket of apples. She could not crumble. She must be strong now for Adair, who was finally doing what she should have done years ago—weeping for the loss of those she loved.

Elsbeth put a comforting arm about her mistress. "There, now, lass, weep," she said softly. "God only knows what is to become of us now."

Chapter 9

Conal Bruce, the laird of Cleit, looked down at the trencher before him on the high board. "What the hell is this?" he demanded to know. He pushed at the gray glutinous mass with his spoon.

"I think it's porridge," his older half brother, Duncan Armstrong, ventured.

"It's burned too," the laird's younger brother, Murdoc, noted.

"Who is cooking today?" Conal asked.

"I think Sim," Murdoc said.

"Conal, we need a cook," Duncan told the laird. "We can't go on like this just because you won't put another woman in the kitchens."

"Every time I bring a female into the keep, one of the men gets her with child, and then she's gone with her bairn, and more often than not the man follows her. We can't lose any more men at arms, damn it!" His gray eyes were stormy with his annoyance.

"There's a simple answer to the problem," Duncan said. "Find an older woman. One with some common sense, not looking for a man. Willie Douglas is offering a group of English slaves he recently acquired for sale at the Michaelmas fair tomorrow. If we get there early we'll have our pick of the best he has to offer. Willie's a careful man. He only carries off the strong and healthy."

The laird sighed. "Well, at least I can take a look," he agreed. "I'm tired of always being hungry, and if I show up at Agnes Carr's cottage for a meal one more time she'll be trying to get me to handfast with her again."

"She's a fine and friendly woman is Agnes," Duncan said.

"Aye, a bit too friendly," the laird remarked. "When I marry I want a woman I know I can trust to be faithful. A woman who is mine alone. Is there any man in the borders who hasn't ridden a mile or two between Agnes's pretty, plump thighs?"

His two companions laughed knowingly, nodding in agreement.

"Some cream might help the porridge," Murdoc suggested. "At least it's nourishing. And it's all Sim cooked for our supper. I think the men are trying to tell us something, Conal."

"Then they had best stop giving the cook a big belly," the laird said dourly.

"We've bread and butter, and a bit of our mam's jam left too," Duncan said cheerfully. "And there's ale."

"We'd best eat up before the porridge hardens into rock, and then get to bed if we plan to go early to the Michaelmas fair," Conal Bruce said, and he poured a dollop of thick cream into the trencher. Tasting it, he said grimly, "It doesn't help, I fear, but 'tis all we have. Butter me a bit of that bread, Duncan. With luck tomorrow we'll find a slave woman as ugly as a toad with warts, but who can cook like an angel. Don't forget to say your prayers tonight before you sleep, brothers, that God will grant us that miracle."

Duncan and Murdoc chuckled.

In the morning the three departed the laird's stone keep for the fair, which was held each year in a sunny glen near the village of Craigsmur. It was late September, and while the sun was a bit slower to rise than it had been a month ago, the day was still fair and warm. As they approached the glen they could see the pendants flying from the pavilions that had been set up. The Michaelmas fair was a time to socialize with one's neighbors; buy and sell cattle, sheep, and other goods; eat and drink; and maybe even handfast with a lass for a year. The three brothers, known to all in the area, were hailed and welcomed as they arrived. They shared the same mother, now deceased. Duncan Armstrong was the youngest son from his mother's first marriage. He had come to Cleit with her when she had married James

Bruce, his stepfather. He was just two years older than his half brother, Conal Bruce, the laird of Cleit; and seven years older than Murdoc Bruce, their youngest brother. James Bruce had been killed in a border raid. Their mother had died only the year before.

The three siblings tethered their horses and sought William Douglas. They found him in the middle of the fair with a group of slaves beneath an awning. "Conal Bruce, 'tis good to see you," William Douglas greeted the laird effusively. He nodded to Duncan and Murdoc. "Are you in the market for something? I've some fine stock today just brought from over the border. They'll not last."

"I need a cook, Willie," the laird said. "A sensible older woman who won't be spreading her legs for the men in my keep, and then finding herself with a full belly."

"I have just what you need," William Douglas said. "Actually two such women. I'll let you have one cheaply. I'm keeping the other to give my wife. I took them because they're healthy and strong. Elsbeth, stand up so the laird can get a good look at you."

Conal Bruce stepped over to the woman. She had a very angry look on her face.

"Can you cook without burning the porridge?" he asked her.

"I can," Elsbeth said tersely.

"Where were you taken?"

"Stanton. I cared for its countess for her entire life," Elsbeth replied.

"Do you have a man?"

"Dead, thanks to yon borderer and his men," Elsbeth said.

"Can you cook something other than porridge?" the laird wanted to know.

"I can cook anything you want, sir," Elsbeth answered. This man looked decent, she thought. Pray God he was.

"There are no other women in my keep," the laird said. "Our mother died, and since then every cook we have had has managed to get herself a big belly. Can you keep yourself from the men, Elsbeth?"

"I want no man but my Albert," Elsbeth said harshly. "I'd kill any who tried to have me, sir. I'll work hard for you."

"I'll take her," Conal Bruce said to William Douglas. "What do you want for her, Willie? She seems a good woman who will do her duty and be obedient."

"A silver groat would suffice," came the reply.

"Half a groat, and you're overcharging me. God knows how long the woman will live. She is a bit long in the tooth," the laird remarked. "I'm doing you a favor. Legally her term of servitude will only be a year. After that she could leave me."

William Douglas closed his eyes a moment and sighed deeply. "Very well," he finally agreed. "A half groat."

"I can't go with him," Elsbeth said. She turned to the laird. "You seem a fair man, sir. I'm sure you would be a good master, but I can't go with you without my lady. I've hardly left her side since her birth, and I'll not leave her now." She stood straight, looking him in the eye, her hands on her hips. "Please, sir, buy my mistress."

"Why would I need another woman in the keep?" the laird wanted to know.

"Well, sir," Elsbeth said cannily, "if there's no other woman in the keep, who has kept it clean for you . . . ? Who has done your laundry? I can see from the color of your shirt 'tis not been washed properly in a long time. Who makes your candles, your soap, your conserves? Who makes the salves, the ointments, the syrups, and the other medicines necessary to keep you and your people healthy? And another woman would be company for me, sir. A lonely woman, no matter her resolve, can often fall prey to temptation."

The laird and his brothers laughed at this none-too-subtle threat.

"She's right, Conal," Duncan Armstrong said. "The keep is a pigsty, and if Elsbeth is to spend her time in the kitchens cooking for us we could really use someone else to clean and wash and do all those other things she has mentioned."

"Very well," the laird said. "I'll buy the other woman. Willie, what do you want for her? And do not say three silver pennies, for I'll not pay it, and if Elsbeth won't come without her then I'll take someone else, or seek elsewhere."

William Douglas looked thoughtful for a long moment. Then he reached down among the seated captives and dragged a woman up. She was dirty like the others, her dark hair matted, but her face was swollen and bruised, and she was shackled at her ankles. She pulled back from him like a scalded cat, hissing imprecations at Douglas. "Her name is Adair, and I curse the day I took her," he said. "She's given me naught but trouble since that moment. If you take her you'll not thank me, Conal Bruce."

"Scurvy Scot!" Adair shrieked at him. "I'll kill you if I can!"

"And she would too," Douglas said. "She's attempted to run away three times now, which is why she's shackled."

"What happened to her?" the laird asked. The girl had bruises on her arms and her legs as well as her face. She had been badly abused, yet she was still defiant.

"I had to beat her," came the taciturn reply. "It was the only way I could control her. She's as hot-tempered a wench as I have ever known."

"He did not treat my lady with respect," Elsbeth spoke up. "And he tried to bed her. Imagine! A border cur attempting to have my precious child, with her noble blood. Well, you did not, did you? His cock shriveled like a dried leaf. And he beat her for it, sir. I'd kill him myself, given the chance!"

Duncan Armstrong and Murdoc Bruce snickered at this.

"The old bitch lies!" William Douglas said angrily. "Give me the half groat and a silver penny, Conal Bruce. You can have the pair of them, and good riddance, I say!"

"I am not a slave, sir," Adair said, drawing herself up to her full height. "I am her ladyship the Countess of Stanton, half sister to the English queen. I wish to be returned to my home at Stanton as soon as possible."

Conal Bruce reached out and, wrapping his hand in Adair's long black hair, yanked her to him with a single sharp motion. "Be silent, madam," he murmured against her lips. "Or Douglas will sell you into a stew where you would not last a week." He turned and, digging into his purse, drew out the half-groat coin and the silver penny. "Unshackle the wench, Willie. I'll take the pair of them, and

I suspect I'm paying you too much, but I need the damned cook, and if the girl makes her happy then so be it." He handed the borderer his coins.

William Douglas bit each coin and tested the weight of them in his palm. He smiled and said, "You've got a bargain, Conal, and we both know it. The girl will warm your bed this winter, and the older woman will keep your belly full." Pocketing the coins, he spit in his hand and held it out to the laird. "Done!" he said.

Conal Bruce spit in his own hand and clasped the borderer's hand with it. "Done!" he agreed. "Now unshackle my property, Willie, and we'll be on our way. I'll be wanting a decent dinner this day, and the kitchen will have to be cleaned first."

William Douglas took a key from his belt and, putting it in the padlock on the shackles binding Adair, unlocked it. The shackles fell away, and Douglas jumped back quickly, avoiding a kick that Adair aimed at him. "Go on with your new master, bitch," the borderer snarled at her.

Adair felt a hand clamp about her upper arm. She turned startled eyes to Conal Bruce. "I will not run, sir," she said. "My Elsbeth could not keep up with me, and to where would we flee? I have lost all sense of direction these past days."

The laird loosened his grip slightly. "Given what Douglas has had to say about you I will take no chances. Elsbeth, come!"

Elsbeth hugged her sister, Margery, and then followed after Conal Bruce and his brothers to where they had tethered their horses. As they passed an awning beneath which were spread an array of ducks, geese, and chickens, Elsbeth pulled on the earl's jacket. "Buy a goose, sir, and I'll cook it for your supper tonight," she said.

He did not answer her, but he did stop and purchase a large bird, already plucked and ready for roasting. He handed it to her. "What else?" he asked her.

"I'll have to check your kitchen, sir," Elsbeth said, "but if you have no bread we might buy a few loaves, and some apples and pears."

He nodded and bought the required items, again handing them to her, and more to Adair. By the time they had reached their horses they were well laden. "Duncan, take Elsbeth up behind you. Murdoc, carry the foodstuffs." He mounted his own horse, reaching down to pull Adair up behind him. "The ride is not long," he told her. "Two hours, no more."

Adair said nothing. She was already contemplating an escape for herself, and for Elsbeth. If she could escape England's king, if she could ride all the way from Windsor to Stanton alone, she could surely escape this Scot's captivity. But first she had to learn where she was—and it must be done quickly. It was already the twenty-ninth day of September. In another month the cold weather would have set in, and after that the snow. They had to go soon, but first she had to learn how far from England William Douglas had brought them. And how far Stanton was. Not everyone had been carried off. Surely all the men had not been killed. There had been one herd of cattle not yet down from the high meadows. She could—she would—begin again. She hardly noticed the passage of time as they rode, but she did notice the rugged hills around them, and few dwellings.

"There is Cleit," Conal Bruce finally said.

Adair looked ahead of them. There stood a gray stone keep on a hill ahead. It was not a large structure, such as Middleham or Windsor, but it still had a very formidable look to it, and did not appear particularly welcoming.

"How do you live?" she asked him as they rode.

"I have some sheep, some cattle; we raid, and hire out our swords," he answered.

"There are no other women?" she said.

"Nay," he answered her.

"Why not?" Adair wanted to know.

"No need for them," the laird replied, "except perhaps a cook."

"Men cannot keep a house," Adair remarked.

"Aye, I've come to realize that, but my men are lusty lads. Every cook I've had since Mam died has been sent off with a big belly," he admitted.

"If that is the case, what is to become of me? I won't be prey to your men, sir," Adair said firmly. "I am no whore."

"Are you really a countess?" he asked her. "The Countess of Stanton?"

"I was until King Henry stripped me of my title," Adair said.

"King Henry? I thought your king was Richard," the laird said.

"King Richard was slain at Market Bosworth, and Henry Tudor now claims England's throne. Andrew, my husband, fought for King Richard. He was killed, and I was punished for it. Now I am plain Mistress Radcliffe," Adair explained to him. She did not tell him that her lands had been taken from her, for she refused to accept it.

"So you're no virgin," he remarked.

"Nay, I am not," Adair responded.

"Good," the laird replied.

"I am not a whore, sir," Adair repeated.

"My lord," he corrected her. "I am Conal Bruce, the laird of Cleit. Women are useful for cooking, for cleaning, for washing, and for bedding. Naught else. I did not buy you to save you, Adair Radcliffe. You must earn your keep."

"I will keep your house for you, my lord," Adair answered him, "but I will not be your whore. I will clean and scrub for you. I have all the talents of a lady born, and know how to manage a household. My father was King Edward."

"But your mother was not Edward's queen, I suspect. Your mother was that king's whore, and you will be mine. Beneath the dirt and grime, beneath the swelling and the bruising you suffered at the hands of Willie Douglas, you are a beautiful woman. I have a sharp eye, Adair. You now belong to me, and I will use you as I see fit. However, I think you will need time to recover from your recent tribulations, and I am content to wait until you do so. If my lust overcomes me in the interim I shall go and visit the cottage of Agnes Carr, like all the men do."

"How reassuring it is for me to find you are such a gentleman, my lord," Adair said pithily. "And in the meantime you will give me leave to be your housekeeper, I assume. I shall do my best to serve you."

He laughed as they crossed the little drawbridge of the keep and entered beneath the portcullis into the courtyard. "I shall expect nothing but the best from you, Adair." And, pulling his horse to a stop, he slid easily from his saddle, turning to lift her down. "Welcome to Cleit, Adair Radcliffe," he said.

It was not Stanton, Adair thought, looking about the dusty courtyard of the keep. It was grim and dirty. The stable did not appear particularly sturdy, and the scrawny chickens scratching about in the dirt had obviously not been well cared for in recent weeks. It would not be difficult to hate Cleit.

"Murdoc," the laird called to his younger brother, who was now struggling with all the supplies they had purchased at the fair, "show Elsbeth and Adair to the kitchens." He looked at Elsbeth and said sternly, "I'll expect that roast goose for my supper."

Young Murdoc gestured to the two women and led them into the keep. "He's not as hard as he sounds," he told them. "Serve him well, and you'll find he's a good master. He doesn't beat his servants," Murdoc reassured them.

They followed him down a small flight of steps from the outside of the keep and into a kitchen. There was no fire in the hearth, and much of the equipment was dirty and in a jumbled heap. The two women looked about despairingly.

"You'll need some wood for the fire," Murdoc said, seeing their distress.

"And water," Elsbeth said. "Where is the well, laddie?"

"Here in the kitchens," he said. "Our mother did a wonderful thing and had a well dug, for she said much time was wasted running back and forth into the courtyard for water, especially in bad weather. She also didn't like the servant girls lingering to talk with the men. She thought it led to trouble, and more often than not she was right." He grinned engagingly. "I'll go get you some wood, and start a fire." He dashed off.

"As soon as I learn the lay of this land," Adair said when he had gone, "I'll plan our escape. We must get back to Stanton before the snows."

"I'll not see Stanton again," Elsbeth said fatalistically.

"Nursie!" Adair cried, suddenly frightened.

"Oh, do not fret, child," Elsbeth replied. "I'm not dying, nor am I likely to anytime soon, but I know in my heart that I'll not see Stanton again. Nor will you. There is nothing to go back to, Adair. The hall is gone. Not a stone of it remains, and there are weeds growing where it once stood. The few Stanton folk remaining are old, infirm, or too young to help you rebuild. If they survive the winter it will be a miracle. And most of the men were slaughtered in the orchard or by the cattle barns. The king has not relented in his punishment. Your lands are gone. Your title is gone. Stanton is gone."

"Then what am I to do?" Adair cried, feeling the tears pricking at her eyelids.

"For now you will help me clean this kitchen, and prepare the laird his roasted goose," Elsbeth said. "I am too tired to think beyond that, and so are you. Come, and let us look about to see where we may begin."

They discovered a pantry where dishes and food could be stored. But it was empty of any foodstuffs. Elsbeth shook her head but said nothing. There was a cold larder where game could be hung, but there was no game hanging. Elsbeth muttered something beneath her breath that Adair could not distinguish. When they reentered the kitchens young Murdoc had returned and begun a fire for them in the great hearth. He was stacking more wood in the woodbox.

"Thank you, laddie," Elsbeth said. She turned to Adair. "Find me a cauldron so I can begin heating some water, and we can begin to clean some of this muck. 'Twill not all be done in a day, but I'll need enough things to cook supper. Where is the spit?"

"Let me help you," Murdoc said. "I'll get the water for you."

Adair sought among the jumble of cooking equipment and finally found a large cauldron. It was heavy, and she struggled to bring it over to the hearth. Together she and Elsbeth hung it, and Murdoc drew bucket after bucket of water, which he then brought across the kitchen and poured into the great kettle. When the kettle had been filled he brought a bucket of water and set it on the big kitchen table along with the foodstuffs.

Then he left them.

"A well-brought-up laddie," Elsbeth noted.

They cleared the table briefly, and scrubbed it with boiling water. They had no sand or soap, and Elsbeth mumbled that this kitchen was poorly fitted, and things were going to have to change. The table finally cleaned, Elsbeth set Adair to crumbling one of the loaves while she chopped apples and pears. Murdoc returned to say that his brother, the laird, wanted to know if they had all they needed.

Elsbeth exploded. "Nay, laddie, we most certainly do not. I need butter and cream, among other things. There isn't a scrap of food in the pantry. Not even an onion!"

"I can go into the village over the hill and fetch you butter and cream, Mistress Elsbeth. I think there might be some onions, leeks, or shallots in my mother's old kitchen garden. You'll find it through the larder door," Murdoc said.

"I'll go," Adair said. The little garden was overgrown, but amid the weeds she found a treasure of herbs and root vegetables. Adair resolved to weed the garden on the morrow and, discovering a row of onions, pulled a few to bring inside. "The garden is there, and I'll start to restore it tomorrow," she told Elsbeth. "We'll harvest what we can, and prepare the garden for next spring," she said enthusiastically.

"Good," Elsbeth responded. "Now clear away all this clutter for me, dearie, and I'll begin to prepare the goose." She was relieved that Adair had stopped speaking about returning to Stanton. It did not mean she was not contemplating it, but for now, at least, she would not act rashly or foolishly. There was nothing left at Stanton for her mistress, and while she had not been born and raised to be a servant, at least Adair was safe for the time being. Elsbeth had seen the way the laird had looked at the girl. Who knew what could come of it? But at least that was a new direction, and all the old directions that they had once followed had come to naught.

Adair gathered up all the kitchen accoutrements and moved them to the pantry, since there was nothing in it at this point. She sought three pewter plates among the disorder, and mugs and spoons. These she put in a stone sink and, taking water from the kettle over the fire, poured it over the tableware. She let them soak and the water cool until she was able to wash and dry them. "How many men will be in the hall, do you think?" she asked Elsbeth. "You can't feed all of them with one goose."

"You'll have to go up and ask the laird," Elsbeth said.

"Me?" Adair answered.

"I'm trying to cook here, child. Go on now. The man won't eat you. Not the way you look and smell," Elsbeth said bluntly. "You're hardly an enticing treat."

"I know," Adair replied. "Do you think I can get a bath after everyone has been fed? And where are we to lay our heads, Nursie?"

"Go and ask the master how many in the hall for supper, and then we'll have another look about. Usually there's a sleeping space or two for the help."

Adair was saved a trip to the hall at that moment by the arrival of young Murdoc Bruce, who was accompanied by two boys.

"I've brought cream, butter, and a wheel of cheese," he announced, very pleased with himself. He directed his companions to place the requested items on the big table.

"Bless you, laddie," Elsbeth said. "Now tell me, how many must I feed tonight? This poor wee goose is barely enough for you and your brothers."

"Oh, lord, Mistress Elsbeth, there will be at least twenty men besides my brothers and me," Murdoc said. "What can you do?"

Suddenly Adair spoke up. "Can you fish, sir?"

Murdoc grinned. "Aye. 'Tis only after the noon hour. I'll go and catch a few trout. Can you make do with some fish, Mistress Elsbeth?"

"I can," she told him, and with a wave he was gone, taking the two boys with him.

"Go into the kitchen garden and see what you can find to put in the pot, child," Elsbeth told her mistress. "And then you'll have to find something to serve the food on, as we have no trenchers. And utensils."

Adair went into the pantry and found a hanging basket. Taking it outside with her, she searched the little garden. She found carrots and some small cabbages, and dug a few more onions. She also picked some parsley and dill. Someone had obviously kept the garden for a time after the death of the laird's mother or else there would have been no vegetables. She had spotted both spinach and lettuce among the weeds. Taking her finds back into the kitchen, she prepared them at Elsbeth's direction. Adair wasn't entirely unfamiliar with cooking. Stanton had not been an overly formal household. She had finally finished paring and cutting the vegetables, and then dusted off a stack of wooden plates she had discovered on a high shelf in the pantry by the time Murdoc returned carrying a goodly string of fish. And while he cleaned the fish for Elsbeth, Adair took a cloth and small bucket of water and crept up the stairs into the hall. To her relief it was empty. Hurrying to the high board, she scrubbed it down as best she could.

When the laird of Cleit sat down to his table that night he was very surprised to discover the meal set before him. There was a goose roasted and stuffed with bread, apples, and pears; a broiled trout sprinkled with dill; a potage of vegetables, bread, butter, cheese, and baked apples with heavy golden cream. His men at the trestles below were oddly silent, and he wondered why. "What are they eating?" he asked Murdoc.

"Elsbeth made them a savory stew of vegetables and fish; and there is bread and cheese, and stewed apples," Murdoc said. "She says she would like to speak with you after the meal in the kitchens, if it would please you."

"Why were you in the kitchens?" the laird wanted to know. "You are not to go sniffing around either of those two women. I'll not have it!"

Murdoc burst out laughing. "You need not worry, big brother," he said. "Elsbeth is more maternal than seductive. As for her companion, I saw the way you looked at her, though I cannot see what you find so alluring about the wench. She's sharp-tongued, short-tempered, and smells like a cesspit. But part of your good dinner is thanks to me. I brought the wood and started the fire in the hearth again. It had been allowed to go out. *And* I caught the fish you so enjoyed, and that our men enjoyed."

"Oh," Conal Bruce said.

Duncan Armstrong chuckled as he spooned the baked apples and cream up from his plate. "I think we have a treasure in this Elsbeth," he said.

"Aye," the laird admitted. "Perhaps she was worth the half groat Willie Douglas wanted, though I should never tell him that."

In the kitchens Elsbeth and Adair ate a supper of vegetable potage and toasted cheese and bread. They were tired, not just from their long day, but from the last few days. Adair had wept for several hours after they left Stanton, but since then she had hardened herself to whatever was going to come. Finally Elsbeth stood up.

"I'll go up to the hall and collect the plates and spoons," she said. "You get some hot water in that stone sink." She bustled off up the stairs. When she returned some minutes later carrying a pile of plates she was followed by young Murdoc, who was aiding her, and had an armful of goblets and spoons. "Thank you, dearie," Elsbeth said to him. "Now run along back upstairs, and join the rest of the men. I do thank you for all the good help you have given us today."

"Your dinner was the best we've had in months!" Murdoc said enthusiastically as he left the kitchens.

Elsbeth chuckled, pleased.

"The water is hot for washing," Adair said.

"I'll wash; you dry," the older woman replied. "You don't want your hands all roughened and unladylike."

"It would appear I'm hardly a lady anymore," Adair remarked softly.

"You was born a lady, you've been raised a lady. You'll always be a lady!" Elsbeth said sharply. "You've fallen on hard times, my chick, but times change."

"I've discovered where we will sleep," Adair said. "There's an alcove off the pantry with two bed spaces in the stone walls. The pallets seem clean and free of vermin, but I took them outside and shook them out nonetheless, and I've scrubbed the stone spaces. But there are no coverlets. We'll have to use our cloaks tonight."

"You wished to see me, Elsbeth?"

They both turned to see the laird standing in the kitchens behind them.

"Aye, my lord," Elsbeth said. "Might we sit at the table? I'm not as young as I once was, and I am fair worn out tonight."

"Of course." He smiled at her. "That was a fine dinner you served up tonight."

" 'Twas not easy, my lord. The kitchen was a jumble of everything, and all of it filthy. We cleaned what we needed, but tomorrow we have a great deal of work ahead of us to put this kitchen back in its proper order. There is much we need. I'll want a strong lad to chop the wood and bring it in, to draw the water, and to sharpen the knives—to run my errands. There are no foodstuffs in the pantry. No flour, or salt, or a sugar loaf. No spices. I saw chickens in the court when we arrived. Where are they kept? I must have a daily supply of eggs, milk, butter, and cream. I'll need a woman from that village where young Murdoc sought supplies for me today to bake bread for me each day. It's a miracle, it is, that I was able to feed your men tonight. Where is the game for the larder? Not a deer, a rabbit, or a bird to be seen hanging." She stopped but a second to catch her breath. "We need soap and sand for the washing. And a broom. We cannot clean your hall without a broom. And beeswax to polish the furniture. And there are no coverlets for our sleeping spaces either."

While Elsbeth rattled on, Adair studied the laird from beneath her dark lashes. He was very, very tall, standing several inches over six feet. His hair was every bit as black as hers was. It was not long, but it touched the nape of his collar, and it was straight as a poker. Dark gray eyes peered from beneath eyebrows so thick that the hairs tangled themselves. He had a high forehead and a long nose. His lips were full, but not thick. His hands fascinated her—large and square, with long fingers. They were surprisingly clean, Adair noted.

"And we'll need some kind of a tub for washing ourselves. My lady is used to bathing on a regular basis. And I'll need a woman to help with the washing. If I am to cook for you and your great lot, and Mistress Adair is to keep your hall clean, then we cannot be expected to do the laundry as well. Certainly your good mam, God assoil her soul, had women servants."

"They departed shortly after she died, for my men can be rowdy at times. My mother's presence is what kept them tolerable," the laird admitted. "I thought we could do without them, but I have obviously been mistaken. I will send you with my brother, Duncan, to the village tomorrow, and you can pick your own helpers."

"That is most generous of you, my lord," Elsbeth said.

The laird stood up. He walked into the cold larder and opened a wide cabinet, pulling forth a small round oak tub. "Where do you want it?" he asked Elsbeth.

"Before the fire, my lord. Thank you."

He gave her a slight bow and left the kitchen.

Adair laughed. "You are truly astonishing, Nursie. This is a whole new side of you. And I did not know you could cook so well."

"I've spent my life looking after you, my chick, but Margery and I both learned to cook from our mother. I often helped the cook at Stanton when it became too much for her. She was very old, you know. But come, and let us fill the tub for you. I'll bathe after you have finished. Let me look where he found the tub. There must be a drying cloth or two there."

"My gown is filthy, sweat-stained, and torn," Adair said. "How can I wear it again after I have bathed?"

"I'll wash your chemise while you are bathing. It will be dry by morning. We'll air your gown in the cold larder overnight, and I'll repair it. It will have to do until I can persuade the laird to find some material from which we can make new garments," Elsbeth said.

Together the two women filled the oak tub. Elsbeth found some large drying cloths where the tub had been stored. Adair stripped and climbed into the tub. Taking the girl's clothes from her, Elsbeth went into the cold larder to hang her mistress's gown, but first she stepped outside and shook it as hard as she could to free the dust.

Adair wasn't certain who was more surprised when Conal Bruce walked back into the kitchen. She scrunched down to cover herself as much as she could, her heart hammering nervously. His eyes widened briefly, but then he handed her a cake of soap.

"I found it in my mother's chamber. I thought it might help," he told her. Then, turning about, he left the kitchen without another word to her.

"Thank you," Adair managed to squeak after him. She brought the cake of soap to her nose and sniffed. It had the fragrance of woodbine. Dipping it in the water, she lathered herself and scrubbed with the little cloth Elsbeth had given her. The dirt began to slough from her body, and Adair began to feel better. She bent over and splashed water onto her head. She rubbed the soap into her hair.

"Where did you get the soap?" Elsbeth asked, returning into the kitchen proper.

"The laird brought it," Adair said.

"And saw you like that? As naked as your mother made you?" Elsbeth gasped.

"I scrunched down, Nursie. He saw nothing, and he did not linger. He said the soap was his mother's. Then he was gone. God's wounds, this feels good! I don't think I've ever been so long with a bath. Would you rinse my hair for me?"

Elsbeth poured a pitcher of warm water over the girl's head. Adair washed her long locks a second time, and once again the older woman rinsed it for her.

"You should have clean water," Adair told Elsbeth as she arose from the tub and was wrapped in a drying cloth.

Elsbeth shook her head. "Your water is still warm enough, and the soap will make up for the other deficiencies," she said, removing her chemise and climbing into the little tub. "Take my chemise, child, and wash it out for me while I get clean."

Wrapped in the drying cloth, Adair made her way to the stone sink where her own chemise was soaking. She added Elsbeth's. Then she waited while Elsbeth used the soap, taking it afterward and using it on the two chemises. She rinsed the two garments. Both women sat by the kitchen hearth, drying themselves and their hair.

"May I come down?" a voice called.

"Who is that?" Elsbeth demanded to know.

" 'Tis me, Murdoc Bruce. The laird said you did not have coverlets for your bed spaces. I've brought them for you."

"Leave them on the stairs, laddie, and thank you," Elsbeth called back. "We're not garbed to receive visitors."

Murdoc chuckled. "They're here when you want to fetch them," he said. They heard the door from the stairs to the hall above close.

Elsbeth went and fetched the two chemises from the sink, hanging them over a drying rack she had found near where the tub was stored. The tub would have to be emptied on the morrow. She ran halfway up the stairs to fetch the coverlets that Murdoc had brought them. Adair's dark head was already nodding as she sat by the warm fire. "Come, my chick," Elsbeth said, helping her mistress up. "We must get to bed." She led Adair to one of the sleeping spaces. "Get in," she said, and then spread one of the coverlets over the girl, who was already asleep.

Elsbeth went back into the kitchen. She moved the drying rack, setting it before the fire, to which she added several logs. It would last and not go out in the next few hours while she slept. Tomorrow was going to be a busy day for both of them. She would send Adair to choose several servants for the keep while she restored the kitchen to its proper order. And it was time the laird and his men went hunting. Winter would be upon them soon enough. The cold larder needed to be filled with game. She would mention it to him once again. She couldn't be expected to feed Conal Bruce and his great lot of men without the proper supplies. Elsbeth took up the other coverlet and lay down to sleep.

When she awoke again she could see the sky through the larder window, dark yet, but lightening to gray with every passing moment. Elsbeth sighed. She was still very tired, but she knew she had to get up. The keep would soon be stirring, and the men would want their breakfast.

The laird was once again surprised by the meal put before him. Eggs poached in cream and dusted with parsley, warm bread, cheese, and ale. He watched as, below the high board, Adair brought his men loaves of bread, hard-boiled eggs, and cheese. She did not speak with any of the men, nor did she make eye contact. When one of his men reached out to catch at her skirt she slapped the hand without hesitation, and gave the man a look that should have frozen him where he sat.

"Keep your paws to yourself, you border cur," she snarled at him, and made to move on with her pitcher of ale.

There was a ripple of laughter from the man's companions. Stung, he reached out swiftly and yanked her onto his lap. Adair never hesitated. She poured the ale over the borderer's head, and then hit him with her pitcher as she leaped from his lap like a scalded cat and fled back to the kitchens. The man jumped up to follow her, roaring his anger.

"Sit down, Fergus," the laird said in a cold, hard voice. "Just so you all understand me, the wench is *mine*. She is not to be tampered with, bullied, or threatened by any of you. Do I make myself clear? As for her companion, the same rules will also apply. I do not intend to go back to burned porridge again for every meal because you men cannot control your randy cocks. And now, I suspect, you will all go without your ale, because it is unlikely the girl will venture above stairs again for a while." Conal Bruce sat back down.

"She's feisty," Duncan Armstrong murmured.

"She'll tame. All women can be tamed eventually," the laird said.

"You'll need patience with this one, brother," Duncan replied.

"I think you know that I'm not a patient man," the laird remarked.

"She's a real beauty," Duncan continued. "She's obviously bathed now. The hair is glorious, and her features are perfect. I've not gotten close enough yet to see what color her eyes are. Have you?"

"They're like large violets," the laird said quietly. "I can see now that she's cleaner that Elsbeth has not lied. Adair is obviously a lady."

"You'll have to do something about her clothing, Conal. The gown she is wearing has certainly seen far better days. I imagine the cook, Elsbeth, could also use a new garment or two. Didn't Mam have a small storage compartment where she kept materials? I'm sure I remember that she did."

"It's in her bedchamber," Murdoc spoke up.

"That's right!" Duncan agreed.

"I will tell the women that they may take what they need from the compartment," the laird said. "And now, brothers, I have errands for you this day. Take a cart and fetch supplies for the kitchen. There is nothing. Elsbeth will want flour, salt, a sugar block, spices, a daily supply of milk, cream, and butter. Several wheels of cheese. A broom, for she says there is none. Beeswax, soap, and sand," the laird finished.

"She gave you quite an earful last night." Duncan chuckled. "Was there anything else she wanted or needed of you, brother?"

"A baker; a boy to chop wood, haul water, and run errands; and perhaps a maidservant to help Adair," Conal Bruce said. "Duncan, you choose. Make certain the women are sensible, and old enough to avoid the blandishments of the men, and the lad strong enough to do what he will need to do."

"And what will you be doing, my lord," Duncan asked, "while we are following your instructions?" He grinned at his brother mischievously.

"I'm taking the men and going hunting. Mistress Elsbeth also told me the cold larder is bare and a disgrace, and she can't feed us all if she has no meat."

Duncan and Murdoc laughed. Then Duncan said, "It would appear for now that our new cook is running the keep, Conal."

"As long as the meals are on time, and as tasty as the last two have been, the woman may have her way with me," the laird told his brothers.

His brothers laughed again.

"I'll go to the kitchens and make certain that Mistress Elsbeth needs nothing more before we start off," Murdoc said.

"And I'll go and harness the horses for the cart," Duncan replied.

In the kitchens Elsbeth assured Murdoc that for now she needed nothing more than she had asked for, and she thanked him. When he had gone she turned to Adair, saying, "I'm sorry, my chick, that you won't get a bit of an outing today, but lord knows this kitchen will be done faster with the two of us."

The two women set to work cleaning and organizing the kitchen. By the time Duncan Armstrong and Murdoc Bruce arrived with the supplies and three servants, Elsbeth was ready for them. There was Flora, a widow, and her young son, Jack. Flora would be doing the baking. The other woman, Grizel, would help Adair in keeping the keep clean and tidy. It wasn't quite midday when they arrived. Murdoc and the boy lugged a side of beef into the cold larder and hung it there.

"Why, bless you!" Elsbeth said. "We'll have several good dinners from that."

"If you have the help you need, Nursie, I will go to the hall with Grizel to see that it is ready for the laird when he returns from hunting," Adair said quietly. She turned to Grizel, who was an older woman. "Bring the beeswax and the broom. You sweep, and I will polish."

Grizel wielded the broom with vigor, and soon the stone floor of the hall was swept clean. "Will there be rushes?" she asked Adair.

"Nay. There were none before, and I don't particularly like them. They attract vermin, and the dogs feel comfortable peeing in them. The hall will only stink. Go down to the kitchens and see if you can help Elsbeth. I will finish the table myself. 'Tis almost done," Adair told her. Then she set about polishing the last end of the table. When she had finished she stepped back and smiled. The high board looked quite nice. It was old, and it had seen many a supper upon it, but it had been previously well cared for, she noted.

"I have not seen the board look as well since our mother died," she heard the laird's voice say. "If you are a lady, how is it you know how to polish a table so well?"

"Even England's queen knows how to polish a table and cook a meal," Adair replied as she turned to face him.

He moved closer to her. "How would you know that?" he said.

"Because she is my half sister, and I spent ten years—from the time I was six until I returned to Stanton—in the royal nursery with her, my lord," Adair answered him.

He moved closer. "Are you telling me the truth, Adair, or is this just some flight of fancy you have concocted?"

She drew herself up and looked him straight in the eye. "I do not prevaricate, my lord. Until I was six the only father I knew was John Radcliffe, the Earl of Stanton. When our home was attacked by the Lancastrians I was sent away with Elsbeth, and only then told that King Edward was my natural father. The title of Stanton devolved upon me. I was the Countess of Stanton in my own right. Both my husbands gained the earldom through me. Andrew, my second husband, as I have previously said, was killed with King Richard. I do not lie about who I am. It is not in my nature to lie, my lord." There were tears in her eyes now, but she never looked away from him, even when a single tear rolled down her pale cheek.

He stopped the tear with his finger. "You have eyes like wet violets," he told her in his deep, husky voice. He had never met a woman like Adair before. She was so brave that it almost hurt his heart to look at her, but he would not be the first to break their gaze.

Adair swallowed back a rush of misery. "I will go and tell Elsbeth you are back, my lord," she said in a tremulous voice. She would not cry. Not before him. Not ever again. She would not cry! She turned to leave him, but he put a hand on her shoulder. She froze. "Please, my lord, I must return to the kitchens." She would not face him.

"You know that I want you," he said quietly.

She shook her head wordlessly. She could not answer him.

"When I saw you among Willie Douglas's captives your defiance burned bright. It was like a beacon beckoning me onward, and I followed. I have probably been a fool to bring you into my keep. Eventually your beauty and spirit will cause me difficulties, and I am a man who prefers peace and quiet above all things."

She whirled about. "Then let me go! Help Elsbeth and me to return to Stanton!"

"No!" he said fiercely, and yanked her into his arms. "I will never release you, Adair. You are mine, and I will have you sooner than later!" Then his mouth descended upon hers in a passionate kiss such as she had never experienced. His lips burned on hers, and they demanded much of her. Her heart. Her soul. Her body.

For the briefest moment Adair wanted to succumb to the kiss. It excited her, and tempted her with a promise of something wonderful to come. Her mouth yielded to his, but then something within her cried out, warning her. This man was dangerous. She would lose herself if she let him make love to her. She had to force herself to pull away from him. "You are far too bold, my lord," she cried, and then, turning, fled the hall and down the stairway into Elsbeth's kitchens, where she would be safe from the laird of Cleit.

Behind her Conal Bruce stood as still as a statue, his male member hard and throbbing. He had kissed many women in his day, but none had affected him quite like this. Adair was wrong, though she might not know it. He would have her. And soon.

Chapter 10

The Scotland into which Adair had been brought was not a peaceful place. Its king, the third James Stewart, was hardly beloved among his rough barony. He had inherited his throne when he was but eight years of age. His mother, Marie of Gueldres, was the niece of the Duke of Burgundy. She had been brought up in a civilized court, and brought her influence to Scotland when she had married James II, to whom she gave four sons and two daughters in the eleven years of their marriage. Her eldest son, James III, looked like her, with his olive complexion, dark hair, and fine dark eyes. Sadly she died when he was eleven, and two years later the other good influence in James's life, Bishop Kennedy, died.

It was then that the Boyd family staged a political coup, seizing the boy king at Linlithgow, and taking him to Edinburgh. There Lord Boyd dispensed with those who had aided him in his endeavor, forced the young king to stand with him, and for the next four years controlled the government. He arranged a marriage for the king with Margaret of Denmark, daughter of King Christian. The union officially brought into Scotland those islands that had been virtually Scots anyway, the Shetlands and the Orkneys. The marriage took place in 1469, and while the king had been deemed by Parliament capable of ruling four years earlier, it wasn't until his marriage that James III took up the reins of government. One of his first acts was to drive the Boyd family from their power base.

But James III was not a man who gloried in martial endeavors or rough ways. He was artistic in temperament, and unsuited to rule over the rough northern land into which he had been born to rule. And Scotland was a lawless country beset by economic troubles. Its nobles were constantly fomenting trouble with the king or with one another. And the powers in England and Europe were always interfering with Scotland's government, and subverting its earls either against the king or against one another.

The king's passions were for the arts. Matters of state interested him but little. He surrounded himself with a group of artists, poets, writers, intellectuals, architects, and craftsmen, even excluding his nobility from his council. Those few nobles who understood something of James III's personality nonetheless resented his attitude. As for those nobles who were less sensitive, they disliked the king and were jealous of his friendships with others. Still, they did not object to his weakness when it came to punishing them for their lawlessness. James was always willing to be bought off for hard coin. It helped him to pay for his extravagances.

Scotland was beset with famine and depression, yet the king did not see it. He collected beautiful jewelry and exquisite manuscripts. He purchased a fine altarpiece by the artist Hugo van der Goes that showed James and Margaret at prayer. The king supported a group of poets, and oversaw the minting of beautiful coinage. He had the great hall at Stirling Castle built by his favorite architect, Robert Cochrane. As James was very particular about his royal prestige, the addition to this castle pleased him greatly. He loved entertaining there once it was finished. And he could not have been more delighted than when the pope elevated St. Andrews from a mere bishopric to an archiepiscopal status in 1472.

All of it, however, meant little to Scotland's nobles. This king with his flair for beautiful clothing and accessories, this royal Stewart who spoke perfect French but knew nothing of the Gaelic language of the Highlands, was an anathema to them. And yet the one area of government in which the king would involve himself was diplomacy. He worked very hard in 1478 to arrange a marriage between his sister, Princess Margaret, and the English king, Edward IV's brother-in-law, Lord Rivers. Unfortunately the match could not go forward, as the princess, who had been having an affair with Lord Crichton, found herself pregnant. And after that the king's reign began to descend into chaos.

Convinced his younger brothers were plotting against him, he ordered them arrested. The elder, the Duke of Albany, escaped. The younger, the Earl of Mar, did not, and died under suspicious circumstances in the king's custody. Their supporters were naturally angered. Albany had fled to England and sought help from Edward IV, who declared him King Alexander IV. The border fighting, usually sporadic, turned into a war, with Richard, Duke of Gloucester, leading the English armies into Scotland accompanied by Albany. James moved to meet his brother, but his nobles turned on him, murdered his favorites, and took him back to Edinburgh a captive. Then, to the complete puzzlement of Richard of Gloucester, Alexander, Duke of Albany, became his older brother's closest adviser and friend. Gloucester returned to England having regained the town of Berwick.

But Albany's about-face was a short one. He had always believed he could be a better king than James. He rebelled a final time against his sibling, joining forces with a Douglas before fleeing to France. The following year he was killed in a tournament accident. Now the nobility turned its eye to the king's eldest son, James, a tall boy with flowing red hair and great charm. Jamie, as his father called him, was equally at home in a rough Highland hall and in his father's great hall. And the ladies adored him. He was the Scots nobility's kind of man, although he was also his father's son. Highly educated, as befitted a Renaissance prince, he spoke several languages, including Gaelic. He was a great athlete. And he was ready to be king. But he was not yet ready to rebel openly against his father. It would have upset his mother, and the boy loved her deeply. The young prince bided his time.

Most of Scotland's quarrels with England over the past few years had taken place on the far east side of the countryside near Berwick, while Stanton, in its remote northwest corner of Northumbria, had not been disturbed. Adair had known little of these wars, for they had never affected her. Now she learned that Cleit was in the borders just to the east and some miles from Stanton. The countryside around them was rough and wild. Adair began to realize that returning to her home was going to be a more difficult task than she had anticipated. Perhaps she would be advised to go to Hillview and seek Robert Lynbridge's help. And she knew she would have to leave Elsbeth behind. Her beloved Nursie could not make the kind of trek Adair would have to make. She would ransom her later on from the laird, and Margery from the wretched Willie Douglas. Conal Bruce could certainly find another older woman to cook for him.

With the addition to the keep of Flora, her son, Jack, and Grizel, there was a need for additional sleeping accommodations. A pallet was found for the boy, and he slept by the fire in the kitchen. Elsbeth shared a bed space with Adair, while Flora and Grizel shared the other. Learning of it, the laird decided that his new servants could make the keep's attic habitable, and quarter there. But Adair would not move.

"Let Flora, young Jack, and Grizel share the attic," she said. "I am content with my bed space here." As she intended making her escape soon, she decided it would be easier to slip out the kitchen door than to have to make her way from the top of the keep.

"Her ladyship likes her privacy," Duncan Armstrong noted, amused. "I thought you would have her in your bed by now, Conal." His blue eyes danced as he wickedly teased his sibling.

"She needs gentling, and that takes patience," the laird told his elder brother.

"I never knew you to have a great deal of patience," Murdoc chimed in, winking at Duncan. "Adair is a fine, spirited woman, big brother. Are you certain you aren't afraid of her? Fergus still has a bump on his head from where she hit him with the pitcher."

His brothers' taunts were irritating, but Conal Bruce wanted Adair to come to him more willing than unwilling. He instinctively sensed that they could give each other a great deal of pleasure if that were the case. He had never been a man to force a woman. He had never needed to resort to force. But Adair was not easy, and she had worked very hard to avoid him since that one time he had found her polishing the table in the hall. He had gone to the kitchen the day after and told her she was to serve the high board only. Grizel would see his men were served.

Today as she poured ale into their goblets he had managed to brush against her hand with his. The great violet eyes had met his, startled. Her cheeks had colored, but she had said nothing. Then she had brought in a bowl of rabbit stew, cheese, and bread. He had ordered her to cut him a slice of bread and cheese, and she had done so. He had thanked her as he took it from her, and their fingers had touched. Adair had bitten her lip, and, seeing it, he smiled at her. She had not returned the smile but rather backed away to wait for his orders, standing behind his chair as she had been told to do.

She would not be his whore, Adair told herself. He couldn't make her. But, of course, he could if he wanted her. And she could see he wanted her. How long until his patience with her ran out? He was handsome. And she wasn't a virgin. What would it matter if she lay with him? A coupling between a man and a woman was nothing special, and often pleasure could be gained by it. And men usually trusted their mistresses. She might even gain his permission to ride out eventually. And it would certainly be easier to find her way back to Stanton a-horse than afoot. But let him yearn for her first. Let him believe he had conquered her resistance and gained a victory. Men liked victory in both war and in love.

Conal Bruce watched Adair as she cleared the board. She was very fair. She was wearing a new garment, a simple gown with no discernible waistline, a square neckline, and long, fitted sleeves. It had been obviously fashioned using her old gown, and was the dress of a lady, not a servant. The color was discreet, a dark red. The boy, Jack, was helping her. He hurried away with the plates and goblets as Adair bent to sweep the crumbs from the high board. He could see the faint swell of her breasts as she worked, her eyes averted from his.

Reaching out with a single finger, he pushed the digit into the valley separating her breasts. "Look at me," he commanded her. The finger was enclosed between the warm flesh. Their eyes met. "How long will you make me wait, Adair?" he asked her quietly.

"My lord"—she found her voice was shaking as she spoke—"I am no whore."

"You are a woman who has known a man," he said low. "How long have you been widowed now? A year? Do you not long for passion again, Adair? Or perhaps your good lord did not know how to give you pleasure. Perhaps he only took it."

"Andrew was a good man," she defended her dead husband.

"I will be good to you too," he promised her, and he withdrew the finger from between her breasts even as he took her hand in his. "Such a little hand, Adair, and it is so cold. Let me warm it for you." He took the hand between his own.

For a brief moment she let herself enjoy the sensation of being seduced, but then she told him, "You are very fortunate to have found me, my lord. I am a lady, as your mother, God assoil her good soul, was." Adair crossed herself piously. "I have restored your household to a semblance of order, and I will keep it that way. You were wise to expend your silver purchasing Elsbeth and me."

"And now I would have value for my coin," he said, amused by her desperate attempt to turn him from his purpose. "I did not buy a housekeeper when I purchased you, and you cannot be so foolish as to believe that I did. And no one else thought it."

"Are you so in need of a woman that you must buy one for your hall?" Adair demanded to know. "I told you that I am no whore."

"Nay, you are not," he agreed. "But you will be my mistress, my honey love. I saw your reaction when I took your hand in mine."

"I do not know what you mean," Adair desperately denied.

"Aye, you do," he said, and he pulled her into his lap.

Adair struggled to rise. "Please, my lord," she whispered. "Do not shame me before the others, I beg you." She could feel tears pricking at the back of her eyelids. She wasn't ready for this. Not yet! Not tonight!

"Be easy, my honey love," he told her. "None other will accost you. They know that you are mine alone." He held her against him, stroking her dark hair. "Put your head on my shoulder, Adair, and let me love you."

She relaxed briefly against him, and his grip on her loosened. Feeling it, Adair pulled away from him and fled the hall and down the stairs into the kitchens.

Duncan Armstrong and Murdoc Bruce burst out laughing, but their mirth was cut short, for the laird arose and followed after Adair. His look was black, his face determined.

"God's blood," Murdoc said low. "He means to have her tonight."

"He's fallen in love with her," Duncan replied softly. "Our brother has fallen in love with his English slave. Only love would drive a man to that kind of madness."

Adair heard him behind her. She practically fell into Elsbeth's arms at the bottom of the stairs. "Nursie!" was all she could say. And then the pair were almost bowled over by the laird as he reached the bottom of the staircase.

Elsbeth immediately grasped the situation. "Now, there, my lord, perhaps this is not the best time for what you want." Her arms tightened about the now sobbing girl. "There, there, my chick. All will be well. Nursie is here for you."

With a smothered oath Conal Bruce stamped back up the stairs.

When she was certain he had gone, Elsbeth set Adair back from her embrace. "Aha, you baggage!" she said. "And what was that all about? As much as it grieves me to say it, sooner or later you must go to his bed."

"I know," Adair answered. "But not tonight. I am not ready yet. Let his desire for me burn hotter and brighter."

"What is this talk?" Elsbeth said, not just a little shocked. "You sound like . . . like . . . I do not know what you sound like, but I do not like it. What mischief are you planning? And do not gainsay me, for I know you too well to be lied to, Adair Radcliffe. You are up to something."

"I am going to make him lust so strongly for me that when I do yield myself to him, he will let me have whatever I want," Adair said.

"And what is it you want?" Elsbeth demanded to know.

"A horse, for when I have one I shall ride back to Stanton," Adair responded.

"Without me," Elsbeth said firmly. "Stanton is gone, child. It is not there anymore for you, or for anyone else. We need a good home, and we have one here at Cleit. Tease the laird. Make him fall in love with you, and then make him wed you. A lady needs a husband, Adair, and the laird has no wife. With the death of our good duke, Richard, and with King Henry's displeasure toward Stanton, England is a closed door for you. You must face that you have no title. No home. No lands any longer."

"I do have Stanton!" Adair declared stubbornly.

"There is no Stanton," Elsbeth replied wearily. "You have nothing anymore but a single gown and a bed space in the kitchens of a border keep. There is no shame in starting again, my chick. Get this fine young border lord to wed you, and be happy. Really happy for the first time in your life," Elsbeth advised.

"You do not understand," Adair said sadly.

"Nay," Elsbeth said, " 'tis you, my chick, who refuses to accept what has happened. Even if you managed to return to where Stanton once was, you would have no house, no cattle, no people. And sooner than later King Henry will give that land to someone he wishes to bind to him. You never heard from Lady Margaret after you returned from court; nor has your sister, the queen, written to you. You know a lady must have influential friends, and you have none, Adair. The life you once lived is over and done with, my child. You must make the best of this new life."

"I am tired," Adair replied. "I want to go to bed." She disappeared into the little chamber with the two bed spaces.

Elsbeth shook her gray head despairingly. She had never thought she would betray Adair, but she was going to warn the laird of Cleit about her mistress's foolish and futile desire to return to where Stanton once stood. Not immediately, because her mistress could suddenly face their situation and change her mind. But if she saw that Adair was going to do something foolish, then she would go to the laird. She had sworn to John and Jane Radcliffe long ago that she would protect their daughter, and she would. She would protect Adair even from herself. Slowly she climbed into her own bed space. Adair was pretending to sleep, although Elsbeth knew very well that she wasn't. She slipped beneath her coverlet, pulling it up over her shoulders, eventually sleeping herself.

But later Adair seemed to have quieted, and Elsbeth considered that she was facing the painful reality of their situation. It was a great relief to believe it, but Elsbeth knew she would have to watch Adair closely, for it was not often she gave up when she had made a decision to do something.

Upstairs in the hall, Conal Bruce sat by his fire with a dram cup of his own potent whiskey in his hand. He was alone, for he had threatened his two brothers with serious injury if they remained. He was not of a mind to be teased further. His male member ached with its need, but he would be damned if he would go and visit Agnes Carr's cottage. He didn't want Agnes's warm and blowsy charms tonight. He wanted Adair. He wanted her mouth, soft and willing. He wanted her body, eager and yielding. Each time she came near he smelled the elusive fragrance of woodbine, and his senses reeled. She had been in his keep for a month now. The days were growing shorter. The nights longer. And he was suddenly lonely.

What the hell was the matter with him? She was his slave. She belonged to him. He had paid Willie Douglas a silver penny for Adair. Not one of King Jamie's black pennies minted from cheap copper, but a real silver penny, full weight. He could order her to his bed. He *should* order her to his bed. She was his! And then he heard Adair's voice in his head: *I am not a whore.* No, she wasn't a whore. She was a lady, and a man needed to woo a lady. Even if she had fallen on hard times and was now his servant. But, of course, the problem with wooing Adair was that his desire for her was already great. And each time she came near his lust rose sharply, pricking him like a spur. He groaned and swallowed the whiskey. They could not go on playing this game.

In the morning Adair brought the small individual trenchers of oat stirabout to the high board. "Elsbeth has put chopped apples and grated some cinnamon into your oats," she told the three brothers. "She says she hopes you like it."

" 'Tis good having a woman back in the kitchens," Duncan Armstrong said, smiling. "And a clean shirt when I want one," he added.

Adair smiled back at him. "A well-ordered household is best," she agreed.

"We've rebuilt the henhouse in the courtyard for Elsbeth," Murdoc said to her.

"I saw when I went to gather eggs this morning," Adair replied. " 'Tis a fine job too, Murdoc." She turned to Conal Bruce. "Do you think, my lord, we might have a milk cow or two? 'Twould be less costly, and if we get a heavy snow it will be difficult to send to the village for our dairy supplies."

"We used to have several milk cows," the laird said. "We ate them after Mam died, for we longed for meat more than milk," he admitted.

"That was because you were all too lazy to hunt," Adair responded. "I would remind you, my lord, that the cold larder is but half-filled. We need it full before the winter sets in, or you will go hungry. Elsbeth can do just so much."

"She is right," Duncan agreed. "We can hunt today, brothers."

"Elsbeth will be very pleased," Adair told them. Then she curtsied and hurried away. She had found a small room off the kitchens where it was obvious that once the lady of the keep had had an apothecary. There was even a small pot of camphor gum on a shelf, along with some other nondescript jars she had not yet inspected. She had been gathering materials for the last few days to make salves, ointments, and elixirs. She planned to begin on that task today. "They're going hunting," she told Elsbeth as she returned from the hall. "I'm going to spend my day making the medicines. Flora, you clear the board, and Grizel will clean the hall today. Jack, fetch me a crock of goose fat from the pantry, and put it on my table in the apothecary."

"Sit down and eat," Elsbeth said. "You've had nothing yet."

The sound of footsteps made them all turn as the laird entered the kitchen. "Elsbeth, give us some bread, meat, and cheese to take with us today. Adair, I would speak with you privily." He took her arm and drew her into the pantry. "I don't want a resistant woman in my bed," he told her. "But I can be patient no longer."

Adair blushed at his candid words, and then she realized her back was against a tall cabinet. She could not flee him now.

He wrapped her single thick braid about his hand, pulling her against him. He ran a finger from his other hand along her lips, the gentle pressure pushing those lips slightly apart. Adair tasted the finger, and, unable to help herself, her violet eyes closed as he rubbed the finger back and forth along her mouth. A little sigh escaped her unbidden. He smiled softly. "You want to be loved, my honey," he murmured against the delicate curl of her ear. "Nay, you are not a whore, but you are a woman." He drew the finger away, and his lips met hers in a gentle but fierce kiss. "You want to be loved," he repeated. "Tell me that I lie, Adair. That you have no curiosity to know what it would be like to be loved by me, to lie naked in my arms and find pleasure."

"You are cruel, my lord," she whispered back to him.

"You torment me, my honey love," he said low. "I need you in my bed."

"Do you not have a cotter's woman to serve your lusts?" Adair asked him.

"I want none but you." He groaned, and his hand found the swell of her breast beneath her gown. Fingers kneaded the tender flesh.

Adair whimpered softly as a thrill of excitement shot through her. His hand was gentle on her breast, yet his touch aroused her in a way she had never before been stirred. She could not deny him, though her arms hung at her sides, unrestrained.

"Such a sweet little breast," he murmured. "I would see it uncovered and as God fashioned it, my honey love."

"Please," she pleaded with him. "They are all in the kitchen, my lord."

"Tonight you will sit in my lap by the fire, and I will kiss you, and I will caress you, Adair. And you will not be afraid of me, will you?" He released his hold on her breast and on her braid.

"You do not fool me, my lord," Adair said. Her courage was returning now that he was not so close. "You will take me to your bed tonight because you desire me, and you own my person. But before I let you have my person, there is something I would have of you, my lord. I will not lie with a dirty man. When you return from the hunt and have had your dinner, I will bathe you and wash your hair. And the bed we lie on will be fresh and smell as sweet as you will, for I will see to it today."

"I had a bath two months ago," he said. "In the stream at the foot of the keep."

"Did you use soap?" she asked him, pushing him back from her.

"Soap? We were swimming," he exclaimed.

"Then you were not bathing," Adair said implacably. "Tonight I will wash you in hot water, and we will use soap, my lord. And I will have a brush."

"Conal, where are you?" Duncan Armstrong stuck his head into the pantry. "We're ready to go." He looked quizzically at his brother.

"Are we agreed, my lord?" Adair demanded to know, looking up into his face. He had gray eyes. Stormy gray eyes.

"Must we use soap?" he wanted to know.

She nodded. "Aye."

He nodded. "I have never been a man to avoid a challenge, Adair," he told her. And then, turning, he was gone with his brother.

"What was that all about?" Elsbeth wanted to know. They were alone.

"He cannot be deterred from bedding me, Nursie, but before he does I will give him a bath," Adair told the older woman.

Elsbeth laughed. "You will make a gentleman out of him, my chick," she said.

"Nay." Adair shook her head. "He will never be a gentleman, but if he would be my lover he will at least be clean. And in a few days I will have my horse," she said triumphantly. "The winter is almost here, Nursie, and I must reach Stanton before the snows. Tomorrow is All Hallow's Eve. I will be gone by Martinmas."

Elsbeth did not argue. It was useless to argue this matter with Adair, but she would not allow her mistress to deliberately walk into danger. "I'll have Grizel clean the laird's bechamber," she said.

"We'll air the mattress, and the feather bed too," Adair answered. "And there must be fresh sheets. And when that is done Jack can take the bathtub up to the laird's chamber. We'll fill it after supper, before I wash him."

Just as the sun was setting Conal Bruce, his brothers, and their men returned home. They had killed a stag, which they would take a day or two to dress before hanging it in the cold larder. They had several strings of grouse, ducks, and rabbits, as well as three geese and a pheasant. Elsbeth praised them mightily, and then served them a dinner of roasted beef, broiled trout, and fine October ale. When she brought out a dish of pears poached in wine, and some sugar wafers, the brothers were ecstatic.

"Ah, Mistress Elsbeth, will you marry me?" Duncan Armstrong asked her with a mischievous grin as he slipped an arm about her ample waist.

Elsbeth cackled. "You wouldn't be able to keep up with me, Master Duncan," she told him, slapping the arm away. "I am a one-man woman, and my man is gone." She bustled off back to her kitchens, where Adair was sitting with Flora, Grizel, and Jack. "They're almost done with the meal," she said. "Go up to the hall now, my chick."

Without a word Adair arose and left the kitchens.

"So she's come to an arrangement with him then?" Grizel said.

"There's many a woman who would be happy to be in the laird's bed," Flora remarked. "They say Agnes Carr has tried to handfast with him."

"Agnes is a whore," Grizel replied bluntly. "A good-hearted lass, I'll give you, but a whore. There isn't a man for twenty miles around who hasn't traveled the road between her legs now and again."

"The laird needs a wife," Elsbeth said.

"Aye," Grizel agreed. "He does. If your lady can bind him, Elsbeth, then good luck to her, say I. She's been wed before?"

"Twice," Elsbeth said.

"And no bairns?" Grizel asked.

Elsbeth shook her head. "The first was a lad of fourteen. The marriage was a proxy one, and he appeared with her uncle one day. He never bedded her, and was killed in an accident before any damage was done." Elsbeth thought it best not to say that poor FitzTudor had been killed by Scots borderers.

"And the second?" Grizel prodded.

"The son of a neighbor. 'Twas a good match, but he was killed with King Richard at Bosworth. She bemoaned the lack of a bairn, but perhaps 'tis better, given what has happened to her," Elsbeth said.

Grizel nodded. "Aye. The raiders who took you would have killed the bairn, for they have no use for them. 'Tis a mercy, actually, for to steal the mam and leave the bairn would cause its death anyway. At least your lady has not that sorrow to suffer. 'Twas Willie Douglas who took you, wasn't it?"

"Aye," Elsbeth answered.

"He has a black heart," Grizel said.

"He kept my sister for his wife," Elsbeth replied.

"His wife is a poor, frail mouse of a creature, but he loves her, they say. If your sister is strong she'll be safe," Grizel responded.

"Margery will cut his throat given the opportunity," Elsbeth said.

Grizel laughed. " 'Twould be a service to us all if she did," she answered. "Did he rape your mistress? He always fucks the pretty ones."

"He tried," Elsbeth said, "and she fought and cursed him so fiercely that his manhood shriveled up to nothing. He was furious, so he beat her instead."

"Poor lass," Grizel said. "It really shriveled up?"

"You couldn't even see it at all," Elsbeth said. "He would have killed my chick had not one of his men reminded him that she would bring more unscathed. He's a man who seems to like his silver. Go up now, you two, and clear the rest of the board for me. Jack, my lad, bring in more wood for the night. And tomorrow you must chop."

The two serving women went up to the hall and cleared away the remaining cups and plates. Looking about, they saw the laird, his brothers, and Adair by the fire talking. Seeing Grizel and Flora, Adair called them over and asked them to have enough hot water heated for the laird's bath. When Duncan and Murdoc began to laugh she sweetly told them they would be hauling the water for the bath up to the laird's bedchamber, and as there was hot water already waiting they might as well begin now.

Now it was Conal Bruce who laughed at the look of surprise on his siblings' faces. "Go along, laddies. I am more than ready to be washed by my fair lassie. We'll just wait here by the fire until you have all in readiness."

"You give as good as you get," Adair noted as the two brothers left them.

"I do," he said meaningfully. "Do you?"

"Aye," she told him. "You did well today. The cold larder is almost full now. Another deer or two; a few more braces of fowl, and we will be ready. Elsbeth would visit the village and see if she can purchase some hams once the pigs have been slaughtered, my lord."

"There are few of those nowadays," the laird told her, "but let her go and see what she can find. Scotland grows poorer by the day."

"Why?" Adair asked him. "England is not poor."

"Trade brings wealth, and we have little to trade with the rest of the world," he said. "And the king is more interested in spending the monies in the royal treasury on jewels to adorn himself, and on works of art. A man cannot eat art or jewelry. He is a weak king, is our Jamie. Scotland needs a strong king."

"How long has he been king?" Adair asked.

"Since he was barely out of leading strings," the laird said. "The best thing about him is the queen. She is a fine lady, a good and pious woman. She's given Scotland four fine princes and two princesses. She is a woman who knows her duty. A pity her husband does not. I am not an important man, but even here in the borders we hear rumors that the earls are not happy."

"Will there be a war?" Adair asked. She hated war. Her life had been ruled by war. Was there no place where peace reigned?

"Perhaps, but 'tis not likely to last long. Either the king will win or his opponents will win. Compromises will be made, of course. The young prince will make Scotland a fine king one day. But why would you be interested in such things, my honey love? You were made for loving, and not for weighty subjects."

"My lord, I spent ten years in the royal court of King Edward,"

Adair answered. "I was surrounded by such *weighty* subjects. I listened and I watched. 'Twas only prudent, for I might have been married into an important family one day. My knowledge would have been considered valuable. One needs important friends and influence to get ahead at the court. As the king's brat, and with a title in my own right, I had some small value to my natural father. Sadly, he did not use that value wisely, but then, he was always a greedy man. He had a lust for life like no one I have ever met."

He was surprised by her knowledge and her observations, and perhaps a little taken aback by them. But then he concentrated on her beauty, and everything else faded away for Conal Bruce, the laird of Cleit. And while they spoke his brothers and the two serving women trekked back and forth from the kitchens through the hall and up to his bedchamber, each carrying two buckets of water with every trip they made.

Finally Grizel came over to Adair. "The tub is full," she said.

"Are there two full buckets by it for rinsing?" Adair asked.

"Elsbeth told us," Grizel said.

Adair stood up. " 'Tis time, my lord, for your bath."

Duncan and Murdoc snickered behind her.

Conal Bruce glowered at them.

"Grizel," Adair said. "Come with me, for you will have to take the laird's garments. Give them to Elsbeth. Is there a nightshirt for him?"

"I don't sleep in a damned nightshirt!" the laird exploded, and Grizel and Flora jumped nervously at his tone.

"Neither do I," Adair said calmly. Then she took his hand. "Come along, my lord." And she led him from the hall, followed by Grizel.

Flora fled to the kitchens before the two men might remember she was there.

In his bedchamber Adair removed the laird's worn boots. "See if you can bring some life back into these," she told Grizel. She yanked the coverings from his feet. "Burn them," she said. "They are rotted and they stink. Stand up again, my lord."

He was fascinated by her efficiency. She stripped his clothing off quickly, handing each piece to Grizel with a pertinent comment.

"This can be cleaned. Wash these. Burn that. This needs mending. If he doesn't have another shirt, can one of you do it before morning? And if he does have another shirt, see that it is clean and in good repair. I can see we will have to do some sewing. Get into the tub, my lord. You don't want the water to get cold."

He climbed in and sat down, his knees sticking up awkwardly.

Grizel took his clothing and departed the room.

Kneeling by the tub, Adair took up a small piece of cloth, dipped it in the hot water, rubbed soap lavishly over it, and began the task of scrubbing him. "I could not find a brush for the bath," she told him as she rubbed the soapy cloth over his broad shoulders and long back, washing, rinsing, washing, rinsing. "Your neck is filthy," she noted, and she scrubbed so hard that he yelped in protest.

"Are you trying to take the skin off of me, woman?" he demanded of her.

"I wouldn't have to scrub so hard if you weren't so dirty, and if I had a brush," she told him as she attacked his ears. "Can you remember the last time you used soap, my lord? Probably not since your good mother died. Shame on you! I know she raised you better, for your brothers have genteel manners."

His chest was lightly covered in dark hair. Andrew's chest had been smooth. Adair washed the laird's chest and his arms silently. He lifted a foot up, and she washed it, pushing the cloth in between each toe. He had very big feet, but then, he was a big man. She washed the other foot. The nails on both his hands and feet needed paring, and she would see to it before he got into bed with her. Next she attacked his dark hair, her fingers digging into his scalp to loosen the nits he certainly had living there. He protested again, and in reply she poured half a bucket of warm water over his head. Then she washed his head a second time, and rinsed it.

"I'm starting to smell like a damned flower," he complained. He reached out to grab her, but Adair slapped his hands away.

"You smell far better now than when you got into this tub," she told him. "Stand up, my lord. I am not finished yet." Adair stood up as Conal Bruce lumbered to his feet. She washed his buttocks, which were tight and round, and the backs of his legs, which were firm. "Turn about," she said sharply, and plied her cloth down the front of his long legs, which, like his chest, were lightly furred, and over his flat torso. She wanted to avert her gaze from his manroot, but it was impossible. Gritting her teeth, Adair quickly washed his genitals. "There," she said brusquely. "You're done. You can get out now."

He stepped out onto the bit of cloth she had spread on the floor for him, taking the drying cloth she held out to him. Slowly, carefully, he dried himself off, and then, wrapping the fabric about his waist, he went to his bedchamber door, opened it, and called out, "Duncan! Murdoc! To me!" And his brothers ran up the stairs from the hall. "Take this damned tub back to the kitchens," he told them. "Empty it first out the window. And keep your randy eyes in your heads," he warned them, for he saw them stealing looks at Adair in her chemise as she knelt to pare his toenails and fingernails.

Duncan and Murdoc lifted the tub by its rope pulls and, going to the window, Murdoc pulled it open as Duncan struggled to hold the tub. Then they dumped it over the sill, the water splashing on the rocks below. The two brothers quickly closed the shutters, and then as quickly departed the bedchamber. Turning, Adair saw the laird turning the key in the lock of the door. Her heart began to hammer against her ribs.

Conal Bruce set the door key on the table by the bed. "Now, Adair, as I have kept my promise, and you have thoroughly washed me, you must keep your promise. Take off your chemise and let me see you."

Wordlessly she drew the sodden garment off and carefully spread it over the chair by the blazing hearth. Then she faced him, meeting his gaze, for she would not show any fear. She stood tall, and while he let his eyes wander slowly over her body she reached up and, undoing her braid, loosed her long black hair, tossing her head as she did.

" 'Tis a good thing Willie Douglas did not see you like this," the laird said. "You are worth far more than a silver penny, my honey love." He smiled a slow smile at her, and held out his hand. "Come here to me, Adair."

Her legs felt heavy. She was surprised that she could move at all, but she walked across the chamber to him, shivering slightly as he drew her into his arms. A hand stroked her hair, following the line of it from the top of her head to the small of her back. The touch of his body against hers was startling. It had been a long while since she had felt such a sensation, and the soft curls on his chest tickled her. His hands cupped her buttocks and brought her hard against him. Adair gasped with shock that this new and closer contact with him brought her.

"If not now, when?" he demanded of her, looking down into her face.

"I . . . I don't know," she whispered, unable to take her eyes from his.

"Then now, honey love," he told her as his mouth met hers in a torrid kiss.

To her surprise Adair almost swooned as his strong arms wrapped about her and his lips teased at hers. She was awash in the sensations that were overwhelming her. Her lips softened against his, letting his tongue gain entry into her mouth. Andrew had never kissed her like this. There was a fierceness in the laird's kisses. Andrew had always been gentle with her, as if she would shatter if he were not. But Conal Bruce, while not rough, was hardly gentle. He demanded, and, to her surprise, Adair found herself giving in to those unspoken demands.

He took her face between his two hands and kissed her closed eyelids, her forehead, her cheeks. "This is different for me," he said, sounding surprised. "It is not like it is with Agnes Carr. With Agnes I want to hurry my satisfaction. With you I want to take my time, honey love, because I don't think I want it to ever end." He caught up one of her hands and pressed a hot kiss on the palm. Then he led her to his bed.

Adair had to admit she found herself a bit confused. With Andrew the lovemaking had been tender, yet she had never felt the emotions inside of her that she now felt building. "It is not the same with every woman?" she asked him softly as he laid her down upon her back.

"Nay, 'tis not," he told her, smiling. "Nor, I am told, is it the same with every man. Or so says Agnes Carr, who has known more than her share of the lads." The laird kissed Adair's lips lightly.

"Oh." So with each man it was different, or it was supposed to be. Andrew had promised her pleasure after their wedding night, but Adair had never really felt any. She had lied to him, of course, and told him she had, because the fault was surely hers and not his. Perhaps if she had been able to give him a child it would have been different. She had not found his husbandly attentions unpleasant, but she had felt nothing like he obviously felt as he labored and groaned over her body. And each time when he had finished he would kiss her, roll over, and sleep while Adair lay in the darkness and wondered why there was no pleasure. She had been afraid to ask him.

Now suddenly this rough Scotsman was touching her body with his big hands, and Adair was being assailed by feelings such as she had never before known. His mouth pressed into the hollow of her throat, and the sound he made sounded very much like a beast growling. He licked the graceful column of her neck with a wet, hot tongue, and Adair felt a quivering beginning deep within her. The greedy mouth closed over a nipple, suckling hard, while his fingers kneaded her other breast. She whimpered with a growing need she didn't even understand. The burning tongue began a slow exploration of her torso, and her breath came in short, quick bursts as his tongue pushed into the cavity of her navel.

The softness of her skin, the faint fragrance rising from her warm body set his senses awhirl with his growing desire. Her plump mons was pink and devoid of hair. The faintly shadowed slit dividing it excited him. He ran his tongue along it, dipping between the flesh to taste her rising juices. He moved himself so he might part the two halves, and there nestled amid the moistness was her love bud. He began a delicate exploration of it with the pointed tip of his tongue.

Adair cried out with her surprise. Andrew had never done that, and yet she didn't want the laird to cease his actions, which were exciting her more than she had ever before been excited. "Oh, yes!" she heard herself say, and she blushed.

He lifted his dark head. "It pleases you, my honey love?"

"*Yes!*" she managed to gasp as her head began to spin.

For a little while longer he flicked his tongue over and around the sensitive nub, but then, his own need rising, he stopped, kissing her mouth to still her protest as he mounted her body beneath him and drove himself into the hot moisture of her sheath. She was tight at first, but then her body yielded to his manhood.

Adair caught her breath sharply as she felt his entry. He was bigger than Andrew had been, and she was surprised at how easily she took him in. He stopped when he was fully sheathed, and she could sense him looking down into her face.

"Open your eyes, Adair," he growled. "I want to see the pleasure rising in your beautiful violet eyes, my honey love."

"Nay," she half whispered. "I have never known the pleasure men speak of, my lord. If I disappoint you, you will surely send me back to Douglas. I would kill myself first!" All thought of Stanton had suddenly fled from her mind.

"Your husband gave no pleasure? Was he cruel?" the laird wanted to know.

"Nay, never! Andrew was gentle and kind. I pretended for him because I could not bear for him to know," she confessed.

"Ah, my honey love, I have already given you a little pleasure adoring your little love bud. Your juices began to flow, which eased my passage within you. Trust me, and I will give you real pleasure," Conal Bruce promised her.

"I am afraid," Adair said.

He laughed. "Nay, not you. You're a lass who does not know fear, Adair Radcliffe. You are anxious, but afraid? Nay! Now open your eyes and trust me."

Slowly she opened her eyes, and his own locked upon her as he began to move slowly at first, and then with increasing rapidity within her. Unbidden she wrapped her legs about his torso. It seemed as if her body was suddenly acutely attuned to his. She sensed the length and thickness of him. She savored the heaviness of his seed sac as it slapped against her bottom. And then suddenly something was happening to her. Adair felt as if she were about to burst into flames with the heat that suffused both her body and mind. Her head spun, and then the wave overtook her. She cried out as the intense pleasure rose up to take control of her body and soul. She heard him groan. His body stiffened, and then through the sweet haze surrounding her she felt his juices filling her. And somewhere in their passion her eyes had closed once again.

For some minutes only the sound of exhausted breathing could be heard within the bedchamber. His weight on her was heavy, but she was so worn with their exertions that she could not move. Finally he rolled off of her, but then he gathered her back into his arms so that she lay atop him. Her heart-shaped face was pressed into the curve between his shoulder and his neck. He felt the soft puffs of her breath on his skin. He did not have to ask. He knew that she had felt her first real pleasure in the arms of a man. And Conal Bruce had to admit to himself that he had felt the kind of pleasure with Adair that he had never before known in the arms of any woman. "I'll not be sending you back to Willie Douglas," he told her softly. "From this day forward I am the only man you will ever know, my sweet honey love. And you'll not sleep in the kitchens any longer, Adair. You will sleep in my bed, because you belong in it—and to me."

"You have had your way with me," she replied, her voice shaking slightly. "Let me go now, my lord."

"Nay," he said. "You are mine."

"Nay," she told him. "Your silver cannot buy my heart. Only I can give you that."

"I don't want your heart," he told her cruelly. "I want all of your body, and my silver has bought me that, Adair. You are mine. I will never let you go!"

"I am just a body to you then?" she cried. Well, what else had she expected? Adair asked herself. Love? She had seen little of that between a man and a woman in her lifetime. Of all those she had known, only Richard of Gloucester had had a deep and abiding love for his wife, Anne. There had been no others, and she was a fool, she decided, to bring love into the picture. She was the laird's new mistress now. Naught else. He had made her the whore she had sworn never to be.

"Aye," he agreed. "But that body pleases me as no other ever has. And you cannot deny that what you felt in my arms you have never felt with another. Now go to sleep, my honey love. When my strength has been restored with a bit of rest I will want to taste your sweet charms again. This night is not yet ended." And, reaching out, he drew the coverlet up over them.

Adair bit her lip. She would not weep. She would not!

Chapter 11

When Adair awoke after the long night she was lying on her belly, and the laird's arm was over her. Slowly she turned over. There was the faintest light showing through a narrow crack in the shutters. She had to get up and go to the kitchens. Elsbeth would already be preparing the morning meal. Gingerly Adair attempted to escape the arm confining her, but it suddenly tightened.

"Where are you going?" he growled at her.

"It is almost dawn," Adair told him. "I have to get to the kitchens, my lord."

"Not yet," he said. "I want more!" And he was atop her.

"Is your lust not yet quenched?" Adair demanded to know. "Three times we coupled in the night. I hardly had a moment's rest satisfying your needs. I must get to the kitchens. Do you imagine Elsbeth can do what she does all alone?" *Dear heaven!* She could feel his manroot already hard with his cravings.

"Elsbeth has the others. I have you," he said, his knee pushing her thighs apart. "I would rather have you for my breakfast than a trencher of porridge, my honey love."

"I must go," Adair insisted. "I have my duties to perform."

"Your first duty is to me, and you are very ready, I can see," he murmured in her tangled hair, the tip of his manhood pushing into her. "You are hot and wet, and you want me every bit as much as I want you, even though you will deny it." He slipped deep into her. "Don't you, my honey love?"

"No!" she said stubbornly. How could he know? How could he be so infuriatingly knowing? She could feel him throbbing within her. "No!"

"Aye, you little liar," he half laughed as he slowly withdrew, and heard her little whimper of protest. "Say you want me, Adair!"

"No!" she insisted. But she did want him. She wanted him deep within her, making her explode with those wonderful sensations he had made her feel thrice last night. "Let me go, you great Scots ape!" Her balled fists beat a tattoo on his chest.

"Enough, woman!" he roared at her. And then he began to move on her, his manroot pushing deep, withdrawing slowly over and over and over until the woman beneath him was sobbing with the pleasure that they were both experiencing.

She was being a little fool, Adair thought. He wanted her. She wanted him. Why was she acting like a silly girl? The fiery intensity was beginning to blaze within her. "Yes, damn you, I want you!" she cried, and then she soared as her crisis overtook her.

Her surrender forced him sooner than he would have wanted. He felt himself being drained by her hungry maw. No woman had ever weakened him like this. He groaned and, barely satisfied, rolled off of her. He could hardly keep his eyes open, and fell back asleep before he knew what was happening to him.

When he began to snore lightly Adair crawled from the tumbled bed. The extra bucket of water, cold now, was still on the ledge by the hearth. She picked the little washrag up and cleansed herself of his juices. She took up her chemise from the chair by the fire. It was dry now, and warm. She donned it, and then pulled her green gown over it. Her footwear was in her bed space. Adding two small logs to the fire so it would not go out, Adair slipped quietly from the chamber and down the stairs.

Grizel was already in the hall, adding fuel to the hearth and lighting the candles. She nodded as Adair hurried past. In the kitchens Jack was bringing in the wood for the day. Elsbeth already had her kettle of porridge cooking, and Flora was eating her breakfast at the table. Adair went into the little alcove where her bed space was located, and found her shoes. Putting them on, she ran her fingers through her hair until all the tangles were out, and then rebraided the heavy mass into a single thick plait.

"Come and eat," Elsbeth called to her as Adair reentered the kitchen. She plunked a small bread trencher full of cooked oats before the young woman. "I can see he's as vigorous a man as he would appear to be." Then she chuckled.

Adair glared at Elsbeth, but said nothing. She reached for the pitcher of cream, and splashed some onto the hot porridge. Then she began to eat. She was just beginning to realize that she felt sore all over. She had been well used by the laird, and if she were honest with herself she had to admit that after her initial shyness she had enjoyed his lusty attentions very much.

But it puzzled her that the bed sport with her dead husband had never been as satisfying. Adair sighed. If she were honest with herself she had to admit her relations with her husband had been downright dull. She had been fond of Andrew. She had even convinced herself that she loved him. He was fair to look upon, kind, and thoughtful of her. But never in all the time they had been married had he once roused her senses to the fever pitch that Conal Bruce did last night. Not once. Not twice. But four times! She had not realized that a man could perform so lustily and so often in so short a period of time. She put her spoon in her mouth and was surprised to find it devoid of oats. She had already scraped the trencher clean.

Seeing her bemusement Elsbeth slapped a thick slice of warm bread dripping with butter and honey before Adair. "You look fair worn," Elsbeth remarked.

"I did not get a great deal of rest," Adair admitted wryly as she ate the bread. But then suddenly she jumped up. "Oh, lord! The laird has no clothes to wear!"

"Sit down," Elsbeth said. "Flora has taken him up his garments. You had best get to work making him some shirts. He has but two. 'Twould be a good task to start today. Grizel and Flora can serve the hall this morning."

When the laird came down from his chamber Adair was nowhere in sight. The two other serving women were busily bringing the meal to the high board, where his two brothers were already seated. Conal Bruce joined them.

"Now where are those flowers hiding?" Duncan Armstrong asked, sniffing loudly.

The laird swatted at him, and his siblings burst into raucous laughter.

"You have the look of a man well satisfied," Duncan continued. "Was she worth the silver penny you expended to get her out of Willie Douglas's clutches?"

Conal Bruce grinned. "Aye. She's probably worth half a groat at least," he said.

"How many times?" Murdoc boldly asked.

"Four, and I was ready for her again but that when I awoke she had gone," the laird said. "Have either of you seen Adair this morning?"

The two shook their heads.

"Agnes Carr would be jealous," Duncan remarked. "I doubt you ever stuck her four times in a night. I don't think I've ever done it that much myself," he mused.

"You will when it's the right woman," the laird said, chuckling.

"Four times," young Murdoc said enviously. "I didn't know a man could do it that much at one time." Murdoc was sixteen.

His brothers laughed at his observance.

"You will one day, youngling," the laird promised. "Grizel, where is Adair?"

"In the kitchens, my lord," Grizel said.

"Tell her I want to see her," the laird replied.

Duncan and Murdoc eyed each other knowingly, and chortled.

"Yes, my lord." Grizel curtsied, and disappeared from the hall. She returned some minutes later to say, "Mistress Adair begs you will excuse her for now, my lord. She is cutting several new shirts for you, and does not wish to stop in the middle of the task, for it would be difficult to begin again."

"You will return to Adair and say that when the laird calls her she is to come with all possible haste," Conal Bruce told the serving woman.

Grizel curtsied again, and left the hall.

"The lass is sewing you new garments," Duncan said. "Can you not be a bit more reasonable, Conal? 'Tis a thoughtful act. She saw your need and sought to fulfill it."

"Aye, Conal," Murdoc agreed. "I wish she would sew some shirts for me."

"She has to learn that I am her master," the laird said stubbornly. "Remember I paid a silver penny for her."

"I would say taking your mighty cock four times in a single night was more than repayment, Conal. She has worked hard to restore a sense of order to our home. It has not looked as good or been run as well since our mam died."

"She is mine!" the laird replied.

"No one denies that," Duncan answered. "But she's a lady, Conal, for all her hard luck, not a common whore."

"Nay, sir, I am no common whore. I am the Bruce's whore," Adair said as she joined them. She turned a fierce look on the laird. "What do you desire of me, my lord?"

"That when I call you, you come," he said testily.

"I have other chores than to serve in your bed, my lord," Adair answered sharply. "Your clothing, the garments of your brothers, all need refurbishing. And the cold larder is not yet full for the winter, which is nearer today than it was yesterday. Today I will sew for you, and you will hunt again for the keep's sake. If it pleases you, of course, my lord." She mocked him with a curtsy, her violet eyes flashing with defiance.

"Come sit in my lap," the laird said.

Duncan and Murdoc looked at each other warily, but then to their surprise, and after only the briefest hesitation, Adair sat down in the laird's lap.

"Good," Conal Bruce purred. "You are becoming more obedient."

Adair bit back a pithy reply. The sooner he believed himself in charge, the sooner she could get about her tasks for the day.

"Now you will kiss me," the laird ordered her.

She gave him a quick peck on the lips.

" 'Twas not well-done," he told her. "Again, my honey love."

The look she shot him would have destroyed another man, but then she kissed him hard on his mouth, lingering just long enough to elicit a whistle of approval from Duncan.

" 'Tis better," the laird allowed, "but not yet good enough. Again, Adair."

Adair slipped her arms about his neck now, and pressed herself against him. Her lips met his in a slow, sweet kiss. "Ummmm," she murmured against his mouth as she rubbed herself suggestively against him, and she kissed him again, her tongue pushing into his mouth to tease his. She sighed a deep sigh, and kissed him a third time in leisurely fashion. Finally drawing away from him, she asked softly, "Is that better, my lord?"

"Aye," he drawled, nodding at her.

"Then," Adair said, jumping from his lap, "I shall return to my sewing." She curtsied. "Good hunting, my lord." And, turning, she was quickly gone.

Duncan Armstrong and Murdoc Bruce had stared openmouthed and not without some envy at Adair's wicked performance. Their brother sat silent, his need bulging in his breeks for them to see. Briefly Conal Bruce was without words. It was Duncan who finally broke the strain of the situation.

"What a lass!" he said admiringly.

"Maggie doesn't kiss me like that," Murdoc complained.

"No one that I know kisses like that," Duncan responded.

"I will probably end up killing her," Conal Bruce said, finding his voice once more. "We all know that women are good for cooking, cleaning, birthing bairns, and fucking, but little else. Adair has be-witched me. I can't seem to get enough of her, and I am half-ashamed to admit it. No woman has ever affected me this way. And she takes as much pleasure in our coupling as I do. Yet each time I have her, I want more of her almost immediately. 'Tis madness, brothers. Right now I want to drag her from the kitchens and take her back to bed for the day. But I know she's right. The damned cold larder needs to be completely filled before the winter comes. When we were out yester-day I saw the bens to the north already white with new snow." His member, which had ached painfully, did not ache as much now. He stood up, wincing just slightly. "Let's go hunting, lads." The laird of Cleit strode from his hall.

"Something is happening," Duncan said. "Something I never thought to see."

"What?" Murdoc wanted to know.

"Not yet, youngling," his elder told him, putting an arm about his youngest brother as they walked from the hall in Conal's wake. "And who is Maggie?"

Grizel slipped from the shadows where she had been listening. She hurried down the stone stairs into the kitchens. "They've finally gone," she announced.

Adair looked up relieved from the table, where she was cutting shirts from some fine linen she had found in the laird's deceased mother's chamber. "Good," she said. "With luck I can have a new shirt for each of them when they return tonight."

"I'll help you sew when I've finished my chores," Flora volunteered.

When the hunters returned shortly after sunset that evening with two roe deer and a string of geese, they found three shirts carefully folded, with one set at each of their places at the high board. Surprised, they took the shirts, unfolding them and holding them out, and then against their own frames.

"There's one for each of us!" Murdoc said excitedly. "Let's try them on!"

"Not yet," they heard Adair's voice say as she rose from a chair by the fire. "You have not yet had your baths, Master Murdoc and Master Duncan. You cannot wear clean shirts on a stinking body. The tub awaits you in the kitchens."

The laird roared with his laughter at the looks on their faces.

"Oh, you as well, my lord," Adair said sweetly, and his laughter died.

"I washed yesterday," the laird protested. "You practically scrubbed the skin from me," he complained.

"Do you wish to bed me again tonight, my lord?" Adair asked him. "I will not get into bed with a man reeking of his own sweat and that of his horse. And if you think to force me, be advised that after I finished these shirts I spent my time exploring your fine keep. There are half a dozen places I could hide, and you would not find me."

"I never knew English ladies had such delicate sensibilities," he grumbled.

"You'll need the least washing," she said dulcetly.

The three men followed her downstairs to the kitchens, where the tub had been set up. The women servants stripped them of their garments, and each man washed himself under Adair's direction. Since women's duties included helping to bathe the men in the household, neither the laird, his brothers, nor the serving women were embarrassed by the nudity. The men joked, remembering how their mother would supervise their ablutions. When they were dry they were handed clean chemises and their new shirts, and given back their breeks, which young Jack had brushed and aired while they bathed.

"You'll have to go barefoot," Adair told them. "Jack will clean your boots for you tonight. Now, if you'll go back upstairs to the hall we'll be bringing your supper up shortly." She shooed them from the kitchens.

"She's getting above herself, and taking over my keep," Conal Bruce said.

"Thank God she is," Duncan said. "Since Mam died everything has gone from bad to worse. But Adair knows how to run a man's household, and I'm glad for it. You should be too, Conal. You may want her on her back pleasuring you, but I'm happy to have a clean hall, decent clothing, and good meals. So you be content with the Adair you want, and I'll be content with the one who does all the rest to keep this house a civilized one. I suspect Murdoc would agree with me, eh, youngling?"

"Aye, I do," Murdoc Bruce replied. "Adair's a good woman, Conal. You had best treat her well or you will face me."

"Jesu!" the laird swore, disgusted. "What a pair of precious bairns you two are."

Duncan laughed at the insult. "Do you want to go back to burned porridge and a flea-ridden hall? We're living like fine lords now. And do you notice that the men are no longer fighting all the time? In a few weeks' time Adair has brought order to Cleit that you couldn't. The women civilize us."

"Until one of them gets a big belly," Conal Bruce grumbled.

"The only one that is likely to happen to is Adair if you keep futtering her four times a night," Duncan mocked. "No one is going to chase after Elsbeth or Grizel. And young Jack watches over his mother like a dog with a favorite ewe sheep."

"I'll admit 'tis better now with a small household of women," the laird said. "I like my porridge with grated cinnamon, and a warm wench in my bed."

"Then go gently with Adair, little brother," Duncan Armstrong said.

"You had best tell her to go gently with me," Conal Bruce replied. "She is not easy. And she has a temper on her. I own her. I paid good coin for her. She is my slave, yet she behaves as if this were her home, and not mine. I never knew a more disobedient creature than Adair Radcliffe. I'm amazed Willie Douglas was able to catch her at all."

His two brothers laughed at this.

The serving women began bringing in the evening meal, and the three men went to the high board, while below them the keep's men at arms sat at their trestles, eager for their supper. Meals were now a good time at Cleit. Even the dogs in the hall were being fed better. One young wolfhound had, Conal Bruce noted, attached itself to Adair. At first she had not paid any mind to the animal, but he had persisted, and she had given in. Her face when she talked with the animal was entirely different from the face she usually wore. It was softer and sweeter.

One day the laird took Elsbeth aside. "Your mistress has made friends with one of the dogs in the hall," he said casually.

"The wolfhound," Elsbeth said. "I know. She had one at Stanton. He was very old and frail. His name was Beiste, and he had been with her since she was a child. That blackhearted Douglas killed the poor animal when it attempted to protect Adair. Severed its noble head before her eyes. She wept for days after. Beiste was really all she had left."

"Thank you," Conal Bruce said.

The winter had slipped in suddenly a bit early. Adair had been taken as much by surprise as the others, and swore angrily to herself now that her opportunity to escape Cleit was gone for the interim. Oddly, she was finding herself happy, although she would never admit it. And she was coming to like Cleit. She was also not ready yet to admit that Elsbeth was right. Stanton was gone. Her life as the Countess of Stanton was gone. But if it really was gone, what was to become of her? Elsbeth had said, and Grizel and Flora agreed, that she had to get the laird to wed her. All well and good for them to say, Adair thought. Conal Bruce was a rough man with no real respect for women at all. How could she overcome that? All he thought about was gratifying his lusts. He made her think of her father, whose appetites were never quite satisfied. But of course, he was not Edward IV, with his charm and his way with all people no matter their station. Conal Bruce was a rough-hewn Scots borderer, and she doubted she could ever raise him up from his primitive behavior.

She was noble-born. A king's daughter, albeit from the wrong side of the blanket. Still, it did not lessen her blood or breeding. It had allowed her to inherit a title in her own right, for all the good that did her now. Henry of Lancaster had stripped her of her title. Had scorned her mother while carefully avoiding the subject of her father, which would, of course, have given insult to his wife, who was sired by the same man. And now, despite everything she had been through, she was brought low. A slave, bought and paid for by a crude border lord who thought her only value lay between her legs.

Briefly she felt despair, but then she decided that while her half sister, if put into this situation, would probably have died of shame within a week, she was not Bess. She was Adair Radcliffe, and she was stronger. Life had given her oatcakes when she wanted sweet cake. Well, she would eat her oatcakes, grow stronger, and find a way to get her sweet cake again. Conal Bruce was having his needs well cared for right now, thanks to Elsbeth, Flora, Grizel, and herself. But because

Grizel had very sharp ears, Adair had learned that Conal Bruce would have to free her and Elsbeth in a year and a day's time, for that was the law of the Michaelmas fair. And if they chose not to remain at Cleit he would be out of luck. She had until then to gain his true affections so that he would marry her. It was difficult to admit to it, but Adair knew she would not be going back to Stanton. Elsbeth was right: Stanton no longer existed. Their life was here in the borders of Scotland. At Cleit. The winter came, and it was a bitter one.

And then with the spring a visitor came to Cleit. He was Alpin Bruce, the laird's cousin. Tall, and perhaps a bit too handsome, with dancing amber eyes and rich chestnut hair, Alpin Bruce arrived just as the sun was setting one late April day. The laird greeted his kin, but Adair noticed there was little warmth in the greeting. Nor did Duncan Armstrong or Murdoc Bruce appear very glad to see the man. But the laws of hospitality made a place at the high board for the visitor. As the three women brought the food from the kitchen and placed it on the table, Alpin Bruce's eye lit on Adair.

"Who are the wenches? I had heard all your serving women had left you after your mother died," Alpin Bruce said.

"Adair is my housekeeper," the laird replied tersely. "And my mistress, cousin."

"Indeed," his guest remarked with a grin. "Is she as capable in bed as she seems to be in the hall, cousin?"

"I am efficient in all I do, sir," Adair snapped.

"Adair! Go to Elsbeth. Flora and Grizel will serve the board," the laird said sharply. He knew his cousin, and he didn't like the way Alpin was eyeing Adair.

"Yes, my lord," Adair said, tartly sketching a curtsy, and she withdrew.

Alpin Bruce laughed. "A spirited lass, I can see. Have you had to take a strap to her bottom yet? Taming her must be a pleasure, cousin."

"Adair is amenable, but not easy," the laird told his cousin. "And I do not beat my women, as I have heard it said that you do. I like a spirited lass."

Alpin Bruce smacked his lips at Adair's retreating form. "I envy you the long winter nights you have had this year, Conal," he said.

"Why are you here?" the laird asked bluntly.

"What?" Albin Bruce pretended to be insulted. "Can I not come to visit my favorite cousin without there being some ulterior motive for it?"

"Nay, you cannot," Conal Bruce answered him.

Alpin Bruce laughed. "Well, as a matter of fact I have come on a mission. Old Jamie sitting in Stirling has decided that he hasn't hoarded enough wealth while good Scots folk starve. He is demanding the revenues of Coldingham Priory."

"What?" The laird looked genuinely startled.

"Aye, he wants them, and says he will have them," Alpin answered.

"But those revenues belong to Lord Home," the laird said. "They have always belonged to the Homes."

"King Jamie will have them for whatever purpose he desires. Perhaps another musician, or silk garments for his new favorite, or mayhap he will build another castle, but nay. Not that. Cochrane was hanged, wasn't he?" Alpin Bruce laughed.

"But how does all of this concern me, for surely you haven't come just to bring such news? What do you want, Alpin?"

"Lord Home plans to defend his rights to Coldingham, and needs to know his friends are willing to sustain him. He has already gained the support of the Hepburns, the Red Douglases, the Campbells of Argyll, and the bishop of Glasgow, among others."

"Is Lord Home planning to go to war then?" Conal asked dryly.

"If he must," came the answer. "If King Jamie is allowed to seize the revenues of Coldingham from the Homes, who will next suffer financial ruin at his greedy royal hands? He must be stopped now. It is rumored that some of the earls would set the king aside and put his son upon the throne. The young James is a grand laddie."

Conal Bruce considered, and then he said, "There is naught I have that the royal Stewarts have given the Bruces of Cleit, and so there is nothing they could take from me. To rebel against the king, even a bad king, is dangerous, Alpin. And it is especially dangerous for a bonnet laird like me. I know of an English noblewoman who was stripped of both her lands and a title that she had been born to because her husband backed the wrong man in a dynastic battle."

"This isn't England," Alpin said. "Besides, the king will die sooner than later. His heart, they say, broke with the death of good Queen Margaret. He's like a beast gone to ground to die. He has holed himself up in those fine chambers that Cochrane built for him. He listens to his lute player, and reads copious treatises of scholarly import. And he counts his gold. But he cares little for his people. Plague has broken out in Edinburgh, but the king doesn't give a damn."

"I won't support the king openly," Conal Bruce said, "but neither will I support a rebellion. The Homes don't know me. If their fight comes to a bad end they will more than likely buy their way out of it. But bonnet lairds like me are always chosen to be punished, for an example must be made so that future rebels are warned against their own folly. Who sent you to me?"

"The Hepburn of Hailes. I serve him as a captain," Alpin said. "We cannot all be lairds with our own keep, cousin."

"An accident of birth," Conal Bruce said. "You are the youngest son of a younger son. I am the eldest son of a laird of Cleit."

Alpin Bruce grinned. "If Cleit is to have an heir you had best wed soon, Conal. You are past thirty. A wife, however, would not tolerate that pretty mistress of yours. If necessary I shall be glad to take her off your hands."

"Perhaps I shall marry Adair, Alpin. You are right. It is past time I took a wife," Conal Bruce answered easily.

Adair listened in the shadows of the hall to all of the conversation between the cousins. She had not gone to the kitchens, but rather taken a leaf out of Grizel's book. Was he jesting with his cousin about taking a wife? Time would tell. That he was a cautious man where Cleit was concerned she found interesting. He was clever not to involve himself in rebellion, but neither to refuse to support Lord Home's cause. And she was learning a good deal of gossip about the Scots king. Having grown up in a royal court, Adair found the politics of Scotland fascinating. The conversation was now turning to less important things, and so Adair slipped down the stairs to the kitchens.

When Flora, Grizel, and Jack had gone to their attic quarters, and Elsbeth was already snoring in her bed space, Adair returned to the hall to make her final rounds of the night. As the laird's housekeeper it was her duty to see that the fires were banked, the candles snuffed, and the door barred before retiring to join the laird. As there was a guest, she went to be certain the bed space had been properly furnished. To her surprise Alpin Bruce was not there. He had probably gone to pee. She smiled to herself. It was a good thing she had not yet set the bar across the door. She was relieved to see that Flora had made up the bed space nicely. And then she heard his voice behind her.

"Come to tuck me in, Mistress Adair?" He was standing so close to her that she could not move. "Or have you come to offer me the comfort of your fair body?"

She felt his big hand on the nape of her neck as he forced her forward. "Let me go at once," she said in a hard voice. "Let me go, and I will not tell the laird of your misbehavior, Alpin Bruce."

He laughed low. "And if I don't, Adair? What will you do?" He loosened his garments, releasing his swollen manhood. Then, with the same hand, he yanked her skirts up and sought to find entry into her body.

For the briefest moment Adair was frozen with fright, but then the fear dissipated, and she screamed at the top of her lungs, struggling to break his grip on her neck as he held her pinioned down, preparing to do rape. She was at a great disadvantage, and then to Adair's surprise his grip on her released, and he howled in pain. She struggled to a stand, whirling about as her skirts fell about her. The young wolfhound who had befriended her had come to her rescue, sinking his fangs into her attacker's snowy white buttocks.

Adair wanted to laugh, but instead she stepped quickly from the bed space and said, "Beiste! Release!"

The dog instantly obeyed, stepping back and growling low to hold Alpin Bruce at bay.

"I will tell the laird of this incident," Adair said softly.

"And I will tell him I fucked you because you begged me to do it," Alpin Bruce replied.

"He won't believe you," Adair replied. "And how will you explain the dog bites in your bottom?"

"Aye, how will you, Alpin?" The laird was now with them.

"Your wench is hot-blooded, cousin," Alpin Bruce began, leering at Adair.

"What happened?" The laird directed his question to Adair.

"I was making my final rounds of the evening, my lord. I did not see your cousin, and I came to make certain the bed space was ready. He came up from behind me and attempted to have his way, but the dog attacked him when I screamed," Adair explained.

"She lies!" Alpin Bruce said.

"Nay, the one thing I can be certain of with Adair is that she does not lie," the laird said. "You, however, do. I told you that this lass was mine, and yet you could not keep your cock in your breeks. Turn around and bend over, so I may see what damage the dog has done to you." And when his cousin had obeyed the laird looked at his cousin's buttocks. They were now very bruised, but the dog had done only enough damage to free Adair. His teeth had just slightly pierced the skin, and the bleeding was negligible. "I'll tend to your wounds myself, Alpin, so there will be no gossip about this incident. Adair, go and fetch what I will need from your apothecary."

When she had gone the laird grabbed his cousin by his neck and shook him hard. "Listen to me, you bastard," he growled. "If you ever come into my house again, and accost someone under my protection, I will kill you! Do you understand me, Alpin? I will kill you!" Then he struck the man several hard blows. "Do you understand?"

"I understand!" his cousin whimpered, tasting the blood from a very loose tooth.

Adair, returning with the supplies that would be needed, saw that Alpin Bruce's eye was now blackened; a reddish purple bruise was beginning to show on his other cheek; and his nose and mouth were bleeding. She did not ask what had happened.

"Go to our bed," the laird said in a hard voice. "I will take care of him."

"Yes, my lord," Adair replied, and left the hall.

The laird bent his cousin over and cleansed the wounds. Then he put a healing salve on them. "Stand up," he said, and when his cousin faced him, Conal Bruce drove his fist into the man's middle several times. "She is mine! You will remember it," he said, and, turning, departed the hall.

Gasping for breath, pain radiating through his entire body, Alpin Bruce crawled, whimpering, into the bed space. He could not sleep on his back; nor could he rest comfortably on his belly. Turning on his side, he silently cursed Conal Bruce as he attempted to find some rest.

In his bedchamber Conal Bruce faced Adair. "I cannot protect a mistress as well as I can protect a wife," he said bluntly. "It's past time I had one."

"You championed me very well, I thought. Did you beat him after I left?" she asked him softly, reaching up to touch his face with her hand.

"A little," he admitted. "Don't you want to marry me?"

"Do you love me?" Adair asked him.

He looked totally befuddled by her question.

"Do you love me?" Adair repeated.

"I don't know what you mean," he answered her honestly. "I want to wed you."

"Why?" she queried him.

"Why?" His tone was irritated. "Why?"

"Aye, why?" Adair repeated.

"So I can protect you," he said.

"You protected me very well tonight, and I am not your wife," Adair replied. "My first marriage was a fait accompli before I even knew it. I did not like him. My second marriage was arranged because it was believed a woman could not protect Stanton without a man; and that was certainly proved when Willie Douglas came raiding. I was fond of Andrew. I suppose I loved him after a fashion. He was a good man. But the next time I wed it will be because the man I marry loves me. Really and truly loves me. My uncle Dickon loved his wife devotedly. And that is what I want from my husband. Will I marry you? Nay, my lord, not unless you learn to love me, and will say the words to my face. And I will know if you lie to me."

He was astounded by her words. Every woman he had ever lain with wanted to wed him. What was the matter with her? "You are mine!" he growled, pulling her roughly into his embrace, looking down into her beautiful jewel-colored eyes.

"Yes, my lord," Adair said, and her tone was just faintly amused.

"My name is Conal!" he almost shouted. "You have been with me seven months, and not once have I heard you say my name aloud."

"You did not give me permission to do so," Adair responded reasonably. "Remember, my lord, I am your slave. You paid a silver penny for me." The violet eyes were now dancing mischievously.

"Say my name!" he ground out. She was mocking him, damn her!

"Conal," she murmured against his lips. "Conal. Conal. Conal."

"I will probably kill you eventually," he told her, kissing her a hard kiss.

"Why?" she asked him. "Am I not obedient to your will, Conal? Do I not keep your house well, and please you in your bed, Conal?"

"You will marry me," he told her.

"Nay, I will not until you love me. The day after Michaelmas, Elsbeth and I will be, under both Scots and English law, free of our enslavement. If you do not love me, Conal, I may not remain. I will go back to Stanton," Adair told him. "You've made me your whore, but I do not have to remain your whore."

"Aye," he said low, "I am going to kill you."

She wrapped her arms about his neck and pressed herself against his hard body. "How?" she murmured against his lips. "How will you kill me, my lord Conal?" The tip of her tongue snaked out to run over his lips. She rubbed suggestively against him.

He could feel the nipples of her breasts against his chest. The heat from her mons was turning his manhood rigid with desire. There had never been a woman who satisfied him so well, and he knew that there would never be one like Adair. He wanted her. But what was this love she prated about? He didn't understand, and so he kissed her another fierce kiss. And then he kissed her over and over again until she was limp in his arms. Pushing her onto the bed, he stripped his clothing off, tossing it carelessly from him. And when he turned back to her she had removed her chemise and lay naked for him to enjoy. He stood for a long moment looking down at her. Love? Was it this hungry longing he felt for her? Nay. What he felt right now was nothing more than pure lust.

"What are you thinking?" Adair asked him, seeing the confusion on his face. She lay on her side, propping herself up on an elbow.

"That before I kill you I am going to enjoy your delicious little body," the laird told her, joining her on the bed. His big hand swept down the curve of her hip. "Did you enjoy Alpin's attentions?" he asked her jealously.

"I have already told you that the fool had nothing of me. Do you want to know exactly what happened, Conal? He pushed me face first into the bed space. His hand was holding me down by the nape of my neck. His other hand was attempting to loosen his clothing, and I screamed. Beiste came to my rescue, and I was able to stand. Then you came. That is all that happened. I had not had the opportunity to be certain the bed space was properly made, and was checking it. Since I had not yet barred the door, I assumed he was outside peeing, or talking with one of the men."

"He wants you," the laird said. "I could see it in his eyes even after I beat him."

"He will never have me, Conal," Adair said quietly. "Learn to love me, and I will wed you. Not love me with your body, for you already do that."

"But what other way is there to love a woman?" he asked her.

"With your whole heart," she said softly.

"I do not understand," he answered her.

"And until you do I cannot wed you, my lord," Adair told him. "This time I will marry only a man who loves me, and whom I can love in return."

"I do not know or understand the kind of love you speak about," he told her honestly. "But I have heard it said that true love brings unhappiness as well as happiness, Adair. Is it not better to marry for more sensible reasons?"

"I should rather know true love, whatever it may bring me, than to know only loneliness of the heart for the rest of my life, Conal," she replied candidly. Then, reaching up, she drew his dark head down to her and kissed his lips sweetly.

"If I put a bairn in your belly I will not have it born on the wrong side of the blanket," he told her. "You must swear you will wed me if you are with child."

"I was born on the wrong side of the blanket," Adair responded.

"You were a royal brat, and that is different. You know it is."

"Then if you would have a bairn born on the right side of the blanket, Conal, you had best learn what true love is all about," Adair advised him. "Now make love to me, my lord, for you know I am as lustful as you are."

He obliged, losing himself in the passion that blazed, but the matter of love hung between them.

In the morning after he had seen Alpin Bruce gone from the keep, the laird rode out to the cottage of Agnes Carr, which was on the far side of the nearby village. A big red-haired woman with pillowy breasts and full hips, she greeted him delightedly.

"I had heard you have taken a mistress. Some little English wench you bought from Willie Douglas last Michaelmas. Have you grown tired of her this soon, my lord?" She held out her arms to him and enfolded him in a lusty embrace.

Conal Bruce gave the woman a brief kiss on her lush mouth, and then he said, "Give me some of that whiskey you keep, Agnes. I have not grown tired of Adair. In fact, I would marry her, but she will not have me." He sat down on the settle by the hearth.

"Will not have you? Is the lass daft then, my lord?" She poured him the whiskey in a pewter double dram for she suspected he needed it. "Here," Agnes said, handing him the cup, and sitting opposite him on a three-legged stool.

Conal Bruce took a gulp of the whiskey. It hit his stomach like a fireball, and made his eyes water. "Where the hell do you get this stuff?" he asked her, but, not waiting for an answer, he continued, "She says she will wed me only if I love her, Agnes."

"Ahhh," Agnes Carr said, feeling not just a little jealous, but she smiled, nodding. "A clever and wise girl, I'm thinking, Conal." At least she had him as a friend.

"What the devil does she mean, love her? I do love her," he said.

"You *make love* to her, my lord, and that is an entirely different thing," Agnes answered him. "She wants you to love her with your whole heart."

"But how do I do that?" the laird asked, an almost desperate tone in his voice. "I don't even understand what that means, and if I don't understand it, how can I do it?"

Agnes sighed. "True love, my lord, is like a will-o'-the-wisp. When you love with your whole heart you would do anything for your woman. Even give your life for hers. And a life without her is un-thinkable, for it is empty and lonely. The sound of her voice makes you happy, and your first sight of her after a long day fills you with joy. Your own life without her is simply miserable." Agnes shrugged. "I know that wiser folk than I could probably explain it better, my lord, but that is how I see it."

"And men are really capable of these feelings, of this emotion, Agnes?" He swallowed the whiskey remaining in his cup. "She says she will know if I lie to her."

Agnes Carr chuckled. "Wise, clever, and hard as rock," she said. "Why I do believe, my lord, that you have finally met your match? And I suspect—although you are not yet aware, or even able to admit to it—that you love this lass, or at least have begun to love her. I have heard it said that your keep is habitable once again, and the food is edible. Grizel is my aunt. She tells me your lass is beau-tiful to look upon, and kind of heart with the servants and your men. Of course, when a lass walks about shadowed by a great dog, the men are apt to behave respectably. I suppose this means I'll not be entertaining you in my bed anymore," she concluded with a re-gretful sigh.

"I fear not, Agnes," Conal Bruce told her with a small grin. "I suspect the kind of love Adair wants from me precludes a man's visiting an old friend for a bit of a tumble."

Agnes nodded. "It does, my lord. Still, I have many friends, including your two brothers. Duncan Armstrong brought the laddie to me just last week for tutoring. I must say that young Murdoc is an enthusiastic pupil. One of the best I've ever had. I was honored to have his virginity off of him."

"Treat him well, Agnes," the laird said. "As for Duncan, he had best treat you well. And you will never lack for anything as long as I am laird of Cleit." He stood up. "I had best get back to the keep. I am told the countryside may be in a bit of a turmoil, for King James wants the revenues of Coldingham Priory off Lord Home. Keep yourself close, lass." He walked to the door.

"Who told you?" she wanted to know.

"My cousin Alpin Bruce came yesterday. He's in service to the Hepburn of Hailes. Lord Home is looking for allies."

"What will you do?" Agnes asked him.

"Bide my time," the laird responded. "I cannot afford to offend the king, and I cannot afford to offend Lord Home's dignity. Such is the fate of we bonnet lairds," he told her ruefully. Then he blew her a kiss. "Take care, Agnes." And he was gone out her door.

Agnes Carr watched as the laird of Cleit rode away. Then she chuckled to herself. The little English wench had ensorcelled Conal Bruce. He didn't know it yet, but he was already in love with the lass; yet from what Grizel had said, Agnes Carr had no doubt that Adair would leave the laird if he could not admit to his feelings. "Poor laddie," she said aloud. "Poor, poor laddie."

Chapter 12

The party of horsemen making its way to Cleit Keep was not large. The man at arms on watch counted ten men, lightly armed. He called down to alert the keep of their visitors. The horsemen galloped into the courtyard and dismounted. Conal Bruce hurried to greet them, his face impassive as he recognized Lord Home, the Hepburn of Hailes, and his cousin Alpin Bruce.

"Welcome to Cleit," he said to Lord Home and the Hepburn. Then he shot his cousin a fierce glance. "You are not welcome here, Alpin, and you know it. Come into the hall, my lords, and take refreshment." He led his visitors into the keep. When they had been settled with dram cups of his own whiskey, the laird of Cleit asked, "How may I serve you, and what business brings you to Cleit?"

"I am disturbed to learn," Lord Home began, "that you will not support me, Conal Bruce, in the matter of Coldingham Priory."

"But neither will I support the king," the laird answered. "I made that perfectly clear to my cousin when he last came. That was the message I sent to my lord Hepburn."

"What prevents you from taking sides in this most serious business?" Lord Home asked quietly. He sipped at his whiskey thoughtfully.

"My lord, this matter is between you and the king. I have no part in it. I am a simple man of no importance. A borderer. A bonnet laird. Naught else. But if the king wishes to take his revenge on you he will strike out at your supporters, not necessarily at you. He will punish people like me to make his point—men of little significance with no great family or friends to defend them. I have what you see about me, my lord. A small keep, some livestock, a bit of land, a village. My people rely upon me for their safety and well-being. I cannot afford to take sides either against the king or against you, my lord. Please understand, for I mean you no disrespect."

"That is not quite how your cousin Albin explained it to Patrick Hepburn," Lord Home replied. "He said that you reminded him the Bruces were blood kin to the Stewarts, and that you would defend their rights to the death."

"My cousin is a liar, my lord, and he always has been," Conal Bruce replied steadily.

"I did not lie!" Alpin Bruce shouted.

"You are a liar, cousin, and the reason you have told this lie is because you wished to make yourself important in the eyes of your master, and because you were foiled in your attempt to rape my mistress," the laird answered coldly. "Liar, debaucher, and now fool. Have the wounds on your buttocks healed yet?"

"I fucked her! I fucked her, and she loved it!" Alpin Bruce yelled.

Lord Home and the Hepburn of Hailes looked at each other curiously.

"My cousin attempted to force my mistress. He failed in his endeavor, and when Adair called for help her dog fastened his teeth in Alpin's fat arse. I'll wager you did not sit for a week or two, cousin," the laird mocked. "Now, get out of my hall. I am pleased to entertain Lord Home and the Hepburn, but I told you, you are no longer welcome in my keep. If you come back again I will kill you, Alpin. Do you understand me?"

Alpin Bruce flung his dram cup across the chamber and slunk from the hall, muttering curses beneath his breath as he went.

"Is she worth the danger Alpin put himself in?" Patrick Hepburn asked, amused.

"You will see for yourselves, my lords, for both of you are too far from your own homes to return today. You will spend the night, of course. Flora," he called to the serving woman, "go and tell Elsbeth that we have guests for the night. There are ten of them, two to sit at the high board with me."

"Aye, my lord, at once," Flora said, and hurried off.

"Where is this paragon that your cousin covets?" Lord Home wanted to know. He was a tall, distinguished older man with snow white hair who had once been Scotland's ambassador to England. His blue eyes were curious.

"At this time of day she will be in her gardens," the laird answered. "She has spent the spring restoring my late mother's kitchen and herb gardens. She is an English captive Willie Douglas brought over the border last autumn. I bought her at the Michaelmas fair. I want to marry her. 'Tis past time I had a wife."

"If you want to wed her, then why don't you?" the Hepburn of Hailes asked.

"She's been wed twice before, and widowed twice. She says when she marries again it will be because the man loves her," the laird explained. "I don't understand her, but she will make me a suitable wife," he said, shrugging his shoulders.

Lord Home laughed. "A most unusual woman," he said. "Will she join us for the meal, Conal Bruce?"

"Aye, she will," he said. Then he continued, "My lord, we have not yet concluded our earlier conversations, and I would not offend you."

"I will admit I am not pleased that you will not support me against the king," Lord Home said quietly, "but aye, I do understand your position. There is talk, however, of making the king step down, and setting his son upon the throne. If that were to happen where would you stand, Conal Bruce?"

"With the crown, of course," the laird answered Lord Home.

The older man laughed heartily. "You are clever, my lord." He chuckled. "With the crown indeed, but with which king?"

"Whichever wears the crown," Conal Bruce replied with a small grin.

"A humble bonnet laird indeed," Patrick Hepburn said. "Your wits are too nimble by far, I am thinking, Conal Bruce." He chortled. "Our young Jamie would like you."

The laird did not ask to whom the Hepburn of Hailes referred. He knew the reference was to Prince James. There was more afoot here than just the matter of Coldingham Priory. He was not certain he wanted to know. Any hint of treason could destroy him. And while a king sat on Scotland's throne, suggesting he be replaced with his son was indeed treason. He moved the subject back once again to Cleit. "You will not hold it against me that I cannot publicly support you, my lord?" he asked Alexander Home. "Mind you, I do not disagree with your position. The king has no right to take the revenues that are yours and have been your family's for many years."

"There is no quarrel between us, Conal Bruce," Lord Home said.

At that moment Adair entered the hall. "I am told we have visitors, my lord," she said, coming forward. She wore a soft light wool gown, pale violet in color. It brought out the color in her eyes and made her pale skin seem paler, especially with her dark hair. She curtsied to Lord Home first, and then to the Hepburn of Hailes.

"This is my mistress, Adair Radcliffe," the laird said. "Adair, this is Lord Home, and Patrick Hepburn of Hailes."

"You have refreshment? Ah, I see that you do," Adair said. "What brings you to Cleit? We do not often have the pleasure of visitors, my lords."

"Jesu!" Patrick Hepburn burst out. "No wonder your cousin covets her. Madam, I do not believe I have ever seen so fair a woman as you are." He caught up her little hand and kissed it.

Adair colored becomingly as she withdrew her hand from his grasp. "My lord, you flatter me, but you must cease, for the laird is a jealous man, are you not, Conal?"

Her eyes were twinkling mischievously.

Patrick Hepburn chuckled and said, "He tells us that you will not wed him."

"I will wed him when he learns to love me, and admits to it," Adair said seriously.

"But what if you find yourself with child, madam?" the Hepburn asked.

"Then it shall be born on the same side of the blanket that I was," Adair told him.

"I cannot believe a lass as well-spoken and mannerly as you are, madam, was bastard-born. Your very looks belie a common background," the Hepburn answered.

Adair laughed. "While I was bastard-born, my lord, neither of my parents were common folk. My mother, God assoil her good soul, was Jane Radcliffe, Countess of Stanton, a baron's daughter."

"And your sire?" Lord Home inquired, now curious. There was something about the girl that was vaguely familiar.

"My sire was King Edward, Lord Home. We have not met, but I remember seeing you at his court when I was a child. I remember thinking you very impressive in your black-and-red tartan. After my parents were slain I was raised in the royal nurseries."

"Of course!" Lord Home exclaimed. "You are the child they called the king's brat. You do not look at all like your sire, but you have a way of holding yourself, of tilting your head, that is very reminiscent of Edward of York."

"But how did a lass such as yourself end up here at Cleit?" Lord Home asked.

"Come and sit by the fire with me, my lord, and I will tell you," Adair replied, seeing his cup refilled, and she did. The Hepburn of Hailes listened to her story as well.

Conal Bruce was surprised that these two border lords, every bit as rough as he was, albeit more powerful, were so interested in Adair's story. Women were useful, and they could certainly give pleasure, but to sit and listen to them prate was something he had not anticipated of his guests. But they were not only curious about Adair's tale; they were openly fascinated. The laird wasn't certain he shouldn't be jealous.

Finally Adair concluded her history, and she arose. "I must see to the meal, my lords. Please excuse me." She curtsied to them and hurried from the hall.

For a long few moments no one spoke, and then Lord Home said to Patrick Hepburn, "She can be valuable to us. What luck to find her here. At Cleit, of all places!" He turned to Conal Bruce. "Your mistress was raised in Edward IV's court, and her knowledge of the people now there will help us in dealing with the English."

"My lord, what do you mean? I do not understand you," Conal Bruce said.

"Adair Radcliffe will know intimate details of the new king and his queen. Details we could not possibly learn except from one of their intimates. This can aid us in our diplomatic efforts with England. We cannot afford a war."

"I will not let her go," the laird said. "You cannot take her from me!"

"Nay, nay, man, we only want to talk further with her. And not this visit," Lord Home reassured him.

"I thought you did not know what love was?" the Hepburn of Hailes said.

Conal Bruce looked puzzled.

Patrick Hepburn laughed. "You love the lass," he said simply, "else the thought of her leaving would not disturb you so, Conal Bruce."

"Nay," the laird declared. "It is just that I do not want the keep to return to the state it was in a year ago. Adair keeps order here."

The Hepburn laughed all the harder. "I suppose," he remarked, "that there is no help for a fool who cannot face the truth, but, my lord, you had best admit to it before you lose her. And she would not want love from you if she herself did not feel a certain gentle tenderness toward the laird of Cleit."

"You think she loves me?" Conal Bruce asked, surprised. What was this love they all talked about? He didn't understand it, or what was meant by the word. He needed Adair. He lusted for her. Was that not enough?

"You would have to ask her that question, my lord," the Hepburn said with a smile. "But the lady appears to me to be as stubborn as you are. If she has said she will not wed you without the assurance of your love, then she is unlikely to admit to her own feelings for you, I fear. Love, Conal Bruce, is a game of both emotions and power."

Adair returned to the hall, and the meal was served. The two guests were very impressed with the meal put on the high board. There was a large bowl of freshwater mussels with a mustard sauce, and a trout broiled with butter and white wine on a bed of watercress. There was a capon that had been roasted stuffed with bread, onions, and apples. It sat on its platter surrounded by a sauce of lemon and cherries. There was a small ham, a rabbit pie with a flaky pastry crust, a brown gravy that was flavored with red wine, and a potage of vegetables. There was fresh bread, sweet butter, and two cheeses. The cups were kept filled with good wine. And finally there was a plum tartlet that was served with heavy golden cream.

When he had finished the last bit of the tart, Lord Home sat back with a sigh. "Even in your mother's day, God assoil her good soul, the food at Cleit could not be described as superlative, Conal, my lad. But tonight's meal was one of the finest I have ever eaten. I may be forced to steal your cook," he said.

"Alas, sir, you cannot," Adair told him with a smile. "Elsbeth is my old Nursie. She has been with me my entire life, and when Conal bought her from Willie Douglas she would not go with him without me. I shall tell her how her meal pleased you, though."

"Was she with you in the royal nursery?" Lord Home asked, curious.

"Aye, she was," Adair answered him. "She is all I have left of what once was my life, my lord. I could not do without her."

"Is the life you live now so unhappy for you, then?" Lord Home wondered.

"In England I was her ladyship the Countess of Stanton. Here at Cleit I am the laird's whore," Adair said bluntly. "I know that Henry Tudor will not relent in his judgment, and I shall never again bear the title I was born to, but I would aspire to more than just the laird's mistress, my lord. Every woman is bound by a certain modicum of pride in who she is, and my honor, like yours, has its limits."

Lord Home was very affected by Adair's words, for it was not often that a woman impressed him. This young woman, however, did. "I had planned to speak with you on a certain matter another time, my lady, but perhaps, as you speak of honor, now might be the time for me to ask you if you would be willing to tell me what you might about the new English king. He had made a certain treaty with our king, and I am curious as to whether he will keep his word, or if he means to keep Scotland at bay in this manner."

"We hear nothing of the world here, my lord," Adair replied. "As for my loyalties to Henry Tudor, I have none, despite the fact that I am English. This king is clever. His throne is not yet entirely secure. The monarchs in Europe think his claim weak, and will, given the chance, seek to destroy him. He needs to prove that he is strong. That he is capable of successfully defending his throne. He does it in ways that make him appear strong, yet in ways that will not offend those who did not support him, but are powerful and wealthy. Those who can eventually be brought over to his side, men who can be of aid to him at some time in the future. He listens to his mother, who is most clever.

"So he permits those new men who have come to his court to libel and defame his predecessor in an effort to bolster his own legitimacy. He listens to it said that King Richard, his own wife's beloved uncle, murdered my half brothers, when he knows it is not so. But he will not say it. The princes were safe at Middleham while my uncle was king. The page who slept in their chamber at night told me of two men who entered the castle with word that the king was dead, and Henry Tudor was England's new king. And that same night he was awakened and, from the dark corner where he lay, he saw the poor helpless princes smothered, and their lifeless bodies removed from Middleham. He came to Stanton for safety, and was killed when the blackhearted Douglas raided my home. But I digress.

"You ask about Henry Tudor. He makes harsh examples of those without the power to defend themselves so he might appear resolute in his intention to rule. I stood before him and he was cruel. Having taken the title that was mine, and not my husband's, having taken my lands, he told me to whore for my bread as my mother had, and sent me from Windsor. And my half sister, now England's queen, remained silent by his side. I made my own way back to Stanton.

"Henry Tudor is a hard man. He will do whatever he must to hold on to what he has taken. There are those with stronger claims on England's throne who still live. The mother who raised him was my governess, and educated me. She was ambitious for her son, and he learned from her. But she was also careful not to show that ambition, or offend any who might one day be of help to her. Lady Margaret is educated, devout, knowledgeable, and thoroughly skilled in politics. Though he would never admit to it publicly, nor would the lady acknowledge it, she is his most influential adviser. But tell me of this treaty your king has negotiated with England." Adair sipped thirstily from her cup, her interest in what he would say open.

"Our good Queen Margaret died last year," Lord Home began. "The treaty is still being negotiated, but I wonder if it should be signed when it is settled. Our king is to wed King Edward's widow, Elizabeth Woodville. Prince James is to marry one of the queen's younger sisters. What is holding up the finality of this is the return of Berwick. We want it back. King Henry is not certain he wants to give it back."

"Your king would be a fool to marry Elizabeth Woodville," Adair said frankly. "She is still beautiful, I will admit, but she is venal and greedy. And from what I have heard of his character, he would leave her to her own devices as long as she left him to his. And her loyalties would first lie with Henry Tudor, not James Stewart. Heaven help your Scotland in that case.

"As for your prince marrying one of my half sisters, I would also advise against it. Mary and Margaret are dead. Elizabeth is England's queen. Cicely is married. There are but three left. Anne is almost thirteen, Catherine ten, and wee Bridget eight this year. Anne is closest in age to your prince, but my half sisters have been carefully raised by the king's mother to be docile, domestic, and hopefully fecund. And any English princess married to Scotland would give her first allegiance to England. Is Berwick really worth the troubles Elizabeth Woodville and one of her daughters will bring to Scotland?" Adair inquired. "If it were my decision, neither would put a silken slipper across the border."

Both Lord Home and the Hepburn chuckled at her observation.

"Your counsel is invaluable, madam," the older man said to her. "Women should be sent as ambassadors to all foreign lands, for as females are considered unimportant and lacking in intellect, no one pays a great deal of attention to them, and they listen, thereby learning a great deal more than a man."

"How liberal and extreme you are in your thought, my lord," Adair said dryly.

The Hepburn grinned at her bold words. "Nah, he is not really, madam."

"Do you flatter me then, my lord, to gain more information from me?" Adair gently teased Lord Home.

"You are too clever for me, madam," Lord Home said graciously. "You have been of great help to us, Adair Radcliffe. It is a pity your own king was so intent on solidifying his own position that he threw away someone who would have been a loyal friend despite her lack of importance."

"I did not know Henry Tudor but from a distance until the day I stood before him. All I had heard of him had come from his mother's mouth, and mothers are wont to speak only good of their offspring. It was my half sister's betrayal that hurt me. We had been friends from the moment I came to court. We played and learned and shared secrets with each other. We shared a bed. Yet she said naught in my defense. She would not even look me in the eye. Lady Margaret was little better, but then, while I have intelligence I was never her best pupil, and I had no importance or stature any longer," Adair finished with a small smile.

"Nay, I suspect you were her best pupil," Lord Home observed. "Perhaps you are not docile and domestic like your half sisters, but you are clever, Adair Radcliffe."

"Cleverness has done little for me, my lord," Adair remarked dryly.

Conal Bruce had listened with growing amazement as Adair had spoken with Lord Home. Until this evening the pedigree and background of the woman he called his slave had meant little to him. But here he sat in his own hall while this slip of an English girl had spoken with authority and certainty with one of the most powerful border lords in all of Scotland on matters that were virtually foreign to the laird of Cleit.

Finally Adair arose. "I must apologize, my lords, but Cleit is small, and we can offer you but bed spaces here in the hall. I will be certain they are in readiness for you now. My lord's brothers have seen to your men, and they will bed down in the stables."

She curtsied, and went off.

"Do what you must, man, but get the wench to the altar," Patrick Hepburn said. "You're a fool if you don't. The children she gives you will bring much honor to your family. Now, what am I to do with your cousin, my lord?"

"Does he serve you well?" Conal Bruce asked.

"Well enough," the Hepburn answered.

"Then keep him in your service, for I do not want him coming again to Cleit," the laird replied. "We have never gotten on, and he always causes me difficulty."

Patrick Hepburn nodded. "If we have a war perhaps I can get him killed for you," he said half seriously.

Lord Home gave a sharp bark of laughter.

"It is good to have friends," the laird replied with a grin.

Adair returned to say their beds were ready when they chose to retire. "Will you see to the rest, my lord?" she asked Conal Bruce. "I should like to retire to bed."

"I will join you shortly," he replied, dismissing her.

"Good night, then, my lords," Adair said with a curtsy.

The three men watched as she left the hall. A serving man refilled their dram cups with the laird's whiskey, and disappeared from the hall. The trio sat watching the fire and talking until finally the laird stood up and, stretching his length, bowed to them.

"I will bid you good night, my lords," Conal Bruce said, and then he left them to make certain that all the lamps and candles were extinguished. He set the heavy bar across the door to the keep, wondering as he did so how Adair managed it each night. When he returned to the hall to add wood to the fire for the night, both of his guests had found their sleeping spaces, and Lord Home was already snoring loudly. Conal Bruce then made his way upstairs to his own bedchamber, where he found Adair still waiting for him. The shutters on the window were open, allowing in the soft summer air. He could see a moon rising over the hills through it.

"You are not in bed," he said to her.

"I know how much you like to undress me, so I waited," Adair told him.

"Aye," he said as she stood up and turned her back to him. He slipped her gown off her shoulders, and watched as it slid down her slender frame to the floor. Then, reaching about her, he unlaced her chemise, drawing it wide open and pushing it to the floor with the gown.

Adair stepped away from the garments and, bending, picked them up, folding them carefully, placing them in a small trunk. "Now it is my turn," she said softly. She stood naked before him, unbuttoned the bone buttons on his jerkin, unlaced his linen shirt, and drew both from his big frame. Her fingers tangled themselves in the dark curls on his chest and, bending her head, she kissed each of his nipples in turn. "Sit, and I will take your boots from you," she told him. Then, taking each of his feet between her legs, she slowly drew off each boot. She undid his breeks and slid them over his lean hips, her hands sliding down his legs teasingly. His interest was already stirring, but Adair pushed away, saying, "First you must undo my hair, Conal." She turned herself about, her buttocks brushing against his groin.

His fingers felt clumsy as he undid her thick braid. He spread the long sable hair out, marveling as he always did at its thickness, its shine, how it rippled down her graceful back. Grasping a handful, he closed his eyes and brought it to his nose, inhaling the fragrance of woodbine that emanated from the tresses. Then his hands moved about her body to cup her two breasts in his hands. He felt the weight of the soft flesh in his palms as he brushed the nipples lightly with the balls of his thumbs.

Adair leaned back against him, her eyes closed as she enjoyed the sensation of his hands. "I need a hairbrush," she told him. "It has been months since I was able to properly attend to my hair. I can do just so much with the little comb that Jack carved for me last winter as a Twelfth Night gift."

"I'll buy you a brush at the midsummer fair," he promised her, pushing her hair aside to drop a kiss on her rounded shoulder.

"And a packet of needles. We have but two left," she told him.

His fingers tightened about her breasts as she pressed herself back against him. "You are a greedy wench," he told her. *Jesu!* He had had her with him almost nine months, and she could still engage his lust quicker than any he had ever known. He rubbed his manroot between the crease separating her bottom.

She turned in his embrace, slipping her arms about his neck and letting the fur on his chest tickle her nipples. "If you expect me to keep making your clothing you will give me the needles," she told him. The tip of her tongue flicked around the outline of his mouth several rotations. Reaching down, she stroked his length. "You are so greedy, my lord," she teasingly scolded him. "Your laddie is already eager for sport."

"Aye, he is," the laird agreed, "but I am going to teach you something different tonight, my honey love. Before he visits your sweet sheath, he would bury himself between your lips. Kneel, Adair." He gently pushed her down before him.

"I have heard such things are forbidden," Adair whispered, staring fascinated at the manhood before her. "Holy Mother Church . . . Will we be damned if I do it?"

"Why?" he asked her, amused.

"It is wrong!" Adair cried.

"Is it? Holy Mother Church says keeping a mistress is wrong. They say that every time a man mounts his wife it should be for the sole purpose of creating a child and nothing more. They say a man's and a woman's bodies are not for pure enjoyment, but only for procreating another soul onto this earth. Dried-up old men with no knowledge of women and passion. Or sodomites who plow between a lad's buttocks for pleasure, not procreation. And yet I know a woman's body is meant for enjoyment, as is a man's. There is naught wrong if we both gain pleasure from it. Take me in your mouth, Adair."

Her small hand wrapped itself about him. Slowly, hesitantly, she opened her lips and took him in. He was thick, and he was warm.

"Suckle me, my honey love," he crooned to her, his hand on her dark head. "That's it! That's it! Gentle, now. Be mindful of your teeth, for he is a delicate lad."

Shy at first, Adair grew bolder with confidence. She sucked upon him. She ran her tongue around the tip of him and tasted a salty drop of his juices. Soon she found she could no longer contain him within the cavern of her mouth.

Sensing her dilemma, he drew her to her feet and kissed her a long, slow kiss. "You did well, my honey love," he told her. "Very well."

"It has made me feel very lustful," Adair whispered.

"Then we must satisfy your lust," he said with a grin.

"Nay! I am not ready," she told him. "On your back, my lord! It is my turn."

Fascinated by her sudden boldness in their bed, for Adair had always preferred to be led to passion than to lead, he lay down upon his back and allowed her to have her way with him. She crouched over him; then, bending, she began to lick him. She pulled at the hair on his chest with her teeth, making little growling noises as she did so. She brought a fire to his belly with her hot tongue and her little kisses. And then suddenly she pulled herself up and pressed her sex down onto his face.

Surprised, he lost his breath for a brief moment, but then he foraged with his tongue until he pressed through her nether lips and found the center of her desire, which he proceeded to tease and taunt with his tongue. "Witch!" he groaned into the moist, sweet flesh as he brought her satisfaction, and lapped at her juices until she was whimpering with her delight.

"Fuck me!" he suddenly heard her beg him. "Oh, Jesu, Conal, I am so hungry for you. I need you to be inside of me! Oh, hurry!" And then Adair was on her back, and she felt him enter her in a single thrust. She almost screamed aloud, but pushed her fist into her mouth to prevent the cry from erupting forth.

He rode her to her pleasure, but he did not leave her, for he had not yet had his. Slowly he began to pump her, going deep, withdrawing. And at first slowly. Slowly. He sensed her beginning to climb again, and his movements became faster and faster. This time she did not hold back. Adair's scream of unadulterated pleasure burst forth at the same time as his roar of gratification. He thought his juices would never stop flowing as they jerked forth in a fierce staccato rhythm that filled her and left them both weak. There was nothing to say. Conal wrapped his arms about Adair and they both fell asleep.

He awoke in the night to find the moon washing over their bodies. Adair lay curled on her side, her black lashes tipped silver in the light, her sable hair covering her shoulders. He lay watching her for some time before he fell back asleep. He considered how empty his life would be without her, and knew he would do whatever he had to in order to bring her to the altar. He wanted bairns with her. He wanted to spend the rest of his life with her. Was that love? He didn't know, and he wasn't going to say he loved her when he still wasn't certain what love was. He didn't want her accusing him of lying.

Lord Home and the Hepburn of Hailes departed in the morning. Both had kissed Adair's hand and thanked her for both her hospitality and her information.

"Prince James will be grateful of your advice, madam. He is not yet of a mind to wed, being young and filled with the lusty juices of a lad," Lord Home said.

"Our Jamie is as randy as a ram in spring," Patrick Hepburn remarked. "And the lassies all flock to him. He'll be a grand king one day."

Then the two men were mounted, and left Cleit with their men at arms, Alpin Bruce among them. The laird noticed his cousin's eye was blackened, and wondered how he had sustained his injury. He later learned that Alpin had come up behind Grizel as she gathered eggs in the henhouse that morning. Spinning the woman about, he had thrown her into the hay, only then gaining a look at her face. It was all the time Grizel needed. Jumping to her feet, she had hit Alpin Bruce a blow, and as he howled with the injury she had grabbed up her basket of eggs, and run for the kitchens to tell her companions. And the shock of the brief attempt on her virtue relieved by his yelp, she had laughed at the incident with Elsbeth, Flora, and Jack. Adair laughed too, but the laird was furious.

"The fool cannot keep his cock in his breeks," he grumbled. And then he too had laughed, for, seen from behind, Grizel appeared a younger woman. He could but imagine his cousin's surprise when the face suddenly presented to him was that of an older, hook-nosed woman with a pointed chin. Grizel's appearance was apt to frighten those who did not know her. "I hope you gave him the evil eye, Grizel." The laird chuckled.

"There was but time to black it, my lord. And I have not run that fast since I was a lass, but I broke not one egg," Grizel replied, and her companions laughed all the harder.

Midsummer was suddenly upon them, and a small fair was set up in the laird's village. A small group of tinkers set themselves up in the midst of it, and families from the keep and the nearby crofts brought their pots to be repaired. One old woman among them told fortunes for a copper. Seeing Adair, she reached out to grasp her hand and peered into it. Her brow furrowed.

"You have known cruel sorrow, and you have been grievously wronged, but you cannot go back," she wheezed. "Still, you will find happiness if you are wise enough to seize it. To do so you must slough off the past and listen to your heart, for your heart speaks true, my lady countess."

Adair gasped, surprised at being addressed by her old title. "How do you know . . ." she began, and the old crone held up her hand.

"I see what I see, my lass," she told Adair. "I do not understand it myself."

Conal Bruce pressed a copper into the fortune-teller's hand. Then he held out his own. "And what do you see for me, Gypsy?" he asked her.

The old woman took up his big hand. "I see great happiness for you, my lord, provided you do not spend too much more time considering your problem." She nodded slowly. "You have already found the answers you seek. You have only to admit to it. That is all I see."

He laughed and gave her another copper before they moved on. "She speaks in riddles," he said to Adair, but he had understood exactly what the old woman was saying to him. He had found love with Adair, and he knew it. If only he dared to admit it to her. They stopped at a booth selling ribbons, and he bought her a length of scarlet silk for her dark hair. "And I promised you a hairbrush, lass. We'll go and find one now."

She looked so pretty today in her light wool skirt of red Bruce plaid, which came to her ankles. With it she wore a linen shirt, its laces open at the neckline, for the day was warm. About her waist was a wide leather belt, and on her feet were black slippers.

Adair smiled up at him, surprised. It was the first gift he had given her. "I should like a brush," she said, "and I thank you for the ribbon."

They stopped at a booth selling small bits of dough that had been fried in oil and dusted with cinnamon. Together they devoured a plateful of the delicious confections. As they turned to go from the booth they were confronted by Lord Home, the Hepburn of Hailes, and a party of men, among them a very tall and handsome young man with bright blue eyes and red hair. Conal Bruce immediately sensed who the young man was, although he had never before seen him or met him.

"My lords," he said, and bowed, waiting for Lord Home to introduce him.

"Bruce, 'tis good to see you again. We have come to join the games to be held later today." He drew the young man forward. "My lord, this is the Bruce of Cleit. And this, Conal Bruce, is Scotland's hope." He did not say the handsome young man's name.

"You honor me, Your Highness," the laird said, bowing low.

"Alexander Home has told me of his recent visit to your keep, my lord," the prince said. "I am pleased to meet a man who is loyal to the crown." The blue eyes twinkled in friendly and amused fashion. The prince was a young man in his mid-teens.

"Your Highness must understand my need to be prudent," Conal Bruce replied.

"We all have a need to be prudent these days," the prince responded. Then his eyes turned with interest toward Adair. "And who, Conal Bruce, is this fair creature?"

Before the laird might speak Adair did. "I am Adair Radcliffe, Your Highness."

"I am told you are his mistress," Prince James said, ignoring everyone else around him. His admiring glance was unmistakable as it swept over Adair.

"I am," Adair said. She recognized his interest.

"I think I envy your bonnet laird that he has so beautiful a mistress," the prince murmured low, and taking up her hand, he kissed it a lingering kiss.

"You flatter me, Your Highness," Adair said, curtsying.

He bent and whispered in her ear, "I would do far more than flatter if you would permit it, madam." He kissed the palm of her hand now.

"Again you flatter me," Adair said, "but I know Your Highness will understand that I must refuse his kind and generous proposal, for I have a certain loyalty to the Bruce."

"No loyalty to your prince?" James Stewart said low.

"I am English, Your Highness," she told him with a mischievous smile.

The prince laughed. "You would still be as clever were you Scots, madam," he said ruefully. "It is with regret that I must accept your decision." He tipped her face up to his and kissed her softly on her lips. Then, turning to Lord Home, he asked, "When do the games begin?"

"I believe they are starting shortly," Alexander Home replied. "Come along, Your Highness, and we will join them. I believe you wished to take part in the caber toss."

Adair saw the look on Conal's face, and she almost laughed, but instead she put a hand upon his arm and said low, "Control your temper, my lord. He will be king one day, and you do not wish to offend."

"He had no right to kiss you," the laird growled.

"It was but a kiss," Adair murmured. "He wanted more, but I refused."

Conal Bruce grew red in the face. "*More?* He dared?"

Adair laughed. "Why would you care, my lord? I am but your slave. Actually you would have gained great favor with him if you had offered me to him. Now let us find that hairbrush you promised me. Tonight I shall teach you how to brush my hair."

He was close to exploding. Prince James wanted to futter Adair, and she was not in the least offended. And why was she taunting him that she was his slave? He had never treated her like one, and God only knew she had never behaved like one. "I will buy your brush," he said coolly, "and then I am going to take part in the caber toss."

He was jealous, Adair realized. Now, why would he be jealous? He didn't love her. Or did he? Was he in love with her but too proud to tell her? She almost giggled, but refrained from showing her amusement. Unless he admitted to his love for her she would leave him on the last day of September, for her term of servitude would then be up. The Stanton she had known and loved was gone, but the village was certainly still there. She would go home, and if Elsbeth would come with her, fine. If not she would go alone. She had traveled alone before. The borders between England and Scotland were no worse than the highways between London and the north. Only the terrain was rougher.

They found the peddler selling brushes and combs. Adair chose a simple brush of pear wood with boar's bristles. The laird haggled with the man over the price, but one was finally reached that suited them both. Then together they walked to the nearby open field where various contests of a physical nature were taking place. Archery butts had been set up in one area. There were footraces being run in another. Several very brawny men were casting great stones in slings across a field. Finding the place where the caber toss was being held, the laird immediately pulled off his linen shirt, handing it to Adair. Then he stepped into the line of men waiting their turn.

Adair moved to the sidelines and was surprised to find the prince there. "I thought you were joining in the games," she said to him.

"I have already had my turn," he told her. "Did you come to watch me?"

Adair laughed. "Nay, I came to watch the Bruce."

"I made him jealous, didn't I?" James Stewart said, slipping an arm about Adair's supple waist. "I saw it in his eyes."

"And so you kissed me anyhow," Adair replied, a small smile on her lips.

"How could I resist so beautiful a woman?" the prince asked her, pulling her close to him. His other hand slipped quickly into her blouse, and he fondled her breast.

"Stop this instant!" Adair said low.

"He can't see us," the prince replied, and fondled her other breast. "Jesu, madam, you have the sweetest tits." He stole another kiss from her.

Adair stamped upon James Stewart's foot and yanked his hand from her bodice. "Shame on you, laddie!" she scolded. "I know that Conal Bruce is of little importance, but one day you might need his goodwill. He is a stubborn man, and a proud one. Do not shame him in this fashion. And do not shame me. I will shortly be his wife."

The young prince looked appropriately contrite. "I will apologize, madam, but you must share the blame for my bad behavior. You are really quite delicious, and a most tempting confection to resist."

"I can see you have been very spoiled, Your Highness," Adair teased him.

Then, turning away from the prince, she looked to see Conal Bruce taking his turn at the caber toss. His back glistened with sweat. His muscles bulged with the effort he was expending lifting the great log. He ran forward a few paces, and then heaved the wood across the field. There was a long moment of silence, and then a great cheer arose from the assembled spectators.

"There's none who can beat that toss," a man standing nearby said.

Adair turned to Prince James. "Would you like to try, Your Highness?" she taunted him wickedly, her violet eyes dancing.

The prince laughed. "Nay, madam, I must give way to the better man in this case," he said. And then he gave her a wink before turning to Lord Home.

Adair walked over to where the laird stood breathing hard. She slipped his shirt over his head. "You will catch a chill if you are not careful," she told him, standing before him and half lacing the shirt up. "I do not expect you are an easy patient. You won, you know. They say it was a most grand toss."

"I did it for you," he told her.

"Why?" she asked.

"To prove to you that I am the man for you, my honey love," he replied.

"I know that, Conal, but until you love me there shall be nothing more between us than there is now. Perhaps that is enough for you, but it is not for me."

"You belong to me!" he said fiercely, looking down into her face.

"Only until the end of September," Adair reminded him.

"Nay! You will be mine forever!" he said.

"Not unless you love me," she replied as stubbornly.

"You are an impossible woman," he raged at her.

"And you a most difficult man," she countered. "Why can you not love me? Or why can you not say you love me if you do?"

"You are going to wed me, Adair. I will not permit another man to treat you as the prince did. Had he been another I would have slain him where he stood."

"Then you love me," Adair said quietly.

"I don't know," he told her. "What the hell is love anyway?"

"When you find the answer to that, my lord, then I will consider marrying you," Adair told him. "I'm going back to the keep now."

"Not without me," he said.

"I am capable of walking back myself," she insisted.

"There are clansmen from all over the border here today," he replied. "You could be accosted by some stranger."

"Then I will warn them to keep their distance, for I am the laird of Cleit's mistress, and he is a very jealous man," Adair snapped back at him.

His hand grasped her wrist hard. "You will walk by my side, Adair," he snarled.

"Yes, my lord. I will walk by your side, but as your slave should I not be several steps behind you?" she cooed at him.

"Shut your mouth, woman," he roared.

"Yes, my lord," Adair said in dulcet tones, and when he glared angrily at her she smiled sweetly at him in return.

Chapter 13

After midsummer the weather was dank and rainy. The cattle and the sheep grew fat in the borderland meadows. Sometimes Adair would stand on the heights of the keep, looking toward England. She wondered who had survived last year's raid on Stanton, and if the king had given her lands to a new lord. And what of Robert Lynbridge and his family? When had they learned of her disappearance?

He had not yet told her that he loved her, and the summer was fast coming to an end. September loomed, and at the end of that month both she and Elsbeth were free to either stay or go. She could not, would not wed him if he did not love her. And she could not remain as his mistress. Adair began to debate with herself about her situation. The truth of the matter was that she was just as stubborn as he was in this matter of love.

Yet she had said she would go, and she would. If she did not follow through on her word he would think her weak. He would make her his victim, and she had never been anyone's victim. When Henry Tudor had thrown her out of Windsor she had gritted her teeth and managed to make her way back to Northumbria. When she had found her home destroyed she had managed again to survive, and keep her Stanton folk safe. Well, if she had to walk all the way back to Stanton she would. And she would make her home wherever she could. Surely there was a cottage left. And if she was alone, then she would be alone. She was Adair Radcliffe, the lady of Stanton, and she needed no one's help. She spoke to Elsbeth about her plans.

"You'll go alone, my chick," her old Nursie told her. "I love you best of any in this world, but I cannot stop you from your own foolishness. We have a home here, and the laird loves you. He would wed you if only you would say yes."

"He does not love me or he would say it," Adair replied. "How can I stay, Elsbeth? How can I wed a man who has so little care or respect for me?"

Outside of the kitchens the rain poured down, but the hot fire in the hearth took the damp and the chill from the room. They had somewhere along the way acquired a large, fat orange cat who had become Elsbeth's especial pet. The cat, a rather excellent hunter, kept the kitchen, the larder, and the pantry free of rats and mice. Elsbeth spoiled him outrageously, and he now snored in her lap.

"Conal Bruce is not John Radcliffe or your uncle Dickon, my child," Elsbeth said. "He is not a civilized English gentleman like Andrew Lynbridge or his brother, Robert. He is a rough-hewn Scots borderer, but his heart is good. He cares for you. I see it in his eyes when he looks at you. But like many men he has not the talent for speaking what is in his heart. You must accept that, Adair.

"Why would you go back to Stanton? There is nothing there for you. You love Conal Bruce, though you will not tell him. You have a chance at happiness, my child. Do not walk away from it. Not now. Not when you are carrying his child," Elsbeth concluded. "The bairn deserves to know his father, and you deserve a good husband."

Adair's mouth fell open. "What do you mean, now that I am carrying his child?"

"You have had no bloody flux since early summer, my child. Were you not concerned by its absence? Flora and Grizel do the laundry, and they only recently mentioned the lack of bloody rags," Elsbeth remarked.

"Oh, Jesu, I am a fool!" Adair cried. "I have been so busy helping Conal to earn a bit of coin for his cattle without his realizing I was helping him that I did not notice. Well, perhaps I did notice recently, but I put it from my mind."

"The bairn will probably come in the very early spring," Elsbeth said. "You must tell the laird, Adair."

"If I tell him he will force me into marriage," Adair said low.

"If you do not tell him within the next few days then I must," Elsbeth answered. "This child will not be bastard-born when his father wants him, and he will."

But Adair was afraid to tell Conal of the coming child, even as he struggled with telling her that he loved her. September was half over now, and the hunting for the cold larder had begun again. The weather, so rainy the summer through, had turned clear and sunny. The laird and his men were out every day, even on the one day it had rained. It was a hard storm, and Conal Bruce returned home feeling ill. By morning he was burning up with fever. He struggled to get from his bed.

"We have to hunt. The grouse are scarce this season, and I haven't seen a single deer in days," he told her.

"You can't go. You're sick," Adair said.

"But we need the game for winter," he protested. Then he fell back on his pillows. He was pale, and his forehead was dotted with beads of sweat.

"Your brothers can go," Adair told him. "You are staying in bed, my lord."

"Ah, you lustful wench, you just wish to have your way with me," he teased her weakly, attempting to leer, but then he began to cough.

Adair smiled at him. "I am going to prepare one of my evil potions to give you," she said. "You are to remain where you are. I won't be long." Adair turned and left the bedchamber. Down in the hall she found Duncan Armstrong and young Murdoc. "Your brother is sick. It was being out in that storm yesterday. Have none of you any sense that you did not return home when it began to rain?" she demanded of them. "Eat your food, and then you must take the men hunting again. Conal tells me the game has been scarce."

"He's not well enough to hunt?" Duncan asked.

"He's burning with fever," Adair said. "He must remain in bed, and I must dose him to rid him of the evil humors that plague him."

"If he has agreed to remain abed then he must really be ill," Duncan noted. "Tell him not to worry. Murdoc and I will take the men and do the hunting."

"I will need your help," Adair told the brothers quietly. "This is not a simple thing, and Conal must remain in bed for several days. He will be more at ease if he knows you have been successful. The cold larder is empty, but it is just September. There is time yet to fill it, but if you should find a deer today I know Conal would rest easier for it. Now I must go to my apothecary and brew a potion for him to ease his cough and his fever."

"He loves you," Duncan said.

Adair flushed. "He has not said so."

"Oh, but he does!" young Murdoc added.

"Then he had best say it, or I shall have to go," Adair replied. Then she went off to make the medicines she would need for the laird.

"We can't let him lose her," Duncan said. "She loves him too. I see it."

"She's with child, Elsbeth says," Murdoc replied. "But we cannot tell."

"Jesu!" Duncan swore. "Why not?"

"Because Elsbeth wants Adair to tell Conal," Murdoc said.

"She'll say nothing, and she'll leave him if that blockhead of a brother of ours does not admit how he feels about her." Duncan groaned.

"There's a little time," Murdoc soothed his older sibling.

Duncan stood up from the high board. "Come on, youngling, we had best go hunting while we figure out how to bring the two most stubborn people in Scotland to reason. Neither of them, it would appear, knows how to compromise, and they must."

The two brothers left the keep with a part of their men, and spent the day hunting. Good fortune rode with them, for when they returned that evening they brought with them two roe deer and three strings of grouse. Adair was delighted, and praised them for their efforts. Her news, however, was not as good. The laird was no better. In fact, she was certain that his fever was higher now than it had been in the morning.

"We have kept cold cloths on his head all day, but the fever is stubborn. I will have to make a fever reducer of yarrow, oil, and honey," she said. "I have already made a syrup of lemon, mint, and honey for his cough."

"You look tired," Duncan said to her. "You must take care of yourself as well, Adair. You cannot get sick, for who then would care for us?"

She looked sharply at him. What did he know? And who had told him? "I will be all right, Duncan," she replied to his concern.

At the evening meal she sat with them, and both Duncan and Murdoc kept sneaking looks at her. Adair didn't know whether to be angry or laugh. They knew. Of course they did, or their concern wouldn't have been so great. As the meal ended Adair knew she had to do something to relieve the tension. "If either of you tells your brother," she said, "I will find a way to repay you in kind. And I am a patient woman," she warned them. Then Adair left them, going down to the kitchens, where Elsbeth was kneading the bread that would be baked very early in the morning. "Which one of them did you tell?" she demanded. "Murdoc, probably. He adores you. And who else have you told?"

Elsbeth looked up from the table, her arms floury. "Your secret will be out soon enough, my lady. Aye, I told young Murdoc because I knew he couldn't keep the secret. That way when one of the brothers tells the laird you can't blame me." Elsbeth plopped the dough back in a large bowl and covered it with a towel before placing it in the warming oven to rise. "So you had best tell Conal Bruce before they do."

"You're a wicked old woman," Adair said, "and I will blame you. I hope the three of you will at least wait until I have cured him of his illness." Then she left the kitchens, pausing halfway up the stairs, as she was certain she had heard Elsbeth chortling. As she walked through the hall she asked Duncan Armstrong to see the keep was secure for the night, and thanked him when he agreed. Then she hurried up the stairs to the chamber that she shared with the laird.

Flora arose from his bedside, where she had been seated. "He is restless, Adair. And the fever burns hot in him," she said. "I've been changing the cloths for his forehead, but they do not seem to help."

"Stay with him then awhile longer," Adair said. "I was going to wait until morning to mix this new remedy, but I will go and do it now." She left the bedchamber, going downstairs again to the little room that served as her apothecary.

She had a basket of fat yarrows, and, selecting one, she cut it, scooping the seeds out first, and then the soft flesh. She spread the yarrow onto an earthenware dish, mixing it with a bit of olive oil and some very thick honey. She took dried mint leaves and put a few into her mortar, grinding them with her pestle into a very fine power that she blended well into the mixture. Then with her fingers she rolled the ingredients into little balls, setting them onto an iron rectangle. The little chamber had a small oven built into the wall. Adair lit a fire in the firepit beneath the oven. Then she slipped the flatiron into the oven so that her remedy would bake. While she waited she cleaned up the apothecary and got down a small stone jar with a quartz lid.

When the little medicinal spheres had been baked dry, Adair removed them from the oven and set them on the counter to cool, removing several and slipping them into her pocket. Then, blowing out the candles by which she had worked and making certain the firepit beneath the oven was banked, she hurried from her apothecary and back upstairs to the laird's bedchamber. Flora was now nodding in her chair. Adair gently touched her shoulder. "Go to bed," she said softly. "You have been a great help to me."

Conal was moaning and tossing in their bed. Adair poured a small cup of wine and, sitting on the edge of his bed, tried to awaken him, but he was caught in the throes of the fever and just muttered her name. Putting an arm about his shoulders she raised him up, and with her other hand pushed two of the pills into his mouth. Then she took the cup, holding it to his lips, and encouraged him to drink. He took two swallows and then coughed, but she saw the pills had gone down. She tried to give him another sip, but he pushed her hand away.

"Adair," he managed to say.

"I am here, Conal. You are very sick. Sleep now, my love," she told him.

"Do not leave me, Adair," he moaned.

"I am here, Conal," she reassured him. "I will not leave you."

"Ever?" His voice was a whisper.

"Go to sleep, Conal," Adair said, and loosened her grip on him, lowering him back to the bed. She sat by his side the entire night, and he slipped deeper into his delirium. In the morning she sent his brothers and their men to the coldest running stream in the area with orders to bring back enough icy water to fill the oaken bathing tub. And when it was full, before the water could warm, Duncan Armstrong carried his brother from his bedchamber and lowered him into the tub he had brought from its alcove.

The icy water partially roused the laird, and he struggled to arise, but Murdoc and Duncan held him in the tub until Adair told them to take him back upstairs. Together they dried him with rough cloths. At first he began shivering violently, and then the fever returned to hold him in its fierce grip. The laird attempted to fling off the coverlets they kept piling upon the bed, but they would not let him, and Conal Bruce poured sweat.

"We're either going to kill him or cure him," Duncan Armstrong said grimly.

Adair nodded. She was very pale, but her look was a determined one.

She loves him, Duncan Armstrong thought. *She really loves him.*

And then the laird's fever broke, and he grew quiet again as they changed the soaked bedclothes and his sopping night garment. Adair rubbed his chest with a mixture of goose fat and camphor, covered it with flannel, and pushed several more of her pills between his lips, making him drink the wine she poured into the goblet. And then Conal Bruce grew quiet. His breathing was normal. His skin was cool to the touch. Looking out of the window Adair saw the sun was close to setting.

"Go and get some rest," Duncan said. "You've been at this for two days. He's safe, and you must take care of yourself now, Adair."

"I'll send Grizel to sit with him for a few hours," Adair said. "You must be tired too, Duncan. Thank you for your help. I could not have done it without you."

He nodded and gave her a warm smile. Then he said, "You're a headstrong lass, Adair. I admire your courage, but do not allow your pride to overrule your good sense."

"Tell your brother that," Adair replied softly. "Aye, Duncan, I love him. But I must know that he loves me before I can wed him. It cannot be for the sake of the child I carry. It must be because he loves *me*. Loves me first, and before all others. I cannot otherwise be happy or content." Then she left the chamber.

Duncan Armstrong stared after her. He could only imagine what their child was going to be like. Then he chuckled. Certainly this episode of serious illness would bring Conal to his senses, and he would admit to Adair what was in his heart: that he loved her, and would love no other. They could not go on like this. Could they?

Conal Bruce awoke the next morning feeling as weak as water, but he also felt better. Adair was dozing in the chair by his bedside, and he remembered through his confused thoughts that it had been she who had struggled so hard to break the burning fever that had gripped him. "I love you," he whispered softly, but she did not stir, and he was relieved. He was obviously still weak from his illness. His eyes closed, and he fell back into sleep. When he awoke again Adair was gone from his side, and it was Flora who sat at his bedside. "Fetch Adair," he ground out to the startled woman.

Flora jumped up. "Yes, my lord, at once," she said, and scampered from his bedchamber.

He lay back against his pillows and waited. When she finally entered the room she was carrying a bowl and a spoon. "What's that?" he demanded by way of greeting.

"I've brought you some broth," Adair said quietly. "It will help you to rebuild your strength, Conal. And later Elsbeth has nice milk custard for you."

"I want meat!" he told her.

"You would spew it before it reached your belly," she answered him quietly, sitting down on the edge of the bed. "Now open your mouth and eat your broth." And she pushed the spoon between his lips as he opened them to protest. "There. Isn't that tasty? We had to kill a chicken to make the broth, but it was old and had ceased laying."

"You are treating me like a child," he grumbled, but the soup was good, and he was hungry. He did not think anyone had ever fed him in all his life.

"You have been very sick, Conal, and you are not strong enough yet for many things. It will take several days before you can leave your bed, and it will be a week or more after that before you are strong enough to venture forth again."

"I am not some elder," he said irritably.

"Nay," she said soothingly, "but you are very sick, Conal. You must not fret. Duncan, Murdoc, and the men are hunting. There are already two deer and a dozen grouse in the cold larder. By October you will be ready to hunt again with them." She spooned the last of the broth into his mouth. "There. You've eaten it all." She dug into the pocket of her gown, drawing out one of her pills. Setting the bowl and spoon aside she fetched the wine, pouring it into his cup. "Here, take this," she said.

He took the pill and swallowed it down with the wine, handing her the empty cup. "One of your evil potions?" he teased her weakly.

Adair nodded with a small smile.

"Why can't I get up?" he wanted to know.

"You are still sick, Conal, even though your fever is gone. Your chest is filled with evil humors, and you have not yet rid yourself of them. Now lie back. I want to rub some of this ointment on your chest." Reaching for the jar on his bedside table, she removed the lid and yanked his nightshirt up.

"The damned stuff stinks," he complained as she smeared the unguent over his skin. "What the hell is in it?" Her hand on his chest felt wonderful.

"It will help you to cough up the sickness from your chest," she said as she finished. "Go back to sleep, Conal. I'll be back later," Adair promised as she recapped the jar and set it back on the bedside table. Then she was gone before he could protest any further. She hurried to the kitchens, and washed the oily ointment from her hands.

"How is he?" Elsbeth wanted to know.

"Complaining," Adair answered with a small smile.

"Then you've beaten his sickness," Elsbeth replied.

"Not quite yet, but I am close to success," Adair said.

Conal Bruce improved daily, and after a few days Adair allowed him to spend part of his day in the hall by the fire. By month's end he was fully recovered and planned to join his brothers hunting on the first day of October. Adair had not been sharing his bed while he had been ill, and he intended to tell her that she was to return to him that night.

They sat at the high board that bright morning. Flora and Grizel brought the small round bread trenchers of porridge, setting them at each place. A bowl of hard-boiled eggs, a pitcher of cream, a hot cottage loaf, sweet butter, and cheese were placed on the board. Fresh cider was served in the polished wooden goblets. The laird thought it seemed quiet that morning. The women servants were subdued. His brothers hardly opened their mouths. He listened for the sound of distant thunder, but heard none. And then as he prepared to leave the hall the storm hit.

"I won't be here when you return, my lord," Adair said quietly. "It is October, and my year-and-a-day period of servitude is now concluded. I will be returning to Stanton. Elsbeth has decided to remain with you, and both Flora and Grizel are competent to manage your household." She curtsied. "I thank your lordship for his kindness."

Conal Bruce's mouth fell open with his initial surprise. And then as she made to turn away from him he began to shout. "What the hell do you mean, you wicked vixen? You cannot leave me. I will not permit you to go!"

"*Permit?* You will not permit me to go? I have been your slave for a year and a day, my lord. I have served out my term of bondage. I have given you good service, and I am now free again. Free to do what I wish to do. To go where I choose to go. You have no rights over me, Conal Bruce. None at all."

"Why do you want to leave me?" the laird asked her, attempting to calm his anger and his wildly beating heart.

"Why should I remain?" Adair replied softly.

"I have offered you marriage. Is that not an honorable proposal?" he said.

"You want an unpaid housekeeper," Adair answered him.

"Then I will pay you to remain. Six groats a year, your board, and two gowns," the laird offered her. "The coins payable today, October first, each year you remain with me. You may make the gowns whenever it pleases you from the cloth in the keep's storage chamber."

"So you admit that all you wanted of me is to be your housekeeper. You are insulting. I was born the Countess of Stanton, not a servant. Farewell and good hunting, my lord," Adair said angrily.

"How do you propose to get back to Stanton?" he demanded of her.

"I have feet," she said scathingly. "I managed to find my way from London to Stanton without anyone's aid." She looked defiantly at him.

"You'll be killed, raped, or worse," he told her. "A woman alone, tramping over the hills to England. Have you lost whatever wits you had? You aren't going anywhere!"

"Conal, in the name of all that is holy, tell Adair the truth," Duncan begged the laird. "Tell her that you love her, because it is obvious to everyone in the keep that you do. And she loves you, but she is as stubborn as you are and will not admit to it."

"You cannot make him say what is not so, Duncan, for if I understand one thing about your brother it is that he is an honorable man. He does not love me."

The laird stood tongue-tied. He wanted to tell her. He wanted to cry out that he did indeed love her. But before everyone in the keep? His men? The servants who had now come up from the kitchens? His brothers? They would think him a fool, and he would not be made to appear as if he were. He stood silent.

Adair looked at him. She was angry, but still her eyes filled with tears. "Farewell, my lord," she said, and turned to leave the hall.

"Conal! You can't let her go," Murdoc cried. "She is carrying your child!"

The laird of Cleit felt as if he had been hit a monstrous blow in his belly. His chest felt tight and actually painful. Then his anger exploded as he stepped forward and grasped Adair's arm in a hard grip. "You bitch! You would leave me, and not tell me you were carrying my child? Know that our bairn is the only thing that prevents me from strangling you where you stand, Adair."

She slapped him as hard as she could with her other hand. "*Our bairn?* Nay, my lord. *Your* bastard!" And when she went to slap him a second blow he grabbed the wrist of her hand in a terrible grip. "You are hurting me!" she cried.

"Holding you thus is the only thing now that keeps me from killing you," he snarled. "Understand one thing, Adair. You are going nowhere. You are mine. You were from the moment we met, and you will always be. I have asked you to wed me, and now you will, for my bairn will not be born without its name."

"I will not wed you, Conal, and you cannot force me, for you do not love me. I was married the first time by proxy, and knew naught of it until I was faced by a pockmarked boy crowing his sovereignty over me. A second time for convenience. But if I marry again it will be for love and no other reason, for now I have nothing to offer a husband but my own love and loyalty. I am no more the Countess of Stanton. I am no longer a landowner. I have only myself to give, and I will not give myself away to a man who cares so little for me that he cannot say he loves me, and mean it from his heart."

"You are going nowhere," he repeated in a tight voice. Then he dragged her from the hall, and upstairs to their bedchamber. Forcing her into the room, he closed the door behind her, and taking a key from his key ring, he locked the door. "We will discuss this further when I return from hunting," he told her.

"There is nothing to discuss," she yelled through the door as she heard him walking away and back down the stairs.

Back in the hall Conal Bruce turned to his brothers and his servants. "I have locked the recalcitrant wench in my bedchamber. Elsbeth, neither you nor the others are to go near that door while I am gone. Let Adair's temper cool a bit. By evening I expect she will be more reasonable."

"More likely her heart will be further hardened against you, my lord," Elsbeth told him. "Why do you not just tell her you love her, and be done with it?"

"What makes you think I do?" he asked of her.

Elsbeth snorted derisively, while Flora and Grizel were both wearing knowing smiles upon their faces.

Behind him he heard his two brothers snickering, and he could sense the grins upon the faces of his men. "She will see reason eventually," Conal Bruce said. "She does not want our child born on the wrong side of the blanket like she was."

"She knew nothing of her true sire until she was six," Elsbeth reminded him. "She never felt bastard-born, for John Radcliffe loved her dearly. She was his daughter no matter who got her on her mother. She does not really understand the consequences of a bastard-born child, for she never had to, even in the royal nursery."

"My bairn will not be born labeled bastard," the laird said. "She carries my child. I am willing to wed her. The priest will wed us, by proxy if necessary."

But Adair continued to prove difficult. She would not even speak to Conal Bruce when he returned from hunting that day and released her from her prison. She stamped down into the hall, ate her meal, and went into the kitchens. When the other servants had retired to their quarters in the attic, Conal Bruce sat grimly waiting in the hall for Adair to return. When she finally did she ignored him as she went about her duties for the evening. Then she prepared to return to the kitchens.

"Where the hell do you think you're going?" he demanded of her.

"I have concluded my duties for the day," she said. "I am now going to bed."

"You sleep with me, Adair," he said fiercely.

"You did not say that bedding me would be part of my duties for the six groats a year I am to be paid," she returned sweetly. "I must insist on at least ten groats if I am to fuck you on a regular basis. And you have not yet given me my coins for the year ahead," Adair reminded him. She held out her hand, palm turned up.

"Then you plan to remain," he countered, ignoring her demand for payment.

"Elsbeth has convinced me this evening that walking the many miles to Stanton might not be wise, given my condition. And then too I have considered seeing the look on your face when I birth your bastard. Especially if the child in my womb is a son. You do not have any other bastards, do you?" Adair asked him venomously.

Conal Bruce gritted his teeth. "Nay, I do not," he said. "At least, I know of none."

"Then this will be your first," she said. "How exciting for you. I am told it is quite an event for a man to have his first bastard."

"I may kill you despite the bairn," he snarled. "Get upstairs to our bedchamber!"

In bed she lay curled away from him. He did not press the issue although he longed to hold her, to caress her, to kiss her, to fill her with his lust.

The following day he sought out the priest in the nearby village and presented his problem.

The priest shook his head. "If she will not have you, my lord, there is little you can do to force her. If she had a guardian that would be a different matter, for it would be he who made the match."

The laird considered the problem, and then asked, "Who could be her guardian?"

"The lady is not a child now, but if a blood relative could be found you could make a match for her with him," the priest answered.

The laird thought on the matter for the next few days. It was his brother, Duncan Armstrong, who came up with the solution.

"Adair is King Edward's daughter," Duncan said. "King Edward the Fourth descends from King Edward the third a good century back. Another of his descendants was wed to our King James the First. This would give Adair and Prince James a blood tie. The prince is considered of age. Could not he be designated Adair's guardian? And if that were the case, could not he, as Adair's legal guardian, arrange a marriage agreement for you with Adair? The connection is tenuous at best, but there is still a blood tie," Duncan finished.

"If I ask the prince for a favor," Conal responded, "then I owe him a favor in return. There is trouble brewing between the king and his nobles."

"That trouble has been coming to a head for years," Duncan remarked. "The king will not be able to hold on to his throne for much longer. Scotland wants and needs a strong man to lead it. This James Stewart is nothing like his father. But his son is a combination of both his father and his grandfather. Like this king he is an educated man, but unlike this king he speaks the language of the Highlands, and is a fine athlete. He is a soldier, and a great lover of women. He does not scorn the company of the earls. Our prince is the kind of man we want as king."

"But the king lives, and is in good health," Conal said.

"The king lives, but he deeply mourns Queen Margaret. He has shut himself up in Stirling and will make no decisions. Sooner than later the clans will force him from the throne and put his son in his place," Duncan said. "But if they think to rule the lad they are wrong. The prince will be king."

"And in return for the favor I ask him I will be beholden to Prince James. What if I am expected to join him when the earls decide to replace the king? What if they take their gamble at the wrong time, and lose, and I am named a conspirator?" Conal Bruce asked his oldest brother.

"Life is a gamble," Duncan said dryly. "You have to decide what you want more, Conal. Do you want your son born legitimate? Or do you choose to cower here at Cleit, taking no chances and believing that you are safe? Safe for what?"

"Do you know where Prince James is now?" the laird asked his brother. He was stung by Duncan Armstrong's sharp words. Duncan had been his mother's second-born son by her first husband, William Armstrong, the laird of Duffdour. His older brother, Ian, was the current laird. When their father had died, Euphemia Armstrong had remarried the laird of Cleit. Her oldest child remained at Duffdour. Her daughter was being brought up by the girl's future husband's family. Only Duncan had come with her to Cleit. But Duncan Armstrong was a man who moved easily through the borders. He knew many, and he knew much.

"Aye, he's at Hailes with the Hepburn," Duncan said. "Do you want me to go to him and ask his help?"

"We'll go together," Conal Bruce said.

"You're not afraid to leave Adair alone?" Duncan asked.

"Adair is not going anywhere. Murdoc will keep her amused, and Elsbeth will make certain that she does nothing foolish," Conal said. "We'll go tomorrow."

Duncan nodded. "Aye, you're right to go now. The sooner the better. She's the perfect wife for you, you know." He chuckled.

"That termagant? You have odd ideas, big brother," the laird replied. "I'd not have her but that she is carrying my child."

"You're a bad liar, Conal," Duncan told him. "You love her, and she loves you. I do not understand why neither of you can admit to it and be done with it. She nursed you like a bairn in your recent illness. She would scarce leave your side even to sleep. I'll be glad when you two come to a peaceful arrangement."

Conal Bruce announced that evening that he would be leaving Cleit on the morrow for a few days. "Duncan is going with me. Murdoc will have charge of the keep. Adair, you may have the run of the keep again, but should you attempt to flee Murdoc has orders to lock you in our bedchamber. Do you understand?"

She glared at him. "Where would I go? Elsbeth continues to assure me that Stanton is no more. All I want to do is sleep in recent days. I am weak from puking, and can hardly eat a morsel. I am hardly able to escape my confinement, my lord."

"Do you understand?" he repeated.

"Aye, I understand," she snapped at him. "Where are you going?"

"Duncan and I have business at Hailes," he replied.

She asked nothing more of him, and he left her sleeping when he departed the following morning. They rode from sunrise until almost sunset. With autumn the days were growing shorter each day. Arriving at the Hepburn's keep, they joined Patrick Hepburn and Prince James in the hall. The last meal of the day was being served, and it was not until after they had all eaten and were seated before the hearth that Conal Bruce set his problem before the prince and his host.

When he had finished his host burst out, "Jesu, Bruce! Have you not told the wench you love her yet? You would not have this difficulty if you did."

" 'Tis not manly to gush about love with a woman," the laird said, flushing.

"Hell, Jamie is forever telling women he loves them. He's already had one bastard, haven't you, you young devil? Women need the reassurance of the words 'I love you' to reassure them that their man actually cares. There is nothing to it. If you are afraid, do it at the height of passion, Conal Bruce."

"She won't believe me at this point," the laird replied. "She has waited months for me to say it, but I could not. She threatened to leave me after her year and a day of servitude was up, and she would have but that my youngest brother blurted out that she was with child. We have fought bitterly since then. If I tell Adair now that I love her she will not accept my words as truth. But I cannot wait to convince her. Our child must be born legitimate." He sighed. "I need your help, Your Highness."

"How can I be of help to you, my lord?" young James Stewart asked.

"The priest tells me that if a male blood relation of Adair's were found, and he would agree to a marriage between us, then she must accept it. Adair is King Edward the Fourth's natural daughter. That king descended from Lionel of Antwerp and Edmund of Langley, King Edward the Third's third and fifth sons. You, my lord, also descend from King Edward the Third through his sixth-born child, his fourth son, John of Gaunt, Duke of Lancaster. It was Gaunt's granddaughter, Lady

Joan Beaufort, who married King James Stewart the First, your great-grandfather. Therefore you and Adair Radcliffe are related by blood. Her natural father is dead. Richard of Gloucester is dead. She had no other male relations. If you would become Adair's legal guardian and formally agree to a match between us, she would be forced to accept it."

The Hepburn of Hailes whistled slowly. "I would have never considered you capable of such deviousness, Conal Bruce," he said admiringly.

"It is worthy of a Florentine," the prince agreed.

"Actually I cannot take credit for the thought, Your Highness. It was my brother Duncan Armstrong who brought it to me."

"It matters not," the prince responded. "While the connection between your lady and me is tenuous at best, it nonetheless exists. I know a priest in Jedburgh who is conversant with the law. Let us see what he has to say about the matter. We'll ride out tomorrow morning." He turned to Patrick Hepburn. "What say you, my lord?"

The Hepburn nodded. "There is a lass in Jedburgh I would be delighted to visit once again," he said with a wicked grin. "My wife need not know."

The following day the four men, in the company of twenty of the Hepburn's clansmen, rode into Jedburgh. While Patrick Hepburn's men drank in a nearby tavern, and the Hepburn himself was entertained by an old friend; the laird, Duncan, and the prince sought out the priest, whom they found in a small religious house on the town's edge. Seeing the young man, the brown-robed priest's eyes lit up with pleasure. He knelt and, taking the royal hand, kissed it in a gesture of respect.

"How may I serve you, Your Highness?" he asked as he rose back to his feet. He invited them to sit, and offered them small cups of wine.

"This is Conal Bruce, the laird of Cleit, who is my friend, Father Walter. He has come to me to help him solve a difficult situation which may require your knowledge of the law." The prince explained how Adair had come into Conal Bruce's possession, and that now that she was with child he wanted to wed her. "But the lass is recalcitrant, good Father. She will not accept the laird's offer, but she must for the bairn's sake. Her close male relations are dead; however, the lady and I are related by blood. A feeble thread binds us, but nonetheless it does exist. Could I be made this lady's legal guardian so that I might arrange the match between this relation and the laird, if for no other reason than the sake of the bairn's immortal soul?"

Father Walter thought for several long and silent minutes. Then he said, "Explain to me the line of descent for you both, Your Highness."

The prince did, and when he had finished the priest said, "It is a thin connection indeed, Your Highness, but it is my learned opinion that the lady, like all of her sex, needs to be protected from her own foolish and headstrong passions. Aye, she must have a guardian who will make a sensible decision for her. If she will not accept it for her own sake, surely her maternal feelings will make her do so for her child. Especially given the stain of bastardy that she herself carries." He turned to the laird. "And while you must certainly atone for your lusts, my lord of Cleit, I commend you for accepting the responsibility of your unborn child and the weak woman who is its mother. Do not hesitate to beat her regularly once you are wed. The Bible recommends it. It is for her own good, and she will be a better and more obedient wife to you for it. I will draw up the papers, Your Highness. If you will come back in a few hours it shall be done."

Outside in the street the prince burst into merry laughter. "I suspect if you ever beat her she would kill you the first chance she got." He chuckled.

The laird nodded. "Aye, she probably would," he agreed.

"I am always astounded that men of the cloth who have no association with women seem to know how they should be treated," Duncan Armstrong said.

"Aye, they forget that they came into this world from a woman's body," the prince said. "Still, if Father Walter says the agreement he is drawing up is legal, then it is."

The three men joined the Hepburn clansmen at the tavern, where they ate and drank until it was time to return to Father Walter. He had two documents spread out upon a table. The first gave the prince charge over his blood relation, Adair Radcliffe of Stanton, to do with her as he would. The line of descent between the two was carefully illustrated. It was signed by Father Walter, and then the prince, and sealed with the priest's official ring. The second parchment was a marriage contract between Conal Bruce and Adair Radcliffe, as sanctioned by her guardian, Prince James.

Several days later the laird of Cleit returned home in the company of the prince, the Hepburn of Hailes, and his oldest brother. He was greeted by Murdoc.

"All has been quiet," Murdoc told him. "And Adair is not angry with me. I much enjoyed her company," he told his brother.

"She will continue to be angry with me," Conal told his youngest brother. "Especially when she learns what I have done." And then he explained to Murdoc how he had gotten around Adair's resistance to marrying him.

Murdoc's blue eyes grew troubled. "If you force her she will never forgive you."

"What choice have I? Would you let my son be born a bastard?" the laird asked.

"Nay, but can you not wait a bit? Perhaps you can bring her around. All you need do is tell her the truth. That you love her."

"And do you believe she would accept my word now?" Conal Bruce replied.

Murdoc looked crestfallen. "I don't want Adair to be angry with you anymore, Conal. It cannot be good for the child she carries."

And then the subject of their conversation came into the hall. The young prince thought that Adair was probably one of the most beautiful women he had ever seen. He envied Conal Bruce, but the truth was, had she not been with child he might have considered making an attempt to steal her from the laird. *I would not have hesitated to tell her that I loved her*, James Stewart decided. *And eventually it might have even been the truth.* He smiled winningly at her as she came forward to greet him.

"Welcome to Cleit, Your Highness," she said, and she curtsied.

"Thank you, madam. I have brought you news of an interesting sort, which I hope may please you," James Stewart said. He was going to tell her. He was not going to let Conal Bruce's youngest brother talk the laird out of doing what he must do. The prince knew enough about women to know that Adair would be far angrier two months from now than she would be learning the truth today.

"The day has been gray, and your ride a chill one. Come and sit by the fire. I will bring you wine myself," Adair replied. She made him comfortable and fetched a goblet of wine for the prince, noting that Conal stood by his side. "Will you have wine, my lord?" she asked him coldly and, not waiting for his answer, brought it to him. Then she smiled at the prince and asked him, "What news do you bring?"

"I have learned, madam, that you and I are related by blood. We both descend from King Edward the Third through his three of his sons. That being so, I shall call you cousin."

"I am honored that you do, Your Highness," Adair answered him, smiling, but there was something more. She sensed it.

"Your father and he you called father are both dead, cousin. You have no brothers living, or any other male relations in England. It would seem your only male relatives are here in Scotland now."

"My lord!"

The prince held up a hand, warning her to silence.

Adair, having been raised in a royal court, responded as she had been taught in the face of authority. *Jesu*, she thought, *I am little better than Bessie*.

"As your male relation I have moved to become your guardian," the prince continued. "The legalities were approved in Jedburgh several days ago."

"I am too old to have a guardian," Adair protested, "and you too young to be he."

"No woman is too old to have a guardian," the prince chided her, "especially when she is given to stubbornness, cousin. The laird of Cleit has made you an honorable offer of marriage, which you refuse to entertain even though now you carry his bairn. I cannot allow you in a fit of female pique to deliberately smear this infant with the stain of bastardy. You will marry Conal Bruce. The contract is drawn and signed. There but remains a visit to the priest, which we will make tomorrow. I will remain to witness these nuptials, as will my lord Hepburn."

Adair was speechless with both surprise and shock. She had never considered that her life could be turned upside down in such a fashion with no care to her feelings. But then, from the moment she had been carried over the border more than a year ago, nothing had gone as she had anticipated. "I cannot wed a man who doesn't love me," she protested weakly.

"He does love you, but he is, it seems, incapable of saying the words aloud," the prince responded gently. He might be young, but James Stewart knew a woman's heart much better than men twice his age, like Conal Bruce.

Adair looked up at Conal Bruce. "You would do this? You would force me?"

"You leave me no choice, my honey love," he replied.

Adair shook her head wearily. "Three words, my lord, and I would have wed you willingly. Gladly! But now should you say them I could never be certain that you really meant them. You no longer need my consent, and I will never forgive you for that."

"You accuse me of being coldhearted, Adair, and yet while I have never said those words to you, neither have you said them to me," the laird answered her. "Do you love me, my honey love? Do you?"

She looked into his eyes. Her own were filled with tears. "Aye," she said to him. "I love you, Conal. For the first time in my life I love a man wholeheartedly and without reservation. It is to my sorrow that you cannot love me in return." Then she turned, and, her head held high, Adair left the five very surprised men standing in the hall.

Finally the laird swore softly. "Jesu, I cannot force her to this," he said.

"If you do not take her to the priest tomorrow it will but convince her that you really do not love her," Duncan said, and the others nodded in agreement. "It will take time and a great deal of patience on your part, but she will forgive you this."

"I hope so," Conal Bruce, the laird of Cleit, said, "because I do love the difficult wench with every bit of my own heart."

"You're a damned fool, brother," Duncan Armstrong said, and his companions nodded in agreement.

Chapter 14

$\mathcal{S}$he couldn't stop crying despite Elsbeth's soothing voice, which pleaded with her.

"You will harm the child if you do not cease your greeting," Elsbeth said. "Your bairn will have a name. Be glad, my chick."

"He does not love me," Adair sobbed, pummeling the pillows of her bed.

Elsbeth gritted her teeth. "Of course he loves you, and you know it to be so!" she snapped at the young woman. "It is regrettable that that big border brute cannot manage to look you in the eye and then get those three tiny words out. But he cannot, it appears. Men can make a great to-do over nothing, it would seem. Still, it does not change how he feels about you, my chick. Why else would he have gone to such trouble to wed you?"

"What trouble?" Adair sniveled.

"Going to Prince Jamie and patching together a blood tie." She chortled. "I see the fine hand of Duncan Armstrong in that. Your man has not the wisdom to have figured that connection out, but his elder brother does. Yet once he had a bit of hope in his hand the laird hot-footed it to find the prince and make that hope a reality. If that isn't love, I don't know what is," Elsbeth said.

"He just wants his child born legitimate," Adair said, sniffing.

"He could as easily legitimize the bairn after its birth," Elsbeth said. " 'Tis the mam he wants first and before all, my child. He loves you."

"I cannot believe it unless he says it to me," Adair replied. She was so tired, and she felt horribly weak. All the fight had suddenly left her.

301

She turned onto her back and closed her eyes. "I need to sleep, Nursie." Her eyes closed of their own volition.

Elsbeth sat by Adair's bedside until she was certain that her mistress was sleeping soundly. Then she arose and returned to the hall, where the five men were now having their meal. The table was a bit subdued. "Is it not enough?" she asked the laird. "Is something wrong with the food, my lord?"

"Everything is excellent, Elsbeth. How is Adair?" he answered her.

"Sleeping, my lord, and I believe she will sleep through the night. I would make preparations for a wedding feast. When will you go to the church tomorrow, my lord?"

"I am sending for the priest to come to the hall so it may be easier for Adair," he told Elsbeth.

But Elsbeth shook her head and clucked disapprovingly. "Nay, my lord. You must take her up on your horse and ride to the church with her for all to see, else she will believe you are ashamed that you are making her your wife. And you must wed her before the altar and all who would enter the church to see. Then you will set her upon your horse and ride back with her to the keep to celebrate."

The prince nodded his agreement. "Aye, Conal. Women put much store in public displays like that. She may not say anything, but she will notice that you have publicly put her forth as your bride and wife."

Patrick Hepburn chuckled. "The lad is barely out of leading strings, but his knowledge of women is phenomenal."

The men about the table laughed.

"I'll go and plan the wedding feast then, my lord," Elsbeth said with a curtsy.

"Are there any flowers left in Adair's garden?" the laird asked.

"A few by the south wall," the woman replied.

"Will you have a bridal wreath made for her head?" the laird said.

His companions chuckled and winked at one another.

"Be careful, brother; you might actually say those dreaded words to Adair if you continue on in such a tender manner," Duncan teased.

Elsbeth chuckled. "I'll see that it is done, my lord," she promised him, and then hurried from the hall. In the kitchens Flora and Grizel were waiting. "There will be a wedding on the morrow," Elsbeth said. "Jack," she called to Flora's young son, and he came from the pantry, where he had been sharpening the carving knives.

"Aye, mistress?" he said.

"Early on the morrow go and pick some flowers from Adair's garden for her bridal wreath, laddie. You must go early, for your mother will have to make the wreath. My fingers are too gnarled and stiff now to do such work. The wedding will take place in midmorning. Adair's gown is the color of lavender, so pick flowers to match and blend."

The boy nodded, and then went back to his knives while Elsbeth, Grizel, and Flora began preparations for the wedding feast. Coming from the pantry the boy saw how busy they were, and went up to the hall to clear the high board. Then he made up the bed spaces for the guests. Duncan and Murdoc shared a bedchamber on the second level of the keep. Jack saw the fire needed more wood, and he added it. The laird and his men were now dicing and drinking. He watched them for a moment, and then returned to the kitchens to wash the dishes. His mother and Grizel were still busy chopping and sifting. Elsbeth was already kneading the extra bread they were going to need.

When the women finally found their rest that night, all was in readiness for the morrow but for the cooking, which would begin early. Jack had agreed to remain behind during the hour of the ceremony itself so that his mother and the others might slip into the church and see Adair married to Conal Bruce.

It was a bright and clear late October day when the sun finally rose the next morning. The men in the hall were served first, and the laird was pleased to see the day-old round trenchers filled with oat stirabout sprinkled with cinnamon, fresh bread, butter, bacon, and eggs cooked with heavy cream, cheese, and black pepper. He saw Elsbeth hurrying through the hall with a small tray, and smiled. Knowing how upset Adair had been, he had not gone to bed until late, and had risen early while she still slept. He wanted no altercations with her today if he could avoid it.

Adair was still sleeping when Elsbeth entered the bedchamber. She set the tray down on the oak table by the window, and gently shook her mistress by the shoulder. "Wake up, my child. It is your wedding day, and 'tis a fair one. I think it a good omen."

Adair could hardly force herself awake at first, but then she finally managed to open her eyes and keep them open. She still felt weak and tired. "My wedding day," she said wanly. "A third husband. Let us hope this one lasts longer than the others."

"So you are resigned then to accepting Conal Bruce as your husband?" Elsbeth asked. "Good! Now you are being sensible, and all will be well, I promise you, my chick. Here is your breakfast. Eat it while it is hot." She brought the tray to Adair and set it on her lap. "I've fed the men in the hall, and the wedding feast is being prepared."

Adair gave her a weak smile. "And what am I to wear?"

"That lovely lavender wool gown we made this summer," Elsbeth said cheerfully. "Jack picked some flowers, and Flora has woven a nice bridal wreath for your head."

Adair began to cry again. "What is the matter with me, Nursie? I weep like a maiden at the least little thing these days," she sobbed.

Elsbeth set the tray to one side and enfolded Adair in her arms, comforting her. "There, my chick, it is the way of a woman with a child in her belly. They weep, they rage, they are euphoric, and all without reason. It will pass, I promise you. Now eat your breakfast," she said, putting the tray back.

"Take the trencher away," Adair said. "I cannot bear the smell of the oats these days." She buttered a piece of bread lavishly and laid some of the salty bacon on it, gobbling it down. Then she sipped at the watered wine Elsbeth had brought her, before she began to eat more bacon and bread. When she had finished eating Elsbeth helped her to wash in the basin, and then she donned the gown Elsbeth had fetched.

The gown was fashioned of soft light wool in a lavender color. The bodice was fitted, and it fell straight from just beneath her breasts. The neckline was a small, square opening. The sleeves were long and tight. The hem was sewn with a darker purple silk ribbon. The only decoration on the gown was the same ribbon edging the neckline.

"It's too tight," Adair complained as the garment settled itself.

"Where?" Elsbeth asked, and then she saw. Adair's breasts were growing larger in preparation for her child. "Stand still," she said, and she carefully pulled some stitches out on the side of the gown beneath Adair's arm. "Is that better, my chick?"

Adair took a deep breath in, and nodded. "We must hope the gown will not burst all its stitches before the day is over, Nursie," Adair remarked with some small show of humor. "The laird is a jealous man."

The door to her bedchamber opened, and Conal Bruce came in. "Go downstairs now, Elsbeth. I will bring my bride when the time is right." He turned from the older woman to Adair. "I have brought you your bridal wreath," he said, handing it to her. "I see you have not fixed your hair yet. Sit down, and I will brush it for you."

She did not know what to say to him. She had already said it all. Wordlessly she sat down and handed him the pear-wood brush he had bought for her at the midsummer fair. Slowly, carefully, he began to brush her long sable hair. The brush slicked down her tresses from the top of her head to the ends of her hair. She actually found it quite relaxing, and closed her eyes briefly.

Finally he stopped and said, "How will you dress it?"

"As I always do. In a single plait," she responded.

"Let me. I have watched you do it enough. I think I can," Conal replied, and proceeded to weave her hair into the thick single braid she favored. When he had finished he bound the ends with the bit of silk ribbon she handed him. "Give me your wreath," he said, and she handed him the circlet that she had been holding in her lap. He set it upon her head. It was fashioned of several small pink late roses, some lavender, and white heather. The fragrance from it was elusive but there. "There. Now you are ready, and I am ready to take you to the priest." He stood up, drawing her to his side.

Adair's hand was icy cold. And then she realized that when she married Conal Bruce the lady of Stanton would cease to exist. But Stanton was already gone. She was not quite ready to forgive him for his high-handed behavior toward her, for his inability to say he loved her, but the truth was, she had had no real choice in either of her previous marriages. Few women did. She could have been killed that day

William Douglas came raiding. She might have been sold into a brothel to be used by man after man until she had died. And no whore mistress would have honored the year and a day of servitude. Fate had treated her in a kindly fashion. "I am ready to go down," she told him.

He led her downstairs and out into the courtyard, where he set her upon the saddle of his great stallion. Then he mounted behind her, one arm holding her gently before him, the other gloved hand filled with the animal's reins. They rode out from the keep's courtyard, followed by Bruce clansmen with their red-and-black plaids blowing behind them. Leading the party was Prince James, Patrick Hepburn, and the laird's two brothers. And behind the procession came a cart carrying Elsbeth, Grizel, and Flora. There was a light wind, but the sun shone brightly, and the sky above them was bright blue.

There was something exciting, Adair considered, about riding beneath such a clear sky on such a beautiful day in the arms of her lover. And he was obviously and patently proud of this marriage that was about to be formalized, she realized, given this public display. He was not ashamed that his bride was English, or that she had been his servant. He publicly exhibited his love for her. *Love? Aye, love!* He did love her! Would he have been so bold otherwise to brandish their wedding day like a great banner before his clansmen and -women? But she still wanted to hear him say the words to her, Adair thought. She would teach him to say them. She smiled to herself.

They reached the village over the hill from the keep, and when they arrived at the small stone church they stopped. The laird dismounted and lifted Adair from the saddle. The priest was awaiting them at the door. Blessing them, he led them into the church, which was crowded with villagers. Elsbeth and her party were distressed to see there seemed no place for them, and then a pretty woman of undetermined age came forward and led them to the front, where places were made for them and they could see all.

"Thank you, mistress," Elsbeth said.

"Agnes Carr," the woman answered.

Elsbeth nodded. "Elsbeth Radcliffe," she returned the introduction. She, like her companions, had heard of Agnes Carr and her warm-hearted nature. That good nature obviously extended to much more in her life than just the lads, Elsbeth decided. She gave Agnes Carr a friendly smile, and then turned to where Adair and Conal now stood before the village priest.

As the bride's legal guardian it was Prince James's duty to release her into the custody of her husband now. He did so, bowing elegantly to Adair and kissing her on the cheek. Then, putting her hand in Conal Bruce's, he stepped back. The ceremony was quickly concluded, for there was no Mass, as standing for too long a period was difficult for Adair of late, and the laird had the utmost consideration for her. Having been proclaimed husband and wife under God's law and the law of Scotland, the newly wedded couple turned, walking down the short aisle to exit the church.

"Hardly seems worth all the fuss," Agnes Carr said with a chuckle. "She's a bonnie lass, your mistress. And from the look on his face it isn't just because he's given her a big belly. The laird loves her, and I can tell you that he's never loved a lass before."

"She loves him too," Elsbeth said. Well, here was a bit of gossip to cheer Adair with the next time she fell to weeping.

"Agnes, my lass." Duncan Armstrong put an arm about the woman. "Come and meet someone very special," he said with a grin.

"You and your brother had best be back in the hall with the prince for the feast," Elsbeth said sternly. Then she turned to Agnes Carr. "Come with us, Mistress Carr, and join the wedding feast. You can meet the prince at the keep." Her look dared Duncan to argue, and he laughed.

"We're coming now, Elsbeth," he promised her. "You are a fierce old dragon, but you cook like an angel. I'd marry you myself, if you would have me," he teased her.

"Well, I won't!" she told him, chortling. "Why, a fine lad like you would be the death of me, though to die so would be wonderful, I'm thinking." Then she let him help her into the wagon, shrieking with surprise when he pinched her bottom.

Laughing, Duncan Armstrong left the giggling women, rejoining his brother and the prince. "Elsbeth didn't want us to be late to the feast," he explained to James Stewart. "But, mindful of your wicked nature, she invited Agnes Carr to the feast. There are plenty of nooks and crannies in the keep where you may take Agnes for your pleasure. She's a grand lass with a big heart and a great appetite for loving, Jamie."

The prince grinned, delighted. "She's a buxom lass," he noted. "I'll look forward to meeting her, Duncan."

They returned to the keep, where the hall was ready to receive the wedding party. Elsbeth had hired several women from the village to aid them that day. Back in her kitchens she began to direct the service with the élan of a military commander at a battle. There was salmon, courtesy of the prince and Patrick Hepburn. There was trout, freshwater mussels with a mustard sauce, and creamed dried cod. There was a whole boar that had been roasted with an apple in his mouth, a side of beef packed in rock salt and roasted over a slow fire, as well as venison. There were platters of grouse, and others of ducks roasted black and served in a sauce of pear and apple, as well as several capons stuffed with bread, sage, onion, and celery, and goose. There was braised lettuce and spinach. Fresh bread, butter, and two cheeses—one soft, the other hard. There were candied violets and rose petals as well as marzipan. The rich red wine never ceased flowing, and the October ale had only recently been brewed.

The guests were well fed and content when the men began to dance to the shrill wail of the pipes. They danced a dance celebrating the wedding, with the bridegroom leading them. They danced the sword dance, skipping nimbly between sharpened blades, their tartans in red, green, black, blue, white, and yellow swirling about them. And amid the celebration, Duncan Armstrong and Prince James sought out Agnes Carr, leading her from the hall.

"You can have the chamber I share with Murdoc," Duncan generously volunteered, grinning.

"Join us for a while," the prince invited as they entered the room. He turned Agnes about to him, and smiled down into her face. "Would you mind?" he asked her.

Like so many women before her, Agnes Carr, normally practical and sensible for all her profession, melted beneath the prince's gaze. " 'Tis fine with me, my lord. I know Duncan Armstrong, and if you are his friend then I know you are a gentleman too." Her mouth curled up in a smile as she slid her arms about his neck and pressed her generous bosom to his broad chest.

James Stewart smiled back at Agnes Carr. "I had been told you were a fine and welcoming lass, Aggie, and I am happy to see the truth was spoken of you." He undid the laces of her skirt first, and then her petticoats, lifting her from them. He undid the ribbons of her shirt and drew it over her head, stepping back to view her nakedness. "Aye, Aggie," he drawled. "You are indeed a fine figure of a woman," he said as he admired her full hips and her large breasts. He turned to Duncan. "I'll race you!" he said, laughing as he began to pull off his own garments, and the two men were quickly naked, tumbling onto the big bed Duncan usually shared with his younger brother, where Agnes was already awaiting them.

"Plenty for all!" she said, chortling as each of them reached for a breast, and soon the bed on which they lay was a tumbled mass of bedclothing and bodies.

The young prince had an insatiable appetite for female flesh, and a very large manhood with which to indulge that appetite. While Duncan held the woman firmly between his legs, his big hands playing with her large breasts, the prince slithered between Agnes's plump thighs and began to forage between her nether lips with his practiced tongue.

Agnes was skilled at seduction, and she was skilled in the act of love, but she had never before entertained two men at once. Nor had she ever known such a lover as the young prince. She moaned her delight as the royal tongue drove her to ecstasy. Then the prince mounted her, and very shortly she was screaming her pleasure as his big manhood drove her almost mad with its skillful thrustings. And she had no time to recover herself, for as the prince rolled away from her, panting with his exertions, Duncan Armstrong was atop her, laboring fiercely.

"That's my lass," he whispered in her ear as he fucked her, and her nails raked down his long back. He pushed her legs over her head and plunged deeper, and she screamed her enjoyment as the prince watched, his own youthful libido roused once more to a fever pitch.

The older man howled with delight as his juices spewed forth, and once more the prince took his place.

Agnes Carr knew she had never been fucked so well or so enthusiastically in such a short period of time. The young prince atop her was tireless, it would seem. His thick and long cock plunged deeply again and again. She could not help herself. Her nails raked the flesh of the royal back, and in response he fucked her harder until she was weeping her pleasure, and only then did he withdraw from her, kissing her tears and praising her for a fine lass. The trio rested for a brief time, and then Prince James was once again ready to enjoy Agnes Carr's charms.

While the royal cock entertained itself in Agnes's rear passage, Duncan Armstrong withdrew quietly, donning his garments swiftly and leaving the room. He returned to the hall and sought out his younger brother. "We're sleeping in the hall tonight," he told Murdoc. "I gave the prince our bed. Agnes is with him. They are giving each other a very good time. He'll not say the hospitality at Cleit was wanting," Duncan said with a rich chuckle. "The lad is insatiable, but he's kind with a woman. Agnes will owe us a debt after this night," he said with a grin. "I doubt no man has ever fucked her quite so well as young Jamie Stewart, nor will any man equal him. This will be a night she long remembers."

"I think Conal and Adair are about to leave the hall," Murdoc said. "Our sister-in-law seems not so angry now." Then he smiled happily. "We're a real family again, Duncan. There's a lady of the keep as well as a lord, and soon we'll have a wee nephew."

"Or niece," Duncan remarked. "Aye, it hasn't been this good since Mam died."

"She'd like Adair," Murdoc said softly.

His eldest brother nodded in agreement.

Adair had left the high board to make certain there was enough wine and ale for the many guests still in the hall. Then, with a whispered word to the laird, she slipped away. Conal Bruce went to each of the trestles below the high board and thanked his guests for coming to their wedding. "There's plenty of wine and ale left for all," he said. "Enjoy yourselves!" he told each group of men and women remaining. Then he too departed the hall.

The high board had been long cleared, and the hired servants had departed back to the village over the hill. Elsbeth locked the door down into the kitchens after Flora and her son had gone to the attic. Grizel was now sharing the bed spaces off the kitchens with Elsbeth, who was frankly grateful for the human company. The two women now slept, Elsbeth with the orange tomcat on the pillow by her head.

"Someone is in your brother's chamber," Adair told her husband, "and it is not Duncan or Murdoc. There is a woman in there, and she is being used mightily. I heard the bedsprings creaking and the sounds of pleasure as I passed by."

"It's the prince, I suspect, with Agnes Carr," Conal answered her.

"Your whore is in my house?" Adair said, wondering if she should be outraged.

"She isn't my whore, and she never was. Agnes is a warm-blooded lass who is always glad to share herself with a like-minded lad," the laird said. "Duncan knows the prince, though young, is a man in every way, and has a great appetite for women. Agnes was willing to aid the laws of hospitality. Prince James will remember Cleit as a hospitable keep, and it cannot hurt to please him. He will one day be king."

"You are showing signs of ambition, *husband*," Adair murmured.

"Not for myself, lass," he replied, reaching out to touch her belly. "For him."

"It could be a daughter I carry," Adair reminded him.

"Nay, I have gotten a son on you, my honey love," he told her.

"I cannot yet forgive you," Adair said.

"But you are no longer angry?" he asked.

"I had lost my anger when I awoke this morning," she replied. "It seemed rather futile and foolish in the face of reality to maintain such a choler. And I would have a peaceful house, Conal. Besides, you cannot help it that you are a fool." Adair sighed.

"I suppose we must accept that," he responded dryly.

"Aye, we must, or we will quarrel again, and it is not good for the bairn," Adair murmured softly. She had removed her gown and was clad only in her chemise. Now, seated upon the bed, she undid her plait and began to brush her hair.

He took the brush from her and sat down. "Nay, honey love, this is my task." The brush began to slick through her tresses. "I love your hair," he said softly. "It is so soft and so rich in color. One moment it is sable, and in another instant the light touches it and it has the blue sheen of a raven's wing." He took up a lock of her hair and pressed it to his lips. "It suits you, *wife*."

A small shiver rippled down her spine. His voice, his words, excited her. It had been so long since they had shared themselves. Adair felt herself melting with the love she knew she had for him. But then she stiffened her spine. He needed to be punished. He couldn't think he might wheedle her with sweet words when he would not say the three words she longed to hear from him. "We must have a care of the bairn, Conal," she said softly. "I have never been with child. I do not know what is permitted and what isn't."

"I'll ask the village midwife tomorrow," he told her as he drew off his own garments and laid them aside. "I will not let you deny me, Adair; nor will I let you deny yourself, my honey love. Our lust has always been very equal." He stood up and put the brush away in her trunk. When he turned back she was tucked into their bed. He joined her, and they lay side by side, not speaking until Conal Bruce sat up, propping the pillows behind him. Then he pulled her so that she half lay between his long outspread legs. He drew her chemise up over her protest. "We will not couple until I know it is safe for us to do so," he told her, "but I do not see why you and I cannot still enjoy each other in sundry other ways." He began to fondle her breasts.

"Oh, please be gentle," Adair begged him. "My breasts are very tender."

"And sensitive, I see," he murmured as her nipples grew tight and hard to his eye.

She shivered under his touch, feeling the stirrings of desire within her fertile body.

He continued to play with her breasts for some time, his warm breath against her ear. Then his hand moved to caress the beginnings of her belly.

"Conal," she begged him, "please stop."

"Why?" he taunted her, tweaking her nipples.

"Because I want you, you devil!" she admitted.

He smiled behind her head. "I do not know if I should pleasure a woman who cannot forgive me," he whispered softly in her ear.

"Then I cannot pleasure you either," she told him. "Please, at least wait until we have spoken with the midwife."

"You're a hard woman, Adair Bruce," he told her.

Adair giggled. She could not help it. "You are a hard man, my lord. *Very hard.*"

He laughed aloud. "It's our wedding night."

"There's a bairn in my belly, Conal. We had our wedding night long ago," she told him pertly. "Fetch my chemise. I am cold."

He got out of their bed, his lust for her visible. *What a waste of a randy cock,* he thought as he picked up her chemise and handed it to her. He donned his own chemise and poured himself a cup of wine, sitting by the warm hearth to drink it. When he finally returned to bed Adair was already asleep. He reached out and touched her face gently with a finger. She was so beautiful, and she loved him. He had to gain the courage to say those three words to her before their child was born. Conal Bruce joined his wife, but his mind was yet active. In the chamber next to his the next king of Scotland was enjoying himself with a woman. Aye, he would remember Cleit's hospitality, but it would not · be enough to wipe out the debt that the laird owed the prince for making his marriage to Adair possible. What would he ask? Conal Bruce knew he would have no choice but to repay the debt, and repay it with whatever was demanded. Would it endanger his small holding? His family? It mattered not. He finally fell into a troubled slumber.

*   *   *

In the morning the hall had been cleared of the last of the guests, many of whom had fallen asleep at the trestles, filled with too much wine and ale. Enough of his clansmen who served as men at arms had remained sober in order to protect the keep, and they virtually ran the last of the guests out. They sat eating their food stoically as the laird entered the hall. Adair was already there overseeing everything.

Prince James came into the hall. He was full of energy, and smiled at everyone. "Good morning, cousin!" he said cheerily to Adair, who waved him to the high board.

Patrick Hepburn, Duncan Armstrong, and Murdoc Bruce appeared, looking somewhat the worse for wear. They had been up very late drinking and dicing.

"Sit down and get some food into you," Adair ordered them.

"Perhaps a wee drop of the hair of the dog that bit us might help," the Hepburn suggested as he lowered himself gingerly into a chair.

"Flora, fill their goblets," the lady of the keep said as Grizel brought trenchers of oats and platters of food.

The Hepburn blanched at the sight of the platters, but bravely lifted the goblet to his lips, as did his companions.

The laird caught his wife's eye and grinned. Adair grinned back.

"I am happy, my lord, to see that you enjoyed our hospitality," she said.

"I will attempt not to die in your keep, madam," Patrick Hepburn told her.

"The prince enjoyed his evening as well," Adair continued. "Did you not, Your Highness? I have heard that Agnes is a most accommodating lass."

"She's a braw girl, cousin," the prince replied. "I shall be visiting her when I am once again in the vicinity." And he chuckled.

"You mean you had a wench, you young devil?" the Hepburn said. He looked aggrieved. "You did not offer me a wench, madam. If I had had one I should not have drunk quite so much, and not had the aching head I have this morning. And worse, I lost a groat and three silver pennies dicing."

"Alas, my lord, there was only one wench. We are a small keep," Adair said sweetly, and her violet eyes were twinkling at the Hepburn as she spoke.

"I'm afraid I wore poor Aggie out," the prince said. "Send her home in the cart, Conal Bruce. She served her prince very well."

"I'll take care of it," Adair told her husband. She left the hall and went upstairs to the bedchamber where she knew Agnes Carr would be lying. Opening the door, she saw the girl sprawled facedown and naked on the bed, her red hair awry. *Lucky wench*, Adair thought. Then she gently shook the girl's shoulder. "Agnes, awake. You must go home now."

Agnes Carr slowly lifted her head from the bed. "Am I still among the land of the living?" she groaned.

"Aye, you are," Adair responded. "And the prince says he'll be visiting you when he is next in the vicinity."

Agnes Carr groaned again. "Never have I been fucked so much in one night by one man," she said. "The laddie has a thirst that is unquenchable, and energy that never flags." She rolled over and, seeing it was Adair, Agnes gasped and grabbed at the coverlet in an attempt at modesty. "My lady!" She struggled to get to her feet, fell back onto the bed, and then Agnes Carr blushed for what was probably the first time in her life.

"The prince's reputation precedes him," Adair said with a small grin. "And 'tis said there isn't a lass he's fucked who ever had cause for complaint."

Agnes managed to retain a sitting position now. "I can attest to that, my lady."

"You have done my husband and me a goodly service by keeping young Jamie Stewart amused last night. Come to the hall when you are ready and have something to eat. Conal will send you home in the cart."

"Praise Jesu for that," Agnes replied. "I do not think I can walk more than a few steps. And I haven't been this sore since I was a virgin newly sprung."

Adair laughed. "When you are ready," she told the woman, and left her to recover herself. Adair returned to the hall. There she found her guests preparing to leave Cleit. The Hepburn's clansmen had already gone to the stables to see to the horses. "My lords," Adair said, "I thank you for coming, and wish you a safe journey."

"You will probably see us sooner than later," Patrick Hepburn told her, and he took her hand and kissed it. "Are we forgiven then, madam?"

"In time, my lord," Adair said, "but until I am able to forgive Conal I cannot forgive his companions in this deception."

"Fair enough," the Hepburn replied with a smile. He was a big, tall man with russet hair and warm brown eyes.

The young prince now stepped forward. "I did not kiss the bride, did I?" he said, and mischievously kissed her lips, leaving Adair a little breathless with her surprise and the knowledge that his lips had been deliciously warm and ardent. "Your hospitality equals that of far larger homes, madam," James Stewart said. Then he pressed a coin into her hand. "For Agnes," he said. "She is more than deserving."

Then, escorted by Conal Bruce and his brothers, the Hepburn and the prince went into the courtyard of the keep to join their men. When they had gone Adair spied Agnes Carr in the shadows. The woman stepped forward.

"I couldn't face the men quite yet," she said.

Adair nodded. "Come and have something to eat," she invited.

"If I might go to the kitchens . . ." Agnes Carr said.

"Of course," Adair replied, realizing that Agnes actually felt a bit embarrassed by her situation. It was one thing to give comfort to the local lads, but she had just spent several very active hours in a prince's bed. A prince who would one day be Scotland's king. She led Agnes to the kitchens, telling Elsbeth to feed her. "When you are ready just go into the courtyard and the cart will be awaiting you," Adair told Agnes. She pressed the coin in Agnes's hand. "From *him*." Then, as she walked slowly up the stairs to the hall, she heard the women in the kitchens begin to question the exhausted Agnes.

"What was he like?"

"Is he as passionate as they say?"

"Is his manhood as large as is rumored?"

Adair giggled and reentered the hall to find her husband had returned.

"What makes you laugh?" Conal asked her.

"The women are querying poor Agnes on the prince," she told him.

Conal Bruce smiled himself. "Agnes Carr will be famous now, having had the prince for her lover. And he will visit her again when he comes."

"*When?*" What did he mean by when? Adair wondered.

"Every favor done requires a favor to be done in return," the laird said slowly. "The prince helped me when he took it upon himself to be your guardian, for that allowed me to wed you."

"It allowed you to coerce me into wedlock," Adair corrected him.

He ignored the barb. "The Hepburn has asked me to allow a group of gentlemen to meet at Cleit now and again. It seems that being insignificant has certain advantages after all," the laird said dryly. "No one would suspect that a plot was being hatched here, and a plot is to be devised."

"What plot?" Adair asked half fearfully.

Conal Bruce shook his head. "I don't know," he said.

"But you can surmise, can you not, Conal?" Adair inquired of him.

"Aye, I can. Conditions in Scotland grow worse with every passing day, and the king does not seem to care. His diplomatic attempt with England has failed. The prince will not marry one of your half sisters; nor will Elizabeth Woodville wear Scotland's crown. The king has retreated to Stirling, where he indulges himself in his hobbies and mourns Queen Margaret. None of this helps Scotland. I am not a man to rebel, but even I realize that something must change."

Adair sighed and nodded. "This frightens me, Conal, but you cannot refuse the prince after what you asked of him. Why did the Hepburn come to you with this request? Why not young James Stewart?"

"The prince does not wish to be accused of fomenting a rebellion against his father. He is a fine son, but King James has never been capable of ruling properly. He has not been a good king. He is a decent man, but there is an arrogance about him that comes from his French mother. Scotland can no longer tolerate his rule. The lords will depose him and put the prince in his place as regent. The king may then be catered to without the responsibility of governing, but Scotland will have a strong ruler again."

Adair was thoughtful for a moment, and then she said, "I have never known of a king who was removed from his throne who was not in the end killed. When you have two kings there is always the temptation for rebellion from the weaker faction."

"The prince wishes no harm to come to his father," the laird said with conviction. "I believe him, Adair. He is a competent young man."

"I believe him too," Adair agreed, "but I also know it is the nature of those surrounding such an affair to seek to solidify their man's position. It was given out that my half brothers were murdered by the Duke of Gloucester in the Tower. But that was a lie. The truth was that Uncle Dickon had sent the boys to Middleham for their safety. They were murdered shortly after the duke's death at Bosworth by those within the Lancaster faction, although despite his cruelty toward me I do not believe King Henry would have given such an order."

"Then you think one of the prince's adherents will kill the king?" the laird said.

"I think it is highly likely, although the prince will not give the order; nor will he even wish to know who did the deed," Adair replied.

"Then I am not comfortable sheltering the conspirators," the laird said. "I cannot do it knowing what you have told me. You are wiser in these matters than I am, my honey love. You understand the mighty and their ways. I do not."

"You have no choice, Conal," Adair told him. "They will make their conspiracy whether you will or no. And poor old King James will be tumbled from his throne, and the prince will be crowned in his stead. Better we be on the prince's side in this matter."

"But why must we take sides at all?" he asked her.

"Because we must. You will not be allowed to stand aside, casting your eyes to the heavens while these events unfold about you, Conal.

Everyone in Scotland will be asked to take sides. No one will have any choice."

"She's right, you know." Duncan Armstrong had come into the hall and was listening to the exchange between his brother and Adair.

"What will the Armstrong of Duffdour do?" Conal Bruce asked about his mother's eldest son, who had been born, like Duncan, to her first husband.

"Our eldest brother will carefully weigh and balance all the options in the matter, and then, being a canny fellow, he will choose to stand with the prince. Ian will not be a knife at our back, Conal. He knows what is involved, and will seek to obtain the best advantage for his own clansmen," Duncan said. "Ian is no fool. Ask the Hepburn's permission to invite him when you are asked to host the gathering. It cannot hurt the Bruces of Cleit or the Armstrongs of Duffdour to both be represented. There will be far more important men, men with rank and power, but we will represent the simple border lords, and remain prominent in the prince's memory. Our families may even benefit some by our early show of loyalty to a new king."

"What if the Highlands rally to the king?" Conal asked. "The Highlands have always been loyal to the Stewarts."

"The Highlands are like the rest of us. They do what is to their own advantage," Duncan replied. "Aye, they'll come to the king if he calls them, but how hard they will fight for him is another matter. And when the prince's forces triumph they will be very quick to make their peace with him."

Adair was fascinated to listen to the two brothers' conversation. It would seem, she thought, that all power was directed in a similar way, no matter the country. It had been much the same in England, with the York and Lancaster factions jockeying for position. She realized as she listened that her husband was not as astute at political intrigue as was his Armstrong brother, or, for that matter, as clever as she was. He was truly a plain border lord, but he was a good man for all his rough ways. *I am fortunate in this husband. Now if he will just not get himself killed in some damned war*, she thought.

In early afternoon young Murdoc came home complaining that

Agnes Carr would not allow him in her cottage after he had driven her home in the cart. His brothers laughed heartily at his discomfort, and told him that the prince had worn the woman out. She would not be ready to entertain a randy cock for several days.

"We need more whores," Murdoc complained, and his brothers laughed all the harder. "Well, Conal, I know what you do, but what do you do, Duncan?" the aggrieved young man demanded to know.

But Duncan smiled mysteriously, and said nothing much, to Conal's amusement and Murdoc's irritation.

Adair was curious as to how they would know when the prince or Patrick Hepburn would come again. "I cannot entertain a houseful of men if I do not know when to expect them. Our winter larder will go just so far."

But Conal told her, and Duncan agreed, that they would not receive any prior notice. Those involved would just appear. Adair sent the men of the keep out once more in the short and cold days to seek more game for the larder. She liked finding herself in the thick of things again, but she would not have Cleit's hospitality criticized. And as if the forces of nature understood her dilemma, game was suddenly in great supply. Soon Cleit's winter larder was filled with the carcasses of deer, game birds, and three wild boar hanging from the heavy iron hooks. And fish was caught, to be smoked and salted. Adair was satisfied that Cleit would not be found wanting.

The first snow came, spreading its mantle of white over the border hills. It glistened in the moonlight on the cold long nights. The village midwife had been consulted, and advised the laird to contain his lust.

"Your wife is not in the first flush of her youth, my lord. She is already three years past twenty, and this is her first bairn. I would, for her sake, advise that you contain your lustful nature until after your bairn is born. Cleit needs heirs, and it took you long enough to wed," she half scolded him.

Adair was relieved at the midwife's verdict. She was sick more times than not with the child growing in her belly. But she had to admit that Conal Bruce knew how to soothe her. Twice each day he brushed her long hair. And at night he caressed her breasts gently, and then his big hands would enclose her burgeoning belly in a tender embrace as he talked to his child. And as November came to an end Adair could feel the faint stirrings of the infant within her. Now she began to wonder if she would give him a son for Cleit, or if it was a daughter that she carried.

December came and went as her belly grew larger. They celebrated the Christ's Mass in the hall, with the priest coming from the village in deference to the lady of Cleit. The hall had been decorated with branches of holly and pine. They had found a great log in a wood that was dragged in to be the hall's Yule log. Fresh candles made over the autumn months blazed in every corner.

"You look happy again," Elsbeth noted one icy morning as she brought her mistress fresh bread, butter, and bacon.

And Adair realized that she was happy. Really happy for the first time in a very long while. She looked around her clean, warm hall with its Christmas decor. The furnishings were comfortable. The young wolfhound she had christened Beiste in honor of her old dog snored before the fire. Her husband and his brothers sat at the high board with her, eating and laughing. She didn't know when it had happened, but suddenly all the anger and bitterness had gone from her heart, and she was finally content.

Chapter 15

The days were now growing longer, and on February 2, which was known as Candlemas, Adair presented the priest with a year's supply of candles for the village church. Lent came with its fasts and its fish. Suddenly one day strangers began arriving at Cleit, and Adair realized that the prince's adherents were coming for a meeting. Whether they had met at other obscure keeps before she had no idea. She went to the kitchens to warn Elsbeth and the others.

"There isn't enough fish," Elsbeth told her.

"I doubt they will worry about a Lenten fast," Adair replied. "Roast a boar. There are two left. And three of the geese. Make six rabbit pies and a large vegetable potage. Send Murdoc and young Jack to fish. They must break the ice if they have to, but we must not be found wanting by our guests."

"It's a great deal of food," Elsbeth noted. "How many are there?"

"I have no idea," Adair replied. "But I would rather we cook too much than be embarrassed by not having enough." But to Adair's relief her guests numbered less than two dozen, including the men at arms who had ridden in with their masters.

Ian Armstrong had been sent for, and he had come, for Duncan had explained it all to him. The laird of Duffdour was unmarried, and much resembled Duncan. They were several years apart in age. Adair, her great belly before her, greeted each of her lordly guests as they entered Cleit's hall. She wore a dull red gown, but even close to delivering her child she was beautiful. Conal was by her side, as was Duncan, who knew all of the men involved in what was now a conspiracy to dethrone King James. The prince was not with them, for he could not be seen to be involved, although he knew all that transpired.

There were Alexander Home and Patrick Hepburn, both the prince's closest friends. There were the earls of Angus and Argyll, representing the Red Douglases and the Campbells of Argyll. There was the bishop of Glasgow himself, who ate a heaping helping of roast boar and devoured at least half a goose, while eschewing the trout. They paid no attention to Adair after having greeted her, and so she listened as they planned.

"We must do this as quickly as possible," the Earl of Argyll said.

"Aye," the bishop agreed. "We don't need a civil war. The Mac-Donald would only use it to consolidate his power in the Highlands even more, and the prince doesn't need that, does he?"

"The lad can charm the MacDonald," Patrick Hepburn said.

"The MacDonald is a wily fox," the bishop replied.

"What of the king?" the Earl of Angus asked. "I need assurances that my family and I are safe from him. After all, 'tis my clan that is believed to have kidnapped young Jamie in order to foment this rebellion."

"The king will be locked away at Stirling," the bishop answered him.

"If an accident does not befall him first," Arygll murmured.

"The prince will not condone murder," the bishop said quietly.

"Two kings are dangerous," Angus responded. "Two kings are too many kings."

"The prince truly believes that this can be done without any harm befalling his sire," Patrick Hepburn said quietly.

"Certainly he knows better," Arygll replied sanguinely. "Jamie must know in his heart that his father cannot live if he is to rule Scotland successfully. There are those who will foment rebellion in James the Third's name just to cause trouble for his son and to gain their own advantage. And the English are not above involving themselves. With luck the king will die in battle, and we will not have his death on our consciences."

"The king is not a man for fighting," Lord Home said grimly. "What if he attempts to solve this diplomatically?"

"We will give him no choice but to fight," Angus replied as grimly. "We do not have any option. If we mount this rebellion it must either end with our prince on the throne, or all of us hanging from the gallows at Edinburgh Castle for our treason, my lords. And as many of our clansmen as our enemies can find as well. We all have much at stake in this conspiracy, and it is too late to go back now."

"My lords, calm yourselves," the bishop said in silky tones. "I will personally absolve you from the sins of treason and any murder that may ensue over this matter. We are civil men, and we all agree that King James, the third Stewart of that name, must be removed from Scotland's throne for Scotland's sake. And we are all in agreement that his son, the fourth James, must replace him. I have prayed long on this before involving myself with you. It is God's will that we do. Of that I am certain."

"Angus is right," Patrick Hepburn said. "When shall we muster and march?"

"I would suggest immediately after Easter," the bishop replied.

"We will light the signal fires throughout the border when the time is right," Angus said. "Where shall we meet?"

"Why not Loudon Hill?" the bishop replied. "As a battle was fought there almost two hundred years ago I think it appropriate we mass our forces there."

The other men in the hall nodded in agreement.

"My lords," Ian Armstrong spoke. "Will any of the Highland clans join us?"

The Earl of Angus shook his head. "It is unlikely. The Gordons of Huntley will certainly support the king, and they are very influential among the northern families."

"I have it on the authority of the bishop in Aberdeen," the bishop of Glasgow said, "that there is one family who may declare for Prince James. 'Tis a small branch of the Leslies. The Glenkirk clansmen. Their laird is a forward-thinking man, but of course the Gordons may attempt to stop the laird of Glenkirk if this is so. They certainly want no other family eclipsing theirs in the region."

"We have enough men, and the right on our side," Patrick Hepburn noted. Then he stood and lifted his goblet. "To James Stewart, the fourth of that name," he said.

The other men stood and raised their goblets. "To the fourth James!" they answered the Hepburn. Then they all sat back down and continued eating.

Adair had noticed that none of the gentlemen at her table wore their plaids, or any other sign of their clan affiliation. She realized this was so they could not be identified if someone should notice them coming and going from Cleit and remark upon it publicly. She was grateful, for though she agreed with what they were doing, she still feared for Conal, his brothers, and the child in her belly.

She was not unhappy when she came into the hall the next morning to find her visitors had all departed in the very early hours of the dawn, when they were less apt to be seen.

And then on the second day of spring her waters broke, and Adair went into labor with her first child. The midwife was sent to come from the village over the hill. Elsbeth left the cooking to Grizel and Flora that day in order to be by her mistress's side. And it was not an easy labor. Adair tried to be brave, but as the day went on her pains became harder and harder. And they came closer and closer. There was no birthing table or chair to be found in the keep. A lack, Adair thought grimly, she would remedy as soon as possible. She paced the bedchamber she shared with Conal until she was no longer able to walk or even stand. The pains grew stronger and, unable to help herself, she shrieked, and tiny beads of sweat dappled her pale forehead.

In the hall below the laird and his brothers waited for someone to bring them word of the birth. They drank Bruce whiskey, and diced for stones. The day faded into night. Grizel served the table twice. Outside they could hear the wind rising, and heavy rain hitting the wooden shutters. The fire in the large hearth that heated the hall crackled and snapped as it burned. Then suddenly Beiste arose from his usual place, his head cocked toward the stairs. Slowly, slowly Elsbeth descended, a swaddled bundle in her arms.

Walking to the laird, she offered the bundle. "Your daughter, my lord. Bless her, for she'll not live the night through, I fear. Murdoc, my lad, ride for the priest, for the wee mite must be baptized."

"*Adair?*" Conal Bruce was pale with fear, and his brothers were surprised. They knew, though he said it not, that Conal loved Adair, but she was, after all, only a woman.

"She's had a difficult time, my lord, but she will be fine once she gets over the disappointment of losing her bairn. She needs you," Elsbeth said.

Conal Bruce took the infant from Elsbeth. She was so terribly tiny and pale. She had a little tuft of black hair upon her small head. Her eyes were closed, the lids shadowed purple. Her nose and mouth were miniatures of her mother's. She was scarcely breathing, and he felt the tears welling up in his eyes. His daughter. This was his daughter. And she was dying.

"What is her name?" he asked Elsbeth.

"Adair has not yet named her. She is waiting for you, my lord," the woman answered him. "Will you go to her?"

"Aye," the laird said, and, the baby still in his arms, he crossed the hall, mounting the stairs to the corridor that led to their bedchamber.

Adair lay wan and listless in their bed. Her cheeks were wet with tears. The midwife had just finished tidying everything up. Seeing the laird, she bowed and murmured her regrets. Then she left the room. Conal sat down on the edge of the bed, and carefully tucked the baby into the crook of Adair's arms.

"I am so sorry," Adair whispered. "I wanted to give you a son, and 'tis naught but a daughter who is not even strong enough to live."

"She is too beautiful," the laird replied softly. "God sent us a perfect little angel, but he grew jealous and wants her back. We cannot argue, my honey love." He ached with her sorrow and her disappointment. "What is her name?"

"May I call her Jane after my mother?" Adair asked.

" 'Tis a good name. Jane Bruce. Aye." He reached out and touched the infant's cheek with the tip of his finger. The child did not stir. "I've sent for the priest, Adair."

She nodded. "Aye. We must baptize her at once." Adair looked down at the baby in her arms. "She is beautiful, isn't she?"

He reached out and took her hand in his. It was like ice. Bringing it to his lips, he kissed the little hand and kept it in his own. "Very beautiful," he agreed. Then he sat holding the infant's hand as she cradled their daughter.

The priest arrived bearing his oil, salt, and holy water. Elsbeth and Murdoc stood as godparents for the baby. The priest baptized Jane Bruce, who did not even let out the faintest cry as the water was laved over her tiny round head, and a cross signed in holy oil was sketched upon her forehead. She did make a small moue of distaste as the salt was smeared upon her tiny lips. The priest and godparents departed immediately after the deed was done, while Conal Bruce sat by his wife and daughter's side the night long. By the time the spring sun arose over the hills the infant had breathed her last. A grave was dug for her on the hillside, and Jane Bruce was buried in a little wood coffin that a carpenter in the village had quickly built when the midwife brought him word of the tragedy.

Adair grieved deeply for her daughter. "Better you had kept me as your mistress than wed me," she said to Conal. "I have failed to give you a son, as my mother failed to give John Radcliffe one."

Hearing her, Elsbeth spoke up. "The earl's seed was not fruitful seed," she said. "None of his three wives conceived of him. Not once. Your mother was not barren; nor was he who sired you."

"We will have other children," the laird added in an attempt to comfort her. "Sons and daughters too, my honey love. I will gladly give them to you."

Adair wept at his words. She had wept a great deal in recent days. Her breasts ached with the milk she had readied for her child, until Flora mixed an herbal draft that helped to dry the milk up. It was some weeks before the sadness began to ease for Adair. The weather grew milder with each passing day. Easter came, and then several days afterward the beacon fires appeared upon the hillsides, calling the supporters of Prince James to gather at Loudon Hill, as had been previously arranged. Conal Bruce, his brothers, and their men departed the keep.

Adair had not wanted her husband to go. "You'll be killed!" she told him. "The last time I sent a husband off to war he never returned. What will happen to us all if you die in battle? I beg you do not go!"

"I owe the prince my allegiance," the laird of Cleit told his wife. "I am an honorable man. Clan Bruce is an honorable family. I must go."

"You repaid the favor done you," she cried. "You allowed the conspirators to meet here at Cleit. Do not go, Conal, I beg you!"

"I will come home to you, riding my own horse," he told her.

Suddenly it didn't matter that he couldn't tell her that he loved her. Adair swallowed hard and brushed the tears from her cheek, nodding. "Godspeed, my lord," she said. "Return to me safely. All of you." She included her brothers-in-law in her blessing. "But please be careful. I need you, Conal."

"To make another bairn," he murmured low as he bent to kiss her lips.

"Aye," Adair answered him. "To make another bairn, my lord." Then she had stood on the keep's hilltop watching as the men of Bruce and Armstrong had ridden off, banners flying. She was both relieved and surprised when they returned some ten days later. No battle had ensued, for the king, not comprehending that his heir was a willing party to this rebellion, had refused to fight. Instead he had treated with them diplomatically, much to the disgust of the Earl of Angus and the others. They didn't want this James upon Scotland's throne. They wanted his son. This king was useless, and what little prestige Scotland had was almost gone. But James III had promised the lords that he would consult with them more frequently. He would seek their advice and that of his son, Prince James. The rebel army faded away from Blackness on the Firth of Forth, where they had attempted to engage the king's forces; but wisely it did not disband, for past experience had taught the earls that James III was not to be trusted.

Adair didn't care which king sat on Scotland's throne. She was just relieved to have Conal home safe, and his brothers with him. Her happiness was infectious, and the sorrow over her daughter's loss had greatly dissipated. She had come to understand that Conal simply wasn't a man for pretty speeches. He was not like any of the men previously in her life, who knew how to weave an enchantment around a woman with words. He was a rough border lord. Her husband. And she did love him.

Perhaps it had been the loss of wee Jane that had made her realize that the life she was now living was the life she was going to continue to live. England was a memory, and Stanton was gone. When she thought back on the last two years, Adair understood how fortunate she was to have been brought to Cleit. Her fate could have been so much worse. Her child's death had brought Adair to the truth that she did want children. She wanted Conal Bruce's children. He had been patient with her, and now she meant to repay his unspoken love in a way that would be most pleasing to both of them. She intended to seduce her husband.

They had not coupled since Jane's birth. The laird was eager for the pleasure of his wife's body. The night of his return she had left the high board, murmuring an invitation in his ear before she departed the hall. Duncan, far quicker than young Murdoc, had waited a short while and then stood up.

"The lad and I are going to visit Agnes," he said, pulling his sibling up from his chair. "We'll not be back until morning, so lock up, Conal."

"I had heard that Agnes has not been satisfied with any lover since the prince," the laird remarked. "Jamie has ruined her for the rest, I fear."

Duncan chuckled. "That is why we are going together," he explained. "It takes two men to please the wicked wench now, and Murdoc is not averse to sharing; nor am I. We'll keep her busy the night long, and have her exhausted by the dawn. She has a particular fondness for our little brother. What he lacks in finesse he makes up for in his youthful exuberance and enthusiasm. I've seen him fuck her for almost an hour without flagging," Duncan said with a broad grin. "A bit dull for me after a while, but I must admit to standing in awe of his endurance."

Conal Bruce laughed aloud and, standing, ruffled Murdoc's dark hair. "Our father, God assoil him, would be proud of you," he told his younger brother. "Go along then. I will see you both in the morning. We must continue to drill our men, for this business with the king isn't over yet. By summer it will surely be settled one way or the other."

"Which way?" Murdoc asked.

"The king's way, but which king is the question," the laird said. "I think the sitting king too weak to withstand his son's ambitions."

"But the Highlands will rally to the king," Duncan noted. "Their forces are great in comparison to Prince James's."

"The Highlands will rally," Conal Bruce agreed, "but will they stay the course and fight? That, brothers, is the question that needs answering, and so we will not know until the day of that future battle in which we shall either live or die."

"Good night," said Duncan, deciding he was not of a mind to debate the issue tonight. Conal did not often think deeply, but recent events had brought him to a more thoughtful state of mind. Duncan strolled from his brother's hall with Murdoc by his side. An evening tumbling Agnes Carr was a more pleasant subject to dwell upon than the future, their possible deaths, and the fate of Scotland.

When they had gone the laird made the last rounds about the keep, making certain the fires were banked, the candles and lamps snuffed out, the door barred. Then he climbed the stairs to the bedchamber he shared with his wife. As he entered the room he smelled flowers. No, lavender. And there before the fire was a great tall tub such as he had never seen. Steam was rising from the large vessel. He could just make out the top of Adair's head below the rim of the tub.

Hearing him, she called out in the most dulcet tones, "Come and join me, my lord. You will need a bath after your long trip and before you get into my bed. Take off your clothes. You will find the steps to the tub on the side."

"Where the hell did this great thing come from?" he demanded to know as he eagerly pulled his garments off, impatient to join her.

"Grizel told me that there was a cooper in the village over the hill. I sent for him, explained to him what I wanted, and behold! We now have a tub large enough for us both. Won't it be nice to be able to bathe together, Conal?"

He practically fell over his big feet as he reached the steps to the tub. Climbing up them, he lowered himself into the water, groaning with pleasure as the heat seeped into his aching muscles. "Jesu, woman, you are bringing civilization to our house." Reaching out, he pulled her into his arms, and their lips met.

She nibbled at his mouth teasingly. "I think you are going to like getting clean from now on," she teased him. "Did you miss me, my lord?"

He didn't know what had brought about this change in her, but he had to admit that he liked it very much. He began to fondle a plump breast. "I missed you," he admitted, and was rewarded for his admission with another kiss. "Did you miss me?"

"I did," she allowed, and began to tickle his balls with her fingertips.

Conal Bruce swallowed hard. "Wife, you are going to get fucked," he growled in her ear. "I don't know if it can be done in a tub, but I will surely try."

"Ohh, I hope so," Adair purred against his lips, looking up at him, a naughty smile upon her face. Sliding her arms about his neck, she let him back her against the wall of the tub. She could feel his manhood had grown hard, and was ready to sport with her.

His hand cupped the twin mounds of her buttocks and lifted her up so that she could wrap her legs about him as he slid his lance between her nether lips to impale her. He sighed loudly as he did so. She was tight, hot, and soft all at the same time. It took every bit of discipline that he had to refrain from pouring his seed into her in that moment. Her plump breasts against his chest felt wonderful.

Her nipples were being irritated by his furred chest. She wiggled her bottom against his hands, and tightened her legs about his torso. It was an unspoken signal between them. Conal began to move within her. Slowly, slowly, slowly, with long strokes of his manhood, until the stars behind her closed eyes began to explode, and Adair began to whimper with the pleasure he was giving her. And from the sounds coming from deep in his throat she knew he was being pleasured too.

He could not help himself. His juices erupted and filled her. She collapsed weakly against him, arms still about his neck. When he was able to speak he murmured against her dark hair, "You seduced me, you witch. You deliberately seduced me."

"Did you like it?" Adair asked softly.

"Aye," he drawled.

"I want to do it again," she told him. "But first I will bathe you." Reaching out, she picked up the cloth on the lip of the tub and, dipping it into her jar of liquid soap, she began to wash him thoroughly.

"You are gentler than the first time you did this," he said low, kissing the top of her head. "Then you practically took the skin off of my hide."

"I had two years of dirt to get off of you then," she reminded him. "Now I just have a few days'."

He stood quietly under her ministrations as she bathed him, and then washed his black hair. He did not complain that he smelled like a flower. He actually enjoyed the pungent fragrance of the lavender. Finally, on her instruction, he climbed carefully from the big tub and began to towel himself dry. She followed, taking the second drying cloth for herself. Unpinning her hair, she handed him the hairbrush he had purchased for her almost a year ago at the midsummer fair, seating herself on the edge of their bed.

He could scarcely take his eyes from her naked body as he ran the brush down her long tresses. Was he imagining it, or was that body lusher than it had been a year ago? The laird forced himself to concentrate upon the task at hand. Even her long sable hair seemed more luxuriant than it had been.

"Ummm, that feels good," she murmured. "I'm glad you like to brush my hair."

"You're attempting to seduce me again, madam, and I am onto your game now," he told her, laughing.

She turned her head to meet his glance. "You said you liked it when I seduced you, my lord. I will stop if you have had a change of heart," Adair said.

"If you cease, my honey love, I shall be forced to beat you," he replied. "The priest who made the prince your guardian before we wed suggested I beat you frequently, so you would always remember who was the master of the keep."

"The priest was a fool then," Adair said. "You don't really want to beat me. You want to put me on my back again," she told him with a small smile.

"And do you want me to put you on your back?" he asked, entering into the spirit of their game. He laid the brush aside and wrapped the silken length of her hair about his hand. "Tell me you want to be fucked, Adair," he said against her mouth. "*Tell me!*"

She replied by standing, pushing his legs apart, and then kneeling before him to entertain his burgeoning manhood in her mouth. She suckled upon its length. She licked around the folded skin at its tip. Finally she stood and climbed into his lap to swallow that manhood within her hot, wet sheath. And when he was fully caged by her burning flesh, Adair looked directly into his gray eyes. "Does that answer your question, *husband?*" she purred at him as she began to ride him. Then, closing her eyes, she allowed the sensations of coupling with him to sweep over her. Soon she was soaring to the heights that being one with him created. Leaning back, she felt his big hands on her breasts. His mouth suckled upon her nipples, and then he blew upon them, sending shivers of pleasure down her spine. His teeth nipped sharply at that same flesh, at her neck and her shoulder. She whimpered her acknowledgment of his actions. Her crisis came, and she cried out as it swept over her, falling forward into his enveloping embrace.

But Conal Bruce had not had enough at that point. He held her tightly, allowing her to recover just enough. Then he stood, cradling her in his arms, and, turning, laid her back upon the bed, his manhood still buried within her. He began to pump her, thinking briefly of his little brother, who was probably now fucking Agnes Carr, and would do so for some time. While Conal Bruce did not believe he could keep up such a pace, he did know that when he had finished both he and Adair would be well pleasured.

"*Jesu!*" she moaned in his ear. "You are making it happen again! Oh, God, do not stop, I beg you, Conal!"

"I won't," he promised her, and continued to piston her until they were both practically unconscious with the delight the joining of their bodies was bringing them. And suddenly in a single moment they both touched that blissful oblivion that lovers find. He flew, and he knew she flew by his side as wave after wave of joy pulsed over them.

Afterward they lay together in their bed, fingers entwined in fingers, toes playing with toes, sated and content. For a long while neither of them spoke, and then Conal Bruce said, "You know that I love you, Adair."

"Aye, I know," she replied as incredible happiness overwhelmed her heart.

"Good," he responded. "Then it need not be said again."

"Only if you want to say it," she answered.

"You do believe me, don't you?" He sounded worried.

"I believe you," Adair told him. "I love you too." If he indeed never said it again she would be content, because he had said it. But something told her he would say those three little words again in spite of himself. "Go to sleep now, my lord," she advised him. "I am through seducing you for this night." And, cuddling into his arms, her head upon his shoulder, Adair soon fell asleep.

He lay awake for a little while longer. He had told her that he loved her, and it was the truth. She had admitted her love for him, and this time it was not in anger or sorrow. He wondered now why he had been so reticent to say those three small words. It didn't matter any longer. The matter was settled between them, and healthy children were bound to come of their love for each other. They had a long summer ahead of them, and for the next few weeks they lived in a daze of happiness.

But then, on a night in early June, the signal fires sprang up across the border hills, and a Hepburn clansman rode into Cleit to tell the laird that the king had broken the promises made just a few weeks prior. The prince and his forces were massing. The Highlands were mustering in defense of King James. This time there would be a battle fought, and when it was over and done with there would be one king of Scotland.

Adair fed the Hepburn clansman, and he remained the night, departing at first light back for Hailes. She gave him several oatcakes and dried beef for his daylong journey. He thanked her, and then spoke with the laird.

"My master asks that you come to Hailes with all due haste, for we will march north in two days' time, my lord."

"We will be there," Conal Bruce said. "And my half brother, the laird of Duffdour, Ian Armstrong, will be with us."

Then the messenger was gone from Cleit, and before the sun was even up Duncan Armstrong was riding for Duffdour. Preparations were being made for the laird and his men to depart the following morning. There were thirty men besides Conal Bruce and his brothers residing at the keep. Twenty-five of them would march out with their clan lord, but Conal worried that leaving only five fighting men at Cleit could put Adair and the other women in danger.

She calmed his concerns with her common sense. "Cleit is not an important keep, and only those coming here deliberately and with a purpose are apt to know about it. We will keep the gates locked both day and night; nor will we admit any stranger. The hill upon which we sit gives us a great advantage over the countryside, for we can see if anyone is approaching. The keep is virtually impregnable when the gates are closed. Besides, there is nothing here to steal," she said with a mischievous smile.

"You are not as fearful this time," he noted, taking her hand in his.

"That is because I know you will return to me," Adair said with certainty.

Duncan Armstrong returned late that afternoon to tell Conal that their brother, the laird of Duffdour, would join them at Melville Cross with twenty of his clansmen on the following day. Then together they would meet up with the Hepburn at Hailes.

That night Elsbeth and the women outdid themselves, serving a great feast for the laird and his men. There was salmon broiled in white wine and served upon a bed of fresh watercress, though where enough fish for the hall had come from was not a question anyone asked. Salmon streams were owned only by the mighty, and Cleit did not have one. There was venison stew with carrots and leeks, and rabbit pies with rich brown gravy oozing in steamy runnels from their flaky crusts. There was a side of beef that had been roasted packed in rock salt to preserve its juices. There were capons served with a sauce made from the last of the winter lemons and a bit of precious gingerroot. There was a small boar that had foolishly come too near the keep seeking an easy meal, only to be slain and roasted for his misjudgment. There were mounds of fresh bread, butter, and cheeses. And the ale and wine flowed. The men would ride off their heads on the morrow. Tonight was for feasting, and singing songs of past battles in the keep's hall.

And when finally the men had all gone to their rest, Adair slowly made her rounds, seeing that all was secure for the night. Then she joined Conal in their bed. He was naked and eager for her, but she cooled his ardor gently, for she did not choose to rush this night of all nights. He watched with a burning gaze as she slowly disrobed, placing her garments neatly aside for the morning. Then she bathed herself in a basin, and he grew more lustful as he looked upon her high, full breasts and the curve of her hip.

"Will you brush my hair?" she asked him and, without waiting for an answer, handed him the little pear-wood brush as she sat down on the edge of their bed.

Wordlessly he took up the brush and smoothed it down her sable tresses. After some minutes had passed he set the brush aside and, reaching around her, cupped her breasts within his big hands. His lips placed a burning kiss on her shoulder.

"Ummm," Adair murmured, leaning back against him and watching as his fingers played with her nipples.

"I don't want to leave you," he whispered into her ear, and his tongue licked at the delicate curl of flesh.

"I don't want you to go, but you have your duty, Conal. I know you will never be a great lord, but I love you as you are. Your clan is an honorable one, and it would dishonor the Bruce name should you re-

fuse to support the prince. He will prevail in this matter. I sense it."
She turned in his arms and pushed him back onto their bed. Then,
leaning over him, she began to lick his body with her hot little tongue.
"I will soothe you, my husband, and you will go off tomorrow knowing
you must return home to me." She nipped at his nipples with her
teeth, then licked them quickly before moving down his torso. She
kissed his belly, and her tongue foraged within his navel.

He groaned with delight at her passion, but then he took charge,
catching her in his arms and kissing her until she was dizzy. He felt her
hands caressing him, and, sliding between her soft thighs, he sought
for her love jewel with his mouth and tongue, playing with her until
her pungent milky juices were flowing. Then, mounting her, he filled
her with his lust until they were both replete, their bodies tangled together, their hearts beating wildly with desire satisfied.

"It can only be this once tonight, my honey love," he apologized.
"I must keep my strength for the morrow." Then, with Adair wrapped
in his arms, they slept for several hours.

Conal Bruce awoke with the first scrap of light in the sky. June
brought very long days. Outside he heard a birdcall, and then another.
Beside him Adair slumbered, curled tightly against him. For several
long minutes more he enjoyed the feel of her, the scent of her body in
his nostrils. He would carry this memory into the battle to be, wherever and whenever it was fought. Finally he arose, stifling a groan of
regret as he did. He peed in the chamber pot, washed himself in the
chamber basin, and dressed quickly. As he was pulling on his boots
Adair awoke from her deep sleep.

"Is it time?" she asked him.

"Almost. I'm going to the hall to eat," he said, bending to give her
a quick kiss.

"I will be down shortly," she said as he left the room.

In the hall the men were gathering. Flora and Grizel were bringing
in the trenchers of oat stirabout. Young Jack followed, placing butter,
bread, and cheese upon the trestles. Then, along with the women, he
helped fill the men's cups with bitter ale. Conal Bruce slid into his
place at the high board.

"You look like you had a good night," Duncan said with a wicked grin.

"And you look like you had a hard night," Conal said with an equally wicked grin.

"Agnes wanted to bid us a farewell. Murdoc is still with her. She swears he'll be with us when we ride out," Duncan said. "With Ian's lot we'll number fifty. He's bringing twenty men, and his captain, who was our da's bastard. They're only a few months apart in age. Our father got a son on Mam's serving woman while she was full with Ian. She was furious with him, but she never held it against Tam's mother."

"Fortunately our da had no by-blows," the laird noted. "Mam was very strict. She would have been more than put out with me, the way I treated Adair when I first brought her to Cleit," Conal Bruce said with a smile.

"She would have been more put out with Adair for not wedding you when you first asked her." Duncan laughed. "And here is the wicked wench now, come to bid us farewell," he said. "Good morning, madam."

Adair busied herself making certain that her husband and the others were well fed. God only knew when they would eat decently again. And then the hall was emptying and only Conal Bruce remained. She pressed a bit more bread and cheese on him. "You will be careful," she said quietly. "And you will come home to me safely. We still must make a son for Cleit, my lord."

"We will," he promised her. "This business is not apt to take long. It will be fierce, but brief, I am certain. We will have the summer ahead."

They walked together into the courtyard of the keep, where the men were now mounted and waiting for their laird, young Murdoc among them, looking slightly worn. Adair straightened Conal's red Bruce plaid, burnishing his silver clan badge with her sleeve. He mounted his horse and, bending, kissed her swiftly. Then, gathering the reins in his gloved hands, the laird of Cleit raised his hand and signaled his troop to depart. Only once did he glance back at her, and she waved her hand in reply.

Adair stood at the gates of Cleit Keep, watching as her husband and his men rode down the hill. She stood for some minutes gazing as men and horses gradually faded from her view. Then, with a sigh, she ordered the gates of the keep closed, and retired back into the hall to help the women clean up the remains of the morning meal.

The young Beiste shadowed her everywhere in the next few weeks. He never allowed her out of his line of vision, and insisted on sleeping in her bedchamber at night. It was as if he understood that the master of the house was gone, and it was up to him to watch over Adair.

The countryside was suddenly very still, as if waiting for something to happen. They saw no one, even from the heights of the keep, where a man watched the day long and through the night, for with the brief nights there was really no time when they might let down their guard. Adair ate in the kitchens with Elsbeth and the others. During the day she occupied herself with her small gardens. The herbs, both cooking and medicinal, were growing well now. And she had managed to bring life again into the flower garden that had once belonged to the previous lady of the keep. The time passed very slowly, and then one day the watch on the heights called down that there was a rider who appeared to be making his way toward Cleit.

When he was almost to the gates Adair came into the courtyard. "Do not open the gates until we know who he is," she said.

"He's wearing the Hepburn plaid," the watch called down.

Then the man at arms on the gates opened the small portal window and, peering out, said, "Who are you, and state your business."

"Hercules Hepburn, with a message from my master to the lady of Cleit," came the reply.

"Open the gates and let him through," Adair said.

The man at arms opened half the gate, just enough to allow the rider through. He entered and, dismounting, went immediately to Adair, bowing politely. "My master wanted you to know that all is well," he said, seeing the concern in her face.

Relief poured through Adair. "Come into the hall, Hercules Hepburn, and have some wine," she invited the man. He was a huge fellow standing close to seven feet tall.

Inside she poured the rider his wine, watched while he drank it down, and then refilled his goblet as she invited him to sit by the fire. Seating herself opposite him, she leaned forward and asked, "What has happened? You say my husband is safe?"

"Aye, and the battle decisively won, my lady," was his reply.

"Let me call our folk into the hall, Hercules Hepburn, so they may hear what you have to say," Adair said.

Three of the men at arms came, for the other two remained on duty. Elsbeth, Flora, Grizel, and Jack came up from the kitchens. Gathering about Adair and her guest, they waited expectantly for him to speak.

Hercules Hepburn drained half of his second goblet of wine, and began. "At Sauchieburn on the Stirling plain the battle was met. It was fought near Bannockburn, the very site your husband's ancestor, Robert Bruce, fought a great battle. And in the same month too!" It was obvious Hercules Hepburn was a great storyteller.

"Ahhhhh," his listeners murmured, fascinated.

"The Highlands stood for the king. The earls of Huntley and Craw-ford, their Gordon and Lindsay clansmen, the burghal levees from Edinburgh, and clansmen from many of the northern clans came to support the king," Hercules Hepburn said. "And there we stood, facing their great army, badly outnumbered, but with the right on our side. Prince James was magnificent. He rallied the forces of Angus and Argyll, Douglases and Campbells, the Hepburns, the Bruces, the Armstrongs, the Homes. Even the bishop of Glasgow sent men to the prince's aid. Most good border names, but there was one Highland laird who stood out. He was the Leslie of Glenkirk, and he came with his clansmen to support the prince. A tall man who fought like the devil himself."

"My husband?" Adair said anxiously.

"Alive and well, madam. Not a scratch on him, I am pleased to tell you. But let me continue. The battle went on for several hours, and though outnumbered by the king's forces our men fought far more fiercely. The Highlanders and the others in the king's service fell before us, slaughtered by our swords and spears. And it is said that when

James the Third saw that the battle would not end in his favor, he fled the fray. At Beaton's Mill his horse stumbled and threw him, the witnesses reported.

"Two cottage wives, not knowing who he was, but seeing he was injured, dragged him into the mill for his safety. It is reported that he asked for a priest. One of the women ran from the mill, crying for a religious. She returned with a man who claimed to be one. The king asked to be left alone with the cleric in order to make his confession. Shortly afterward the priest departed. When the two women returned to see what they might do to aid the injured man, they found him stabbed in the heart, dead. They fled screaming from the mill, and sought help from the men coming from the battle."

"*Jesu!*" Adair whispered, and all those listening crossed themselves.

"It is not known who assassinated the old king, but Scotland has a new and undisputed king, James, the fourth Stewart of that name. May God protect him!"

"Aye! God protect our King James!" the assembled responded.

"I thank you for coming and reassuring us that my husband is safe," Adair said. "Do you know when he will return to Cleit?"

"The king asked those who had supported him to come to see him crowned at Scone on the twenty-fifth day of this month," Hercules Hepburn answered her. "Your man will return home to you after the coronation, madam."

Adair nodded. "You will stay the night?" she asked.

"Nay, but thank you," he replied. "There is little darkness in June, half the day left, and a fine border moon tonight to ride by. I can reach Hailes, and then I must return to join my master."

"But you will eat?" Adair tempted him with a smile.

"Aye, a bit of food would be appreciated," Hercules Hepburn admitted.

Elsbeth fed him, admiring his appetite, for this Hepburn had been well named. He was a big man with a great appetite. And then he had departed Cleit. Before he had left Adair had given him a verbal message for her husband.

"Tell Conal Bruce," she said, "that he is not to dally amid the festivities of the coronation, for we have business to take care of here."

"I'll tell him," Hercules Hepburn replied, and then, mounting his horse, galloped forth from the keep, his horse heading north once again.

Chapter 16

On the last day of June, Conal Bruce came home to Cleit. His two brothers and twenty Bruce clansmen rode with him. There were also seventeen Armstrongs in the laird's party, but the laird of Duffdour was not among them. Adair was in the courtyard to greet her husband and his brothers. They appeared tired and worn. Young Murdoc's shoulder was bandaged, and Adair could see the bandage needed changing. She insisted on taking him to her apothecary first. He sat silent as she carefully removed his binding and examined the wound. It was a deep slash, but whoever had tended to Murdoc had seen the injury well cleaned, and there was no infection, although the edges of the long cut oozed just slightly. She cleansed the injured area, rubbed an ointment made from polenta, mint, and salt mixed with a bit of goose fat into it, and rebandaged the wound with clean strips of cloth.

"You'll live," she told him, and he gave her a weak smile.

"It was horrible," he said softly. "I've seen enough blood and carnage to last me a lifetime, Adair. I know a man is supposed to be strong, but I am so glad to be alive. Don't tell my brothers what I said. I don't want them ashamed of me." His eyes filled with tears that began to slip down his handsome young face.

Adair put her arms about him. "It's all right, Murdoc. I won't tell."

"I'm the same age as the king, and yet he was so brave," Murdoc replied.

"I suspect he weeps too in the privacy of his chamber," Adair said. "All men do, though they will not admit to it. I saw my uncle grieve deeply over the loss of his wife and his little son. Being strong and being a man does not mean you cannot sorrow."

The hall quickly filled up, and the women were kept busy bringing food and drink to the trestles, the high board having been served first.

Adair waited for Conal to tell her what she wanted to know. Where was Ian Armstrong, and why was Duncan looking so sad? And then she could bear it no longer. "Where is the laird of Duffdour?" she asked.

"Seated on your left," Conal Bruce said.

Adair turned to Duncan questioningly.

"My brother was killed at Sauchieburn," Duncan said. "As he was unwed Duffdour is now mine, and I am its laird. I will be leaving Cleit tomorrow."

"I am sorry that you have lost your brother," Adair replied, "and yet that loss has made you a man of property and authority, Duncan."

"Cleit is my home," Duncan answered. "I was just a little boy when I came here. I barely remember Duffdour. I did not visit Ian a great deal. He did not like having me about, as he felt it sapped his power to have both our father's sons in his house. He loved Duffdour, and he will not even be buried there. Like most who fell at Sauchieburn, he was buried on the battlefield where he died."

"My uncle died on the battlefield at Bosworth," Adair said softly. "And my last husband, Andrew Lynbridge, and Dark Walter, my captain, and so many good Stanton men too. I am sorry, Duncan, but I do understand."

"Thank you, Adair. I will miss you," he told her.

"You will have to cease your wicked ways now, *my lord*," she addressed him formally. "You are now the laird of Duffdour, and must take a wife to continue your Armstrong family line."

"But where will I find a woman of such eminent good sense as you, Adair?" he teased her. She had lifted the burden of his sorrow from him with her gentleness and practical nature. And she was right: He was going to have to take a wife.

"She is out there just waiting for you, Duncan, but you'll not find her at Agnes Carr's cottage," Adair teased him back.

The men at the high board, privy to their conversation, laughed. Then Conal Bruce repeated what had been said to the men seated at the trestles below the high board. The hall erupted with good-natured laughter, for most of the Bruce clansmen, and not just a few of the Armstrongs, knew Agnes Carr well. A good meal at Cleit and talk of the village over the hill's friendly whore took the darkness of the past weeks from the men. Life was going to get back to normal again.

Adair and the brothers adjourned to their places by the hall's hearth, where a fire took the damp chill off the June evening. Outside the twilight would linger most of the night. The clansmen were now gathered in groups, talking or dicing. Beiste put his large head into Adair's lap and gazed soulfully at her as she scratched his ears for him.

"Tell me about the coronation," she said to Conal. "Was it very grand?"

"More shabby, I would say," Duncan remarked.

"Aye," Murdoc nodded.

"Conal?" Adair looked questioningly at her husband.

"What do you know?" the laird asked.

"Only that the old king was slain by an assassin, or so Hercules Hepburn said when he came to tell me you were alive," Adair answered him.

"Aye, he was slain. Word was brought to Linlithgow, where the prince, now the king, waited. He was devastated, they say, for he thought it could be different. No one knows who did it. Someone undoubtedly in the hire of one of the great lords. It might not have even been ordered by anyone, but just done by someone hoping to curry favor with his master who took the task upon himself," the laird said.

Adair nodded, remembering the young page from Middlesham who had come to Stanton for her protection, and told her of her half brothers' deaths after Bosworth. No man claiming a kingship for himself wanted a rival faction rising up to challenge him.

"The old king's body was borne back to Stirling and placed in the Chapel Royal, where it lay beneath the royal standard until a coffin could be made. The new king rode from Linlithgow with Home, Angus, and Patrick Hepburn. He went into the chapel alone, I was told, and when he came out he gave his hand to each of the three to kiss. When they had the young king left them.

"They brought his brothers, the Duke of Ross and Prince John, to him for it was feared that malcontents on the losing side might take one of the lads, and attempt to form a rebellion around him. The old king was interred at Cambuskenneth beside the queen he had loved. And then we all returned to the palace at Scone for the king's coronation. He ordered that we all be dressed in black, as he would be. His priest, however, prevailed upon him to wear a short cape in a color. He chose scarlet, and the Duke of Ross chose blue. There was a to-do because the king's cousin wanted to wear a green cape. The king would not allow it. While he and Ross showed a bit of color for the people, the rest of us could wear naught but black. The king would see his father properly mourned, for he loved him even if his lords did not.

"Little had been prepared for the crowning. The Highland lords who had survived, and many of those in the far west, did not come. There were several bishops among the missing, including Elphinstone. No order of . . . what do you call it, the order in which the lords may enter?"

"Precedence," Adair told him.

"Aye, precedence! None had been decided, for the parliament had not yet met to appoint office holders for the new king. Angus had been acting as regent for the king, and he decided that Home's manner was offensive. It was, if the truth be known. The king had to soothe them both so that they would behave. Home was in rare form. He quarreled with his brother, the prior of Coldingham. Argyll and Lord Grey were not speaking, and some damned bishop from some unimportant see lectured us all on the sins of our actions coming to pass. The greatest aids to the king were his brother, the Duke of Ross, who is yet a lad; and Robert Blacader, the good bishop of Glasgow who had supported him from the beginning. The rest of the lords squabbled and fought like children."

"Were there any dignitaries from other countries at the coronation?" Adair asked.

"If there were I would not have known them," Conal replied, "but it was a hurried and a very shabby affair to my eye. While Scone is the traditional place of crowning for Scottish kings, nothing had been prepared, and there had been two weeks between the battle at Sauchieburn and the coronation. A slightly moth-eaten gold canopy was found in the palace attics. It was held over the king's head.

"When it was time for the king to be anointed he would permit only his two brothers and the clergy in the chapel with him. The rest of us stood in the doorway attempting to see something. As I was at the back I saw virtually nothing. The Hepburn managed to make his way to the front of the pack. He is no great lord, but few would deny him, for he is the king's closest friend. He told me the king was crowned kneeling, and that his diadem of gold and jewels kept slipping forward on his head because he had such a distaste for it that he had not allowed a fitting the previous day for the velvet lining it needed. They had had to measure from his caps, and it was not right.

"Later in the great hall of Scone Palace I stood in a long line with all of those who had come to see the fourth James crowned. The walls of the chamber were hung with banners belonging to all the clans represented there that day. I saw our Bruce banner in a prominent place, for our ancestor had once reigned as Scotland's king. Home told me that the crown the king wore had been the Bruce's, and because his head was so large all the other kings after him had had to line the crown with velvet to prevent it from falling from their heads. I waited with all the others to pledge my fealty as laird of the Bruces of Cleit. And Duncan pledged for the Armstrongs of Duffdour."

"The king offered me his condolences," Duncan said, "and told me he would pray for my brother. It was a great kindness."

"And afterward?" Adair asked them.

"There was a less than lavish banquet," Conal said. "I have eaten better of my own food in my own hall."

Duncan and Murdoc nodded in agreement.

"There was no dancing? No entertainment?" Adair was surprised.

"It was poorly done," Conal said, "but how could it have been otherwise? The king's father murdered after a battle in which his son took his throne. A court in mourning cannot celebrate the rise of a new king with joy. We are fortunate that no further bloodshed erupted. There are those who are unhappy with the outcome of Sauchieburn, but they will learn that this James means to rule as his father did not."

"The king sent you a message, Adair," young Murdoc said excitedly. "Tell her, Conal. Tell her what he said."

Adair cocked her head and looked at her husband. "What did he say?" she asked.

"He asked to be remembered to you," Conal answered a bit sourly.

"He said," Murdoc told Adair, " 'My lord of Cleit, please be certain to remember us to our fair English cousin. And tell her that we hope to see her at court eventually.' "

"He did? Why, how kind of the king to remember me," Adair murmured in bland tones, but her eyes were twinkling. Conal was jealous. The look upon his face told her that he was jealous. And the fact that he could hardly bear to mention the king's greeting at all told her that he was jealous. Very jealous. Then she arose from her place. "Good night, brothers." She held out her hand to her husband. "Will you come now, my lord, or later?" And she smiled at him.

"Later," he growled.

Adair curtsied and left the hall.

"I would have gone with her," Duncan said with a small smile.

"We'll see how you behave when you have your own wife, and her behavior tries your patience," the laird replied.

"What has she done?" Murdoc asked. "Adair seems most amenable to me."

"She'll want to go to court," Conal Bruce said. "Did you see how her eyes lit up when you prated the king's words verbatim at her? She was raised in a court. It is a familiar place to her. I couldn't wait to leave Scone, and they say Stirling, where the king will hold his court, is very grand. I am not a grand man. I am a simple border lord."

"Whether or not you are right I do not know," Duncan consoled his brother. "Get her with child now that you are home. A child will settle her down, and she will be content to bide at Cleit."

"Aye," Conal agreed absently as he sat staring into the fire.

"You'll not do it here, laddie," his elder brother remarked. "Go to her!"

The laird jumped up, and without another word hurried from the hall upstairs to the bedchamber he shared with Adair, slamming the door open and then shutting it with a very loud bang that rattled its hinges.

"I've been waiting for you," Adair said, flinging off her chamber robe to reveal her nakedness. She began tearing at his garments. "I don't care if you stink of your horse, and Sauchieburn, and two weeks without bathing, I want you, my lord! And I am not of a mind to wait, Conal."

"Jesu, woman," he gasped, surprised, feeling his manhood beginning to swell in his breeks. "I want you too!" They struggled together to remove his boots and clothing, kissing as they did so. And when he was naked he threw her to the bed and, without further ado, pressed his length into her welcoming body. She was warm, and she was very wet. "You've taken no lovers then while I was away," he growled into her ear.

"Not a one," she replied. "Ohh, yes, Conal, like that! Do more," Adair begged.

He reamed her slowly, slowly, going deeper and deeper into her sweetness. Her legs wrapped about him, and he slid as far as he could. Her hair smelled sweet, and her body seemed to fit his perfectly. She moved seductively against him. She moved in time with the strokes of his manhood. She made whimpering little sounds of pleasure, encouraging him onward until his head was spinning. And then too soon his juices filled her, and he groaned, disappointed.

Adair held him in her arms comfortingly. He was still inside her, and she realized that his lover's lance had not lessened in either its size or its intensity. He had spilled his seed, but he was not yet satisfied. And then he began to move in her once more. He used her for some minutes, rested a time, and then began his sweet torture once again. Her pleasure exploded, and his mouth kissed hers, stifling her cries of delight. And still he remained within her, hard and hungry. "You are going to kill me," she whispered to him.

He laughed low. "I have missed you, that's all," he told her. Then he ground deeply into her again, and before many minutes had passed both the laird and Adair found themselves lost in a blaze of fiery passion that consumed them and then left them too weak to move as they fell into a deep sleep, fingers entwined.

A summer stretched before them. The bees buzzed in the heather that grew on the hillsides, and there was peace. Duncan Armstrong had gone to Duffdour, been welcomed by his clansmen and proclaimed their laird. The Armstrongs of Duffdour had pledged loyalty to their new laird. Conal, Adair, and Murdoc missed him, however. Murdoc's wound healed, but his sword arm remained stiff. Despite his distaste for war he practiced each day in the courtyard of the keep, until finally the stiffness released its hold on his body, returning only when the weather was particularly foul.

"Why do you do it when you dislike it so much?" Adair asked him.

"The borders do not remain peaceful for long," Murdoc told her. "My arm may be needed one day to help defend Cleit. Remember, Adair, that I am the youngest of our mother's bairns. I must earn my keep, for I have neither lands nor coin to call mine. And only my brother's kindness allows me a roof over my head."

"When you are older, we will find you an heiress," she told him, and he laughed.

Hercules Hepburn came to bring them news of the king in late July. "The king has stripped his father's late favorite, Ramsay of Balmain, of the title the old king gave him, and given it to Patrick. He is now the Earl of Bothwell," Hercules told them. "And the king is hearing all the cases of the four great criminal offenses."

"What are they?" Adair asked, curious.

"Murder, arson, robbery, and rape," he told her. "Does the English king not hear such cases, my lady?"

"We have courts, with judges," Adair replied. "Sometimes the king will hear a very important case, perhaps an accusation of treason."

"We have not enough learned men," Hercules Hepburn admitted.

"And it is good for the king to involve himself personally. His father was too lenient in his judgments. Our King James is not. He hanged the only son of old Lord Drummond of Perth for causing the deaths of sixty Murray clansmen and women. Young Drummond, a most charming young man, and a favorite of the king's, had been feuding with the Murrays. He fired a church into which they had fled his forces, causing those deaths. He said he meant only to singe their beards, but he had barred the only door. The king judged him guilty and saw him executed, standing by old Lord Drummond's side as it was done. The king said he would show no favoritism in his justice.

"And how the people flock to him. He can go nowhere without being surrounded by the common folk. They love him greatly. When he comes from the Tolbooth, where he has held court, a man goes before him shouting, 'Make way! make way!' But the people reach out to touch his garments, to grab at his hand and kiss it. I have never seen the like of it in all my life," Hercules Hepburn said.

"Have all the lords reconciled with him now?" Conal Bruce asked.

Their guest drank deeply from his goblet. "Some, aye. Others, nay, although they will come around eventually. He called for them all to come to Edinburgh. Some of his closest associates wanted him to charge his father's supporters with treason; others did not. Angus was most vocal in saying that charging a man with treason who had fought for his king was absurd. The king agreed. But he needed to overcome the charge of regicide that some foreign governments are crying."

"England," Adair said softly. "Henry Tudor would seek an advantage."

"Aye, England. Ramsay fled there, and is attempting to encourage their king to invade Scotland," Hercules told them.

"To what purpose?" Adair wanted to know. "Scotland's legal and lawful heir sits on its throne. But tell us what happened when the lords came to Edinburgh."

"Some came and some did not, as I have previously said," the big man continued. "A list of those to be arraigned for treason was put forth, but of all those great names only one appeared. It was the old king's uncle, the Earl of Buchan. Hearty James, as he is called, is a fat fellow. He knelt before the king, bent, with his head touching the king's boots, and our Jamie lifted him up and forgave him. And while neither Huntley nor Crawford nor the other great names were in evidence, there were a goodly number of other lords, knights, and gentlemen come for the king's judgment. And he was fair, fining them, scolding them. He told them his greatest desire is to make Scotland united, strong, and prosperous. That he had no room in his heart for revenge."

"That was exceedingly gracious," Adair noted.

"It smacks of his sire," the laird said.

"Nay, he is nothing like old James," Hercules assured them. "This is a strong king, but he has begun his reign by tempering his victory with mercy. He is spoken of well for it. But of course, when it came time for the king to reward his own faithful, all of his council and friends were telling him what it was they wanted. Angus, however, said nothing. He was taciturn. I suppose he expected the king to reward him without his saying. But then he grew angry at the others, and berated them for their greed and disloyalty. Unfortunately he included the king in his tirade, and when he had finished he slammed out of the chamber. The king could not run after him, although I know it must have hurt him, for Angus has been, along with Bishop Blacader, his closest supporter. So the king gave away those offices and honors he had reserved for Angus to the others. My poor cousin Patrick is now lord high admiral of Scotland, and he hates the sea." Hercules laughed heartily. "Thank God we have Sir Andrew Woods to man our small fleet. Though why Scotland has any kind of fleet is a mystery to me." Hercules Hepburn drained his cup, and Adair quickly refilled it. He gave her a wink, which caused Conal to scowl, and almost caused her to break into a fit of giggles.

"It is so good of you to come to tell us the news, Hercules," she told him.

"I'm glad to pass on to you what I know, but I am also the bearer of an invitation. As Scotland is officially in mourning for the king's sire, there will be no Christmas court at Stirling, but the Hepburn, in his capacity as the new Earl of Bothwell, will be hosting the king, and invites you to Hailes for the New Year. The celebration will be muted, of course, just old friends," Hercules told them.

"I do not know," Conal said, "if we will be able to accept the earl's invitation."

"The king especially asked that his lovely English cousin be invited," Hercules said quietly. "Hailes is not large, but there will be few ladies present."

"My lord," Adair said carefully, putting a small hand upon her husband's sleeve, "it is an honor that the earl does us. Please, may we not go? I should so enjoy it."

Hercules Hepburn hid the smile that threatened to break forth on his face. The lady of Cleit was extremely clever, and her husband was besotted by her. But he had also heard it said that the Englishwoman had been raised in a royal court. She therefore knew the ways of the mighty, and despite her stubborn mate would prevail in her desire to go to Hailes at New Year's. She would not lose an opportunity for her husband and Clan Bruce to gain favor with the new king, or with the Earl of Bothwell.

"What if you are with child?" he demanded to know.

"I am not with child," Adair replied calmly.

"But it is only late summer. You could be with child by late December," the laird persisted. "You have lost one bairn, madam. Will you lose another?"

"If I am with child then," Adair told him, "we can reconsider our decision to go to Hailes, but 'tis only a day's journey away, Conal. I would not offend either the king or the earl by refusing them now. But, of course, you must decide, for you are the laird of Cleit, and I just your wife. Still, if you would make me happy you would send Hercules back to his cousin to say we will be there," she finished. And she smiled up into his face.

Amused, Hercules Hepburn watched the play of emotions across the laird's face. He wanted to be master in his own house, but he also wanted to make his wife happy. And she was certainly giving him every opportunity to preserve his dignity. She had not taken the initiative, as some women might have, and said he was being silly and that of course they would accept the earl's invitation. She had not wept, or sulked, stamped her feet at him, or accused him of wanting to make her unhappy. Instead she was skillfully leading him to the conclusion that she desired. A most formidable woman, the lady of Cleit, Hercules Hepburn decided silently to himself.

"Tell Patrick Hepburn that we will be pleased to accept his invitation for the New Year's celebration, provided the weather will cooperate," Conal Bruce finally said.

"He will be pleased, my lord, and so will the king," came the reply.

This visit Hercules Hepburn remained the night. He was an amusing man who enjoyed telling stories about his clan. When he departed in the morning Adair was sorry to see him go, for they rarely received visitors at Cleit.

The summer came to an end, and one day in October Adair rode out with Conal, Murdoc, and a few of their clansmen to help bring the shaggy short-horned cattle they owned closer to the keep. They had almost reached the herd when they spied another party of horsemen coming from the other direction. The laird swore beneath his breath. The other riders showed no badges of service, which meant they were probably raiders. The laird called a halt to his party.

"Go back to the keep," he said to Adair.

"If I break away from our party someone from theirs will come after me," she replied. "I'll not be sold again, Conal Bruce!"

"We're going to get into a fight," he said. "I can't keep my mind on defending myself and my cattle if I am going to worry about you, damn it!"

"I can fight," Adair said.

"Jesu, woman, do what you are told. Murdoc, take her back and see the gates to Cleit are barred."

Murdoc reached out and, taking the bridle of Adair's horse, galloped off even as his brother urged his men forward again to meet the raiders. When they had gained the safety of the keep and its gates had been slammed shut behind them, Adair slid from her horse and dashed for the keep's battlement, where she might view what was happening. Murdoc was close on her heels. Together they viewed Conal Bruce and his men as they met head-on with the intruders. They both realized at the same time that there was no battle being fought. Instead both parties turned together and rode toward the keep.

As they drew near Adair thought she recognized the rider by her husband's side. She carefully picked her way from the battlement, with Murdoc coming behind her. They climbed down the ladder from the heights into the attic hall below, and then down the stairs, hurrying into the hall from one direction as the laird entered from the other.

Adair immediately recognized the man in her husband's company. "Robert!" she said. "Robert Lynbridge!" She came forward, her hands outstretched in greeting, and embraced him warmly. "What brings you to Cleit?"

"You know him?" the laird demanded.

"He is Andrew's older brother," Adair said. "Andrew Lynbridge, my late husband who died at Bosworth. How is your Allis, and how are the bairns?" She signaled for refreshment for their guest and led him to the hearth to warm himself, sitting down next to Robert on the settle. "I did not ever expect to see you again, Robert," she told him.

"I have been looking for you, Adair. For many months now," Robert said. "We did not know Stanton had been raided until late the following summer, when the king's messenger came to us. He had gone to Stanton, but he found it quite deserted. We rode back with him, and after some time we discovered an elderly couple hiding in one of the cottages. They were terrified we were raiders too, and had come to kill them. When we finally convinced them we were not, they told us a man named William Douglas had raided Stanton, and carried its lady and many others off. Most of the men, they said, had been slain. They spent days with those other few who had not been taken burying the dead. In the winter the others had died, and they were all that was left of the Stanton folk.

"We have been looking for you ever since, Adair. It took us some time to find this Douglas fellow. At first he claimed to know nothing of Stanton, but in time he finally admitted that it was indeed he who had raided it. He remembered you quite well, for he said you were a difficult captive, and he was fortunate to sell you to the laird of Cleit, who had purchased your Elsbeth. Elsbeth, he told me, was as troublesome as you were, for she refused to leave your side unless this laird bought you too, and so he did. Then I had to find out where Cleit was located, and damn me if you are not even more isolated here than at Stanton." Robert drank down his wine eagerly now.

"Why have you come, Robert?" Adair asked him quietly.

"Why, to rescue you," he said as if he thought her simple. "I shall pay your master twice what he obtained for you. And I will pay for Elsbeth's release as well."

"Surely you did not spend years seeking me out just to *free* me," Adair said. "Surely you have come with another purpose, Robert. Yet if the truth be known, I do not choose to return to England. My home now is here at Cleit."

"But Adair," Robert Lynbridge said, "the king has restored your lands to you. I read the message that was sent. It came from the king's mother, Lady Margaret Beaufort, who persuaded her son to have mercy upon you. He will not return your title, and he wants to choose a husband for you to defend Stanton, but your lands are yours again."

Her head spun with his words. *Stanton!* Stanton was hers again! And then she looked up into the eyes of Conal Bruce. The pain she saw in them was like a physical assault upon her person. He loved her. And she loved him. She would not desert him, now or ever. Even for Stanton. "I cannot go back, Robert," she told him.

"But why?" he asked her. "I know that Stanton means more to you than life itself, Adair. And the king is certain to choose you a wealthy husband so the hall may be rebuilt once again. Stanton can regain its small glory. Lord John would want it."

"Rob, I have a husband. A Scots husband who is laird of Cleit. I cannot go back. I do not want to go back. And my father would want my happiness, which is here."

He misunderstood her. "A handfast union is no real marriage, Adair," Robert Lynbridge explained. "Of course you can go back."

"Nay, Rob, I cannot. And I truly do not want to go back. I was married in a most legal union by a priest of our most Holy Mother Church, in the presence of the Earl of Bothwell and the new king himself. Elsbeth was with me, and my lord's two brothers, the laird of Duffdour, and Murdoc Bruce. I am happy here. I am content with my husband and the life that we have together."

"But what is to happen to Stanton?" Robert Lynbridge wanted to know.

"King Henry took it, and it is his to dispose of as he chooses. There is little left of it, save for some empty cottages. What it once was exists no longer. I will write him a message, which I hope you will carry back to England for me and see delivered. If you would like the Stanton lands, I will ask the king to give them to you, although there is no guarantee that he will. Still, as the Lynbridges and the Radcliffes are related by blood, perhaps he will be generous, and it would, of course, please me to know that Andrew's brother now possessed what was once Stanton. And your grandsire would have been delighted. And I will write to Lady Margaret as well, thanking her for interceding for me."

"I would have never believed that you could release Stanton so easily," Robert Lynbridge said in a surprised tone.

"Easily? Nay, not easily, Rob, but I have been gone for over two years from Stanton. The hall is destroyed The Stanton folk are scattered or dead. The only thing that remains of the Stanton that I once knew and loved are my memories. They will reside with me here in Scotland for as long as I live."

He shook his head. "You surprise me, Adair. You have changed greatly from the girl who was Andrew's wife, and whose devotion to Stanton was even greater than any love she might have felt for my brother, God assoil his good soul."

The barb hurt. What right had Robert Lynbridge to criticize her? Would he have come looking for her if the king's messenger had not come to Hillview seeking his aid? She seriously doubted it, even if he had been her husband's elder brother. He had his own lands to attend to, and she had not wanted his help anyway where Stanton was concerned. "Aye, God assoil Andrew's good soul," she said. "He died with honor, and I was proud of him, Rob. But much has changed for me since that day he marched off to join my uncle in his final battle for England's throne."

"Has it changed so much that you would wed a Scot?" Rob asked her bluntly. "This union can be annulled so you may have a good English husband, and your own family's lands back. Once the Radcliffe name meant everything to you, Adair. So much so that my brother must take it for his own if he was to be your husband."

"But for all of Lord John's loving kindness I was never really a Radcliffe, was I, Rob?" Adair answered him. "I was a king's brat, a royal bastard. Naught else. Conal Bruce and I share far more than I ever shared with Andrew. We shared a child."

"You have a child?" He was surprised. She had shown no signs of children with his brother. "Where is this child?"

"Buried on the hillside," Adair said quietly. "Our daughter, Jane, was born late last winter, and lived less than a day. So you see, Rob, my good lord and I are bound together for life. And with God's blessing we will have other children."

Robert Lynbridge turned to the laird. "Forgive my candid speech, my lord," he said. "When a man and a woman have shared a child I know that everything changes. I meant you no offense, and ask your pardon. I did not want my brother's wife to remain here with you if she were not really content and happy. And I am frankly surprised that she would give up her lands for a Scots husband."

"You mean no offense," Conal Bruce said in a hard voice, "and yet you continue to give it. If Adair were unhappy and leaving me would bring her happiness again, I should let her go. A caged bird pining for its freedom does not survive. Does my wife look miserable to you? Or discontent in any manner? Have I stopped her from speaking the truth? Shall I leave you alone in my hall to plead your case again? Nothing will change if I do. Of that I am certain, for Adair loves me, even as I love her."

She almost wept at his words. He had now publicly declared his love for her. She rose to stand next to her husband, and felt his arm slip about her waist. "We would be pleased if you would tarry the night with us, Rob. And Elsbeth will be delighted to see you again. I will make certain that your men are fed and housed, your horses cared for in our stables. And after the meal you will tell me how Allis is, and your bairns."

She had ended the discussion, Robert Lynbridge understood, and so he bowed politely. "I am grateful for your hospitality, my lord, Adair."

Conal Bruce remained relatively taciturn the rest of the evening. He had considered himself and his brothers Adair's family. Robert Lynbridge's visit had disturbed him deeply. He didn't want his wife to have any links left in England. He had never put a great deal of concern into the fact that she had been the possessor of lands herself. He had not known that Adair. The woman he had known had been his servant, his mistress, not a noblewoman who owned lands in her own right. The appearance of Robert Lynbridge had forced him to face the fact that his wife had indeed been the daughter of an English king. She was indeed the half sister of England's queen. This reality made him suddenly uncomfortable, and he did not like it.

He had forced Adair into marriage. Oh, he had been clever—or rather his brother Duncan had been clever. It had all been done in a legal and lawful fashion. Which brought him to another discomfiting point. His beautiful wife was also a very distant cousin to his own king. Who was he to be married to a cousin of Scotland's king and the half sister of England's queen? He was nothing more than a simple border lord. Was Adair really happy with him when even she must be aware that she could do better? Perhaps he should let her go, and have their union annulled. But he couldn't let her go, for he really did love her, and life at Cleit without his honey love would be miserable.

Conal Bruce was not unhappy to bid Robert Lynbridge farewell the following morning. He noted that his wife was cordial, but not particularly warm toward the Englishman. "Do you wish you were riding out with him, and home to England? To Stanton?" he asked her low.

Adair looked up at him with those wonderful violet eyes of hers. "Sometimes, Conal, you can be a dunderhead. Like now," she said. "Cleit is my home, and always will be. Now, I have more important things to consider, like a new gown or two for New Year's at Hailes. I am quite looking forward to it. It will be good to see Patrick Hepburn and the king again. And I must make certain that your clothing is respectable for our visit." She turned and went back into the keep.

"I'll not be dressed up like some damn Gypsy's monkey," he grumbled, following after her. "I'm a border lord, not some perfumed courtier."

"Because you are a border lord doesn't mean you have to go to Hailes looking like a ruffian or smelling like a cow byre," she snapped back. "I intend making you a fur-trimmed gown, and you will wear it, Conal."

He caught her hand and pulled her about. Looking down, he cupped her face between his two big hands, gazing into her eyes. "You are really happy with me?" he asked, attempting not to sound like he was a weakling. "If you are not, if you want to return to England and regain your Stanton lands, I can send after Robert Lynbridge now, Adair. I could not bear it if you were not completely content at Cleit. I will not change, my honey love. I am what I am: a simple man. I do not seek any title but the one I have, laird of Cleit. But you are what you are: a woman with royal blood in your veins. You have held a title and lands in your own right. Cleit will never be more than what it is: a border keep with a herd of cattle and some sheep. We shall not be rich or powerful. Are you certain you can be content, be happy, with a man who has so little to offer you?"

"Do you love me, Conal?" she asked, looking up into his rough-hewn features and the stormy gray eyes with the golden flecks that stared at her so hopefully.

"Aye, I love you," he answered her. "So much so I have discovered that if letting you go would make you happier than remaining with me, I would do it, to my sorrow. I love you, I have discovered, so much that I can actually say the words aloud. Cry them in my hall for all to hear. I love you! *I love you!*" Then he bent and covered her small face with what seemed to her like a hundred kisses.

She began to weep with her happiness. "Now why, Conal Bruce," she sobbed, "would I ever leave a man like you? You are everything a woman desires in a man. You are! I am more than content to remain the wife of a border lord. A man who will remain exactly what he is at this moment: loving, loyal, and noble to his core."

"If you are content then why do you weep?" he begged her.

"I am crying because I am so happy!" she told him, half laughing now.

"I will never understand women!" the laird declared.

"You aren't supposed to understand us," Adair told him. "You are just supposed to love us! Now let me go so I may begin the tasks I need to complete before we go to Hailes at the end of December."

Conal Bruce was relieved that Adair was satisfied to be his wife and seemed to have no regrets over her lands at Stanton. Over the next few weeks he watched as she, Elsbeth, and the other women worked on two new gowns that she would take to Hailes. And he even stood good-naturedly in his hall while they carefully fitted him for a long black velvet coat that would be both lined and trimmed in warm fur. It was a simple garment, he noted, with a deep cuff. He had nothing to complain about, much to his surprise. Even the short-skirted new doublet she sewed for him could not be called ostentatious, even with its embroidered neckline. She made him three new linen shirts, and sewed him hose in the Bruce plaid. When he saw all she had done he was touched.

"I have done what a good wife should," she told him, and then said no more.

For herself she had made, with the help of the other women, two new gowns. Both dresses were cut with fullness from the neckline with a high waist. One was burgundy-colored velvet, and the other a deep purple that was almost black. The sleeves were long and fitted, the necklines high and square. The burgundy dress's sleeves had fur-trimmed cuffs. The purple gown's sleeves had embroidered cuffs that were trimmed with a narrow line of tiny pearl buttons. The hemlines were trimmed with ribbon: the burgundy with cloth of gold, and the purple with embroidery matching the gown's cuffs.

"I imagine styles have changed, but I have no knowledge of it,"

Adair said as she showed him the two garments. "They are a bit more elegant, because I felt it would do honor to the king and Patrick Hepburn. It is an honor to be invited to Hailes."

"I've been to Hailes before," he said. " 'Tis a keep like Cleit."

"Surely bigger," Adair said.

"Aye, bigger," he admitted.

"You were at Hailes when the Hepburn was a mere laird and the king a prince," she reminded him. "It will be different now."

He smiled at her excitement in spite of himself. If there was one thing he was not looking forward to it was a day's ride across the winter hills to Hailes. He hoped for a serious snowstorm, but it seemed they were meant to go, for while there was rain for several days in December that lashed the keep and anyone foolish enough to venture out in it, and while there was a dusting of snow now and again, it would be possible to make the journey. And Adair had not said she was with child. He had no excuses, and they would have to go, for Adair was correct when she said that they could not insult the king or his best friend, Patrick Hepburn, the Earl of Bothwell.

Their clothing was packed, and the trunk would be carried by a sturdy mule. Ten men at arms would accompany them. They celebrated the first of the twelve days of Christmas with a Mass in the hall. Afterward a small feast was served, and the laird presented each of his men with a silver ha'penny in appreciation of their loyalty. They were grateful, as they knew their master was not a rich man. Adair presented her women with enough cloth so each might have a new gown. And Jack was given his first knife. It had a bone handle, and he was very pleased, although Flora professed her concern that her son was not old enough for a weapon.

Murdoc had been given one of young Beiste's first litter. He was well pleased. He had not been invited to Hailes, and so would remain behind as guardian of Cleit Keep. He was very excited at the responsibility that had been given to him, and stood in the courtyard as they prepared to depart the morning of December thirtieth.

"We'll be back in seven days, laddie," the laird told his youngest sibling. "Try not to get into too much trouble while we are gone. And bring Agnes up for your pleasure. Don't spend the night away from the keep."

Murdoc grinned. "I'm glad to have your permission," he replied.

Conal Bruce laughed.

"Travel in safety, and with God's protection," Murdoc said as the laird's group turned to ride off. "I'll see you in seven days."

Chapter 17

*J*t was a long, cold ride to Hailes Castle, but while the day was bitter, the wind was negligible, and the sun actually shone.

"You see," Adair said cheerfully, "our visit is meant to be."

"You won't think so if we have to remain longer because of a storm, or the storm hits us halfway home to Cleit," the laird grumbled.

"This is a wonderful opportunity for you," Adair told him. "The king will get to know you better, and that is to the good."

"I fail to see why," Conal Bruce replied. "I have naught to do with the king."

"There is no harm in being a king's friend," she advised him. "You don't have to go off to court and become involved in politics to be his friend. But this visit to Hailes, the camaraderie that you will share with the Hepburn and the king, will show James Stewart that here in the borders he has a loyal man in the laird of Cleit. You are the sort of man he will want to hunt with, drink and gamble with, my lord. And you are the kind of man who will answer this king's call to arms."

"How can you be so knowing in matters like this?" he asked her.

"You forget, Conal, that I was raised in a royal court. The children who people the court are paid little heed. People gossiping think nothing of their presence. Listening, absorbing, filtering out what is important from what is not important, and keeping secrets are all part of a royal child's education. I learned my lessons well, my lord," Adair told him with a rueful smile. "This visit to Hailes can be to Cleit's advantage."

"You seem to understand this king, and I wonder how that is," he answered her.

Adair laughed. "There is something about young James Stewart that very much reminds me of my own sire. He has great charm and skill with people. You cannot name a time in your short acquaintance with the king that he has ever treated you like an inferior, can you, Conal?"

"Nay, I cannot," the laird admitted, shaking his head.

"And I have heard he has quite a reputation as a lover with the ladies as well, much like my own sire. With that king I found such éclat repugnant. With this one, mayhap it is his youth, but I find it more amusing. Perhaps because James Stewart is not a married man with a houseful of bairns I am less apt to be condemning," Adair noted.

"He looks at you like he would like to eat you," the laird muttered.

Adair laughed again. "He looks at all women, particularly pretty women, like that. He means no harm, and I have not heard it said that he ever forced a woman who refused his attentions."

"That is because no woman ever has," the laird said sourly.

"Are you jealous, my lord?" she teased him.

"Aye, I am!" he admitted strongly.

"But you know you have no need to be jealous, don't you, Conal?" Adair said.

"Aye," he replied.

"Then our visit shall be a pleasant one, and you will not become unduly distressed when the king flirts with me, which he will, I am certain. He simply cannot help himself," Adair told her husband. "This visit could be a fortunate one for our children."

He looked at her curiously. "What do you mean?"

"What will happen to Murdoc?" she countered.

"What do you mean?" His look was confused.

"Duncan has Duffdour. You have Cleit. But Murdoc has nothing to recommend him. What will happen to him? Who will he wed? Can he afford a wife? He owes his very existence to you. His brother. His laird. And when we have sons his value grows even less in importance. I want this friendship with the king for our children, Conal. You will have an heir, but what if we have more than one son? What if we have three sons? One could certainly go to the church, but what of the other? A friendship with the king might give a son a place at court in the king's guards. Or, if he were scholarly, among the king's secretaries. Without the friendship of an important and powerful man our sons could spend their lives roaming the borders, raiding, wenching, and drinking. That is not what I want for my sons. And I want any daughters I bear you to make good marriages. If their father is friends with the king their chances are far better than if their father is simply a border lord of no importance."

"I had no idea that you were so ambitious," he said slowly.

"All women are ambitious when it comes to their bairns, Conal," she answered him with a small smile. "We do the best we can, but we always want better for our bairns, my lord. It is in our nature, I fear."

Now it was his turn to laugh. Then he said, "I will leave all of this in your most capable hands, my honey love, for the truth is I am naught but a humble border lord of no particular importance who has obviously married far above his station."

They stopped once to relieve themselves and rest the horses. They chewed on oatcakes to still their hunger pangs, and sipped whiskey from a flask to force some warmth into their bodies. Adair could no longer feel her feet, and her hands holding the reins of her horse felt icy and stiff. Not to mention her bottom, which ached. She wanted nothing more than a hot bath, which she knew she would be unlikely to obtain in a house full of guests come to be with the king.

Finally, as the winter sun was setting over the western hills, they reached Hailes Castle. It was not a large dwelling, but it was certainly bigger than Cleit. Their horses clumped across the thick wooden drawbridge, which lay over a frozen moat, and into the courtyard of the castle. Patrick Hepburn himself came to greet his guests as their horses were taken away to the stables.

"Welcome to Hailes," the Earl of Bothwell said. "Come into the hall, all of you." The sweeping gesture of his arm included the Cleit men at arms. "There's food and drink for all." He kissed Adair's little gloved hand. "I apologize that my wife is not here to also greet you, but she is near her time and unwell. She awaits us in the hall." He ushered them inside.

"I was not aware you had a wife," Adair said quietly.

"Aye, Janet Douglas. She's the daughter of the Earl of Morton. We wed earlier this year, right before Sauchieburn," the earl said.

"And she is not well? I am sorry," Adair replied.

They entered Hailes's great hall, with its two large fireplaces burning high and bright. It was warmer here, Adair was relieved to find, than the corridors of the castle. Still, she thought it would be a day or two before she completely thawed out from their long ride. She followed the earl to one of the hearths, where a young woman sat in an upholstered high-backed chair, a small black-and-brown terrier at her feet.

"My angel," the earl said. "This is Conal Bruce, the laird of Cleit, and his wife, Adair. They have come to pay you their respects."

The Countess of Bothwell looked up at them and smiled a warm but wan smile of greeting. Adair understood why her husband addressed her as *my angel*. Janet Douglas Hepburn was petite and fragile, with pale blond hair and light blue eyes. Her belly was enormous with the child she was carrying. "You are most welcome to Hailes," she said in an almost ethereal voice. "I do not envy you the ride you have had this day. Even here inside the castle I feel the winter's cold."

The laird bowed, and Adair curtsied to the earl's wife.

"When is your bairn due?" Adair asked her, and saw out of the corner of her eye that her husband and their host were moving away.

"Shortly, the midwife tells me," Janet Douglas Hepburn replied with a sigh. "Sit down and keep me company, unless you wish to join your husband or the other ladies who are all crowding about the king." Her blue eyes twinkled. "He has been eagerly awaiting your arrival," she said.

"I think I will remain with you, madam," Adair responded. "Conal is a jealous man, and has grumbled at me the entire ride over the king's kindness to me."

The Countess of Bothwell laughed, albeit weakly. "Jamie has charm, I will admit. He is a really wicked laddie. He attempted to seduce me into his bed just before Patrick and I were wed, the young wretch."

"I am relieved to say he has not approached me in that manner," Adair lied.

"Yet," the Countess of Bothwell said with another twinkle. "Sit down, my lady Adair, and keep me company, as you are not of a mind to join the others. Have you bairns of your own?"

"We lost a daughter, Jane, last winter," Adair said. "But we are so recently wed that there is time for others. Conal said we could not come if I was with child. So I never told him I am. He will come in late summer, I imagine."

Janet Douglas Hepburn laughed softly. "You are a strong lass," she said. "I wish I were, but I am not. 'Tis most unusual for a Scotswoman. Patrick should really not have sought to wed me, for I am frail, as you can see. My mother did not want it, but I did. I fell in love with him the first time he came to Castle Douglas and I saw him. I pray daily for a son, for if this bairn does not kill me it is unlikely I will ever have another."

"Oh, madam!" Adair cried. "Why would you say such a thing? My stepmother, Queen Elizabeth Woodville, was petite and dainty like you, and she gave my sire ten bairns." She crossed herself quickly. "This is your first child, and you are concerned."

The young countess reached out and took Adair's hand in her own. "You are kind, my lady of Cleit, but I *know* what my fate will be. You are King Edward's daughter? Tell me how that came about."

Adair briefly related her history to Janet Douglas Hepburn. Her companion was wide-eyed with fascination, for it all, she remarked to Adair, sounded like one of those adventurous tales that the minstrels sang about. By the time she had concluded her story it was time for the meal. The earl came to escort his wife to the high board, where to Adair's surprise she and Conal had been seated. But then, looking about, she saw that there were really very few guests. A servant had taken her long wool cape as she stood to repair to the high board. Beneath it she wore a simple yellow wool gown with a high neck and long sleeves, each with a row of tiny buttons carved from wood and stained dark. About her hips was an embroidered girdle of cloth of silver.

"You look like a spring flower, cousin," the king said. He was seated at the earl's right hand. "Come and kiss me in greeting. You have not done so yet."

Adair went to the king's chair and dutifully leaned down to give him a quick kiss upon his ruddy cheek, but James Stewart turned his head, and Adair was shocked to find her lips meeting his. Her eyes widened in surprise, and she sprang back before the kiss could become something it shouldn't. A swift glance told her Conal had not seen, and her sigh was almost audible.

"Another time, cousin," the king murmured mischievously.

She laughed. "I think not, Your Highness," she told him primly, and then sought the seat to which she had been assigned.

The earl had invited a distant cousin, Eufemia Lauder, an attractive woman with dark red hair and brown eyes. She had been widowed twice, and was delighted to have been chosen by her relative to be his guest and the king's bed partner. Eufemia was a practical and discreet woman with no pretensions. She would satisfy the king's lust with enthusiasm while he visited the earl, and not weep when he departed, or beg to know when he would come back. She would accept the gift he gave her with good grace, and then return to her own home. But most important of all, she was respectable enough to be accepted by the Countess of Bothwell and Adair. While Patrick Hepburn knew his king's needs, he would never insult his wife or another woman by forcing them to associate with a woman of dubious reputation. The king did not have a mistress at the moment or else he would have brought her to Hailes. There were two other gentlemen in the hall tonight. One was the earl's brother-in-law, James Douglas, and his wife. The other was the earl's younger brother, Adam, and his wife.

The meal was good, Adair thought, but not as good as those of her own house, and that thought gave her great satisfaction. She was going to tell Conal tonight that she was expecting another child. They were here, and there was nothing he could do about it. Fortunately, other than breaking her link with the moon, she was showing no other signs of her condition. In fact, she felt outrageously wonderful. It was not like the first time, when she had been sick from the very beginning.

When the meal had been concluded they left the high board and gathered about the countess's chair by one of the hearths. The earl's piper played for them, and the men danced together while the women watched from their seats. Finally the earl and the king sat down to play a game of chess. The other three men sat together talking. Adair was glad that they had come, and she suspected that Conal was too. He was laughing with the others, and seemed quite at his ease, though he had thought he wouldn't.

A servant came and asked if she might show the ladies to their bed-chambers, which Adair took to mean that the evening was over. She arose with the others and curtsied to the countess. Then the women followed after the serving woman, who brought them to a high floor in the castle and directed each lady to her own chamber.

The room was not large by any means. There was a small hearth, which was burning brightly. A tiny window was shuttered with a thick wooden shutter, and a heavy curtain was drawn across it to temper the wind that still managed to come through the shutter's cracks. There was a large bed. A single chair. Nothing more; nor could anything else have fit within the space. Their saddlebags had been laid carefully upon the bed. Adair drew out her two new gowns, shook them, and laid them over the chair. Then she hung the bags on a hook that stuck out of the wall by the fire. Undressing quickly, she washed her face and hands in the basin that had been set on the edge of the hearth, and climbed quickly into bed to wait for her husband.

She was almost asleep when Conal came in. He undressed swiftly and climbed into the bed, reaching out for her. "I'm glad you insisted we come," he said softly, and then he kissed her lush mouth, running his tongue around it teasingly. His hand reached out for her breast, which he kneaded as he spoke to her.

"I like the countess," Adair said to him.

"Patrick is fearful she is going to die with the child," Conal said.

"All first-time fathers worry foolishly. Fortunately, those with more experience do not. We're going to have another bairn, Conal. In late summer."

"You lied to me then," he said, his voice tight.

"I did," Adair admitted, totally unashamed. "I wanted to come. There was no harm in my riding right now. But you would have not trusted me to know myself, and then we would have fought over it. Neither of us would have been happy about the outcome, Conal. I can already tell that this is not like the first time. I feel strong. The bairn growing within me is strong. Don't be angry, my honey love," she cajoled him.

"I should beat you," he told her grimly.

Adair snuggled in his embrace. "Ohh, would you spank me?" she teased. Reaching for one of his hands, she drew it around her and placed it on her bottom, wiggling against the hand. "Have I been a bad lass, my lord?" she asked him in a singsong little-girl voice, rubbing herself against him in an outrageously provocative fashion. His manhood was already hard against her thigh.

"You are incorrigible," he said, trying not to laugh. *Jesu!* He was hard as iron. "What if you harmed yourself? Or the bairn?" He was putting her on her back as he spoke, pushing up her chemise as she pushed up his.

"It's too early to be dangerous," Adair told him. "Oh, hurry, hurry, my honey love! I am so hot for you tonight!" She drew him in close, wrapping her legs about him as he slowly entered her wet heat with a groan.

He shivered as his length sheathed itself within her. Would he ever grow tired of this woman? Nay. He would not. No matter how many times he possessed her, each time they coupled was like the first time for him. The excitement of pressing his manhood deep, of feeling her yielding to him—it always seemed new and different. He felt her tighten herself around him, and groaned again. "Witch," he whispered into her perfumed black hair. "I love you!"

Adair let the sensations he engendered within her blossom and grow. She loved the feel of his thick length as he slowly, oh, so slowly sheathed himself within her. Every fiber of her being seemed to meet in that single spot inside of her body. Liquid, fiery, honeyed heat engulfed her until she was burning up. She moaned his name. "Conal! Conal!" And then he began to piston her with long, measured strokes of his lover's lance, and her head was thrashing wildly against the pillows as she whispered over and over again her love for him. Her head was spinning with the incredible pleasure he was giving her. She cried out, unable to help herself. Stars and moons swirled behind her closed eyes, and she flew until she could fly no more. It was then that she tumbled into a velvet darkness that seemed to reach up to enfold her in its warm and tender embrace.

Conal plunged over and over again into her liquefied heat. No matter how hard he worked himself he couldn't find release at first. But then her small hands closed around his buttocks. Her nails dug deep into his flesh, and he felt his passions roaring up to overflow within her. He could not prevent the cry of pleasure that emanated forth from his mouth. A primitive howl that burst forth from his throat surprised him even as they met ecstasy together. And then they slept, entwined in each other's embrace.

When the morning came and they prepared to go down to the hall, the laird of Cleit took his wife into his arms and kissed her a long, slow kiss. "You are a bad lass, Adair, but I do trust you," he told her.

"And I'm sorry I did not tell you I was again with child. But you would have argued with me, Conal. You know you would have," she said.

He laughed ruefully. "Aye, I would have," he admitted.

"And then I would have had to ride off without you, and you would have come tearing after me," she said.

"Aye," he agreed again, "I would have."

"So it really was better that I waited until we were here at Hailes to tell you," she concluded.

"Aye, it was," he said, laughing as he kissed her nose. "Woman, you know me far too well, I fear."

"Aye, I do," Adair told him, and she kissed him back.

Then together they descended into the great hall, where they found the other guests already eating. As the day was clear and again without precipitation, the gentlemen hunted while the women remained indoors playing at cards. That evening, the last night of December, a great feast was held in the hall at Hailes, featuring a large boiled haggis. It was the one bit of the meal that Adair could not manage even to like. Nor, it seemed, could Janet Douglas Hepburn. Her dainty nose wrinkled with distaste. But the king and the other guests ate the slices of stuffed sheep's stomach with great gusto.

There was dancing in the hall that night, with the men and the women doing reels and country rounds. Two pipers and several other musicians, playing drums, flute, and horn, played for them. The king, who had kept a polite distance from Adair until now, chose her as his partner in a reel. Adair had chosen to wear her violet gown this night. Her sable hair became undone in the vigorous dance, and her cheeks were flushed pink.

James Stewart could not resist. He managed to dance her into a corner with no one else the wiser in the merriment of the evening. "You are just too delicious, cousin!" he murmured, backing her against the wall and cupping one of her breasts. Then his mouth descended upon hers in a fiery kiss.

Adair tore her lips from his. "My lord!" She gasped, suddenly aware of the hand caressing her breast, and of how her nipple was tingling. "Cease this instant, you wicked lad! You offend me! Is not Mistress Lauder enough for you?"

"I cannot help myself," the young king said and, taking her hand, placed it where his manhood was burgeoning. "I adore you, Adair!"

"While you insult me, I cannot help but be flattered by the attentions Your Highness showers me with." She firmly removed his hand from her breast and hers from his groin. "But I am an honorable woman. I have a husband whom I love. And I am expecting a child come late summer. I want my husband to be Your Highness's most loyal friend, but he is a jealous man. Granted, Conal Bruce is not important, but a king never knows when he might need an unimportant friend in the right place at the right time," Adair said. Then she gently pushed him back and, taking his arm, discreetly insinuated them back into the general jocularity of the hall, where the dancing had just now ceased.

"You are a clever woman, cousin," the king told her.

Adair smiled at him. "And you are going to be a wonderful king, Jamie Stewart," she told him softly.

At midnight they banged pots, and the local church bell chimed the occasion.

They awoke to a cold, icy rain, and the earl and his guests kept to the indoors that first day of January. They exchanged gifts, and as the day wore on the men got to speaking of the months ahead, of how England must be stopped from causing any difficulties, and how Scotland's new king must be accepted by the other rulers in Europe.

"You must send ambassadors out to the foreign courts." Adair surprised the men by speaking up.

"Scotland has never done such a thing before," James Douglas said.

"And does that mean they should not do it now, my lord?" Adair answered him.

"Why do we need representatives at foreign courts?" Douglas persisted. "Scotland does well on its own, and we have the French alliance."

"The French aid you in war, but in return they expect your aid in battle as well. But there are ways to settle matters other than war."

"The old James was always going on about diplomacy," grumbled Douglas. " 'Tis a lot of nonsense. Might is all that counts in this world, madam, but you would not understand, for you are a woman."

"I was raised in a royal court, my lord," Adair said icily. "Men, being foolish by nature, have a tendency to speak around women as if we cannot hear. I will wager I am far more educated than you are, and I know that it is important for Scotland, if it wishes to be taken seriously by the European powers, to have ambassadors."

"Where would you send my ambassadors?" the king wanted to know.

"England. You would offend King Henry if you did not ask to send him an ambassador first. He may refuse, but then he cannot be distressed when you send ambassadors to France, Spain, and the Holy Roman Empire. I would send men to all the kingdoms of note. Denmark, Italy, Portugal. And you should send someone to one of the smaller Mediterranean kingdoms, so your trading ships will have a place to stop to take on water and fresh food on their voyages to and from the eastern kingdoms."

"What trading vessels?" Douglas said. "We have no trading fleet."

"Once you open up direct relations with the European kingdoms you will find you will develop a trading industry. Trade is very important. It will bring prosperity to Scotland. Surely you are not against prosperity, my lord?"

"Again you sound like old James," the countess's brother scoffed.

Adair turned to James Stewart. "May I have Your Highness's permission to speak most candidly?" she asked him.

"You may, cousin," he responded.

"Your father, may God assoil his good soul, was not a strong king. And he did not have the respect of his lords, I fear. His own mother, your grandmother, Marie of Gueldres, was an educated and sophisticated woman who was his greatest influence. Raised in a Burgundian court, she taught him to appreciate beauty, learning, and the arts. Unfortunately, the loss of his own father at so tender an age left him bereft of the good influence of a strong man, for his lords, and especially those in charge of raising this king, were far too busy maneuvering for position and exploiting their authority to teach him what he needed to know to be a king. Their sole interest was in advancing themselves and lining their pockets.

"And then your father was declared of age to rule, but alas, he did not know how. And these same lords who should have taught him now despised him. Worse, they went out of their way to spite him, to defy him. Is it any wonder your father disliked them in return? Or that he turned to men with interests like himself for friendship?"

"Craftsmen and poets," sneered James Douglas.

"Aye," Adair agreed. "Men like the king himself, my lord. Men who understood him, and could talk with him on subjects that mattered to this king."

"He should have sought the company of his own kind," James Douglas said.

Oddly, the other men in the hall were silent, and appeared to be giving Adair's words some thought.

"He had nothing in common with rough lords who drank and wenched and diced, whose joy was in hunting deer and boar. Old King James was a man of the arts. And none of you made any attempt to understand him, so the situation grew worse as the years passed. Those men who surrounded the king, though they had the same interests as he, were no better than Scotland's lords. They took advantage of their situation and became as arrogant as their rivals. You hanged several of them at Lauder Bridge, I believe, and then opened Scotland to my uncle, the Duke of Gloucester, and the king's younger brother, the Duke of Albany. 'Twas badly done, my lord.

"Yet for all his faults the old king had some good ideas for Scotland, which were never put into effect, for you were all too busy fighting amongst yourselves. He is dead now at an unknown's hand, and this king, who calls me cousin, rules Scotland. He is his father's son in his love of learning and the arts. But he is also a Scots king who can sit in a Highland hall and speak that unpronounceable language of your north. He sees that the world around us is changing. He understands the necessity of sending his ambassadors to other lands because Scotland cannot isolate itself any longer. And Scotland should not be beholden to France for its protection. We should protect ourselves, and diplomacy is a better path to take than war."

Conal Bruce was astounded by his wife's speech. Once again he realized that this woman who was his wife was a better wife than he should have had. For all she had been born on the wrong side of the blanket, she was a king's daughter. There was noble blood on both sides of her family. And he was naught but a simple Scots border lord.

"There is a great deal of merit in my cousin's words," the king said slowly.

"Aye," the Earl of Bothwell agreed, "there is. What can it hurt us to offer our ambassadors to the various lands?"

"The cost alone of sending these men out is apt to be exorbitant," Douglas complained. "If we open an embassy it cannot be a paltry affair, lest Scotland be mocked for a poor showing."

"Your embassies do not have to be grand affairs. We are a small country," Adair told them. "A good showing is all that is required.

Have your agents purchase suitable buildings in each place you put an embassy. Furnish it simply, in an attractive manner. It does not have to be ostentatious. Better it isn't. But have the ambassador you send meet all the expenses of maintaining their embassy. It should be considered a great honor to serve King James the Fourth in such a manner. You must have your lords and other wealthy men who seek your favor clamoring for an ambassadorship. And it must be understood that they cannot just accept the position and remain in Scotland. They must take up their post in Paris, or London, or wherever they are assigned. If their families wish to go, so much the better. A lady serving as her husband's hostess on the day your coronation is celebrated, or on New Year's Day, when Scotland's embassy will be open to the public, will be most charming."

"Aye," the king agreed, "it would. I like your idea, cousin. Scotland can gain a great deal of prestige among the other kings if we open embassies of our own."

"The French won't like it," Douglas said darkly.

"The French do not rule Scotland," the king said sharply. "I will not be told what to do by anyone, but certainly not by the French. And I will pick men to fill these posts who will be loyal to me alone, and not their own interests."

"But choose men with noble titles to do the countries honor," the Earl of Bothwell suggested. "If a man has lands, can afford to maintain one of these embassies, and is true to you, you can create a title or two to fit the situation."

"I already have several men in mind," the king told them. Then he caught up Adair's little hand and raised it to his lips, kissing it fervently. "My dear cousin, I do thank you for offering me such a splendid idea." He turned to the laird. "Conal, your fair wife is a most amazing woman. I hope you appreciate her. You must come to Stirling in the spring," he told them.

Now Eufemia Lauder came over to boldly slide herself onto the king's lap and whisper something in his ear. He grinned and nodded as he reached up to casually fondle the woman's plump breast beneath her gown as they continued to talk.

"What a pity you are a woman, madam," the Earl of Bothwell said. "You would make a fine ambassador for us."

Adair laughed. "I am far more content being the lady of Cleit," she told him. "My New Year's gift to my husband was to tell him of the child we will have by late summer. It will be a son this time, I am certain."

"So you finally told him!" Janet Douglas Hepburn laughed.

The other ladies tendered their good wishes while the men clapped Conal Bruce on his back and congratulated him. He then told them how Adair had tricked him into coming to Hailes by not revealing her condition until they arrived. The men chuckled, and the king shook a finger at Adair with a smile.

"Was it that you longed to see me again so desperately, cousin, that you would prevaricate with your good lord?" he teased her.

"Of course it was," Adair replied, her violet eyes twinkling with mischief. "There could certainly be no other reason, *cousin*."

And good-natured laughter filled the hall.

Amazingly, the next few days remained rain and snow free. The last day of their visit, which was Twelfth Night, arrived. The day was spent in feasting and merriment. There was entertainment in the form of a man with a pack of dancing dogs, and musicians and pipers. There was even a small troupe of mummers who came to perform. The following morning the guests all departed Hailes Castle, thanking their hosts for a grand visit.

"I am so glad we have met," the young Countess of Bothwell told Adair. "Perhaps next summer we can meet again with our bairns."

"You would be most welcome at Cleit," Adair told her. "The keep is small, but I have made it quite civilized."

The two women kissed in farewell.

The day grew grayer and lowering as they traveled the distance from Hailes back to Cleit. The cold was damp and cutting. An hour from their journey's end it began to snow. At first it was but a flurry. Then the snow began to drift down gently. Adair thanked God that they were so close to home, for with each step that they traveled the snow grew thicker and heavier. By the time they reached Cleit they could barely make out more than a few feet ahead of them. And when they dismounted their horses in the courtyard and looked through to where they had come from, the animals' footprints in the snow were already covered, and beyond the keep entrance it was a solid sheet of white.

The winter had finally set in, and it snowed all through the night. In the morning the hills around and beyond them were garbed in white. It remained that way until the spring came. Murdoc reported to his brother that it had been deadly dull while they had been gone. He was most anxious to hear about Hailes, and how they had celebrated.

"Was our cousin Alpin there?" he asked Conal.

"If he was he managed to keep out of my sight," the laird replied.

Elsbeth was outraged that Adair had discovered she was with child and not told the laird until they were at Hailes. "I do not know what has made you so difficult," she said. "Do you want to lose this child too?"

"I won't lose my son," Adair told her old nurse.

"A son, is it?" Elsbeth said. "And you've been given the second sight now, then?"

Adair laughed. "I just sense in my heart that this is a lad I will bear. He will be a strong bairn, unlike my poor wee Jane."

The winter passed slowly, finally melting into spring. The hills began to color green again. Adair's belly had begun to show, and she was well pleased and happier than she could ever remember being in all her life. In late April word came that Janet Douglas Hepburn had given birth to a daughter, baptized Janet, in mid-January. The baby was strong and healthy, but her mother had died at the beginning of April. Patrick Hepburn, grieving for his wife, had brought a wet nurse into Hailes, and then departed to join the king. Their friendship was a strong one, and the king had rewarded that friendship by making the earl master of the king's household, custodian of Edinburgh Castle, and sheriff principal of Edinburgh and Haddington. His brother, Adam, had been made master of the royal stables.

Adair was saddened to learn of Janet Douglas Hepburn's death, but then she remembered that the young Countess of Bothwell had practically foretold her own end when they had spoken at Hailes during the New Year's celebration. Still, she had thought that the Hepburn's wife was simply being affected by the child she carried. Obviously she had not been. Adair shivered with the memory of their conversation as the child within her moved strongly.

Then one night the watch reported signal fires sprouting upon the hills. The English had come raiding. Cleit lit its own fire to warn those beyond them. The courtyard gates were closed, locked, and barred. Cleit had the advantage of its location upon a small hill. The hillside was kept clear of trees and bushes behind which an enemy might take shelter or hide. Cleit would not be an easy keep to take, and raiders usually passed it by for just that reason. The village over the hill, however, was vulnerable, and the laird invited its inhabitants to shelter in the keep. The laird had his men drive Cleit's cattle off on the principle that it would be easier to steal the herd if it were all together than to go chasing after the individual beasts. They would lose some, but not all.

This time the raiders came to the keep and attempted to storm it. The gates, however, held, and Cleit's archers had deadly accuracy. After two days the English borderers moved on in search of easier pickings. When they had gone the laird and his brother had taken a party of their own clansmen and gone after the English, managing to save the village over the hill from too much pillaging and damage. They drove the raiders back over the borders, and then returned home. But the entire spring and summer the border roiled with unrest.

They learned the reason for the unusual activity from Hercules Hepburn, who had come to Cleit to see if they were all right.

"It's the English king," he told them wearily, for he had been involved in several skirmishes over the last few weeks.

"What has happened?" Adair asked him. "We had an uneasy truce, but we had one nonetheless."

"King Henry is unhappy that the old king was overthrown and killed," Hercules answered her query.

"Why should he care?" Conal Bruce wanted to know.

"The old king was easier to manage," Hercules replied.

"Of course he was," Adair said. "He preferred what he thought was diplomacy to war. But this young king is not so amenable, and cannot be managed by England."

"Aye!" Hercules said, nodding vigorously. " 'Tis said Ramsay of Balmain fled to him, and now the English king is encouraging him to mischief. He has based himself in a village called Stanton, and from there controls the raiding parties that come over the border to pillage and rape. He is in league with a man, Sir Jasper Keane, a nasty devil."

Adair grew very pale. "*Stanton?* You are certain it is Stanton?"

"Aye," he responded. "The place was deserted, they say, but the cottages still sound and livable."

Adair felt her anger rising. "How could he?" she fumed. "How could he do such a thing to me? Was it not enough that he took everything I had? Must he now make Stanton a means for his perfidy?" Her face was high with color.

"Adair, do not distress yourself," Conal Bruce begged his wife.

"What is the matter?" Hercules said, confused.

"I was born the Countess of Stanton," Adair told him. "When Henry Tudor of Lancaster took England's throne he took my title and my lands from me, because I would not permit lies to be disseminated about King Richard, who was my uncle. My own half sister sat by his side, now England's queen, and would not defend me or my rights. I returned to Stanton to find my home destroyed, but my village was left. It was from there I was stolen by Willie Douglas and brought into Scotland. Some months ago my late husband's brother came looking for me. The king had restored my lands to me, but I sent Robert back to England with a letter for Henry Tudor renouncing my claim on Stanton, telling him that I was now wed to the laird of Cleit, and content. I asked that he give my lands to my former brother-in-law, Robert Lynbridge. This is the English king's answer."

"But why?" the laird asked his wife.

"Why? Because I did not wait for his mercy and largesse, which I am certain had already been trumpeted about his court. I made a new and happy life for myself. And I made it with a Scot! In King Henry's eyes I am a traitor to England. So he would besmirch Stanton's good name by making it a refuge for a Scots traitor." And then Adair burst into tears. "I will never forgive that Welsh usurper," she sobbed. "Never!"

Conal put a comforting arm about his wife. "There, there, lass, don't greet," he said, and he kissed the top of her dark head.

Adair pulled away from him. There was suddenly a hard line to the mouth he so enjoyed kissing. There was fire in her eye. "I will not tolerate what that Welsh king of England has done," she said. "Does he believe that because I am now in Scotland I cannot strike out at him?"

"Adair," her husband said, "he is a king. You cannot strike out at a king."

"And I am the lady of Stanton, or was," she said. Then Adair looked up at her husband. "I was not responsible for who sired me, Conal, and John Radcliffe knew I was not his blood. But he treated me as if I were. Before I was born he made certain that I would inherit Stanton and its title in my own right. That Edward of York would take care of me should it become necessary. The man I will always remember as my father gave me his name. I am proud of the Radcliffe name, as was my father, which is why any man who wed the lady of Stanton had to eschew his own family and take the Radcliffe name for his own. Radcliffes ruled over Stanton for over six hundred years. The name is an old one. It is an honorable one. I will not allow this Welsh upstart who now sits on England's throne to besmirch my father's name. I will strike out at him."

Hercules Hepburn listened to Adair and nodded with his understanding of her words, but then, he was not wed to the lady; nor was she carrying his bairn. He could understand the worry and the concern he saw on Conal Bruce's face.

"How can you strike out at a king of England?" the laird asked his wife.

"I will destroy what little is left of Stanton," she said. "I will eradicate it from the earth. There will be nothing left but the land. No village, no hall, nothing by which it or the Radcliffes can be identified or shamed."

"You are having a bairn any day now," Conal reminded her.

"Our son is more important to me now than ever before," Adair said. "I will do nothing to endanger him. That I promise you. But when the autumn comes, Conal Bruce, and a fine border moon rides high above the Cheviots, we will go to Stanton and do what must be done. I swear it by almighty God, my lord! I will do what needs be done!" Her eyes were blazing now with her determination.

"And the Hepburns will ride with you, madam," Hercules said admiringly. Then he turned to Conal Bruce. "With your permission, of course, my lord."

"Since I am a wise enough man to know I cannot keep my wife from what she must do," the laird said wryly, "I will welcome the company of the Hepburns of Hailes." Then he took Adair into his arms again, saying, "I can only hope that the son you will soon bear me will have your ferocity, my honey love."

"He will, my lord," she promised him. "He will!"

Chapter 18

*J*ames Robert Bruce was born on a rainy July morning. He was a large infant who entered the world red-faced, howling loudly, and with his small clenched fists waving. Elsbeth cleaned him with warm olive oil, commenting as she did so on the particularly fine attributes he possessed. Then, swaddling the baby tightly, she laid him in his cradle so they might attend to his mother. Conal Bruce stood over the cradle admiring his firstborn son, who looked back up at his father with deep blue eyes.

Adair was both exhausted and elated. She had insisted upon seeing her son immediately upon his birth, and kissed his wet dark head joyfully. This was so different from when their wee Jane had been born. This child was strong. He would live. After passing the afterbirth she allowed Elsbeth and Flora to bathe and refresh her. Then she lay back in a freshly made bed that Grizel had prepared for her.

"Give me the bairn," she said, and when Conal had lifted their son from the cradle and put him into his mother's arms, Adair put the boy to her breast. Immediately the little mouth opened and then clamped down firmly upon her nipple. He sucked noisily, and his mother smiled, well pleased. "I told you I would give you a son," she said to Conal Bruce. "When he has satisfied himself you will take him into the hall to show Murdoc, Duncan, and your clansmen." Adair was extremely pleased.

"He's a braw laddie," the laird remarked, grinning. "You've done well, lass."

Adair laughed. "I have indeed," she agreed.

"You need your rest," Elsbeth scolded her gently.

"Let the bairn take his nourishment, Nursie," Adair said, and Elsbeth smiled at her mistress's use of her old designation.

"You'll need a nurse for the bairn," she said.

"Let Flora help me," Adair replied.

"Leaving Grizel and me with all the heavy work," Elsbeth grumbled. "I should bring another woman in from the village."

"Nay," Adair said. She turned to her husband. "If you are truly pleased with this son I have given you then you will give me something in return."

"What do you want?" he asked her, surprised by the request. He had not thought Adair an acquisitive woman.

"I want you to go to Willie Douglas and get Elsbeth's sister, Margery, for us. Her term of servitude is long finished, but if she is not dead she has remained with him, for she has nowhere else to go. Before I bring another woman from the village I would like to see if you can fetch Margery. She is not a woman the men would seek to futter."

"I'll go tomorrow," the laird said, and Elsbeth burst into tears.

"Thank you," Adair said. "Cease your howling, Nursie; you will frighten my bairn," she told the older woman. She detached her infant son from her breast and handed him up to his father. "Take James Robert to the hall and present him to his uncles and his clansmen," she said. "I must sleep."

"Bless you, my chick." Elsbeth sniffled as she exited the bedchamber.

Adair lay quietly after they had all left her. She was still a little bit too excited to sleep. She had done her duty to Cleit. Conal had an heir. Now she would recover her strength and do what needed to be done by Stanton. She had learned that Ramsey of Balmain had settled himself into Stanton village, and all summer long he had raided across the border from his sanctuary. Every time she thought about it Adair was filled with cold anger. She would bide her time for a little while longer, but then she was going back to Stanton. And when she left it would all be gone forever. No one would ever again besmirch the Radcliffe name or Stanton, because neither would exist any longer.

In the hall below she heard a shout go up, and knew that the Bruce clansmen were giving their approval of the newest member of the family. The infant would be passed about to be admired, and then she knew that either Elsbeth or Flora would bring the child back upstairs, settle him in his cradle, and then sit by it while she slept. Adair's eyes grew heavy as she slipped into sleep. She did not awaken when her husband slipped into their bed later that evening.

In the night Flora brought the baby to his mother so that he might nurse. Awakened, the laird lay on his side watching as his son vigorously suckled upon his mother's breasts. It was, he thought, the most beautiful sight he had ever seen. He slept again, awakening just before the dawn. Rising from their bed, he quickly dressed and left the bedchamber. Shortly afterward he rode out from the keep with his older brother. To his surprise he found Willie Douglas in his own house. He wasted no time in coming to the point of his visit.

"Is Margery still with you?" he asked.

"Aye," Willie Douglas replied. "I kept the old bitch on even after my wife died."

"I'd like to speak with her," the laird said.

"Why?" Willie Douglas demanded to know.

"Her term of servitude with you is past," the laird said. "Her sister wants them to spend their final days together. Elsbeth has become an important member of my household. I am happy to comply."

"If she'll go with you then take her," Willie Douglas said. "She's a sour bitch, and I'm of a mind to take a new young wife. I would have sent her packing sooner than later, for my bride-to-be is healthy, unlike my last wife. She will cook and care for my house. I have no more use for Margery, and do not wish to feed a useless mouth. The kitchens are below. I hear you took the wench I sold you as a mistress. I hope she gave you more satisfaction than she gave me."

"How long did it take you to heal?" the laird asked. Then, as he turned, he said, "The lady is my wife now, Douglas. Speak of her with respect." He left the trader openmouthed and descended into the kitchens. "Margery, sister of Elsbeth, show yourself to me," he called out into the darkened room. "I am the laird of Cleit, and I have come to take you home."

Elsbeth's sister crept from the shadows. She was gaunt to the point of starvation. Her hair was a dirty white, and she was clothed in rags. But there was still a fire in her eyes. "And where is home, my lord?" she demanded to know.

"Cleit, where your sister rules my kitchens, and the lady Adair is my wife," Conal Bruce said with a small grin.

"You might have come sooner, my lord," Margery told him bluntly. "Well, let's go. I am more than ready to leave this place."

"Get your things then," he said.

"Things?" Margery said dryly. "I am wearing them, my lord."

"God's teeth, woman!" the laird swore softly. "You cannot ride as you are. If I miss my guess those ragged bits you are wearing are the same garments you were taken in from Stanton."

"They are," Margery said. "You didn't expect the old miser upstairs to expend a ha'penny on a servant, did you? His wife, God assoil the poor soul, was about my size, but when she died he took her gowns and sold them all in the market. He might have given me one, for it would have cost him naught, and they were old and well-worn, but he could only think of what he might gain. I'd ride naked to your Cleit just to escape that man and this cold stone house of his."

"You can have my cloak for modesty's sake," the laird said, taking it off and putting it about the woman's shoulders. "Come along now. No need for good-byes."

Margery followed him up the stairs and out into the sunshine, where Duncan sat upon his mount, holding two horses. The laird helped the older woman to mount, and then climbed into his own saddle. It wasn't until they were several minutes past Willie Douglas's house that he told his brother of what had transpired. Duncan was shocked.

"And the bastard says he's going to remarry," the laird noted. He looked to Margery. "Who is the unfortunate bride?" he asked her.

"The lass is the daughter of a farmer who owes Willie Douglas money," Margery said. "She ran away once, but her father sent Douglas after the poor little wench. When he caught her he bedded her, with her da's permission. To make certain, he said, that she didn't run again, and understood she would be his wife whether she wished it or not. I can still hear her weeping after he had taken her virginity. And later he bragged to me that when he brought her home he and the lass's father took turns beating her until she fainted. They are only waiting for her to heal enough so they can go to the priest. Between that devil's rough lovemaking and the beating the girl received, she cannot yet walk."

"Why did you remain?" Duncan asked curiously.

"When my service was up his wife still lived. She was a good soul, and so happy to have another woman in the house to keep her company and look after her. And then she died six months ago, and where was I to go, my lord? I would not even know how to return to my cottage at Stanton." She looked to the laird. "Tell me of my sister and the lady Adair. They are well?"

"They are," he assured her. "Adair is now my wife, and we have recently had a son. She said if I were pleased with her, would I go and fetch you to come to Cleit."

Margery cackled. "And so you have, my lord, and I thank you. I do not think I could have lived in that house much longer, and I probably would have taken a knife to Willie Douglas once he was wed and mistreating that poor lass again."

The two men chuckled at her pithy comment.

"You will need time to recover your health, Mistress Margery," the laird said. "But then I know it would please us all if you would enter my service. I am no great lord, and Cleit is not a grand place, but you will have a warm home, good food, new garments when you need them, and the companionship of your sister."

"I would like to return to Stanton, to my own little cottage if I might, for they did not destroy the village that day we were taken," Margery said.

"Regain your health first, and then decide," the laird suggested to her. He would let his wife and Elsbeth tell Margery of Stanton.

They reached Cleit just after sunset. And seeing each other for the first time in almost three years Elsbeth and Margery burst into fulsome tears, weeping upon each other's neck in their joy at the reunion. The laird found his wife in the hall nursing their son.

"Should you be here?" he asked her. "You have just had a bairn, my honey love."

"I had Murdoc carry me down," Adair said. "I woke up, you were gone, and it was lonely in our bedchamber. Where have you been all day?"

"Duncan and I sought out Willie Douglas and brought Margery back with us. She is in the kitchens now with Elsbeth, and they are both weeping at being together again," Conal Bruce told Adair. "Thank God you thought of her. Douglas is remarrying and planned to throw her out. He's a mean brute. The poor woman was still in the clothes he took her in that day, and they are beyond rags. I gave her my cloak so she might ride without embarrassment."

Adair's eyes filled with tears. "I should have thought of her sooner," she replied.

"She said the same thing," the laird answered his wife with a grin.

An hour later the two sisters came up from the kitchens. Conal Bruce was pleased to see that Margery had been able to bathe, and was wearing one of Elsbeth's linen skirts and a clean blouse. She was much thinner than her sister, but the laird suspected that in time, with enough to eat, Margery would regain herself again.

Margery went right to Adair and curtsied. "Thank you, my lady, for rescuing me and reuniting me with Elsbeth. I do not know what would have happened to me if you had not. I had no idea where you both were, and if I had I would not have known how to find you. I am grateful you remembered me."

"I am ashamed I did not bring you to Cleit sooner," Adair said.

"Elsbeth has told me of Stanton," Margery replied.

"Will you remain with us then?" Adair asked her. "Your sister could use your help, as I have taken Flora from her household duties to be my bairn's nurse."

"I will stay, and I am glad for the home you offer me," Margery said. Then she looked at the infant at Adair's breast.

"He's a big laddie"—she nodded—"and bound to get bigger with his great appetite."

Adair laughed and brushed the top of her son's dark head with an indulgent finger. "Aye, he'll be a big lad," she agreed.

The summer passed, slipping into autumn. Cleit Keep stood vigilant on its hilltop. His household was running smoothly, and Adair was up and about again. Conal Bruce began to consider that perhaps her concern over Stanton was now forgotten. But then one evening as they concluded a game of chess before the hall fire she spoke of it.

"Ramsay is still raiding," Adair said. "We need to rid the border of this scourge, and I need to close the book on Stanton, Conal. We must send to the Hepburns at Hailes, and to Lord Home, and your brother, the laird of Duffdour, so we may decide how best to accomplish this."

"Why are you so determined?" he wanted to know. "I thought with Robbie's birth you had decided to put the past behind you."

"I cannot do that until I have destroyed every vestige of what was once Stanton," Adair replied quietly. "Have you learned nothing about me but that I am a pleasing bed partner, Conal? I had thought better of you than that."

The rebuke both stung and annoyed him. "I do not see why you must go gallivanting over the border into England. If you need this thing done then we will do it for you. Why must you go? There could be fighting. There will be fighting. I cannot put you in that danger, my honey love," the laird told her.

Adair sighed deeply. "Before I was your *honey love*, Conal, I was Adair Radcliffe, the Countess of Stanton. And that is why I must be involved. If I were a man you would understand this reasoning."

He laughed ruefully. "Perhaps it is because I cannot see you as a man," he said.

Now it was Adair who laughed, and then she grew serious. "My honor is as important as any man's, Conal. The Welsh usurper now lording it over England has tarnished that honor, my family's honor, Stanton's honor, by allowing a traitor to find shelter on my lands while he causes havoc and destruction on the other side of the border. Henry Tudor does it more to irritate King James, who has much responsibility in his quest to bring a just peace to Scotland and to make it a prosperous place for all its people. James Stewart cannot be distracted by this border nonsense, yet he cannot ignore it and be called fair. And if Ramsay of Balmain is this eager to get his revenge, then just raiding is not all he has in mind. I will wager he is in contact with other malcontents like himself who have as yet said little, but will strike out at King James given the opportunity."

"What of our son? You cannot take him with you if you do this thing, but neither can you leave him to starve," the laird said. "Your place is with Robbie."

"Do not presume to tell me my place," Adair said in a tone that bordered on the dangerous. "And if you were so concerned with our son you would know that I brought a wet nurse in from the village over the hill a month ago. Grizel knew of her. A young widow who lost both her child and her man recently."

"Is it safe to let our son nurse from the teat of a woman who lost a bairn she was nursing?" Conal demanded.

"The bairn was almost two. He strayed from his mam into a meadow, and was trampled by a heifer fleeing a randy bull. When his father ran to rescue the lad the bull caught him up on his horns, and the poor man had his neck broken when he fell back to the ground," Adair said icily. "The wet nurse's milk is healthy, as was her son until this terrible tragedy. The lass was desolate until Grizel thought to bring her to the keep. Our son is thriving at her breast. And my milk is now almost all dried up."

He was amazed by this news. How could he have not noticed this change in his household? But he hadn't. He had come to rely upon Adair's judgment. The house and the servants were her responsibility. More than ever he was coming to realize that she was a stubborn woman determined to have her own way in certain matters. She was not going to rest, nor would she give him any peace, until she had done what she must. "I will send messengers out tomorrow to the Hepburns, the Homes, and the Armstrongs," he said. "We'll need a large force. The king will undoubtedly pay a goodly reward for Ramsay of Balmain," the laird decided.

"We should do the king a greater service and save his treasury if we saw that Ramsay of Balmain died in the fighting," Adair said dryly.

Conal Bruce looked sharply at his wife. "I had no idea you could be so fierce, my honey love," he told her.

"Did you not, my lord?" Adair arose from her chair and settled herself onto his lap, kissing his mouth softly as she did. Her fingers unlaced his shirt, and her hand slipped beneath the linen to caress his warm flesh. She pushed the shirt open as wide as she could and, bending her head, began to lick provocatively at his nipples.

Sliding a hand beneath her skirt he trailed it slowly up her leg to the junction where her thighs met. He played across the warm, silky flesh, finally pushing a single finger between her nether lips to tease her sensitive little love jewel. He yelped softly as her teeth nipped at him. His lance was at the ready. "Ride me, you wicked witch," he murmured into her ear, licking it for emphasis. Moving his hand from under her gown, he enclosed her waist with his hand, and positioned her so that she sat facing him. Pushing her skirts up, he waited eagerly for her to free his manhood, and when she had she mounted him. He groaned as he felt himself slowly entering her hot, wet sheath.

Her palms flat upon his shoulders for balance, Adair encased him within her fevered body. She had kept him at arm's length since Robbie's birth some three months ago, but now she was ready once again for passion. She felt him unlacing her gown to pull it down to her waist. He fondled her full breasts eagerly, and she leaned back with the pleasure beginning to flow through her. He bent his head and took a nipple in his mouth. The jolt that tore through her surprised her. Her nipples were so incredibly sensitive. She moaned and began to ride him slowly, slowly, until he released her nipple and found her mouth with his, his lips possessing hers in a heated debate. Their wet tongues entwined themselves about each other as she continued to ride him. She could feel him within her, swollen, throbbing, and oh, so hot! Her eyes closed. She leaned back to let him go deeper, little mewling noises coming from her throat as she approached the apex of her pleasure. And then she felt that almost imperceptible quiver as his manhood stiffened a final time. They both cried out as they met at the pinnacle. Then Adair fell forward onto his neck and, his own head pressed against her shoulder, he enclosed her in his arms.

Finally, after some moments, he said, "Will you always do this when I give you your own way, my honey love?"

"Always," Adair promised him, laughing weakly. "God's blood, I have missed our couplings!" She arose from his lap on weak legs, falling back into his arms. "Lace my gown," she said. "We are fortunate not to have been caught at our pleasure by anyone."

He complied with her request, saying, "It is not too late to retire to our bedchamber, my honey love."

"You wish to continue this interlude?" she said with a small smile.

"Aye," he replied.

"I will tell Annie to take our bairn and his cradle in with her tonight," Adair said.

"Who the hell is Annie?" he asked.

"The wet nurse," Adair answered him.

"Then most certainly tell Annie to take the lad and his cradle with her. I'll even move it myself. Where does she sleep?"

"There is a small chamber upstairs at the end of our hall," Adair told him. "It is cool in summer, and warm and cozy now that the autumn is on us." She held out her hand. "Let us go and tell Annie," she said.

The passion between them had returned stronger than it had ever been. And true to his word, the laird sent messengers out the following morning to his allies. Hercules Hepburn; Andrew Home, one of Lord Home's sons; and Duncan Armstrong arrived the day afterward.

When Andrew Home heard what Adair wanted to accomplish he nodded in agreement. "My father tells me that there have been rumors of a plot to kidnap the king and take him to England. Then they will place his little brother, the Duke of Ross, upon the throne with a regent chosen by the English king. The plot is said to originate with

Ramsay of Balmain, but no one knew where he was hiding. The king is not concerned, but my father and Bothwell are. And your knowledge of his whereabouts, my lady, is the last piece of the puzzle for us."

"Then here is another reason for us to go to Stanton," Adair said.

"You would go?" Young Home was surprised.

"I must go," Adair told him.

"There will be fighting, more than likely," Home said. "It will be dangerous."

"I will stay on the hills above Stanton, observing," Adair responded. "When it is over and you have slain this traitor, then I will come into the village, and you will help me to do what I must do to salvage my family's good name, and that of Stanton. Not a stone must be left to indicate any habitations were once there. Next spring the grasses will grow again in the little valley that was once Stanton, but it will be gone. And with it all traces of the Radcliffes, but for the burying ground where my mother, my father, and their ancestors lie. And one day all traces of that place will be gone as well too. But King Henry will never again use my lands for his treachery against Scotland, my lords."

"Your cause is just, as is ours," Andrew Home said.

"We should ride soon," Hercules Hepburn remarked, "in the next week or two, before the weather turns toward winter."

"Agreed," Duncan Armstrong said, and Conal Bruce nodded.

A meeting place for them to gather with their clansmen was decided upon.

"The full moon is in eight days," Adair told them. "Can you be ready by then? Better we ride with a bright night sky."

Again the men agreed.

"We'll have our clansmen at the meeting place on that day," Hercules Hepburn said. "I can bring fifty men. How many does Ramsay have? Do we know?"

"I'll send my youngest brother, Murdoc, to reconnoiter for us tomorrow," the laird replied.

"You must consider that Ramsay and his men may also be planning to ride out on the full moon," Adair said. "It is better to trap them in the village than to have to face them in the open. We will lose more men that way."

"Madam, your strategy is worthy of a general," Andrew Home told her.

"If you attack in late morning," she continued, "you will succeed, and no one would expect any attack then. But I will wager that Ramsay of Balmain has become very lax, and believes himself safe, as no one has ever followed him to his viper's nest."

Conal Bruce listened, very surprised that the rough border lords would listen to his beautiful wife in regard to strategy, but they were heeding her. And she was right.

"Is it possible some other Scots are involved with Ramsay?" Adair wondered aloud. "Men whom no one would suspect?"

"We've considered it," Andrew Home said, "and my father believes it so."

"Then we need to learn who these men are," Adair said. "Ramsay and everyone connected with his treason should be expunged."

"One of those men may be your cousin Alpin," Hercules Hepburn said, embarrassed that he had to say it. "The earl dismissed him from his service some months back. He could not keep his hands off the women in the keep. He did no serious damage, but there were so many complaints that even Patrick finally had to pay them heed."

Conal Bruce's face grew dark with his anger. "If he is with Ramsay then I will kill him myself," the laird said. "I will not permit him to bring shame upon our clan."

His companions nodded in agreement.

Murdoc Bruce left before the dawn the following day on his mission of reconnaissance. He was very pleased to have been given such a responsibility. It was a two-day trip to Stanton from Cleit, Adair later learned. Riding the second night by the light of the waxing moon, Murdoc reached a spot overlooking the little valley of Stanton early on the third day. The entrance into the valley was very narrow, which should have made it easy to defend, but Murdoc saw no men at arms posted. Nor were there any men watching upon the hillsides. Ramsay of Balmain obviously felt quite secure. Murdoc had hidden his horse in a copse of trees. He watched as Ramsay's men returned from a raid shortly after he had arrived. The sun was not even yet up, although the sky was blue with expectant dawn. Murdoc lay in the grass upon the valley, observing. When the raiding party reached the village they dismounted, stabled their horses, and, in groups of several men, entered the cottages, where smoke was streaming from the chimneys. After a time Murdoc saw women exiting and reentering the cottages. They were probably captives captured in the raids and brought to Stanton to cook and otherwise service Ramsay and his men. No men were visible, however, until quite late in the day, when they began appearing again from the cottages, where they had obviously been sleeping.

Adair had been correct, Murdoc thought with a small smile. His sister-in-law was a clever woman. Had she not been, he considered, Cleit wouldn't be the comfortable home it now was; nor would his brother have such a fine wife. And even from a distance Murdoc spotted their cousin Alpin. The bastard had turned traitor! And then, to his surprise, William Douglas rode into the village on a large wagon. He was greeted by Ramsay of Balmain himself. Together the men entered one of the cottages. Murdoc wished he could go closer, but his brothers had warned him that if he were caught all would be lost. He was just to observe.

After a time Douglas exited the cottage, and Ramsay's men began loading their recent booty onto the wagon. It was then covered to conceal its contents, and Douglas went back into the cottage. Murdoc did not need to be closer to understand that William Douglas was obviously selling the goods that Ramsay's men stole in return for a share of the profits. This permitted the traitorous lord to finance his treason without involving the English king. And it gave Douglas the income he needed without any risk to himself, or the need to share those monies with men in his employ. It was cleverly done, Murdoc had to admit. He watched that night as the raiders rode out again. They would go a-roving most nights until the snows and cold prevented them unless they were stopped. Murdoc saw them return in the predawn just as William Douglas was climbing up on his wagon seat to depart.

Having seen enough, the young Bruce retrieved his horse and rode for Cleit to tell his brothers and the others what he had learned.

Conal was furious to find that Alpin Bruce was indeed one of Ramsay's men. It would bring shame upon his clan should the information become public knowledge, and the Bruces of Cleit had always been considered honorable men. But they were all surprised to find that William Douglas was involved. Without his help in disposing of the ill-gotten gains, it was agreed, Ramsay of Balmain would have had a more difficult time of it.

"I always thought Willie Douglas deserved hanging," Hercules Hepburn said. "I suppose we shall have to do it. He was never a particularly trustworthy man, but he's involved himself in treason. We'll hunt him down when the business is completed, and render some border justice."

The others nodded in agreement.

"We'll leave tomorrow before dawn," the laird said.

"We're all ready," young Andrew Home replied. "Your hall is fuller with our men, I will wager, than it has ever been. How your cook has managed to feed us all for two days I will never know."

"I actually think Elsbeth and the others have enjoyed it," Adair said with a smile.

And as if to prove her words a great supper was produced that night, with beef and lamb and trout. There was venison, and rabbit pies, and roast fowl of several varieties. There was bread and butter and cheese, all washed down with the laird's October ale. And at least two hours before the dawn, as the men stirred sleepily in Cleit's hall, Elsbeth, Margery, Grizel, and even Flora were placing trenchers of hot oats on the trestles, along with bread and cheese. As the men prepared to depart, the four women moved among them, passing out freshly baked oatcakes and small wedges of hard cheese to be stored in their purses. Cleit's hospitality would never be faulted.

Adair had dressed herself that morning as her husband had never seen. She wore a pair of dark brown woolen breeks that had obviously been made just for her. Her linen shirt was a natural color, and with it she wore a short jerkin of leather that had been lined in rabbit's fur and was closed with small buttons carved from ash wood. About her waist she wore a leather belt, from which hung a thin leather scabbard containing a bone-handled dirk. She had a sash of red Bruce plaid that was pinned to her shoulder with a silver clan badge. The round insignia showed a lion with his tail extended, and above the beast was the clan's motto, *Fuimus*, which translated to *We Have Been*. Her black hair, braided as always in a single plait, was topped with a small flat cap that sported an eagle's feather. She was every inch the clan chief's wife, as the admiring glances of the men in the courtyard told her. Without help Adair mounted her own black gelding.

They rode out even before the sun came over the hills. Anyone seeing them would simply assume another border raid was in the offing. But when night came and they stopped to rest their animals for a few hours, no fires were lit. The horses were slowly watered, and then allowed to graze along the hillsides. The riders sat on the ground eating oatcakes and cheese, drinking sparingly from their flasks. While some slept, others kept watch for any danger that might approach.

Late the second night they reached Stanton and, concealing themselves in the grass and thickets of trees, they waited. Ramsay and his men returned with the dawn, and as Murdoc had told them they entered the cottages of the village. Eventually, as the morning deepened, the women began coming forth to go to the well for water and to gossip. The Scots raiding party prepared to attack.

"I want to go with you," Adair said to her husband.

"You promised you would remain upon the hillside," he reminded her.

"Surely you don't intend to kill the women, do you?" she asked almost fearfully. "The women have done no deliberate treason. Most, if not all, are captives. You need someone to take them to safety so you may do what you must."

"She is right," Andrew Home said. "We want Ramsay and his men. Not the lasses. I would not deliberately kill a woman without cause."

"But how?" Conal Bruce asked. "I will not have my wife endangered."

"If you are in position, and prepared to sweep into the village from the hillsides themselves, you will have more than enough time, even if one of the women sounds the alarm. Let me ride into the village and just ask the women to follow me."

"That's ridiculous!" Conal exploded angrily. "One or even more of the damned wenches is certain to have fallen in love with her captor. She will run screaming, and the others will follow for certain."

"I think you are wrong," Adair replied. "These men will have raped the women now with them. They will have shared them amongst one another, and beaten them. The men will have expected them to cook and clean, and no matter how hard they have tried to please—and some will have in hopes of escaping the brutality—they will have still been mistreated. If someone had ridden into Willie Douglas's camp when I was a captive, and said, 'Follow me,' I more than likely would have, and I was in his charge only a few days. Many of these women have been here for several months. Let me try, my lords. If I fail I will ride up the hills as you are all riding down. The women will scatter when they see you if they do not follow me."

"Jesu, madam, you have courage," Hercules Hepburn said admiringly, "but I am not certain whether you are totally mad."

Adair laughed. "I am not mad, Hercules, I swear it. But this is Stanton. My lands. I must avenge my family's honor. And while, if you all insist I remain upon the hillside while you attack, I will, I should far prefer to have a more active role in these doings." She turned to her husband, as did all the other lords with them. "Please, Conal."

"She should be safe," Duncan Armstrong said. "The men are sleeping, and the women are believed so cowed that Ramsay hasn't even set a watch."

Adair threw her brother-in-law a grateful look.

"I agree," Hercules Hepburn said. "And it would certainly be a huge help to us if we could get the women out of the way. It will be a lot easier to go about our task if they are not there to howl and shriek."

"And one rider whom they will quickly see is another woman will quell any fears the little darlings may have," Andrew Home remarked with a grin.

"Go," Conal Bruce said to Adair. "But if you get yourself killed I shall not forgive you, woman. I'm expecting more fine sons from you."

She laughed. "I think I'm supposed to say something like that," she told him. "It will take me a few minutes from here to ride around to the valley's entry. Watch for me." Then, gently nudging the gelding forward, she moved off.

They watched her go, losing sight of her briefly until she came out upon the narrow track leading into Stanton village.

It was all so familiar, and for just the briefest moment Adair was assailed by her memories. The orchards were still there, although some trees had fallen over the last few years, and they remained where they fell, for there was no one to clear them away. Eventually all trace of the orchard would be gone. She wondered what had happened to the bodies of the men slain there that day. There was the burying ground where her parents, FitzTudor, and so many others of her acquaintance were interred. But not Andrew Lynbridge. She sighed. Would it have all been simpler if Andrew had not died that day at Bosworth? She didn't know. Would never know.

Adair yanked her mind back to the present as she rode into Stanton village. She directed her horse to the village fountain and well, watering him as she stood among the group of shocked women, who had never imagined to see a woman a-horse ride into their midst. Then, with a small, friendly smile, she said in a quiet voice, "I am Adair Radcliffe, the lady of Stanton. Come with me and I will set you free." She did not wait for a reply, but, turning her horse about, she headed down the road and out of the village. And behind her most of the women followed her. The few who did not stood for several long moments as if they had been turned to stone. But as the group of women disappeared from their sight and they saw the horsemen galloping down the hillside, the three women who had not been able to make up their minds picked up their skirts and, running for all they were worth, chased after the others.

Adair did not stop until she had brought the women from the village to the top of the hillock from where she had come. Then she told them, "You will all be freed to return to your own homes when this is over, lasses."

"Who are you?" one of the bolder women asked.

"I have already said. I am Adair Radcliffe, the lady of Stanton."

"You wear a plaid and the badge of a chieftain's wife," a sharp-eyed woman said.

"I do," Adair admitted. "I am also the wife of the Bruce of Cleit."

"Why have you come to rescue us?" another girl asked.

"We did not come to rescue you, but rather to mete out justice to a traitor to King James. Ramsay of Balmain and his ilk have operated beneath the aegis of King Henry of England to stir up trouble here in the borders. Several of the border lords have taken it upon themselves to clean out this nest of traitors. King Jamie does not want a war between Scotland and England. He has too much to do to bring peace within our borders, and to bring prosperity to Scotland. The border lords did not want any women harmed if it were at all possible."

"What will happen to us now?" a woman asked.

"We will try to get you back to your homes," Adair answered her.

The women now grew silent, the first shock having worn off, and they watched as below in the village, house after house was emptied of Ramsay's men, who were dispatched swiftly and without mercy. Adair saw Conal and Murdoc single out a man whom they slew together. She knew without anyone telling her that it was Alpin Bruce, but she could not find it in her heart to be sorry. She did, however, say a quick prayer for his soul. And then Ramsay of Balmain was brought forth from a cottage. A strong rope was fastened about his neck. He was dragged to a nearby tree and hanged from a high branch. For several long minutes he struggled and squirmed on the rope's end. Then, with a great shudder, he died and was still. To Adair's surprise the women with her cheered loudly. Some embraced one another. Others wept with open relief.

Murdoc rode up the hill to tell Adair that the village was now safe. She left her flock of women upon the hillside, promising to return. Then she joined Conal and the other border lords. "The women want to know what will happen to them," Adair told them. "They are still frightened. I have said we will return them to their homes."

"We'll find out from where they have come," Duncan said. " 'Tis probably no more than a few villages and farms. There are no more than twenty of them."

"Do it now," Adair said. "Take them away now so that they do not have to spend another moment in a place where they suffered so much indignity. Those who remain behind can destroy Stanton. We can fire the cottages today, and then batter the walls of what remains over the next few days." There was a grim and angry look in her eyes, and none of the men would argue with her.

Instead, Duncan Armstrong rode up the hill to learn what he could. When he returned an hour later he chose two men from each clan group, eight in all. The nine men went back up the hill, where the women had gathered into small groups. Each clansman brought with him a string of horses, one for each woman he would escort. They would be allowed to keep the horse they rode as recompense for their unlawful imprisonment. Duncan assigned each clansman a group of women, and then waited as the women mounted, and the eight groups rode off. Then he and Murdoc returned down the hill.

The bits of furniture remaining in the individual cottages were piled into the center of each dwelling and then set alight. As the flames rose higher the roofs caught too. Adair remembered seeing those roofs burn over three years ago. They had obviously been rethatched to accommodate Ramsay and his men. The cottages burned into the night. When the morning came the dirt floors were scorched black, the beams and roofs gone, as were the small blackened windows.

For the next few days the stone walls were battered down one cottage at a time. And as each cottage ceased to exist, the stones were carried away to be placed on the hillside. A small dam was built of some of the stones in Stanton Water. And finally there was nothing left to ever indicate that a prosperous village had once stood upon that ground. Even the fountain where the women had come for water had been destroyed, and the well filled in with stones. Stanton was, to all intents and purposes, gone.

Adair walked alone to the hilltop where Stanton Hall had once stood. She looked out over the lands that for six hundred years or more had belonged to the Radcliffes. It was no more. Oh, the land would always be there. But everything else that had made Stanton the Radcliffes' pride was gone. She wept silently for it all. For her mother, for her father, for her beloved old Beiste, and yes, even for young and foolish FitzTudor. And when her tears had ceased and the sadness began to lift from her heart, she turned her face north, toward Scotland. A slight breeze brought with it the elusive scent of heather. Adair smiled. Then she turned and looked down the hill to where her husband was patiently awaiting her. She began to run toward him, and she did not stop until she had reached the shelter of his strong arms. She lifted her small heart-shaped face to him, and Conal Bruce kissed her with all the love he had in his heart for her.

When their lips had parted he turned and shouted to the men waiting for them, "I love her! I love my lady wife, and I always will!"

The Scots raiding party cheered his declaration loudly, Hercules Hepburn, Andrew Home, and the laird's brothers all grinning broadly as Conal Bruce lifted his wife into her saddle. They urged their horses forward, and when they had reached the top of the hill Adair turned to look back but once. Then, setting her face forward, she moved her horse to Conal's side. They were going home. She was Adair, the lady of Cleit, the wife of Conal Bruce, and no one was ever going to take that from her. *No one!*

About the Author

Bertrice Small is a *New York Times* best-selling author and the recipient of numerous awards. In keeping with her profession, Bertrice Small lives in the oldest English-speaking town in the state of New York, founded in 1640. Her light-filled studio includes the paintings of her favorite cover artist, Elaine Duillo, and a large library. Because she believes in happy endings, Bertrice Small has been married to the same man, her hero, George, for forty-three years. They have a son, Thomas; a daughter-in-law, Megan; and four wonderful grandchildren. Longtime readers will be happy to know that Nicki the cockatiel flourishes, along with his fellow housemates: Pookie, the long-haired greige-and-white cat; Finnegan, the long-haired bad black kitty; and Sylvester, the black-and-white tuxedo cat who has recently joined the family.